DOUBLE VISION IN RIPLEY GROVE

DOUBLE VISION IN RIPLEY GROVE

A RIPLEY GROVE MYSTERY, BOOK 2

SHIRLEY WORLEY

Without limiting the rights under copyright(s) reserved below, no part of this publication may be reproduced, stored in or introduced into a retrieval system, or transmitted, in any form, or by any means (electronic, mechanical, photocopying, recording, or otherwise) without the prior permission of the publisher and the copyright owner.

This is a work of fiction. Names, characters, places, and incidents either are the product of the author's imagination or are used fictitiously, and any resemblance to actual persons, living or dead, business establishments, events or locales is entirely coincidental.

The scanning, uploading, and distributing of this book via the internet or via any other means without the permission of the publisher and copyright owner is illegal and punishable by law. Please purchase only authorized copies, and do not participate in or encourage piracy of copyrighted materials. Your support of the author's rights is appreciated.

Copyright © 2020 by Shirley Worley. All rights reserved.

Book and cover design by eBook Prep
www.ebookprep.com

June, 2021

ISBN: 978-1-64457-113-2

ePublishing Works!
644 Shrewsbury Commons Ave
Ste 249
Shrewsbury PA 17361
United States of America

www.epublishingworks.com
Phone: 866-846-5123

Dedicated to my husband, Bert, the love of my life.

ONE

CiCi's face beamed with happiness as she emerged from the dressing room and stepped onto the raised platform. She turned one way, then another, to view the one-of-a-kind wedding dress from different angles in the oversized mirrors. *This is the feeling I wanted to have. The dress is perfect...well, almost perfect.*

Her consultant, Rebecca, noticed the slight hesitation. "Let me bring in the owner. With a few changes, I'm certain she can give you the dress of your dreams."

Tasha and Megan, the maid of honor and bridesmaid, sat nearby on a couch upholstered in muted shades of pink. As her friends oohed over the latest selection, the sound of footsteps drew CiCi's eyes to the mirror's reflection of the hallway behind her. Rebecca appeared first, followed by a petite woman in her midfifties who wore a bold yellow tape measure underneath the collar of her silk blouse. The floral print skirt fluttered when she walked, and her hair, the color of golden wheat, fell in a soft bob just below her jawline. A captivating smile highlighted her flawless skin and clear blue eyes sparkled behind a pair of chic eyeglasses.

Rebecca moved aside. "Miss Winslow, I'd like you to meet Katherine Bliss, owner of Blissful Creations."

When the owner's gaze caught first sight of the dress, she sucked in a sharp breath and clutched a hand to her chest. Her smile faded as she turned an icy glare on her employee. "Who gave you permission to pull *that* dress? Get her out of it and bring it to my office. Now!"

CiCi tensed. Tasha's and Megan's eyes grew wide at the outburst.

"But…the dress was hanging with the available stock. I assumed…I'm so sorry," Rebecca stammered.

Katherine Bliss turned a deaf ear to the apology. She composed herself before removing her glasses and shifting her attention on the bride-to-be. Suddenly, her face drained of color. Her eyes filled with tears as she lifted a trembling hand toward CiCi's cheek. "Jenna? Jenna, darling, is that you?"

CiCi shook her head. "I'm sorry, but you've mistaken me for someone else."

Mrs. Bliss stared, as if frozen in time. Without saying a word, the diminutive owner turned and disappeared down the hallway, leaving the bride-to-be and her entourage in shock. CiCi followed Rebecca back to the dressing room, where her trembling fingers unzipped the dress and carefully returned it to its hanger. Overcome with emotion, the consultant fled the room in tears.

CiCi's stomach tightened in a knot and a million questions raced through her mind as she dressed. *What just happened out there? How could this beautiful dress bring such joy to one person, and distress to another?* While bent to adjust the strap on her shoe, she noticed a small tag attached to a thin silver cord lying on the floor. She picked it up and threaded the tag around the neck of the padded hanger. She turned the tag over, expecting to see the price. Instead, she saw the name "Jenna Bliss" written in calligraphy.

With the consultant nowhere to be found, CiCi carefully tucked the dress inside the clear plastic garment bag and zipped it shut. Draping the bag over her arm, she made her way to the back hallway. She rapped on the pale pink door with the owner's name painted in a feminine script across the upper panel. A muffled voice from within told her to enter.

Mrs. Bliss sat in a tufted swivel chair behind an antique desk, staring out a large picture window that overlooked a small patio. She spoke without turning, her voice flat and void of any emotion. "Hang the dress on the coat rack, Rebecca, then shut the door on your way out, please."

"Mrs. Bliss? Rebecca left, so I thought I'd bring the dress to you myself. I'm sorry if my trying it on caused a problem."

Walking across the room, CiCi hung the garment bag on one of the coat rack's brass hooks. As she did, Mrs. Bliss turned. The charming smile and flawless face from earlier were gone. The woman who stared back now had puffy, red-rimmed eyes, mascara-streaked cheeks, and a runny nose. Her shoulders sagged with a heavy sadness.

"Oh, I'm sorry. I thought you were Rebecca."

CiCi stepped forward and took a box of tissues from the corner of the desk and placed them in front of the distraught woman. Taking the hint, the owner plucked out several tissues and blew her nose as delicately as possible. Once she regained her composure, she squared her shoulders and met CiCi's gaze.

"I apologize for my behavior today. I strive to make every bride-to-be feel special and their shopping experience unforgettable. I failed you in that regard. If you'll give me another chance, I'll personally see that you find exactly the dress you're looking for. But that particular dress is not for sale. Not now, not ever."

"It's truly beautiful, one I would have considered. I read the tag on the hanger. Is Jenna your daughter?"

Mrs. Bliss nodded and swiped at a tear that threatened to trickle down her cheek. "Yes, she is."

"She has excellent taste."

"I designed that dress for Jenna's wedding and sewed every lace embellishment and seed pearl on by hand. It was a labor of love for my only daughter. She went missing last year. When I saw you today, I thought…well, you remind me of her."

CiCi's heart swelled with empathy. "I'm sorry to bring back painful memories."

"It wasn't your fault."

"I know it's none of my business, but I don't think Rebecca meant any harm. I hope you'll give her another chance."

Mrs. Bliss sighed and settled her gaze on the dress in the corner. "I will. The dress being in the wrong place is *my* fault. Yesterday marked one year since Jenna went missing, and I took out the gown to look at…to reminisce. I intended to put it back in the vault, but I got distracted."

"That's understandable, considering the circumstances."

"Enough about me and my problems," she said as she cleared her throat. "Let's talk about the other dresses you tried on today, Miss…I'm sorry, what was your name again?"

"Winslow. Cecilia Winslow, but my friends call me CiCi."

Katherine studied CiCi's face with a renewed interest. "Are you by chance Jack and Helen Parker's daughter?"

"I am. You know my parents?"

"I did…a long, long time ago," she whispered as tears sprang to her eyes. She quickly averted her gaze and grabbed for another tissue. "I didn't make the connection at first. Wasn't Winslow your mother's name before she married Jack? You became Cecilia Parker when he adopted you."

"I did, but I took back my biological father's name after my divorce."

"I see," Katherine said quietly.

It was the way Katherine spoke those two simple words that unnerved CiCi. She paused, not knowing how to respond, and the silence between them grew awkward. "Mrs. Bliss, my friends are waiting. Perhaps I'll come back another time."

"Yes, another time."

CiCi left the office and retraced her steps to the room where she had modeled the wedding dresses. Not seeing her friends, she headed to the outer lobby.

When she had first entered the small boutique, the lobby had taken her breath away. The polished marble floor gleamed, and the light reflecting off the crystal chandelier gave the pale pink walls a shimmery effect. A small sitting area on one side of the room had a rose-colored sofa and a side table that held a vase of fresh flowers.

On the opposite side of the room, two mannequins, each wearing a couture bridal gown, flanked the reception counter. Her heart had pitter-pattered with excitement, a far cry from what she now felt.

Tasha and Megan were chatting on the sofa. Their whispered conversation stopped the moment they caught sight of CiCi. Still unnerved by the owner's outburst, CiCi suggested they stop someplace for lunch.

CiCi sighed and leaned back against the restaurant's booth. "I absolutely *loved* that dress, but I think I need to take a step back."

Megan's eyes flashed with alarm as she pushed a long strand of dark brown hair away from her face. "Wait. You're not having second thoughts about marrying my brother, are you?"

CiCi's gaze drifted to the diamond and sapphire engagement ring on her finger, her heart fluttering at the thought of spending the rest of her life with Chad Cooper, a thirty-two-year-old Ripley Grove detective. "No, no second thoughts. But I feel…oh, I don't know."

Tasha wagged her finger in the air. "Don't let that woman spoil your day. She was unprofessional and out of line."

"Mrs. Bliss? Yes, she was, but after talking with her, I can understand why," CiCi said as she dropped a lemon slice into her glass of water.

Megan's and Tasha's opinion of Mrs. Bliss softened after hearing the heart-wrenching story.

"That's awful," Megan said as the waitress delivered their food.

"For sure. I can't imagine living with that kind of grief." Tasha paused and took a bite of salad. "What do you plan to do now?" she asked.

CiCi paused between bites. "I don't know. That dress was as close to perfect as I could ask for. Even if Mrs. Bliss changed her mind and made the alterations I want, I honestly doubt if I could wear that dress on the happiest day of my life knowing it was shrouded in heartache."

Tasha tapped a finger against her flawless dark brown cheek. "Blissful Creations isn't your only option. There are several couture bridal shops in Johnson County and more just across the state line in Kansas City, Missouri."

"I thought of that, but if I'm going to spend money on a wedding, I want to spend it here in Ripley Grove."

Megan smiled. "A hometown girl who's loyal to the core. Your mother would be proud."

CiCi sighed and pushed her plate away. "Yeah, she would. I wish she were here to help plan the wedding and pick out my dress. If only she'd stayed in remission for another year."

Megan's hand flew to her mouth. "I'm so sorry, CiCi. I wasn't thinking."

"It's okay, Megan." CiCi's eyes misted as she tucked a dark blonde curl behind her ear.

Tasha reached across the table and squeezed her hand. "Megan and I will see to it you find a dress that would've brought a smile to your mama's face."

"Thanks," she said. "I couldn't have chosen better bridal attendants."

Tasha raised her tea glass for a toast. "To best friends."

The others followed her lead and clinked glasses. "To best friends," they said.

"I know what will lift your spirits," Megan said. "Dessert. Dessert makes everything better."

CiCi couldn't refuse, dessert being one of her weaknesses. Despite satisfying her sweet tooth, the incident at the boutique cast a shadow over the rest of the day. What was meant to be a memorable event turned out to be memorable, indeed, but for all the wrong reasons.

TWO

CiCi rolled over in bed the next morning and sighed when she read Chad's text. He'd been called to the scene of a crime before the sun had even thought of peeking over the horizon. She hated going to church without him but knew when they began dating that a detective's job didn't always fall between the hours of nine and five.

After the service, she called to see if he had made it home yet. He had, so she stopped by her townhome long enough to change into a T-shirt and her favorite pair of jeans and pull her wavy hair up into a ponytail. After picking up two sandwiches at their favorite deli, she headed to the first-floor apartment he rented in an older, two-story home.

She parked her Jeep at the curb and walked up the driveway he shared with the man who rented the second floor. Chad's long legs stuck out from under the vehicle and she playfully kicked his foot as she passed by. He scooted out from under the truck and squinted up at the sack of food she dangled from her hand. "Want to eat on the porch or inside?"

"Porch. It's too nice to eat indoors."

She shook her head when he reached for the sack. "Get the grease off those hands while I get us something to drink."

After they had eaten, she sat in a lawn chair and watched as he methodically washed his truck. Her gaze swept across his handsome face and down to the patriotic eagle and flag tattoos covering his shoulders and biceps. His toned upper body glistened with a mixture of sweat and errant soap suds. Muscles rippled as he scrubbed away the dirt and grime. Ratty jean shorts clung to his narrow hips. She shook her head at his grungy size eleven sneakers. It wasn't often she saw him wearing something other than a pair of western boots. A wet lock of dark brown hair fell across his forehead. The sight before her rivaled anything on TV or Netflix, and she wasn't the only person who thought so.

The fifty-something woman who lived in the blue house on the corner walked by with her dog and waved. CiCi returned the gesture, but the neighbor never noticed. Her attention was focused solely on Chad. Down the block, two younger women sat on their respective porches watching the show. Across the street, a teenage girl scrutinized his every move from her stoop. CiCi had heard of neighborhood watch groups, but these people took it to a whole new level.

A spray of cold water made her gasp and brought her to her feet. "Hey! Watch where you're pointing that thing."

"It's the only way I could get your attention. I asked if you wanted me to wash your Jeep."

"No thanks, it can wait." She brushed the droplets of water from the front of her shirt. "For all your marksmanship awards, I thought you'd have better aim."

He sprayed her again, with a gleam in his eyes. His gaze drifted to the front of her shirt, and a dimpled grin appeared. "My aim is perfect, and the results are very satisfying."

She giggled and raced behind the truck to avoid the next blast of cold water. He followed, hitting her again. She bent, latched onto a length of hose, and folded it in half, cutting off his supply of water. Finding himself disarmed, he threw the hose aside and gave chase. Squealing, she made three laps around the truck, but at five-foot-six, her stride was no match for someone six-foot tall. His arms snaked around her waist and brought her to a halt facing him. She swayed, a bit light-headed from the chase, and leaned against his broad chest. The head injury she received during a vicious attack in her home several months ago hadn't improved enough for her to resume strenuous activities.

"Whoa. Are you okay?" he asked. "That was stupid of me. You're not ready to be running around like that."

"Not…your fault." She closed her eyes until her mind settled and smiled as he tucked a wet strand of hair behind her ear. She straightened and glanced across the street. "You have quite an audience today."

"What?" He frowned and looked around. The two women down the street gave him a little wave. "They need to get a hobby," he huffed.

"I'd be willing to bet you *are* their hobby. With the strain they're putting on their eyes, I'm surprised they don't need glasses."

He wiggled his eyebrows and looked down at her wet T-shirt with a wicked grin. "I don't need glasses to appreciate what life has to offer."

"That's called wishful thinking, at least until we say, 'I do.'"

"March seems like a long way off. Maybe we should get married sooner."

Truthfully, there wasn't anything she would like better than to become Chad's wife. She often fantasized about letting his hands explore her peaks and valleys. But she'd decided early on not to complicate matters of the heart with the desires of the body. It wasn't easy, but she was determined to learn from her past. She had married her first husband, Richie, after she found herself pregnant. The miscarriage several months later left her completely devastated, and their eventual divorce only intensified her feelings of guilt. Chad, on the other hand, had put his brief marriage to Vickie behind him and was ready to move on with life.

"We're halfway through September, so March isn't that far away. Even a small ceremony takes planning. Want to go over the guest list?"

He glanced at his watch. "Not now, sugar. I need to shower and change before I leave."

"Where are you going?"

"*Someone* I know has a thirtieth birthday coming up, and I need to pick up her present. Want to catch a movie later?"

"I'd rather know what my present is."

"Not gonna happen." He smiled and gave her a peck on the cheek before going inside.

Wonder what he bought. She took a seat on the porch steps as her mind ran through the possibilities. She sighed. *Guess I'll have to wait and see.* Leaning back to let the sun dry her T-shirt, she closed her eyes and listened to the sounds of life. A bird perched in a nearby tree chirped, children down the street laughed as they played tag, a car door slammed, and a dog barked.

A shadow fell across her face. She opened her eyes and looked up at her reflection in the mirrored sunglasses of Mark Sullivan, Chad's best friend and fellow detective. His face had a rugged handsomeness to it, despite having his nose broken in the past. Though five years older, he and Chad shared the same swagger when they walked, the same mannerisms, and the uncanny ability to communicate with each other without speaking a word.

"Mark. Didn't expect to see you today." She smiled, then quickly looked down to make sure her shirt had dried.

"Chad home?" He took off his Chiefs hat and raked a hand through his thick dark brown hair before taking a seat beside her.

She nodded. "He's taking a shower. Should be out any minute."

"How was your first week back at work?"

"Long. Those thirty hours felt like sixty. One more week of limited duty, then I'll go back to full time."

Chad stepped out onto the porch and stiffened when he saw Mark's expression. "What's wrong?"

Mark's jaw clenched. "We got a problem. Evan wants to meet."

"Who is Evan?" she asked.

"An undercover agent."

"Undercover? What, is someone selling fake raffle tickets again?" CiCi asked.

"No, something a lot more dangerous, and I want the scumbag in charge behind bars." Mark stood and glanced at his watch. "We meet in one hour."

Chad nodded and stepped inside. He returned and stopped in front of her while slipping on a light jacket to conceal his shoulder holster. "Sorry. Looks like we'll have to catch that movie another time."

"I understand. Say, I can pick up that present if you're short on time."

"Nice try, sugar. I'll get it on the way," he said. He pulled her to her feet and into his arms. After a lingering kiss that curled her toes, he whispered in her ear, "And if you're thinking of following me to see where I go, think again."

THREE

The next morning, CiCi backed her Jeep into her usual parking spot at work—in the last row under the shade of a large oak tree. Taking in the low, red brick building in front of her, she hummed along to a country tune on the radio and let her thoughts drift to the past.

She had first landed the job as a researcher at Five Star Real Estate and Appraisal after her divorce. Though she spent most of her time on the computer researching property, compiling market data, and assisting with the preparation of reports, she quickly fell in love with the appraisal side of the business. After weighing the pros and cons of putting her accounting degree aside, she enrolled in a program to become a certified general appraiser. The process took several years and a lot of study, but she never once regretted her decision.

Then in May, tragedy struck when an employee was murdered on the premises. Initially, CiCi had been considered a prime suspect. But as the investigation progressed, police began to wonder if she had been the intended target. By the time the killer's identity became apparent, he had CiCi in his sights, and she almost lost her life after he caught up with her. CiCi shuddered at the thought.

The blaring twang of a guitar signaled a change in songs and brought her trip down memory lane to an end. Her best friend and co-worker, Tasha Green, waved from Five Star's front window. CiCi made her way inside. The aroma of freshly brewed coffee brought a smile to her face. After grabbing a pastry and a cup of java, she headed to her cubicle, ready to attack the waiting mound of paperwork.

Just after lunch, Tasha sashayed across the room with a banana in her hand. Her skirt and blouse were a bright mix of purples, golds and oranges, a perfect pairing against her creamy, dark complexion. "Have you eaten yet?"

"No. I haven't had time." CiCi leaned back in her chair, relieved to take a break from staring at her two computer screens. Her eyes darted to the banana.

"I thought so," Tasha said, handing over the piece of fruit and sinking into the empty seat beside the desk.

"Thanks. I have two reports due Wednesday. I hate to stop, even for lunch."

"Floyd hasn't complained about your work, has he? I noticed you've had several closed-door meetings with him lately. Everything okay?" Tasha used a manicured nail to push back several shiny black curls that fell across her forehead. Those long talons were hard to ignore, and most people, CiCi included, wondered how she ever typed as fast as she did.

CiCi turned away to avoid Tasha's questioning gaze. *Ugh. I hate keeping secrets from her.* "Yes, everything's fine," she mumbled around a bite of banana. She swallowed, then added, "I've been explaining the new file system to Floyd. I don't mind helping, but I'll be glad when he hires a permanent accountant."

"Did he say anything about the company's future?" Tasha asked. "People here are worried, me included. Every day when I come to work, I expect to see the front door locked and a note on the window listing the website of the unemployment office. Having the company name associated with the word 'murder,' not once but twice, is hard for any business to overcome. It's been several months now, but I can't imagine Floyd has recovered from the financial loss."

"Hang in there. I'm positive things will improve soon."

"From your lips to God's ears."

At five o'clock, CiCi clocked out, waved goodbye to Tasha, and headed to her car. The moment she arrived at home, she slumped into a chair and kicked off her shoes. Not ten minutes later, the phone rang.

"Hey, hon. I'll be at your place around five," Chad said. "That should give us plenty of time to grab a bite to eat before our meeting."

"Meeting?"

"Our counseling session with Pastor Young, remember?"

"Is that tonight?" *Darn it. How could I forget?*

"It is, and I'll see you soon."

She raced upstairs to freshen up and change clothes. Chad arrived fifteen minutes later than promised with a phone pressed to his ear. After he disconnected, he leaned in for a proper kiss.

She pressed her lips to his and lost herself in the woodsy scent of his cologne. "Mmm, you smell good." He deepened the kiss and pulled her snug against his body. She moaned with a mixture of pleasure and frustration. "As much as I'd love to stay and continue this, we need to get going."

He reluctantly stepped back before glancing down at her short-sleeved top. "It's supposed to get chilly tonight. You might want to bring a jacket."

In previous premarital counseling sessions, they had discussed what commitment in a marriage looked like, their short-term expectations, lifelong goals, and their philosophies on raising a family. The week they talked about money was a tough one to dance around because of the astronomical amount CiCi inherited from her mother. Chad's pride made him hesitant to combine the entirety of her finances with his, and they were still working through that issue.

As they sat on the loveseat in Pastor Young's office, he led them through a set of questions revolving around their parents and future in-laws. The talk of joining two families together made her feel somewhat lacking.

"Family members often affect the relationship between a husband and wife, causing fights and undue stress," Pastor Young said. "Cecilia, how do you feel about Chad's family?"

Megan, Chad's sister, was younger by two years and still single. His parents had moved out of town earlier in the year to take care of his grandmother. All in all, the Coopers were a close-knit group and were everything she could ask for in a family. And everything her family was not.

"I adore them. Actually, I'm a bit jealous." She hesitated and stole a quick glance at Chad.

Pastor Young gave her a reassuring smile. "It's okay, Cecilia. This is a safe zone. Anything you say will be held in confidence."

Chad squeezed her hand and encouraged her to continue.

"With my mother and grandparents gone, I don't have any relatives left to speak of. My dad and I have been estranged for several years. His drinking and abuse destroyed our relationship during my teen years. After Mom died and left me the majority of her estate, his hatred for me has only deepened." She turned to Chad. "I envy the bond you have with your parents, and I can't wait to become a part of your family."

Pastor Young nodded and turned his focus to Chad. "I'll ask you the same question, Chad. How do you feel about her father?"

Chad forced a smile as CiCi tensed beside him. "Honestly?"

"Of course." The man of God nodded, steepled his hands in front of his chest, and waited for an answer. CiCi removed her hand from Chad's thigh and twisted the engagement ring on her finger back and forth.

"Okay. I know you've said everyone deserves a second chance, but Jack's an alcoholic who's mean and unpredictable. He's caused her enough hurt to last a lifetime. I feel my first and only responsibility is to CiCi, to love her and protect her. I won't encourage her to mend the relationship until he makes drastic changes." He paused and looked over at her. "Whether you want to admit it or not, deep down, you still love him. I know he's your dad, but I trust him about as much as I trust a fortune-teller to pick the winning lottery numbers."

She took his hand in hers and offered a faint smile. "I don't blame you for feeling that way. He's proven over and over how much he despises me. Don't worry about me wanting to rebuild the relationship. He'll have to take the first step for that to happen. Besides, we've not seen or heard from him in months. He's probably forgotten I'm still alive."

"I can only hope," Chad muttered.

FOUR

On Tuesday morning, CiCi found the office abuzz with rumors that revolved around Floyd Master's struggle to keep Five Star afloat. Being associated with murder and scandal was never good for business. One of the firm's real estate agents had heard the company might have to file for bankruptcy, while another was certain a new partner would soon be joining the company. CiCi shook her head, refusing to get involved in the discussion. She had tons of work to finish, and deadlines waited for no one.

At noon, she leaned back in her chair and rubbed her eyes. A door slammed. Her gaze shifted down the hallway. Ashley was leaving Floyd's office and heading for her desk. The college senior and soon-to-be accountant worked part-time and had been hired by Rex, one of the former co-owners of the business. It came as a surprise to all that she stayed on after his death.

When Ashley turned and noticed CiCi watching, a deep frown appeared. After shutting down her computer, Ashley jammed her arms in the sleeves of her jacket, grabbed her purse, and headed for the door.

Tired of the hateful looks, CiCi called out as the young woman walked by. "Hey, Ashley, how about we have a chat over lunch? My treat."

"I'm meeting someone. Besides, you should save your money," Ashley said with an evil smile. "If I have my way, you'll be eating at the local soup kitchen soon enough."

CiCi's jaw dropped, shocked that a junior employee would insinuate her job was in jeopardy. "What do you mean by that?"

"As Uncle Rex's only heir, I'm certain the court will be awarding me his share of the company any day now. When they do, you'll be the first to get a pink slip."

Ashley strode from the building, leaving CiCi stunned. Tasha came from behind her desk and stood beside CiCi at the window overlooking the parking lot. Ashley made her way to an older green pickup, jumped inside, and slammed the door shut. She appeared to be venting to the driver, a male in his late twenties with pitch black, shaggy hair. He shot daggers in CiCi's direction, then stuck his arm out of the window and gave a one-fingered salute as they drove from the lot. The tongue of a fire-breathing dragon tattooed on the back of his hand snaked up his extended digit and added a sinister touch to his sign language.

"You need to keep your eye on her," Tasha said. "She has a lot of anger directed at you, girlfriend, especially since it was your fiancé who shot and killed her uncle. And it's only gotten worse since she heard you were coming back to work and taking over the accounting office."

"That's the reason I do the payroll after she's gone for the day. Staying late is a minor inconvenience if it keeps her from going ballistic."

Tasha shook her head. "I think Floyd wants to fire her but is worried it will look like retaliation now that she's filed a claim for Rex's share of the company. Personally, I think Floyd has been more than lenient with her. Have you heard he may have found a new business partner? I hope so, but I wonder how the new guy will react to having that kind of attitude in the office. It'll be interesting."

The phone rang on Tasha's desk and she scurried across the

room to answer it. CiCi turned to find Floyd standing behind her, hands planted on his hips. His shirtsleeves were rolled up to his elbows, revealing muscular forearms. A frown overshadowed the laugh lines around his eyes as he stared out the window.

"Hey, Floyd. What can I help you with?" she asked.

"Can I have a word with you in my office?"

"Sure." She followed, giving Tasha a shrug as she passed.

CiCi took a seat and watched as Floyd sat behind his aging desk, twirling a pencil between his fingers. In his late fifties, stress over the struggling business had taken its toll. He had lost weight and his trademark salt-and-pepper hair was saltier than it had been a few months ago.

"First, let me say again how thrilled I am to have you back. You've taken a load off my shoulders. I hope you're not pushing yourself too hard."

"Thanks, but I'm fine." His concern touched her. As her supervisor while studying for the appraisal license, she had developed a soft spot for him.

"From what I just saw, I'd say Ashley's not happy to have you back."

She waved off his comment. "Don't worry about it."

"I've tried to be patient, but it looks like she and I will need to have another talk. As you know, she hired a lawyer to stake a claim to her uncle's share of the company. That's why I removed her from the accounting office and reassigned her to the front office under Tasha's supervision. I couldn't chance having her tamper with the books if the court doesn't rule in her favor."

"That was a smart move." CiCi leaned forward and took a deep breath before asking the crucial question. "When will the court make a decision? Do you think she has any chance of inheriting Rex's share of the company?"

"Not according to the phone call I just received from my lawyer."

CiCi suppressed a sigh a relief. "Does Ashley know?"

"No, not yet. Considering her behavior, I can imagine how she'll react to the news. I had an outside accounting firm go over the books after Rex died. As I suspected, his poor decisions left nothing for Ashley to inherit. Now I can move forward with the changes necessary to turn this company around. The lawyers will finalize the paperwork for the new partnership this week."

The phone on his desk rang and he paused their conversation to take the call. "Thanks, Tasha. Give me a minute or two, then send him back."

CiCi stood to leave as he hung up the phone. "Is there anything else?"

"Yes, I've offered jobs to the top three candidates from last week's interviews. All have accepted and will start this coming Monday. I'm glad you were involved in the process. Your observations were spot on, and holding the interviews off-site was a brilliant idea."

"Thank you."

"If all goes well, I'll make the big announcement on Monday. I know the rumors are flying, but let's keep the details to ourselves until then."

"Whatever you say. Why don't I put together a celebration lunch, of sorts, for the new hires and the new partnership?"

He nodded. "That's an excellent idea. Do you mind?"

"I'd love to."

Later that afternoon, CiCi's cell phone rang. She didn't recognize the number, but answered anyway, hoping it wasn't another sales pitch. "Hello?"

"Miss Winslow? This is Katherine Bliss, from Blissful Creations. I hope I'm not interrupting anything."

"No, no, you're fine. How can I help you?"

"I was wondering if we could get together this evening."

CiCi frowned. *Why would she want to meet outside of normal business hours?* "Mrs. Bliss, I'm flattered, really, but I'm not in a rush to buy a dress."

"I'm sorry. I should've been more clear. My request is regarding a personal matter. The sooner, the better—before I change my mind."

FIVE

The beautiful stretch of scenery did nothing to ease CiCi's curiosity as she followed the directions on her phone's GPS. The boutique owner lived on the edge of town, ten minutes as the crow flies, but twenty when she had to navigate the winding, narrow stretch of road that followed alongside a wooded hillside that hid the creek below.

She pulled her Jeep to a stop in front of a small white house with blue shutters and surveyed the exterior as she walked to the entrance. *Ranch-style house, good condition, roughly fifteen hundred square feet, built in the seventies. The large, landscaped lot overlooks a small lake.* CiCi breathed a sigh of relief. *Now it all makes sense. She must've found out I work at Five Star and wants to sell her house. She's going to be disappointed to find out I'm an appraiser, not a real estate agent.*

Mrs. Bliss opened the door seconds after the doorbell rang. She wore a striped apron over a crisp white shirt and a pair of pressed slacks. Her hair had been pulled back on one side and secured with a gold clip. "Please, come in and have a seat. Excuse me while I take a batch of cookies from the oven," she called over her shoulder as she headed toward the back of the house.

A mouthwatering aroma filled the air, and a buzzer sounded

from another room, presumably the kitchen. CiCi took off her jacket and made herself comfortable in the living room. The interior of the dwelling proved to be as charming as the exterior. Light oak hardwood floors matched the sleek mantel over the white brick fireplace. Floor to ceiling drapery flanked the two large windows. Accent pillows in soft shades of rose and orange added a splash of color to the off-white sofa and tufted side chairs. The decorating style mimicked that of the bridal store, making the mental transition from work to home seamless. *This is the best version of "taking your work home with you" I've ever seen. It's beautiful.*

Katherine returned, minus the apron, and placed a tray of refreshments on the coffee table next to a faded photo album. Her hand trembled slightly as she handed CiCi a glass of tea and offered her a freshly baked chocolate chip cookie. "I'm so glad you agreed to come, Miss Winslow."

"Thank you, and please, call me CiCi." She shifted under Katherine's steady gaze. Her host seemed to be studying her features as though committing them to memory. CiCi broke the awkward silence that filled the room by saying, "Mrs. Bliss, you have a lovely home. If you're wanting to sell—"

"Call me Katherine, please. But no, dear, selling my home is not what I wanted to talk about." Mrs. Bliss twisted the ring on her finger and looked away.

CiCi cocked her head to one side. "What *did* you want to talk about?"

"My, this is harder than I thought." Katherine stared at the napkin on her lap before looking up. "I'd like to talk about your family, if you don't mind."

CiCi set her glass on a coaster and struggled to keep a perplexed look from her face. "Um, okay. You mentioned you knew my folks from years back."

"I did. I was very sorry to hear of your mother's passing. Helen was a wonderful woman. She always had a smile and a kind word, no matter who you were. And that laugh of hers—it was infectious."

"It was, and I miss hearing it. If you don't mind me asking, did you attend the funeral? I don't recall seeing you." CiCi nibbled on the cookie.

Katherine shook her head. "I was in Chicago, but I heard it was a lovely service."

"It was."

"I know for a fact your mother loved you more than life itself." Katherine hesitated before asking, "How is your father, Jack?"

CiCi stiffened at the mention of her dad. She set the remainder of her cookie aside and looked at Katherine. Instead of saying her father was a functioning alcoholic, abusive, and had anger issues, CiCi opted to take the high road with a whitewashed version of the truth. "Fine, as far as I know. For reasons I won't go into, we're not on speaking terms."

"I see."

"Katherine, it seems you knew my parents well, yet I don't recall them ever mentioning your name."

Katherine stared out the window for several moments, as though in a trance. When she turned, her eyes glistened with tears. Her voice cracked as she continued, "They say that lightning seldom strikes the same place twice, but it did the day you came to my shop. Yes, I was shocked to see the strong resemblance you have to my Jenna, but to discover *who* you were was a double jolt to my system."

CiCi frowned. "I...I don't understand."

"No, you wouldn't. I wrestled with my conscience all weekend over what to do. After I made my decision, I prayed for guidance on how to tell you."

"Tell me what?"

"CiCi, I'm your aunt. Cecil Winslow, your biological father, was my older brother."

CiCi's breathing hitched and her mind struggled to make sense of the news. Stunned, she stared at Katherine, certain there was a misunderstanding. "That's not possible. None of my biological father's family is alive. They're all dead."

"I'm sorry, but that's not true."

"It is. My parents told me so, and they wouldn't have lied about something like that."

"But they did, my dear."

"Why? Why should I believe you?".

Katherine moved to the sofa and placed the photo album on CiCi's lap. "If there were an easier way to tell you, I would. These pictures will prove what I am saying is true."

CiCi's hands trembled as she opened the book. She glanced at several photos, then slammed the cover shut to hide the familiar faces. Placing the album on the coffee table, she grabbed her jacket and hurried toward the door. "I'm sorry, I…I need to leave."

Katherine followed. She gently touched CiCi's arm and pressed the photo album into her hand. "Please," she pleaded, "take it with you. I know this must come as a shock, and you're sure to have questions. My shop is closed tomorrow. If you'd like to talk, I'll be available. Please, give me a chance."

CiCi took the album and numbly walked to her car. On the drive home, questions and confusion clouded her mind. *What is wrong with me? If what she says is true, I should be happy, thrilled even, to learn I have family. But why didn't someone—Mom, Dad, Katherine—tell me before now? My guess is Jenna didn't know, either. So why all the secrecy?* Her cell phone rang, and rang, and rang. She let it go to voicemail. When she parked in front of her townhome, Chad waited on the porch.

After taking in the troubled look on her face, he asked, "What's wrong?"

She shook her head, mentally exhausted from the weight of the news. Once inside, she draped her jacket over a chair and laid the album on the table. He joined her on the sofa and drew her into a hug as she told him about her meeting with Katherine. "I'm so confused. I don't know what to think or who to believe."

His thumb drew circles on the back of her hand. "You have every right to feel upset. She could be a scammer. Is it possible she somehow knows about your inheritance?"

CiCi shook her head, not surprised he would see a side of the situation she hadn't thought about. "I doubt it. Not even our friends know how much I inherited."

"I'll make a phone call and have a short background check run on her. She may be the owner of a bridal shop, but you need to know if the woman is who she says she is. You could find basic information on the internet, but my info will be verified." He stood, took out his phone, and marched out to the porch to make the call in private. A few minutes later, he returned and sat beside her. "Just to be safe, I don't think you should contact her until I get the report back."

"You're right. I need proof that she's my aunt." Pressure built behind her eyes, forcing her to squeeze them tight to keep the tears at bay. She fisted her hands in her lap. "As much as I'd love to believe her, I'm angry. Angry at Katherine and angry at my parents. If what she says is true, I had a right to know I had family out there. I expect that kind of behavior from my dad, but why didn't Mom say anything?"

"I don't know, but I'm sure she thought it was for the best."

"I'm not a kid anymore, Chad. I should've been allowed to decide for myself," she snapped. "Sorry," she sighed. "I'm just so… so frustrated."

Chad gently squeezed her hand. "Maybe the extra love and attention she lavished on you growing up was her way of making up for losing your extended family."

"Maybe," she mumbled.

She leaned against him and rested her head in the crook of his shoulder. They each fell into a comfortable silence, consumed by their thoughts.

She stared at the photo album on the table as they ate dinner together but refused to look inside. After Chad left, she hesitantly ran her fingers over the worn leather binding, then opened to the first page. An hour later, she closed the book, certain what the background check would reveal. She placed a quick call to Floyd and asked permission to take the following day off.

Tomorrow, she hoped to have more answers than questions.

SIX

The buzz of a cell phone forced CiCi to open her eyes. Blinking against the daylight streaming through the French doors in her bedroom, she reached for the phone. The display read eight-forty-five. *I've overslept—but wait, no, I asked for the day off.* "Hello?"

"Morning, sugar. Did I wake you?" Chad asked.

"Sort of. I didn't sleep well last night. What's up?" She threw back her grandmother's quilt and sat on the edge of the bed.

"I got the report back on Katherine. She is who she says she is. Her record is spotless."

CiCi sighed. "After looking through the photo album, I thought that's what you'd say. I called Floyd last night and asked for the day off. I'm hoping to pay Katherine a visit."

"Need me to come along for moral support?"

"Thanks, but no. I think we'll need some time alone."

CiCi called Katherine and, after apologizing for her abrupt departure the day before, asked if they could meet after lunch.

Katherine, sounding relieved, responded with a reserved eagerness. The drive took a mere twenty minutes. Yet thirty minutes later, she still sat, white-knuckled behind the wheel of her Jeep in front of Katherine's house. She glanced at the open front door where Katherine waited. CiCi took a deep breath, grabbed the album from the passenger seat, and made her way up the brick sidewalk.

Katherine opened the screen door, an anxious smile on her face. CiCi stepped inside. Nervous energy and the aroma of cinnamon filled the air.

"I'm glad to see you brought the photo album. Come. Let's go to the kitchen. I made apple turnovers this morning." Katherine led the way to the heart of the home. "I hope you like them extra sweet. I got carried away with the icing."

CiCi grinned. "Sounds perfect, Kath—um, Aunt…um."

Her host gave a small chuckle. "Why don't we stick with Katherine or Kate? You pick. Ever since my husband died, the only person who calls me Katie is my mother-in-law."

"Are there other Winslows still living?"

"No one but me and Jenna."

CiCi took a bite of a turnover, then turned to Katherine, desperate to have her questions answered. "First, I'd like to know why my mother and father—um, Jack—never mentioned you or Jenna. Sorry, I mean no disrespect to your brother. He may have been my biological father and namesake, but Jack Parker is the only dad I remember."

"I understand. To avoid any confusion, why don't you call your birth father by his given name, Cecil. In fact, I would enjoy hearing it again."

"Okay. So, can you help me understand why we've never met?"

"Our families got together quite often when you were young. After Cecil died, your mother and I remained close. My husband and I were surprised when she married Jack because they came from such different backgrounds. But he made your mother happy, even more so when he adopted you. It wasn't long before things changed, and Jack began racking up hefty gambling debts."

CiCi frowned. "That's something Mom never mentioned." *Could that be part of the reason my mother excluded him from inheriting her family's fortune?*

"It was hard on your mother, but she loved him regardless. After my husband died, I received a modest settlement from his life insurance. When Jack asked for a sizable loan, I had to decline. I was a widow and had Jenna to think of. I tried to explain, but he wouldn't listen. He was furious and refused to let me see you or your mother from that point forward. Helen and I were devastated."

"Why didn't you and my mother stay in contact, despite what he wanted?"

"Your mother loved him, period. His word was law. Jack said if she ever crossed him, he would make her life unbearable. A year later, Jenna and I moved to Chicago, where I opened Blissful Creations." She shrugged. "Life took over. I contacted Helen when I moved back a few years ago, but insisted she not tell him we'd been in touch. After hearing rumors about Jack's temper, I didn't want to cause her or you any harm. Does he still have a gambling problem?"

"Not that I know of. He must have traded one vice for another and took up drinking instead."

"Enough about Jack. Let me walk you through the Winslow family history." Katherine reached for the album, opened the cover, and started at the beginning.

CiCi scooted her chair closer, not wanting to miss a thing. Photo after photo, starting with Cecil's childhood, depicted happier times. There were numerous shots of Cecil, Katherine, and their parents, smiling for the camera. On one page, Katherine and CiCi's mother posed at a family picnic. A few pages further, a pregnant Katherine stood with Helen, Jack, and CiCi in front of a Christmas tree on the town square.

Through alternating bouts of laughter and tears, she discovered a family bound by love, then torn apart by the anger of one man—Jack Parker.

One of the last pictures in the album showed a little girl and a toddler locked in a fierce embrace. They looked like sisters. CiCi knew they weren't. She was the young girl. The toddler must've been Jenna.

"You and Jenna would've been the best of friends," Katherine said. She dabbed a napkin at the lone tear that streaked down her cheek. "Every night, I ask God to send her home. The pain never goes away. It won't until I find her."

"I'm so sorry, Katherine. With my mother's illness last year, I didn't pay attention to the news, much less read about her disappearance. I wish I could do something to ease your pain."

Katherine paused. "Maybe you can."

CiCi took a deep breath, unsure of what Katherine might say. A clock chimed as CiCi waited for Katherine to speak.

"You have every right to say no, but would you talk to Jenna's friends? Perhaps they've heard from her or know where she is."

Stunned by the request, CiCi sat motionless while she gathered her thoughts. "Um, I don't know, Katherine. Have you talked to the authorities? After all, they're the professionals."

"The police have done all they can. They've closed the case and moved on to more pressing issues. They won't even return my calls. I sometimes wonder how competent they are."

"I understand your frustration. My fiancé is a detective, and I assure you he and most of the Ripley Grove Police Department take their jobs very seriously."

"That may be so, but you know as well as I do not every person does their job to the best of their ability. We've all worked with professionals who are not worthy of their title."

"True. Do you remember who was in charge of Jenna's case?"

"Let me think. Alfred Lowman? No, that's not right. Hmm, I think his name was Logan. That's it, Detective Albert Logan."

CiCi winced upon hearing the name. *Now I understand her frustration. Logan is a disgrace to his profession, and I'm not the only one who thinks so. Chad and Mark have complained that his investigative tactics aren't up to department standards.*

Katherine took a sip of tea. "Later on, a Detective Mason was assigned to help with the case. He's such a nice man. Though I hear he's retired now, he calls from time to time to let me know he still thinks of her." She sighed. "CiCi, I'm desperate. I've done everything I know to do. At one point, I even hired a private investigator, but he failed to uncover any information that would tell me where my daughter is. I have nothing to lose by asking for your help."

CiCi looked into the pleading eyes of the grief-stricken woman and her heart broke. *What should I do? I'm a real estate appraiser. I don't have any experience digging up information on a missing person. And yet, how can I say no? She's my aunt, the only blood relative I have left except for Jenna. Besides, what harm can it do to ask a few questions?*

"Okay, I'll talk to her friends." As soon as the words rolled off her tongue, she wondered if she'd made a mistake. *I should've given this more thought. I'm sure Chad won't approve. He might even think I'm questioning the competency of the RGPD.*

"Thank you." Katherine's eyes brimmed with tears. She clasped CiCi's hand in hers and smiled.

"Katherine, to be honest, things are hectic at work right now. I'll do what I can, when I can, and I can't guarantee I'll learn anything new."

"I appreciate anything you can do."

"Have you talked to Jenna's friends yourself?"

"Yes, but not recently. I think they'll be more open with you than they were with me or the police. They'll relate to you. You and Jenna look so much alike you could be her double."

"That's hard to believe."

Katherine stood and left the room. She returned a moment later and placed a framed photo in CiCi's hands. CiCi studied the image of her cousin. Other than the bright streaks of pink and purple in Jenna's blonde hair, the uncanny likeness startled her.

"In my distraught state of mind last Saturday, I saw what I wanted to see—my daughter in her wedding dress. As you can see, Jenna's hair is naturally straight and a shade lighter than yours—well, when she's not adding crazy colors to it. But the resemblance is there." Katherine took the photo back and lovingly stroked her finger on the glass over Jenna's cheek. Her lower lip began to quiver, but she regained control before looking at CiCi. "What can I do to help?"

"Well, I'll need a list of Jenna's friends, and I'd like to know more about her as a person."

Katherine nodded. "Come with me."

SEVEN

CiCi followed Katherine through the house. They stopped in front of a closed door at the end of a hallway. Katherine paused, her hand lingering on the doorknob. She took a deep breath, squared her shoulders, and pushed open the door.

CiCi's eyes widened. Without a doubt, the small bedroom belonged to a proud University of Kansas student. The crimson and blue décor contrasted with the rest of the house. A large Jayhawk mascot emblazoned the center of the bedspread and pillow shams. The valance over the window had been fashioned from various pennants. An assortment of posters hung on each wall. KU memorabilia sat atop nearly every flat surface, but somehow the room looked organized.

"After graduating from high school in Chicago, Jenna moved to Lawrence to go to college. She chose KU because my husband and I are both alumni. Jenna is somewhat restless. She switched majors several times and dropped out after five years without a single degree." She picked up a photo of Jenna and smiled. "I sold my store in Chicago and moved back to Ripley Grove a couple of years ago to be near her. After she quit school, she moved in with me for a short time. When her boyfriend proposed, they moved in together.

Three months before the wedding, she moved out of his apartment and in with a friend."

"Did they call off the wedding?"

"No, although I sensed things were tense between them. Then, one night she called to say she needed to talk to me about something. I haven't heard from her since."

"How old is she?"

"Twenty-seven."

"So, a couple of years younger than me. Did she work?"

"After college, nothing held her interest until she landed a job at *The Ripley Review*. That's where she met Tyler and discovered her love of writing. She worked at the paper for almost a year, the longest she'd stayed at any job."

"What did the police say? Is the case still open?"

"The case is closed. There were no signs of foul play. Detective Logan believes she left town to fulfill her journalism dream. Someone he spoke to said she talked about moving back to Chicago, where there would be more opportunities in her field. That was news to me. Even so, she wouldn't have left without saying goodbye or keeping in touch. Never. And she wouldn't intentionally put me or Tyler through this anguish."

CiCi looked around the room and was immediately drawn to a unique sunglass holder hanging on a closet door. Two rectangular layers of red suede had been sewn together, and there were twelve one-by-two-inch slits evenly spaced in the top layer. Every slot held a pair of sunglasses, a temple from each tucked into the opening. She ran her fingers over the soft fabric. "Looks like Jenna and I have something in common."

"You collect sunglasses?"

"I do, and this organizer is stunning. I love it. Mine hang from wire loops attached to the underside of a little framed cabinet that holds my collection of novelty flash drives."

She moved about the room. A framed picture on the dresser caught her attention. The photo captured Jenna at a party. A handsome young man with a guarded smile had his arm wrapped around her shoulders.

"That's Tyler Quinn. I don't hear from him much these days."

She studied a photo taped to the mirror. She turned it over and read the names printed on the back. "May I take a few pictures with my phone?"

Katherine nodded. "Sure, and I'll text you their contact information."

CiCi walked around the bed and nearly fell over a box on the floor.

"Sorry," Katherine said. "I should've tucked that in the closet. One of Jenna's friends brought it by last week. She found some of Jenna's things while packing to move."

"Do the police know about the box?"

She shrugged. "I didn't see any reason to tell them. The items inside are of no value to anyone but me."

"Did she own a car?"

"Yes, an old rusty, dark blue Jeep. She didn't need one when she lived on campus, but after she got the job at the newspaper, having a car was expected. She hated wasting money on insurance and taxes and considered a vehicle nothing more than a necessary evil—her words."

CiCi smiled. "I'm partial to Jeeps myself. In fact, I'm still driving the one my mother bought me when I graduated high school. I can't bear to part with it."

"That's another reason the police believe she left town. They never located her vehicle. From its looks alone, I doubt anyone in their right mind would steal it."

"I assume they checked to see if the car had been registered in another state?"

"They did, but nothing showed up."

"It's possible she sold it or junked it. What about credit cards?"

"Not a one. Saw how much debt her friends accumulated by using them, so she refused to apply for one. She didn't own much, but what she had, she paid for with cash."

"What about her bank account?"

"Hasn't been touched since she left. That's another reason I don't believe she left for a better job. She would need money to start over."

"Cell phone or computer?"

"No trace of either. None of her friends had seen her laptop, which had one of those personalized skins with the KU mascot on the lid. She had an old flip phone and the phone carrier eventually closed her account for non-payment." She cast an approving smile at CiCi. "I think you're a natural at this. You've already asked more questions than Detective Logan."

After a while, CiCi felt she'd gathered as much information as she could. She gave Katherine a warm hug before heading home.

CiCi pulled the chicken and rice casserole from the oven and scooped a large serving onto Chad's plate and then her own. Chad set a basket of crusty bread on the table.

"How did your meeting with Katherine go?" he asked.

"Better than I expected. We had a wonderful visit. I think you'll like her. It'd be nice if we take her out to dinner some evening."

"That'd be great. Just let me know when."

As they ate, she filled him in on the reason their two families never had contact.

Chad shook his head. "Your dad leaves a trail of destruction wherever he goes."

"It seems that way. I'm still mad that he and my mother lied to me all these years. I suppose there's nothing I can do now except move forward."

"Did she talk about her daughter, Jenna?"

"Yes, she did. She wasn't impressed with your Detective Logan, and she's not convinced Jenna left town in search of a new job."

Chad grunted. "First off, he's not *my* Detective Logan. Second, I don't know anyone who's impressed with him."

Having finished the meal, they put the leftovers in the fridge and cleared the table before settling on the sofa in the living room. They watched the evening news before browsing through Netflix. They settled on an action film, followed by a comedy. As the credits rolled, Chad glanced at his watch. "I need to go. I've got to be in the office early tomorrow."

"Hey, think you could read through Jenna's old case file when you have spare time?" she asked. "You might spot a clue or something that Logan missed."

He turned a dimpled smile to her. "I'm surprised you waited so long to ask. I've already put in a request for it."

She wrapped her arms around him and snuggled close. "I should've known you'd be one step ahead of me. I appreciate you doing that." She brushed her lips across his. He held his breath, as if waiting for more. He pulled her into him as she deepened the kiss.

"I appreciate your appreciation."

After he left, she stifled a yawn and glanced at the clock, surprised at how quickly the evening passed. Her cell phone dinged. She pulled it from her purse and read Katherine's text containing the contact information for Jenna's friends. A quick reply was sent to acknowledge that she'd received the message. Questions whirled in her mind as she slipped into her pj's, turned out the light, and crawled into bed.

Where did you go, Jenna? Your mother needs to know you're safe.

EIGHT

CiCi felt exhausted by four o'clock the following day. Again, she'd worked longer than she intended. She climbed into her Jeep, slipped on her sunglasses, and rolled her head from side to side to ease the tension in her neck. Letting the engine idle, she called Chad. He planned to hit the gym before meeting up with two former military buddies who were passing through town. Their conversation was brief, but hearing his voice had a calming effect. As she pulled from the lot, she had an idea.

She turned east on Sycamore and drove toward what the locals called the square. Situated in the old part of Ripley Grove, the square was one of CiCi's favorite places to shop and only four blocks from her townhome. An aging limestone courthouse, the post office, and the library were the focal points of the square. Lush lawns surrounding the buildings provided a parklike setting with plenty of benches nestled under mature shade trees. Dozens of shops and businesses, mostly of the "mom and pop" variety, occupied the streets around the downtown landmark. She made a left on Ash and drove a few blocks further until her destination came into view.

The Ripley Review was the city's only source for local news. The building looked tired and needed a fresh coat of paint. But that cost money—money the local newspaper struggled to keep as its subscriber base dwindled. She pushed open the door and went inside.

The brunette sitting behind the front desk had a phone wedged between her shoulder and ear. She held up a finger and continued her conversation. CiCi took a second glance at the familiar face. Though she couldn't recall her name, they had gone to high school together. After the former classmate disconnected, she flashed a smile at CiCi.

"Hey, CiCi. How can I help you?"

The soft voice rang a bell. "Abigail, long time, no see. How've you been?"

"Fine. How about yourself? You were in the hospital awhile back. You doing okay?"

"I'm good," CiCi replied. Hoping to avoid revisiting bad memories, she asked, "How long have you worked here?"

"About nine months now. It's a decent job and Rivera isn't a stickler if I need time off."

"Are those your kids? They're adorable," she asked, pointing to the photos on Abigail's desk. The proud mom smiled as she rattled off names, ages, and hobbies. The two women chatted on for several more minutes before CiCi got to the reason for her visit. "I stopped by to see if Tyler Quinn still works here."

"Sure does." She turned in her seat and craned her neck to look across the room. "There he is…the guy in the dark blue shirt."

"Thanks. Call me if you want to have lunch one of these days." CiCi jotted down her phone number, then walked past a dozen cluttered desks and a handful of workers. Some were on the phone, while others focused on their computer screens. A young man with glasses and shoulder-length hair fixed her with a stare as she passed. When she neared the end of the row, she recognized Tyler from Jenna's photo albums.

Tyler stood in his cubicle-with-a-view, rooting through a file cabinet. He was perhaps in his late twenties and slim. His tousled brown hair and the stubble on his angular face gave the impression he had just rolled out of bed. When he saw her approach, he froze. His eyes widened and his mouth hung open. With a frown, he tossed a file on the desk, then turned his back to her, choosing instead to stare out the window. He remained silent and unmoving, with his hands jammed into the pockets of his chinos.

"Tyler? Tyler Quinn?"

At the sound of her voice, Tyler's head snapped around. His piercing green eyes took in every inch of her face. His gaze lingered on the scar that ran down the side of her forehead. The shocked expression fell away, and his face flushed with embarrassment. "I'm sorry. I thought you were—never mind. My apologies."

Oh my gosh, he thought I was Jenna! But if that's the case, why wasn't he elated to see me? "My name's Cecilia Winslow." She took a tentative step forward and shook his hand.

"I should have realized that. If I'm not mistaken, you survived the incident at Five Star a few months back and were later attacked in your home. I didn't cover the story, but I understand you were badly injured. I hope you're recovering well."

"I am, thank you." *Is that how he thinks of murder—as simply an incident?*

He sank into the swivel chair behind his desk and directed her to an empty seat. It became clear from the way he looked at her that her resemblance to Jenna was difficult for him. His eyes drifted to a spot on the desk. She followed his gaze to a tiny picture of Jenna under the large sheet of plexiglass protecting his desktop.

She sat and gave him a minute to regroup and think of her as CiCi, not Jenna.

Tyler cleared his throat. "What can I do for you, Miss Winslow?"

"Please, call me CiCi. As a favor to Katherine Bliss, I'm talking to Jenna's friends to see if anyone has heard from her since she went missing."

His lips pressed into a tight line. "I can't speak for anyone else, but I haven't. The police believe she left town of her own free will, so the term *missing* is misleading."

"Is that what *you* believe—that she left without telling anyone?"

He was speechless, a quality she found unusual for a reporter. When he leaned forward to answer, a raspy voice shouting from across the room cut him off. "Quinn. In my office, pronto!"

Tyler sighed and shook his head. "Look, can we talk later? How about Peggy Sue's Diner on the square? Twenty minutes?"

After he dashed off towards the editor's office, she turned to leave. Again, she found the young man with glasses staring. She smiled to be polite and retraced her steps to the entrance, where she said goodbye to Abigail.

True to his word, Tyler entered the diner twenty minutes later. CiCi raised her hand to catch his attention. He approached her table and took a seat. At his nod, the waitress brought him a cup of coffee. He studied CiCi's face over the rim of his cup as he took a sip. "I apologize for staring, but your resemblance to Jenna is unnerving. At first glance, I assumed she'd gotten a perm and…well, let's just say you threw me for a loop."

"No need to be sorry. Jenna's mother had the same reaction. As a matter of fact, I recently learned from Katherine that Jenna and I are cousins."

"Is that so?" He leaned back and rested an ankle on the opposite knee. "How is Katherine?"

"Distraught."

"I'm not surprised. I quit visiting her. I'm a painful reminder of her daughter and a wedding that never took place."

"Tell me, do you believe Jenna left town to pursue a writing career?" From the corner of her eye, she saw a familiar face walk through the door. He pushed his glasses up the bridge of his nose, took a seat with an unobstructed view of their table, and placed an order with the waitress.

Tyler stared into his cup. "My gut says no, but I don't know what to believe. She was a small-town girl at heart who loved the simple life. This is where she belonged. It's true she had big dreams about furthering her career in journalism, but that's all it was—a dream. If she thought about moving, she never mentioned it to me. Besides, if she wanted to leave, we would've gone together, maybe to

Chicago. After all, that's where I'm from and I still have connections there."

"Her mother said she never finished college. Is she that good of a writer to land a job without a degree?"

His hand paused in midair, the cup halfway to his lips. Muscles in his jaw clenched several times before he took a drink. "Yes, she was." He lifted his mug and finished the last of his coffee. "Herb, our lead reporter, planned to retire at the end of summer, and Jenna had her heart set on filling his shoes. Rivera told Jenna she would have to write a story worthy of the front page before he'd risk giving her that big of a promotion."

"Did she ..." CiCi sensed she was being watched. She scanned the room and her search stopped on the young man with glasses, who quickly averted his eyes.

Tyler followed her gaze before turning his attention back to her. "Don't worry about Jimmy. He's geeky and a little weird at times, but he's a good guy and a great photographer. Like me, he probably thinks you're Jenna. He won't admit it, but he had a crush on her." He pushed his mug to the side and clasped his hands on the table. "What were you about to ask?"

"Did Jenna find a story worthy of the front page?"

He shrugged. "According to her, she did. In her mind, it was *big*. So big, in fact, she became very secretive. She wouldn't tell anyone what she was working on—not even me."

Those mesmerizing green eyes filled with fire as he spoke. *Interesting. Was he jealous of Jenna's natural talent as a writer, or angry she put her career over their relationship?*

"Did you ask?"

He nodded. "I did, several times. She said I needed to trust her, that she needed to write the story without my help. We argued about it, and she moved out. She promised I would understand once the newspaper printed the article."

"Where do you think she is?"

"I don't have a clue. Of all the possibilities, I hope she left town to follow her dream."

"Sometimes hope is all we have. Me? I'm hoping one of Jenna's friends can shed some light on where she might have gone."

"I wish you luck, but I doubt you'll find her." He pushed back the cuff of his sleeve to check the time. His lips pressed into a tight line. "If you'll excuse me, I have someplace to be."

CiCi watched him leave, puzzled by his response.

NINE

Friday afternoon's appraisal inspection had taken much longer than expected. The building was listed as a two-story, mixed-use property, with an apartment located above the fabric store. But she'd found a discrepancy. Extensive remodeling had been done, and there were now *two* apartments above the retail shop instead of one. After taking measurements and snapping numerous pictures inside and out, CiCi glanced at her watch. There was nothing more she could do today. She climbed into her Jeep and headed home.

The breeze through the open window whipped her hair into a frenzy. Her mind lingered on the last inspection of the day. As per company policy, Floyd would double-check her report, but finding the error bolstered her confidence and left her feeling satisfied. She loved working as a real estate appraiser and was glad to have found her niche in life.

Was that how it was with Jenna? Did she switch majors in college and jump from job to job because she never found her niche until she landed a position at the newspaper? CiCi's thoughts turned to her conversation with Tyler. Something didn't make sense. The police led Katherine to believe Jenna left town to further her career in a bigger market. If that was true, why didn't she go with Tyler and take advantage of his connections in Chicago? *Maybe she didn't leave town. Maybe there's a link between Jenna's story and her disappearance.*

She drove the same route as the day before, parked in front of *The Ripley Review*, and went inside. Tyler's desk sat empty, as did several other desks in the room. Abigail occupied the reception desk, directing a customer to someone who could answer her questions.

When it came to CiCi's turn, Abigail gave her a welcoming smile. They chatted for a minute or two before Abigail told of a recent humorous outing with her children. Her color-blind five-year-old son asked for jello with his meal instead of applesauce. When the waitress brought the small bowl of bright red, jiggly cubes to the table, her son clapped with excitement and exclaimed, "Oh, goody. Chocolate is my favorite!" Both women laughed freely, their voices carrying across the room.

"Cecilia Winslow. I'd know that laugh anywhere."

The gravelly voice drew CiCi's attention to her right, where a tall man in his late fifties stood, his grin hidden behind a thick mustache that matched his dark hair. She smiled. "Mr. Rivera. You're just the man I came to see."

He tilted his head toward the hallway and motioned her to follow. When she entered his office, he gave her shoulder a friendly pat before offering her a seat and settling himself behind a large oak desk littered with papers. "How are you getting along, CiCi?"

"Good. I've returned to work, I got engaged, and life is good. I understand I have you to thank for not printing the picture of me one of your eager reporters took while I was in the ICU." Though his naturally tan skin made it difficult to see, the tough-as-nails editor-in-chief blushed, bringing a smile to CiCi's face.

"A new kid tried to impress me by getting a leg up on Jimmy, our regular photographer. He impressed me all right, enough to can him on the spot." He shook his head. "Reporters today have no sense of decency. They think the world revolves around sensationalism. Your mother, God rest her soul, would've haunted me day and night if I'd printed that picture. Our friendship never stopped her from telling me when she thought I was wrong."

CiCi grinned. "There were no gray areas in her world. Things were strictly black or white, and you always knew where she stood on any given subject."

"That's true," he chuckled. "Now, tell me why you're here. I know you didn't come to shoot the breeze with an old man who's getting crankier by the day."

"I'm looking for answers. I understand Jenna Bliss worked here before her disappearance. Have you heard from her since she left?"

He frowned. "No, I haven't, though I tried to contact her numerous times."

"What can you tell me about her employment here?"

"Why are you asking?"

"As a favor to her mother."

"I see. And she wants you to look into it?"

"She does. I recently learned Jenna is my cousin, so naturally, I want to find her. I figure it can't hurt to ask a few questions."

"I can see the family resemblance. When Jenna first hired on, I asked if she knew you. Said she didn't, so I let the matter drop." He leaned back in the worn leather chair and stared into space as though sorting his thoughts. After a moment or two, he straightened and braced his elbows on the desktop. "I'll tell you what I told the police. I took a chance and hired her to write the obits after she dropped out of college. Turned out she had a natural talent for making the most mundane life seem extraordinary. I was half-tempted to have her write *my* obituary, not that I'm ready to say my final goodbyes just yet."

"Did she have problems with any of her co-workers?"

Mr. Rivera opened his mouth to speak, then paused before speaking. "Nothing to speak of, really. After a while, Jenna asked to cover stories that had more substance, so I let her write a couple of human-interest pieces. Soon, she wanted more. Had her eye on a vacancy we had coming up. I told her she had to prove herself. Then maybe, just maybe, I would consider her for a promotion. Until then, I would leave front page reporting to those better qualified."

"You mean, someone with more experience?" Movement in the

hallway caught her eye. Abigail slowly walked past, carrying a ream of paper.

"Exactly." He shook his head. "All these young kids think they're entitled to whatever job they want without putting in any effort whatsoever."

CiCi nodded. "I know; I work with one. What did Jenna do after that?"

"A month or so later, she quit showing up for work. I assumed she landed another job. I was surprised when the police came asking about her."

"Did she give notice?"

"No, but I'm not surprised. She was mad that I suggested she finish her education. Didn't want to hear it. Said education was overrated."

"I understand she was working on a big story before she left."

He cocked his head. "That's news to me. If she was, it wasn't something I assigned to her. Have you talked to her ex-fiancé? He works here, you know."

"Tyler? I have."

The phone on the desk rang several times. "I don't know what else to tell you, CiCi." Mr. Rivera shook his head and then picked up the handset.

CiCi gave him a wave as she left, and he nodded in return. As she passed a vending machine, a shapely young woman in her early twenties walked by. Without stopping, she snatched the candy bar from the hand of a young man wearing off-kilter glasses. When he looked up, she recognized him as Jimmy, the paper's photographer who had followed her and Tyler to Peggy Sue's yesterday.

"Come on, Serena," Jimmy shouted. "That was the last candy bar without nuts."

She laughed and tossed her dark brown hair over a shoulder as she walked toward the entrance. She turned and faced him when she reached the door. Peeling back the wrapping, she took a slow, dramatic bite of the candy bar, no doubt to taunt him. "What are you going to do? Run to the boss and tattle? Man up, Jimmy. If you want it, come get it." She took another bite, then slowly ran her tongue across her lips.

"No, thanks. I've lost my appetite." He extended a middle finger to push his glasses from the end of his nose back to their proper place, sending a not-so-subtle message to Serena.

"Oh, *that's* real mature." She laughed as he stormed off. She took another bite, then tossed the rest into a nearby trashcan.

After Serena left, Abigail shook her head and looked at CiCi. "Office shenanigans, but one of these days karma will bite that girl in the butt. She should treat Jimmy better, especially since her stories depend on his photography skills." Abigail brushed her bangs out of her eyes. "I can't wait for this week to be over. So, you're asking around about Jenna, huh?"

"How did you...oh."

Abigail grinned. "It never hurts to keep your eyes and ears open around here. When I first started working here, that's all everyone talked about. I thought the picture of Tyler's fiancée on his desk was you until I remembered you were dating a cop."

CiCi extended her left hand and wiggled her fingers. "Chad's a detective, and we're engaged."

"Congrats. I'm so happy for you."

"Thanks. What else have you heard about Jenna?"

"Not much, but you might want to talk to Serena, the gal who just left. She and Jenna weren't the best of friends."

"Oh? Why's that?"

Abigail glanced around to see if anyone was near enough to hear their conversation. "For one thing, rumor had it that Serena was always hitting on Tyler."

"That would make any fiancée mad."

"There's more." She leaned across the counter and lowered her voice. "The senior reporter on staff had planned to retire. Serena and Jenna both wanted his job. Mr. Rivera had a hard time choosing between the two, but everyone thought Jenna was a shoo-in for the job."

"Were they both equally qualified?"

"Serena has a business degree but has her mind set on being a journalist. Jimmy said Jenna had more talent in her little finger than Serena could ever hope to have."

"Then why did Mr. Rivera even consider Serena for the position?"

"She's his goddaughter. She always gets what she wants, by any means possible. According to Jimmy, the next thing everyone knew, Jenna was gone, and Rivera gave the job to Serena."

The phone rang and Abigail returned to her job. CiCi waved goodbye and walked to her car. *Hmm, I guess Rivera had his blinders on when he spoke about kids today expecting something for nothing.*

TEN

CiCi left *The Ripley Review* and headed to the grocery store. As she stood in the aisle rifling through her purse for a coupon, a shopping cart bumped hers. She glanced up and smiled. "Hi, Katherine. Getting a little shopping done before the weekend?"

"No, I'm picking up a few things for Mom. She lives at the Sunflower Village Nursing Home. They supply the necessities, but she's particular about the shampoo she uses."

CiCi's eyes widened. "Wait. *Your mother?* Does that mean I have a grandmother?"

Katherine shook her head. "I'm sorry. Edna Cracken is my former mother-in-law, but I've always called her Mom. Even after my husband passed, we've remained very close."

"Her last name isn't Bliss?"

"She's been widowed twice. When her health started to fail, she moved to Sunflower Village. She's charming, but can be a handful at times, even for her nurses. Would you like to meet her? I'm headed there now."

CiCi checked the time. "Sure. Chad won't expect me at the bowling alley until seven."

"Good. I'll see you there. Edna's in room 102."

Ten minutes later, CiCi pulled into the center's parking lot. Her heart rate kicked up a notch as she approached the single-story building that combined assisted living and nursing home care under one roof. Her own mother spent the last days of her life in a care facility much like this one. It was hard to believe that five months had passed since her death.

As the double doors swooshed open, the sound of flatware clinking against plates and the low murmur of voices told her the residents were eating dinner. She looked around the spacious lobby for Katherine, then approached the reception desk.

The woman at the front desk glanced up and smiled. "You look lost, honey. Can I help?"

"Yes, I'm here to visit Edna Cracken."

"Normally, she'd be in the dining room eating meatloaf with her friends, but she's in a snit today. You'll find her in room 102, down the hallway to your left."

"Thanks." CiCi turned left and followed the signage.

A few seconds later, she entered Edna's room. Soft yellow walls reflected the fading remnants of daylight streaming through the large window. The bed, along with two upholstered chairs flanking an end table, faced a flat screen TV atop an antique sideboard on the opposite wall. Family pictures adorned the walls on either side of the double closet.

While Edna sat in one of the chairs, Katherine stood beside her, lovingly brushing back a strand of hair from the elderly woman's forehead. "Look, Mom. You have a visitor."

The woman's aged face lit up with a smile when she caught sight of CiCi. "Jenna, baby, I've missed you. Come, let me look at you."

CiCi lifted her eyebrows and glanced at Katherine.

"Her vision is poor and she's a bit hard of hearing," Katherine whispered. She leaned over to Edna and said, "Mom, this is CiCi Winslow, not Jenna."

"I'm not losing my mind. I know my girl when I see her."

Katherine shrugged and whispered, "I don't think arguing with her will do any good."

CiCi stepped forward and gave Edna's hand a gentle squeeze. "How are you feeling today?"

"Have you got a cold, dear? Katie, get her a cough drop. There's some in the nightstand." Edna leaned back against the chair and smoothed the lap blanket covering her frail body.

"Mom, what's this I hear about you not eating dinner?" Katherine asked, motioning for CiCi to have a seat.

"I'm not about to sit with Mable after she ate my chocolate pudding at lunch. She knows how much I love dessert."

CiCi opened her purse and pulled out a baggie containing the dessert she had left over from lunch. "This must be your lucky day. I happen to have a slice of homemade banana bread you can have. But there's a catch."

The elderly woman's eyes narrowed. "What's the catch?"

"You have to eat dinner. I hear they're serving meatloaf tonight, and it smells delicious."

Edna's eyes widened. "Meatloaf? With mashed potatoes and gravy? Maybe I will."

"Good. Let me have someone bring you a tray of food, then we'll visit while you eat. How does that sound?"

An hour and a half later, CiCi glanced at her watch. "Oh! I'm sorry, I need to go." She stood and gave a gentle squeeze to Edna's hand before turning to leave.

"Don't forget your jacket, dear. You left it last time you were here. It's hanging in the back of the closet. And don't stay away so long."

"I'll be back to visit soon," CiCi said as she opened the closet door. Jenna's coat was hard to miss amongst Edna's wardrobe. She pulled the lightweight camouflage jacket from the hanger, slung it over her arm, and waved goodbye.

Katherine walked CiCi to the exit. "I can't thank you enough for getting her to eat and playing along when she thought you were Jenna. Once she gets something in her head, there's no convincing her otherwise."

"I enjoyed the visit as much as she did. I'll stop by again

sometime. By the way, I've talked with Tyler and Jenna's boss at the newspaper. No one's heard from her."

"Thanks for trying." Katherine's smile barely hid her disappointment. She turned and slowly retraced her steps to Edna's room.

It wasn't until CiCi had gotten into her Jeep that she realized she still held Jenna's jacket. She shrugged and tossed the jacket into the back seat. Pulling out her phone, she saw two missed calls from Chad. She sent a quick text that she was on her way.

By the time she arrived at The Alley, Chad's Strike Hard, Spare None bowling team was well into the eighth frame of the first game and ahead by fifty pins. She slipped into the chair beside him and gave him a kiss on the cheek.

"You had me worried," he said as he wrapped an arm around her shoulder.

"Sorry," she shouted over the noise. Bowling balls rolled down the lanes, pins exploded, and eighteen machines racked the downed pins in a continuous pattern of organized chaos. "I was visiting someone at Sunflower Village. Time got away from me."

"Oh? Anyone I know?"

"Edna Cracken, Katherine's mother-in-law."

"Chad! You're up!" Mark, Chad's teammate and a fellow detective, shouted over the din. He caught CiCi's eye, winked, and tipped his beer in her direction. She grinned back, then waved to Frank Guzman. He was the third member of the team as well as a fellow officer.

"What's up, missy? Glad you could make it." Pete Mason, the fourth member of the team and a retired detective who owned and operated a security and surveillance company, smiled as he slid his trim six-foot-two frame into Chad's empty chair. After adjusting the velcro straps of his wrist guard, he stroked the thick salt-and-pepper mustache that matched his hair.

"Hey, Pete. How's it going?" She always enjoyed talking to Pete. He was a lovable character who had become a good friend, and he had a sweet tooth that rivaled her own. Questions about Jenna's case popped into her head, but she quickly dismissed the idea of asking for his input. *There's no doubt he would mention it to Chad, but Chad should hear it from me first. He may have agreed to look over Jenna's file, but I'm not sure how he will feel about me looking up Jenna's friends and asking questions.*

"I'm in peak form tonight. I just rolled a five-bagger. You can watch me show your fiancé how it's done."

"In your dreams, old man," Chad said. "You leave one open frame, and I'll catch up. Now, get out of my seat and away from my girl." Pete laughed and slid over to the next chair.

"I hope you two remember you're on the same team," CiCi said.

"Nothing wrong with a little friendly competition. You hungry?"

"I'm starving. I'll take a cheeseburger, fries, and a soda." There was nothing tastier than a burger fried on a greasy grill. As Chad walked away, she called after him. "Oh, don't forget—"

"I know, a brownie or a chocolate chip cookie." He tossed her a grin. "Sugar, if you didn't want dessert, I'd think you were sick."

After the third game, Chad wandered off to put his bowling ball in his rented locker. CiCi popped the last of the brownie in her mouth while he checked next week's schedule. When he finished, Chad took her hand and walked her out to her vehicle. Most of the cars were gone, and the moon cast a soft glow over the lot.

"As captain, I think I deserve a reward for a job well done tonight." Chad pressed her up against the Jeep and smiled. His lips grazed hers as his hands slid beneath her shirt to caress the sensitive skin along her rib cage. She shivered at his touch.

"I thought the wins were a team effort."

"I'm not sharing my prize with anyone." His lips gently skimmed down her neck.

"How about a reward for having the highest score on the team?" She pulled him in for a passionate kiss.

"Mmm. I love chocolate kisses. I can still taste the brownie you ate."

Mark exited the bowling alley and climbed into his vehicle. The engine roared to life, his headlights illuminating Chad and CiCi as they kissed. Mark beeped his horn twice as he drove off, destroying the intimate moment. Chad sighed and shook his head. She gave a little laugh and scooted out from under his embrace, much to his dismay.

"Hey, have you read Jenna's file yet?"

"The paperwork hit my desk as I was leaving work. Don't worry, I should have time to look it over next week." He opened the door to her Jeep.

"Are we still on for tomorrow?" she asked as she climbed into the driver's seat. Before she shut the door, he leaned in for another kiss.

"Definitely. You feeling okay, sugar? You look a little tired."

"I worked longer than I expected, is all. Speaking of Jenna, there's something I want to run by you. Katherine asked—"

Chad's phone buzzed and he pulled it from his pocket and read the screen. His mood changed in an instant. "Sorry, hon, I've got to go."

"That's okay. I'll see you tomorrow. Love you."

ELEVEN

The next morning, CiCi sighed as she hung up the phone. Chad had been called in to work, so it looked as though they wouldn't be spending the day together as planned. The unexpected interruption was a normal part of life, considering his profession.

After a quick shower, she stripped the bed and added the linens to the pile of dirty laundry heaped in front of the washing machine. Between each load, she dusted, paid bills, and folded the clothes she took from the dryer. Once finished, she went downstairs, kicked her shoes off, and settled on the sofa with a tall glass of tea and a book. The mystery was intriguing, but Jenna was never far from her thoughts.

Unable to concentrate, she stood and pulled a small spiral notepad from a buffet drawer. On a clean page, she wrote Tyler's name and jotted a few notes from their conversation. He hadn't given her much to go on, except that Jenna hadn't been happy with her current position at the newspaper and talked of working on a "big story" guaranteed to get her noticed. Something seemed off with his relationship with Jenna, but she couldn't put her finger on it.

She added Jenna's boss, Mr. Rivera, to the list and a summary of their exchange. She found it hard to believe he wasn't aware Serena and Jenna were at odds. Abigail knew it to be so. Jimmy would probably agree, seeing as he also didn't get along with Serena.

CiCi called a couple of Jenna's college friends, hoping they may have heard from her. They hadn't. After adding a few additional notes to the notepad, she slipped on her shoes and chose a blue pair of sunglasses from her collection. There was no point in staying inside on such a beautiful day. She might as well use the opportunity to talk to Serena and the girlfriend Jenna roomed with after she moved out of Tyler's apartment. Before heading to her Jeep, she grabbed a few cookies from the freezer and defrosted them in the microwave. Having home-baked goodies on hand often opened the door to a friendly conversation.

CiCi parked in front of the upscale duplex and compared the address Abigail had given her to those on the residence. From the number of vehicles in the driveway and lining both sides of the street, Serena was having a party. She sidestepped between a lime green VW and a red BMW before bumping her shin on the bumper of a shiny black Ford parked in front of the garage. After walking up a short flight of stairs, she knocked on the door and huffed a loose strand of hair out of her eyes. Muffled music and laughter filtered from inside. She waited, then knocked again. As she raised her hand to try again, the front door swung open.

Serena stood in the doorway, her eyes wide as if surprised.

"Hi. My name's CiCi Winslow. I was hoping you might have a few minutes to talk."

Serena's brows furrowed, and she snapped her fingers. "Oh. Winslow. Weren't you a prime suspect in a murder at Five Star a few months back?"

CiCi winced at the casual ease in which her name was connected to the crime. "Yes, but—"

"I get it," she said, stepping out onto the porch. "Grumpa wants me to write a piece on how you're coping now that the tragedy is behind you. That's a great idea, and I'm the perfect person to write a human-interest story."

A black and white cat appeared and began to rub against Serena's legs. Serena wrinkled her nose in disgust. "Shoo! Get lost, you stupid cat! I've told you before; I'm not feeding you." Using her foot, she shoved the cat across the stoop and into the shrubs below. The feline let out a loud meow before scampering off to safety. "Look, I'd love nothing better than to hear your story, but I don't work on weekends. Check back with me at the office on Monday."

CiCi held up a palm. "I didn't come to talk about me. I came to ask about Jenna."

Serena crossed her arms over her chest. "Why are you interested in *her*?"

"I'm her cousin, and I'd like to find her."

"I see the resemblance, but why ask me?"

"Employees always know more about what's going on in the workplace than the boss."

Serena snorted. "That's for sure."

"So, have you heard from her since she left town? Phone calls, texts…anything?"

"You're kidding, right? We weren't exactly the best of friends. She had a nasty habit of trying to make me look bad. Well, it didn't work, because *I* got the promotion she wanted. I'm sure you saw my byline on yesterday's front-page."

"I did. You have quite a knack for getting to the heart of the story." She watched as Serena relaxed and soaked in the compliment. "Someone told me Jenna had been working on a big story before she left. Do you know what the story was about?"

Serena leaned against the doorframe. "Don't know. I doubt she was working on anything. She may be your cousin, but Jenna was nothing more than a job hopper and college dropout. She probably moved on to avoid causing any more embarrassment for her family and Tyler. He should be glad she's out of his life. His family values money, education, and social standing, none of which Jenna had."

"So, she and Tyler weren't a good fit?"

"Didn't take a rocket scientist to figure that out. Their relationship was doomed from the beginning. Tyler just didn't realize it." Someone inside the house yelled Serena's name. She turned and opened the screen door. "I need to go."

"If you hear from Jenna, would you let me know?"

"Maybe." Halfway inside, Serena stopped and stepped back outside. "How about we make a deal? I'll let you know if I hear anything new, and you do the same for me. I'd love to write the story, especially if she's gotten herself into trouble."

"I'll think about it." *Yeah, probably not. I'd never turn Jenna's life into a three-ring circus for the sake of a headline.*

As CiCi climbed into her Jeep, she realized she'd left the cookies on the passenger seat. Somehow, she didn't feel guilty. It would take more than cookies to sweeten up Serena. CiCi glanced back at the duplex. Serena stood at the window, peeking through the mini-blinds. CiCi started her vehicle and headed to her next destination.

Fifteen minutes later, she turned down Polk Avenue, a street that ran along the lower west side of town. The neighborhood contained a mixture of low-rent properties that struggled to maintain their dignity. Several landlords had let Mother Nature take over, while others tried hard to keep appearances and property values up.

She pulled into an empty space in front of four curbside mailboxes that sat precariously atop a rotted wood post. The rectangular outlines flanking each window were vivid reminders that the single-story structure had shutters once upon a time. The inside had seen better days. Two low-wattage bulbs lit the drab hallway, paint flaked from the cracked walls, and chunks were missing from the cheap peel-and-stick tile floor. *Despite the location and size, the owner could up the value with a few simple fixes.*

She walked down the dim corridor and knocked at the last apartment on the left. A young woman wearing a long-sleeved T-shirt and a pair of baggy jeans opened the door. With a hand that clutched a twenty-dollar bill, she brushed back a strand of dark brown hair from her face, revealing a smudge of dirt across one cheek. Her eyes went straight to the small bag in CiCi's hand. "So? Where's my pop and pizza?"

CiCi had been mistaken for someone else many times, but never for someone who delivered pizza. "Sorry, Heather. I guess I'm not who you were expecting. My name's CiCi Winslow. If you can spare a few minutes, I'd like to ask you a few questions about Jenna."

Her eyes widened as she took in CiCi's face, then a smile appeared. "Oh, right, Katherine left a message and said you might stop by."

The outside door to the fourplex opened and a uniformed young man raced down the hall with a large pizza box and a two-liter bottle of pop. He panted as he looked at his watch. "Twenty-nine minutes. A minute to spare. That'll be twenty-two-fifty-five."

"It should be nineteen-fifty with my coupon." She dug in her pocket and handed him a crumpled piece of paper along with her money.

He frowned, realizing she intended to give him a measly fifty-cent tip. He looked at the coupon and shoved it back into her hand. "That expired two months ago."

Heather read the fine print and scrunched up her nose. "Well, darn."

CiCi reached into her purse, pulled out a five, and handed it to the driver. "Keep the change." The delivery guy smiled, handed the box and the pop to Heather, then turned and left.

"Thanks. You might as well come in. There's plenty for both of us." Heather opened the lid and waved a pineapple, shrimp, and mushroom pizza under CiCi's nose. The smell alone almost made her gag. No way on earth would she ever eat shrimp on a pizza.

"Thanks, I'm not hungry. Go ahead, eat while it's hot. Then we'll have dessert," CiCi said, holding up the bag of cookies.

Heather giggled. "Don't tempt me. I've been known to eat dessert first."

Moving boxes were stacked three rows high against one wall in the front room, making the living space appear even smaller than it was. A four-foot-long breakfast bar, the only dining space visible, separated the living room from the tiny, one-person kitchen. Heather scooped a stack of newspapers from two barstools, then went to the kitchen. CiCi took a seat as Heather returned with two glasses of ice and poured them each something to drink.

"Sorry for the mess. My boyfriend and I take possession of our new place soon. I can't wait to move out of this dump. It's way too small." Heather sat, then grabbed a slice of pizza and took a bite. "So, what do you want to know?"

"I understand you were the last person Jenna lived with. Do you have any idea where she went after she moved out?"

"Nope. Took me by surprise when she left. Until the police came around asking about her, I thought she moved back in with Tyler."

"Think she moved away to find a better job in a bigger city?"

Heather picked off a piece of shrimp and popped it in her mouth. "I guess it's possible. She always was the restless sort. Trying this, dabbling in that. She couldn't pick a college major and stick with it. I really thought she'd settled down after she got hired at the newspaper and met Tyler. I don't know which she loved more—her job or Tyler."

"I heard she didn't like the job."

"Not true. She didn't like writing *obits*," Heather said, tossing the crusty edge of the pizza back into the box. "When her boss started letting her branch out and cover feature stories, she knew she'd found her calling. Trouble was, even though she and Tyler loved each other, working at the same place created problems."

"How so?"

"They were both jealous. Tyler was jealous of Jenna's talent. He was furious when she kept him in the dark about a story she'd been working on. I could sympathize. She wanted to prove to herself, and to him, that for once in her life, she could start something and finish it without any help." Heather reached for another slice and refilled her cup. "She was also jealous of the attention Tyler received from some gal at work. They argued about it. A lot."

"Did she mention a name?" CiCi knew who the woman was but wanted confirmation.

"No. Later, when Jenna struck up a friendship with some guitar player, Tyler accused her of trying to get even. She told him it was work-related, but he didn't believe her. That's when Jenna asked if she could stay here until they sorted things out."

"But she never called off the wedding?"

"No way. She loved Tyler more than anything, and her mom almost as much."

"Are you the one who dropped off a box of Jenna's stuff at her mother's house?" CiCi took a few sips of pop.

"Yeah. I ran across a few things when I started packing. I store extra furniture in the basement and keep the overflow of boxes in the second bedroom where Jenna slept. She didn't bring much with her and didn't seem to mind the cramped conditions. She kept most of her clothes and belongings in her car. With her working two jobs, she never spent much time here."

"Two jobs?"

"Yeah. She worked at the newspaper during the day and waited tables at The Tap & Keg three or four evenings a week."

"Hmm. Katherine never mentioned Jenna worked at a bar."

"I don't think she wanted her mom to know, but Tyler knew. She started working at The Tap & Keg maybe a month before she moved out of his place."

"Is that where she met the guitar player?"

Heather nodded around a mouthful of pizza. "I think so. I had the impression he's the reason she took the job in the first place. She didn't seem infatuated with the guy; she was more like…focused. It's hard to explain."

After she finished half of the pizza, she put the remainder in the fridge. When she turned, her eyes fixed on CiCi's dessert bag on the counter. CiCi nodded, and Heather delved into the sack with a smile and moaned with pleasure at the first bite. She offered a cookie to CiCi, who declined. Not that she wasn't hungry, but eating cookies while the putrid smell from the pizza lingered in the air just seemed wrong.

They chatted like old friends while Heather munched on cookies. After eating her fill, Heather stood and picked up a flattened box and the tape gun. "Well, I'd better get busy. This stuff won't pack itself."

CiCi thanked her for the information and left to the grating sounds of ripping tape. Her stomach rumbled as she climbed into her Jeep. She was hungry, but not for pizza. She drove to one of her favorite places, the Speckled Pig, and ordered a pulled pork sandwich and a drink.

As she ate, she took out her list and summarized what she'd learned. It seemed strange Tyler never mentioned a second job or a guitar player, or that Serena played a part in his separation from Jenna. CiCi wrote down Serena's name and jotted observations underneath. Serena had certainly done her research on Tyler. Had she wanted Jenna out of the way in order to tap into the connections he and his family had in Chicago? Had Serena's relationship with Tyler moved forward after Jenna left? It seemed doubtful, as Tyler still had Jenna's photo under the glass mat on his desk.

CiCi closed her notebook and leaned back against the booth. She checked her phone, hoping to see a text from Chad. Nothing. Calls to a couple of Jenna's college classmates didn't yield any new information. She sighed, pushed away her unfinished sandwich, and opened the notebook again. After a few minutes, she stuffed the pen and paper into her purse and walked out to her Jeep. *A Saturday night with no plans. Might as well head home and see what's on the Hallmark channel.*

CiCi attended the Sunday worship service the next morning. Though a tad long, the sermon was thought-provoking and the music a refreshing mix of contemporary and traditional. She and Tasha mingled with friends and neighbors before heading out to lunch on the square. After the meal, CiCi headed home. With Chad busy for the day, she had the afternoon free to complete a residential appraisal on her laptop. Working from home also hid the fact that she was putting in a few more hours than her doctor recommended.

After she finished, she tidied up the house, hemmed a pair of slacks for work, then spent the evening restocking the freezer with baked goods. The brownies received a generous layer of frosting and the apple-spice bars got a light dusting of powdered sugar. The aroma in the house brought back nostalgic memories of baking with her grandmother.

As she washed and dried the last mixing bowl, Chad called. He planned to head home and go straight to bed. Exhaustion seeped through his voice as he spoke, reminding her again of the physical and mental toll of his job. Before saying goodbye, he said, "Why don't you ask Katherine if she'd like to go out to dinner tomorrow night?"

"That's a great idea."

She called Katherine, who readily accepted the invitation. Their conversation felt effortless, and the time flew by. CiCi enjoyed how natural it felt, especially since they hadn't known each other long. With her mother gone, she hadn't realized how much she missed having family to talk to.

After hanging up, CiCi took a cup of hot tea and a sampling of her baked goods upstairs and snuggled under the covers with a book. Before long, she drifted to sleep with a smile on her face and powdered sugar on her lips.

TWELVE

On Monday, CiCi's computer didn't want to work any more than some of her co-workers. She had several phone messages to return, property info to clarify, a client who shortened the deadline on an appraisal by several days, and another who thought the value of his property had been miscalculated, despite the detailed report backing up her findings. The day was long, and by five-thirty she was more than ready to call it a day.

She rushed home and found Chad sitting in her living room. "I know. I'm running late," she said on the way to her bedroom. "Give me twenty minutes to shower and change."

Thirty minutes later, she reappeared in a pair of cobalt blue dress slacks and a silk blouse tied at the waist to accentuate her soft curves. The diamond pendant that once belonged to her mother sparkled from the delicate chain around her neck.

Chad rose and took her in his arms. "You look amazing," he said, nuzzling her neck.

She pressed her lips to his, enjoying the feel of his embrace and the woodsy scent of his cologne. She stepped back and smiled. "You're looking mighty handsome tonight."

As she reached to straighten his tie, her vision blurred and the room began to spin. The floor shifted under her feet and her heart raced. She swayed, struggling to keep her balance.

"Sugar, what's wrong?" Chad drew her close, providing the support she needed. "I've got you, hon. Just relax. Steady your breathing. In …out…in…out, that's it." When her knees buckled, he caught her and helped her to the sofa.

She leaned her head back, closed her eyes, and let the episode fade. As in the past, an unexplained weakness lingered. When her strength returned, she forced a small lie through her lips. "I'm fine, Chad. Really."

"You sure?"

No, but I'm not about to admit it. "I'm fine," she repeated, hoping to erase the concern in his voice. She ran a shaky hand over her face and straightened. "I didn't eat much today, and work has been stressful with everyone speculating about the new partnership."

"The doctor said you could work twenty hours a week. Are you working more than that?" She looked away and he sighed. "That's what I thought. You've made a lot of progress these last few months, hon, but if you don't take care of yourself …"

"This dizziness is just a little bump in the road."

"Do you know what they call those little bumps in the road?"

She rolled her eyes. "What?"

"Speed bumps. They're designed to slow you down."

She absently touched the scar on the side of her forehead, an everyday reminder of how lucky she was to be alive. *I refuse to be defined by a head injury—or let it slow me down.* "You worry too much."

"From what I'm seeing, I have good reason to."

"I'm *fine*. We need to go. I told Katherine we'd pick her up at six, and we're late."

"Okay," he said, helping her to her feet, "but I want to know if you start feeling off again. Promise?"

"You'll be the first to know." *But no promises.*

After the waiter delivered drinks and took their orders, Katherine lifted her glass. "A toast to the happy couple and my congratulations on your engagement. I wish you a lifetime of love and happiness."

Chad raised his glass and smiled. "Thank you, Katherine."

"We'd love for you to come to the wedding," CiCi said.

"I look forward to it. I'm hoping, CiCi, that you'll allow me to design a custom wedding gown for you—that is, unless you've decided to shop elsewhere."

CiCi placed a hand over her heart. "Thank you, Katherine. I'd be honored. And I never once thought of looking at another store."

Conversation flowed freely throughout dinner, moving from wedding talk, to interests, to funny stories from the past. After sharing a memory of a young CiCi trying to teach Jenna how to blow bubbles, Katherine turned quiet.

"Is everything all right?" CiCi asked, placing her hand over Katherine's.

"Yes, dear. The meal was delicious and the company delightful." She turned to Chad. "I'm sure you know the situation with my daughter, Jenna."

Chad took a drink of water. "I do."

"I understand you've offered to go over Jenna's file to see if there's anything amiss. I appreciate you doing that. It means a great deal to me."

"I'm happy to do it. After all, we're practically family, and family comes first."

He paused and swirled the ice in his glass as though thinking how to continue. CiCi noticed the slight change in his posture. *Detective Cooper has joined the conversation.*

"I'll be honest with you, Katherine," he said, "it'll take a while to give it the attention it needs. I think someone must've dropped the file and tossed the paperwork back in the folder without a second thought. The notes and interviews are a jumbled mess."

"I'm grateful for anything you can do. From what CiCi has told me, you have a keen eye for detail." She sat back and smiled. "And with her asking—"

Suddenly, the glass CiCi held to her lips slipped from her fingers.

Water and ice cubes splashed onto her lap, and the glass tumbled to the floor. CiCi gasped as the icy water soaked her slacks. Chad reached across the table to hand her his napkin.

"Are you feeling okay?" he whispered as a waitress rushed over with extra towels.

"What? Oh, um, yes, I'm fine. Just a bit clumsy," she said, dabbing a napkin against her slacks.

After paying the bill, Chad and CiCi dropped off Katherine at her home. She thanked them for the wonderful evening, and Chad, being the gentleman that he was, walked her to the door. He paused, only turning to leave once he heard the deadbolt slide into place.

"You were right. She's a sweet lady."

"I think so, too."

He held her hand as he drove, caressing the back of her hand with his thumb. After arriving at her townhome, he followed her inside and settled himself on the sofa while she fixed him a cup of coffee. He flipped through the newspaper, picked up a pen, and began working the daily crossword puzzle. She set his drink on the coffee table, kicked her shoes off, and claimed the opposite end of the couch and the front section of the paper.

He paused. "You know, it's strange. Earlier tonight, I had the feeling Katherine wanted to say something more about Jenna's disappearance." She shrugged and he returned to his crossword puzzle, tapping the pen against his chin. A minute later, he asked, "What's a nine-letter word for 'not forthcoming'?"

Her heart rate kicked up a notch, and she sensed him staring at her. She peeked from behind the newspaper and shook her head. "I, uh…I don't know."

"Oh, got it—secretive. How about a five-letter word for meddle?"

She put the paper down. "Are those actual clues, or are you trying to imply something?"

"Bingo." He grinned. "I think you're up to something that has to do with your cousin's disappearance."

"Up to something? Like what?" She dipped her head and gave him the most innocent smile she had.

"You tell me."

She laughed. "Okay. So, Katherine asked if I'd talk to Jenna's friends to see if they've heard from her. I said I would. How could I turn her down? She's family."

"Talking is fine, as long as that's *all* you're doing. If you come across any information that points to her whereabouts, I expect to be the first person you call."

She smiled and returned to the front page.

THIRTEEN

Tuesday morning, Floyd announced plans to close Five Star on Friday, giving the employees a three-day weekend. The following Monday, a mandatory meeting would be held shortly before noon, followed by a catered lunch. Afterward, employees would be free to leave. The directive to finish as many jobs as possible threw the office into a frenzy of activity.

During a break, Tasha voiced her biggest fear. "What if the new co-owner wants to clean house and hire his own staff? I'd hate to look for a new job."

"You worry too much. And didn't you say Floyd offered you the office manager position along with a hefty pay raise?"

"He did, but what if this unknown partner changes Floyd's mind? I mean, why else would we have to tie up loose ends? And when have you seen Five Star spring for lunch? Maybe they should've called it 'The Last Supper' instead. We'll most likely be eating stale donuts and drinking day-old coffee."

CiCi laughed. "Floyd wouldn't treat us like that. I shouldn't say, but the catered lunch is coming from one of our favorite places—Peggy Sue's."

SHIRLEY WORLEY

"Something tells me you had a hand in that decision. Hallelujah. I guess Floyd has more smarts than I thought."

"I believe there will be a lot of positive changes ahead."

CiCi took a call from Chad as she prepared to leave for the day. He didn't feel well and planned to go straight to bed after work. She heard the weariness in his voice and told him to get a good night's rest. Too wired to go home, she glanced at her watch. "Hey, Tasha," she called as she shut down her computer. "I'm going out for dinner. Wanna come?"

As CiCi drove, she shared the bits of information she'd gathered from Serena and Heather over the weekend.

"That's interesting," Tasha said. "What'd Chad have to say?"

"Oh, um, nothing."

"Nothing? That doesn't sound like Chad."

"He knows I'm talking to Jenna's friends."

"And he's okay with you tracking down your cousin?" CiCi ignored the question, looked both ways, then pulled through the intersection. Tasha shook her head. "I'm not a psychic, but I see trouble in your future."

"Look, if the police didn't turn up any new leads this past year, I doubt I will either. If I do, I'll tell Chad and let him handle it. But it's got to be solid information, something worth pulling him away from his other cases. He's offered to look through Jenna's file in his spare time, but he also has a lot on his plate right now."

She pulled to a stop outside The Tap & Keg. The red brick building sat next to a company that supplied transportation for the school district. She assumed the bar saw a fair share of frazzled bus drivers at the end of each day—hopefully not before.

"I've never been here before. What made you pick this place?" Tasha asked as she slid from the passenger seat.

"Jenna worked here part-time." CiCi glanced around. The parking lot had an equal mix of trucks and SUVs, with a few compacts interspersed. "They're not very busy. Maybe it's too early for the evening crowd. Let's see what we can find out."

"I'm starving. I smell grilled onions," Tasha said as she stepped inside.

They stood for a minute, letting their eyes adjust to the dim lighting. Sports memorabilia covered the dark-paneled walls. Neon beer signs hung over the large mirror behind the bar. Liquor bottles in various stages of emptiness lined the glass shelves. An elevated platform and a dance floor occupied the far side of the room. Past the bar, several pool tables and gaming machines sat idle, waiting for players seeking the thrill of friendly competition.

Tasha led the way to the bar. "Let's order a burger."

A handful of older men sat along the bar, the nearest sitting a half a dozen bar stools away from CiCi. The bartender, a man in his early fifties, threw a towel over his shoulder and sauntered toward them wearing a big grin. "I knew you'd come back, blondie. So, what've you been up to since you left?" He placed a soda on the bar and winked at CiCi. "Cherry coke. Still you're favorite, right?" He turned a smile to Tasha. "What'll it be for you?"

"I'll have the same."

When he returned with Tasha's drink, someone from the back of the room shouted for Steve. The bartender yelled over his shoulder, "Pipe down and wait your turn." He laughed and turned his attention to Tasha. "So, what can I get for you ladies? Today, the loaded burgers are buy one, get one free."

Tasha licked her lips. "That sounds great. And add an order of onion rings."

"You got it. Jenna, you still like your fries crispy?" At her nod, he walked away.

Tasha turned to CiCi and whispered, "What're you going to do? He thinks you're Jenna."

She shrugged. "It happens. I'll play it by ear and see where it goes."

A minute later, two older gentlemen in their sixties wobbled from a nearby table and onto the stools to CiCi's right. One man wore a scruffy beard and the other oversized bifocals. It was clear they had been drinking for a while.

"Ain't ya gonna say 'hi' to your old friends?"

CiCi shifted under their stares and smoothed a lock of hair behind one ear. "I'm sorry, I don't think we've—"

"Whoa! That's a nasty scar ya got there, doll. Were ya in an accident?"

CiCi immediately let her hair fall forward. "You might say that, but—"

Bifocal leaned against the bar to keep from falling off his stool. "We've missed ya, darlin'. Haven't seen ya since the fight."

Her brows pinched together. "What fight?"

Scruffy's eyes widened. "Ya mean ya don't remember the big fight?"

CiCi shook her head, and Bifocal bumped shoulders with Scruffy. "Of course she don't 'member," Bifocal slurred. "She got ammonia from the head injury."

"Ya dimwit," Scruffy replied, "she don't have ammonia, she's got anemia."

CiCi and Tasha stifled a laugh. Before Scruffy or Bifocal could answer, Steve walked up and placed two mouthwatering burgers, a large basket of crispy fries, and an order of onions rings on the bar. "Go back to your table and let the ladies eat in peace, or I'll call your wives." Choosing not to give Steve a reason to call home, Scruffy and Bifocal scowled and left.

"Don't mind them," Steve said. "They're semi-retired now, meaning they haven't told their wives they quit working. They leave the house in the morning as usual, spend the day with friends, and stop here before heading home 'from work'. Their wives play Bingo tonight, so they're in no hurry to leave." He shook his head. "What a life."

CiCi bit into her burger and moaned. "Steve, I have something to confess. One, this is a great burger, and two, I'm not Jenna. I'm CiCi, Jenna's cousin."

His mouth dropped. "You're kidding me."

"Not kidding. Remember the woman who worked at Five Star

and was attacked in her home?" She pushed a lock of her hair aside before letting it fall back in place again.

"That was you? Wow." Steve raked a hand through his thinning hair. "So, where's Jenna?"

"That's what I'm trying to find out. Did Jenna ever mention that she planned to leave town?"

"Not to me."

"How long did she work here?"

"Part-time, maybe two or three months? She was an awesome waitress. Made a killing in tips. Everyone loved her."

"Maybe not everyone." She nodded toward Scruffy and Bifocal. "Those guys said Jenna had a big fight with someone before she left. You know anything about that?"

His mouth firmed as he took a moment to wipe the counter down. "There's this band that plays here several nights a week. Jenna had a thing for the lead guitar player. I told her he was trouble, but she wouldn't listen."

"What's the guy's name?"

"Derek Sawyer." He shook his head and refilled their sodas. "She had him eating out of her hand. She hung out with the band, went to practices. It wasn't long before he had Jenna singing the last song of the night with him. Pissed Red off big time."

"Who's Red?" Tasha asked.

"One of the band members."

"So," CiCi continued, "what was the big fight about?"

"Those old farts are making it out to be something worse than it was. With all the noise in here, I couldn't hear exactly what they were saying, but it sounded like she took something, and Derek didn't like it. Didn't see her after that. I assumed she didn't want anything more to do with him and quit."

"Think she left town?"

He shrugged. "Who knows?"

"Does Derek still play with the band?"

Steve braced both hands against the bar and narrowed his eyes. "Yeah, but if I were you, I'd stay away from that guy. He's nothing but trouble. If I owned this place, he'd be outta here. But I don't.

The owner lets me hire and fire as I see fit, but my hands are tied when it comes to the band. I put up with them to keep my job."

When the bartender turned and walked away, CiCi finished her soda and slid a hefty tip under her empty glass. "Let's go, Tasha. I think we're done here for now."

As CiCi pushed through the exit, her shoe caught on the doormat and she fell forward. A well-muscled biker on his way inside reached out and kept her from tumbling face-first to the ground. "You okay?"

"Yes, I'm fine. Thanks."

The biker flashed her a dimpled grin. "Good. You're way too pretty to get your nose skinned up."

Heat flared in her cheeks. She turned and tugged Tasha toward the Jeep. "Let's go."

FOURTEEN

CiCi's morning had been hectic, placating a client who questioned her appraisal and then driving to three locations to take measurements and photos. On her way back to the office, she made a stop on the square. Chad's illness gave her a rare opportunity to pamper him with a jumbo container of Peggy Sue's chicken noodle soup. "Would you add extra crackers and lemon pudding to the order, please?" CiCi asked.

"Sure thing," the waitress said as she tallied the bill.

A short time later, CiCi let herself into Chad's apartment and found him sprawled across the leather sofa with a blanket thrown across his body. Crumpled tissues littered the coffee table and an empty juice bottle sat on a coaster. Surprised to see her, he sat up and gave a weak smile. "What are you doing here?"

"I brought you something to eat." She walked by and placed a kiss on his forehead. "Hmm. You feel a bit warm." Within minutes, a glass of water and two tablets to reduce his fever sat on the table alongside a large bowl of soup and an assortment of crackers. She nudged him toward the dining room and encouraged him to eat. "There's pudding in the fridge. Sorry I can't stay."

"Thanks, hon. Go, I don't want you to get sick."

"I'll call you later. Love you."

She checked on Chad throughout the day. The chicken noodle soup would carry him through dinner, and a recorded football game would occupy his mind for most of the evening. At five o'clock, she shut down her work computer and stopped at Tasha's desk on the way out. "Chad's still sick. I thought I might grab a sandwich and then check out the address I found for Derek Sawyer. Want to come?"

"Sure."

After they'd eaten, CiCi and Tasha cruised down Beaker Parkway. The older neighborhood had undergone a revitalization. Small businesses lined both sides of the street, and many had converted the upper floors into trendy lofts. CiCi turned left at Lemont. Derek's address was in the first mixed-use building to their right. A business occupied the first floor and the upper floors appeared to be apartments.

As CiCi pulled into the lot, a black sedan barely missed clipping her rear bumper. She sucked in a breath as the car sped off. "What an idiot!"

"He was probably texting and not watching where he was going," Tasha added.

As they made their way up the sidewalk leading to the three-story structure, CiCi gazed at the building with an appraiser's eye. It had good bones, with a brick exterior in decent shape, an upgraded porch with a generous overhang, and new landscaping. Half of the third-floor windows were boarded up, indicating one of the apartments on that floor might be undergoing renovations.

The two women stepped inside. The tiled foyer was clean and well-lit with a wide staircase to their left. As Tasha read the names on the six mailboxes near the base of the steps, a young man and woman bounded down the stairs hand in hand.

"Excuse me, I'm looking for—" The pair walked on without

giving a friendly nod or greeting. CiCi frowned. "Well, that was rude."

"I agree." Tasha nodded as she watched the couple head to their car. "Or maybe not."

CiCi looked outside and saw the couple using sign language to communicate with each other. "I guess I judged too soon."

"We both did."

Tap! Tap! Tap!

CiCi and Tasha turned toward the source of the noise. They walked across the foyer. The glass door to a photography studio stood open, so they peeked inside. A man wearing pressed jeans and a blue shirt with the sleeves rolled up had his back to them. His low, sleek ponytail swung between his shoulder blades as he struggled to hang a large portrait on the wall. He stepped back to judge the placement, then reached forward to level the picture.

The framed picture showcased the silhouette of a young woman wearing a filmy peasant top. Her face was turned toward the sunset, away from the camera. She fingered a small, engraved pendant that dangled from the gold chain around her neck. "Cracker" was the only word she could make out. The setting sun gave the woman's blonde hair and gauzy blouse an ethereal feel. It was truly captivating.

The gentleman, who appeared to be in his mid-forties, turned abruptly. Startled by their presence, he took a step back and nearly dropped his hammer. His brown eyes lingered on CiCi's face and he appeared to be at a loss for words.

"Sorry, we didn't mean to scare you." CiCi nodded to the picture. "Did you take that?"

He tossed the hammer in his toolbox and closed the lid before he ventured a cautious smile. "I did."

"You have an extraordinary gift. Is she your wife?" she asked, nodding to the picture.

"Um, no, just a business acquaintance." He glanced at the picture and smirked before walking to his desk at the end of the room. CiCi and Tasha followed. "I'm sorry, the studio is closed.

Were you wanting to sign up for a photography class or schedule a photoshoot?"

She shook her head as she surveyed the space to her left. Tables and chairs faced a large whiteboard. Floating shelves along one wall held an array of cameras, many of them antiques. On the other side of the room, a gallery of pictures surrounded a large desk topped with photo albums. The variety of photographs on the exposed brick wall were stunning.

"No?" he said. "Well, if you're here about the apartment on the third floor, someone put a deposit on it last month. I can give you a call when the apartment across the hall is finished, but that may not happen until next year." She cocked her head, and he smiled at her confusion. "I own the studio *and* the building."

"I see. Then maybe you can help me. I'm looking for Derek Sawyer," CiCi said.

"He doesn't live here anymore. Mind if I ask what you want with that guy? He doesn't seem to be your type."

"I'm looking for a friend of his named Jenna."

"Jenna? Yeah, I remember her." His eyes never left hers. "You must be related. You look like her, except for the hair."

"I'm her cousin, CiCi, and this is my friend, Tasha."

He nodded and stuck out his hand. "Name's Vince Russo, but people call me Flash."

"Nice to meet you, Flash. No one has seen Jenna in the last year and I thought Derek might have heard from her recently."

"I, uh…heard she left town. Chicago, I think it was."

"Her mother doesn't think so. Were you the landlord when Derek lived here?"

He looked at CiCi, then to Tasha. "You with the police department?"

Tasha raised an eyebrow. "Seriously? Do we look like we're with the police?"

He chuckled and rubbed a hand over his chin. "No, I guess not."

"CiCi's on a mission," Tasha said. "Jenna and her mother are the only family CiCi has left, so you can understand why she wants to find her cousin."

He took a seat behind his desk, tapped a few keys on his computer, and then glanced at his watch. "I have an event to photograph this evening. I can give you fifteen minutes. Take a seat and I'll see if I can help."

"Thanks," CiCi said.

Flash leaned forward and braced his forearms on the desk and twisted the ring on his right hand. "So, what do you want to know?"

"Were you the landlord when Derek lived here?"

"No. I lived across the hall from him on the second floor. I bought the building from the previous owner for next to nothing because the place was in such bad shape. Derek moved out a month or two later."

"Were you good friends with Derek and Jenna?"

He shrugged. "Didn't know either of them very well. She seemed friendly when she came to see him; he was just the opposite. Glad to see him go."

He described his interactions with the band members when they came to practice. It was clear Derek wasn't someone Flash wanted as a renter. His tone changed, though, when he spoke of Jenna.

"She was a sweet one, she was. A girl with big dreams, although she was far too trusting. Don't know why she hooked up with that guy. If you ask me, leaving town was the best decision she ever made."

"Did she say where she planned to go?"

He paused and glanced at his computer screen. "Uh, Chicago, I think. That's how I remember it, anyway. Told the police the same thing."

"Has she ever called here to get in touch with Derek since he moved?"

His gaze wandered about the room as he thought over the question. "No, can't say that she has, and the phone number hasn't changed."

"Do you know where Derek lives now?"

"I've got his address here somewhere. He was hoping to get his security deposit back, but that was never going to happen." He opened the drawer of a file cabinet labeled 'Lemont Apartments' and pulled out a folder. After flipping through a few pages, he scratched an address on a note pad, tore off the top sheet, and handed it to CiCi. "That's the only address I have. Who knows if he's still there? If you want my advice, you'd be well off to leave that guy alone."

She read the address, then handed it to Tasha, who glanced at the scrap of paper and wrinkled her nose "He didn't exactly move up in the world, did he?"

"Believe me, that place is more his style," Flash said.

CiCi tucked the note into her purse. She looked up to find him studying her with an intensity that unnerved her. *What is up with this guy?*

"Who else have you talked to?" he asked. "The police?"

"I'll go to the police when I find something worth looking into. For now, I'm just gathering information."

"Personally, I think you're wasting your time. It's clear she's moved on with her life. If she wanted to contact her family, she would've done so by now. Sorry if that sounds harsh, but I tell it like I see it."

"Well, thanks for your help." CiCi turned and followed Tasha out of the studio, certain his eyes bore a hole in her back.

"Wait!" he called. He closed the gap and pressed something into her hand. She glanced down, surprised to see a business card for Captured Moments Photography Studio. "I noticed you're wearing an engagement ring. If you haven't booked a photographer yet, keep me in mind."

"Thank you. I will." She let out a sigh of relief.

Tasha spoke first after they left the building. "Girlfriend, I think you just found your wedding photographer. How great is that? He does fabulous work."

"Yes, he does." CiCi nodded absently as she climbed into the driver's seat.

"Did you notice the way he looked at you?"

"Yeah, and I thought it was creepy."

"What? No. Maybe he's thinking of using your photo for advertising. That could get you a huge discount on a bridal package."

CiCi started the vehicle, but sat staring back at the studio.

"What's the matter?" Tasha asked.

"I don't know."

"Photographer types are always different because they see the world through a different lens." She laughed at her play on words. "Anyway, he tried to be helpful. He gave you Derek's new address, didn't he?"

"He did."

"Then what's bothering you?"

"I don't know. I can't put my finger on it."

FIFTEEN

CiCi would've gone to work, but Floyd had closed the office until Monday. Taking advantage of the free day, she met Tasha and Megan for lunch. Most of their conversation revolved around the checklist for the wedding. Invitations needed to be ordered, a venue selected for the reception, a cake chosen, not to mention the florist, caterer, and photographer. The decisions and expectations were beginning to make CiCi stressed. *Maybe we should elope. Nah, I'd regret it later.*

After Megan returned to work, CiCi turned to Tasha as they climbed into the Jeep. "I need to get my mind off everything bridal, and I'm too restless to sit at home all afternoon. What've you got planned for the rest of the day?"

"Ugh, don't ask. Mom wants to introduce me to some fella at the animal shelter where she volunteers."

"But…aren't you allergic to cats?"

"Yes, and I'm not about to get involved with a guy who has more hair on his clothes than on his head."

CiCi chuckled and slipped on her sunglasses. After glancing in the rearview mirror, she flipped on her turn signal and paused before pulling into traffic. "Maybe we should track down that Derek guy this afternoon. I'm curious why Jenna would let some guitar player come between her and Tyler."

Tasha strummed her fingers on the armrest. "Hard to say, but Flash didn't like him. Maybe this is where you should ask Chad to help you."

"No way. He may have agreed to read through Jenna's file, but if he found out that I'm trying to track down some guitar player, one with a questionable reputation at that, that'd be a whole 'nother discussion." Her gaze darted again to the rearview mirror and her grip tightened on the steering wheel.

"You're right. Cops don't like it when citizens insert themselves into police investigations."

"That's just it—there *is* no investigation because Detective Logan closed the case," CiCi countered. "Even if there were, there's no law against asking questions."

"True, but Chad is a natural-born protector, and he doesn't want anything to happen to you. I doubt he would encourage you to hunt down a person that two people have warned you is nothing but trouble."

"No, he wouldn't," CiCi huffed. "Anyway, if I don't turn up any leads, my taking this a little step further will be a moot point." Her attention alternated between the road ahead and her rear-view mirror as she drove. "Do you recognize that black sedan two cars back? I could swear it's following us."

Tasha turned in her seat and craned her neck to look. "Don't recognize it."

CiCi turned right on Colburn. She looked back. The sedan made the same turn. She veered into the left lane and sped through a yellow light at the next corner. With her foot pressed to the pedal, she jerked the steering wheel to the right and rounded the corner at a higher rate of speed than she expected.

Tasha's eyes widened, and she held tight to the "Oh, Jesus" handle above the passenger door. "What the heck are you doing? We're going the wrong way."

"I know, but that car is freaking me out."

Tasha twisted in her seat. "I don't see it. If it was following us, it's not anymore."

"Good." With a sigh of relief, she loosened her grip on the wheel and reversed direction.

They drove to the outskirts of town, or more like the underbelly of the community. The paved road gave way to a gravel road bumpy enough to jar a few teeth loose. She slowed as she turned down Whitfield and entered the Majestic Gardens Mobile Home Park.

The trailer park had never been majestic, and there wasn't a single garden in sight. The cracked sidewalks were uneven in places. Basic shutters, if there were any at all, hung askance from window frames, and the skirting was missing from most of the mobile homes. Weeds were knee-high in spots, and several porches needed repair. At the cluster of mailboxes, a redhead with a nose ring argued with a short, older woman wearing a floral housecoat and pink curlers.

CiCi turned left at the next street and checked the tongue of each trailer for the lot number. Young men lolled about on lawn chairs and stared as she and Tasha passed. Her twelve-year-old Jeep looked new compared to the other vehicles parked along the crumbling curbs. She pulled to a stop across the street from Lot 8C, giving her and Tasha a good view of the dilapidated structure. Cardboard had been taped to the inside of a broken window at the end of the trailer. The exterior light fixture hung by a weathered piece of duct tape. The screen door, minus the screen, leaned against the deck's railing.

"The place looks abandoned," Tasha said.

"It's not. The trash can on the deck is full, and the truck at the curb has its hood raised."

"Maybe you should've called first."

CiCi shook her head. "I like the element of surprise and talking face to face. How they react is sometimes as important as what they say."

"Have you noticed the looks we're getting from the neighborhood welcome committee?" Tasha said as she eyed the man sitting on the porch of the trailer they'd parked in front of. He appeared to have taken a special interest in their arrival.

"I won't be long. You'd better stay in the car while I talk to Derek. If we both go, we may not have a vehicle when we come back."

The slight drop in temperature and the breeze that redistributed the trash along the street made CiCi shiver when she got out of the Jeep. She reached into the back seat and slipped on the only thing available—Jenna's camo jacket. For having a gazillion pockets and zippers, it felt surprisingly light. After making her way across the street and onto the rickety wooden porch, she glanced back at Tasha for reassurance, then knocked on the door. No one answered, but music filtered through the thin walls of the trailer. She cupped her hands around her eyes and peered through the window next to the door.

Empty beer cans lined the kitchen countertop and dirty dishes filled the sink. The trashcan beside the fridge overflowed onto the dingy linoleum. The kitchen table held a slew of empty candy wrappers, tools, and an amplifier that had its back cover removed.

"You couldn't stay away, could you? I knew you'd come back."

Startled by the words, CiCi whipped around. The redhead with the nose ring stood on the sidewalk in front of the trailer next door. CiCi walked around a cracked birdbath and across the parched lawn. The late afternoon sun behind the woman's head gave the illusion that her hair was on fire. She swayed and struggled to stay upright as she lifted a cigarette to her lips, took a puff, then held her breath before slowly exhaling. A sweet musky wisp of smoke drifted upward as a thin line of blood trickled from her nose.

CiCi pulled a tissue from her purse and offered it to the woman. "Your nose is bleeding." She stepped aside to keep the smoke away from her face.

"Thanks. Can you believe she punched me? One of these days, I'll slap her into next week. I don't care if she is my ma."

CiCi's eyebrows rose. "That woman in the housecoat is your *mother?*"

"Why'd you come back?" the redhead asked, as she swiped the blood from her upper lip.

How far can I ride this misunderstanding? Should I? Of course, I should. "I'm looking for Derek."

"Well," the redhead said, taking a seat on the trailer's exposed tongue, "if I were you, I'd go back to wherever you been hiding. Derek has been looking for you, and he's mad."

The last comment surprised CiCi. "Why?"

The neighbor paused and scrunched up her face. "Why what?"

"Why's he mad?"

"Blames you for getting him in trouble with his boss. Almost got him fired. Said when you took off, that's when everything went south."

"Know when he'll be back?"

The woman giggled as though she'd just heard a joke. "Who?"

CiCi rolled her eyes. "Derek. When will Derek be back?"

She shrugged. "Who knows."

"Is he still playing at The Tap & Keg?"

"Where else?"

CiCi pressed another tissue into her hand before turning and heading back to her vehicle. Tasha stood outside the Jeep, talking to the man they'd seen on the porch. She quickened her step but slowed when she heard Tasha laugh.

"Hey, CiCi. This is Juan. He went to school with my older brother."

"You know Red?" Juan lifted his chin toward the trailer CiCi had come from.

"No, but she thinks she knows me." CiCi smiled at Tasha's knowing look.

"I wouldn't believe too much of what she says. She's stoned most of the time."

"Have any idea what her real name is?"

A motorcycle rumbled down the street, drowning out his answer. It cruised to a stop in front of a truck parked next door. The muscular biker revved the engine one last time before shutting it down. He dismounted, removed his helmet, and gave a nod to their little group. His gaze lingered on the women, his appreciation for what he saw evident in his smile. He unstrapped a large duffle bag from the back of the bike and tossed it behind the driver's seat of the truck. After locking up and grabbing his helmet, he disappeared inside the single-wide mobile home.

"Wow, that's a good-looking hunk of—" Tasha stopped and gave a quick look at Juan "—machinery." She swallowed. "Not that I know anything about motorcycles. At least your friend wears a helmet."

"Too early to call him a friend," Juan replied. "He moved in about a month ago. Rents the trailer from old man Winters. Seldom talks to anyone except Derek or Red."

"Tasha, we'd better get going. Nice to meet you, Juan." CiCi waved, slid into the driver's seat, and made her way back to the main road.

"That biker looks familiar," Tasha said. "Where have I seen him before?"

"Don't you remember? We ran into him as we were leaving The Tap & Keg."

"Oh, yeah. What a coincidence, huh?"

She and Tasha picked up cappuccinos on the way to Tasha's apartment. CiCi also thought she picked up the dark sedan in her rearview mirror. By the time she and Tasha parted ways, the sedan had disappeared.

SIXTEEN

Several hours after CiCi arrived home, her cell phone rang. She glanced at the screen, surprised to see Tasha's name. *What could she want? We spent most of the day together.*

"Hey, it's me," Tasha said. "Remember Juan, my brother's classmate who lives at the trailer park?"

"Sure. Nice guy."

"He called and invited us to a party tonight at The Tap & Keg. I know you usually spend Friday nights with Chad at the bowling alley, but since he's sick I figured it might be a good opportunity for you to check out that guitar player."

CiCi bolted upright on the sofa. "What time are you leaving?"

"Around nine. What are you going to tell Chad?"

"That you have a date with someone you don't know well and need a safety net. He'll understand."

"What if Derek thinks you're Jenna?"

"Hmm, that could be a problem." She paused to think. "Okay, pick me up and come a little early. I'll need to borrow a couple of things from you."

CiCi could count on one hand the number of times she'd been to a bar, and never to The Tap & Keg other than her visit three days ago to talk to Steve, the bartender. She bit her lower lip as she stared out of the windshield of Tasha's Corolla.

Tasha glanced over at her. "That black wig looks better on you than it does on me."

"I'm glad you brought one with bangs to hide my scar."

"I didn't think Jheri curls would be a good fit for you." Tasha chuckled. "You should keep that one a few extra days. I think Chad would like it."

"Let's not talk about Chad. I'm nervous enough as it is," CiCi said as she got out of the car. She tugged at the hem of her short denim skirt and then straightened the faux glasses Tasha often used as an accessory. "Are you sure this wig will stay on?"

"Yes, now let's go. I'm thirsty."

They walked past the outdoor patio, crowded with smokers, and made their way inside. They paused before moving further into the dimly lit room to let their eyes adjust. The interior pulsated with loud music. To their left, patrons leaned against a polished bar that reflected the neon beer signs on the walls. On the stage at the far right of the room, a band energized the crowd with a version of a well-known country song.

Tasha put her mouth next to CiCi's ear. "I see Juan. Follow me."

Juan and his friends had taken over a large table against an outer wall. He rousted two guys from their seats to make room. "I'm glad you came." After greeting Tasha with a peck on her cheek, he gave a nod to CiCi. "Who's your friend?"

CiCi breathed a sigh of relief. *The wig and glasses work.*

"Oh, this is, um, Foxy. Foxy, Juan." Tasha turned to CiCi and smiled, and CiCi narrowed her eyes in return.

"Glad you could join us, Foxy."

Juan made quick introductions around the table. The group included three construction workers, a stay-at-home mom, a welder, a mortician, and two who were happily unemployed.

Juan asked, "What'll you ladies have to drink?"

Tasha ordered a mixed drink. When CiCi declined, Eddie, the

mortician, turned and said, "I know just the thing to work up a thirst." He stood and pulled her to the dance floor before she could protest. She forced a smile and glanced at his T-shirt. It read "Let me be the last person to put a smile on your face." *What have I gotten myself into?*

"A little work humor." He laughed when she caught on to the meaning.

The country music was lively, but the crowd limited her view of the band, particularly Derek. From what she could see, the guitar player was of average height and good-looking with wavy brown hair that fell to his shoulders. Red, wearing low-slung jeans and a skintight tank top, played bass guitar while gyrating to the beat of the music. Her dance moves were clearly enjoyed by the men in the crowd.

When the music stopped, CiCi followed Eddie to the bar where he ordered her a drink without even asking what she'd like. *I bet he doesn't get many second dates,* she thought. "This is quite a place. Been coming here long?" she asked.

"Since I turned legal. Seen a lot of changes over the years."

"I had a friend who worked here. I haven't seen her around and I'd love to get in touch with her."

"Yeah? What was her name?"

"Jenna. Since you're a regular, think you could ask around to see if anyone's heard from her?" CiCi twirled a lock of the black wig around her finger.

"Sure. That'll give me a reason to see you again." He winked and paid for the drinks. "Here you go, sweetheart. Something special just for you."

She took a hesitant sip, then coughed and sputtered as the liquid burned a path down her throat. She held up a finger, gasping for air. "Excuse me for a moment."

"Sure thing," he said. "I'll take the drinks and meet you back at the table."

CiCi wove her way through the crowd and into the restroom, where she rinsed her mouth with tepid water from the faucet. Before leaving, she applied a fresh coat of lip gloss and made sure the wig was secure.

As she stepped into the hall, angry voices could be heard coming from a door leading outside. From the sliver of light around the frame, the door hadn't clicked shut. She crept down the hallway. With her back pressed against the wall, she peered through the crack. The security light cast menacing shadows across Derek's face. Red's eyes went wide when he pinned her against a dumpster.

"What do you mean you *think* Jenna stopped by the trailer? If you weren't high all the time, you'd remember." Red mumbled an apology. Derek stepped back and snarled, "Get back inside. Break's over."

CiCi turned and scurried back down the hall. As she passed the bar, she motioned Steve over. She pushed back a small section of bangs to reveal her scar. The bartender did a double take, then nodded. "Steve, see that guy over there? Whatever he ordered for me, make another one without the alcohol and switch them out when he's not looking."

Steve smiled. "Sure thing, hon."

A chuckle erupted to her left. She turned a scathing look to the guy perched on the stool. Juan's hunky neighbor at the trailer park, smiled back in amusement.

She pursed her lips. "Something funny?"

"Nope." He turned to face her. His eyes narrowed as he studied her face. "You look familiar. Have we met before?"

"No." She turned and left before he had time to ask more questions.

Eddie intercepted her on her way to the table and coaxed her back onto the dance floor. She obliged, hoping to learn more about Jenna or Derek, but asking questions while dancing to a spirited tune proved impossible. When the band played a slow song, she thought it the perfect opportunity to do a little investigating. Eddie had the same idea. His hands roamed over forbidden territory despite her protests.

"Relax, babe. After spending all day with stiffs, I just wanna have a little fun."

"I didn't come for that kind of fun." She pushed away, but Eddie grabbed her arm and pulled her back. Seconds later, a hand gripped his shoulder and he grimaced under the pressure.

"May I cut in?" Juan's hunky neighbor offered a menacing smile and tightened his hold. Eddie grudgingly nodded and stalked off to the bar.

"Thank you," CiCi said as Red crooned the opening line of a Patsy Cline song. "Your timing was perfect. He was about to take a knee."

"I'm guessing you're not talking football." The mischievous twinkle in his eyes prompted her to laugh as he led her across the dance floor. "My name's Mace. Yours?"

"Ci…um, Foxy."

"Well, Foxy, I could swear I've seen you before. I just can't place where."

"Did you come with friends?" she asked.

"Sort of. Derek's my neighbor and we work together. His truck broke down, so I been giving him a lift until he can find the parts to fix it."

"That's nice of you to help him out. So, what does Derek—"

The crowd began to cheer, drowning out her question. On stage, a bleached blonde strutted onto the stage. For a woman pushing fifty, she rocked a leather outfit, boots and several tattoos. She sat down an older model amplifier identical to Derek's. After hooking up her equipment, she slung a guitar over her shoulder and picked a few notes to tune her instrument. The crowd's excitement built with each pluck of the strings.

CiCi leaned into Mace and shouted, "Who's that?"

"First time here? That's Crystal," he said. "From what I've gathered, this is one of her regular stops across Kansas and their dueling guitars are a big hit on the weekends. I imagine that's why there's such a large crowd tonight."

Three hours later, after the music stopped, the musicians busied themselves packing up their equipment. Derek and Crystal were off to one side having a serious discussion, while Mace studied the pair from afar. Derek stopped midsentence when Mace approached and said, "Ready when you are."

Derek glared at him. "Are you hard of hearing? I told you I'd be out in a minute. Go wait for me in the truck."

Heated words were exchanged, but CiCi couldn't make them out. Mace narrowed his eyes, then turned and stormed outside. Crystal shook her head before picking up an amp and leaving. Derek's gaze followed her until the exit door slammed shut. He waited a moment, then picked up his amp and guitar and made his way outside, presumably to Mace's truck.

Wow. Did I see that right? I think Crystal picked up Derek's amp by mistake. He won't be happy when he discovers the mixup. He's got a hot temper, and I wouldn't want to be on the receiving end of it.

SEVENTEEN

On Saturday morning, CiCi's birthday, Tasha and Megan treated her to a facial and mani-pedi. Later, she and Chad enjoyed a light lunch and watched a chick flick at the theater without one snicker or word of sarcasm from Chad. On the drive home from the miniature golf range, his phone rang. She gave a pleading look as he checked the screen. "Please don't tell me you have to work."

The corners of his mouth lifted as he slipped the phone into the holder attached to his belt. "Nope. Today, I'm all yours. While you get ready, I have an errand to run."

"What should I wear this evening?"

"Whatever you like, but nothing too fancy."

As she climbed from the truck, she stifled a yawn. "I might need a nap."

"You and Tasha must've gotten back late. Where'd you two go?"

She froze. *Should I tell him? If he hears where I went and why, he won't be happy, and I don't want to ruin my special day. I didn't discover anything newsworthy, so I think it can wait.* "Nowhere special." She plastered on a smile to dispel the wary look in his eyes. "By the way, where are we going tonight?"

"It's a secret."

"Can't you give me a hint?"

He grinned. "Not unless you tell me where you and Tasha went."

Her mouth opened, then closed. "It's a good thing I *love* surprises."

He chuckled.

After a nap and a long soak in the tub, CiCi pulled together an outfit for the evening ahead. She chose a skinny pair of black slacks and a form-fitting red blouse. The sleeves were sheer, and the deep V of the yoke revealed the perfect amount of cleavage. Casual, yet classy.

When she answered the door, her heart skipped a beat. Chad wore a crisp shirt tailored to fit his broad shoulders, a pair of black slacks, and his Raleigh lizard dress boots.

He let out a low whistle as he twirled her around. "You look fabulous. Are you sure you're thirty? I'm thinking you may have to show ID tonight."

Her smile widened at his compliment. "Thank you. I see you're wearing the boots you proposed in."

"Yep. I only wear them on special occasions." He pulled a small box wrapped in metallic paper from his pocket. "A present for the birthday girl."

Her fingers shook as she fumbled with the ribbon and wrapping. She gasped when she opened the lid. A delicate watch lay draped over a velvet pillow. The silver band had black accents, and the black mother-of-pearl face had small crystals in place of the usual numbers. The words "Our Love Is Timeless" had been engraved on the back. "Oh, Chad, it's beautiful."

"Here, let me put it on you." She held up her wrist while he fastened the clasp. "It's a little loose. We might need to have a couple of links removed."

"Maybe. I think it's perfect as is."

He leaned forward and kissed the tender spot on her neck. "Are you ready to go?" When she nodded, he took her hand and escorted her to his truck. Once seated behind the wheel, he handed her a satin sleep mask.

She looked at him, puzzled. "What's this for?"

"Just put it on, and no peeking."

She frowned but did as he said. "I hope you have your badge handy. If anyone sees me like this, they going to think I've been kidnapped and call the cops."

They made a right after leaving her complex. A few blocks later the truck swung to the left. Numerous stops and turns had her so confused, she gave up trying to figure out where they were. When the truck stopped, Chad helped her from the cab and led her down a winding path. They paused. She heard the faint swoosh of a door opening before he led her forward. Muffled sounds and a sense of energy surrounded her. The mouth-watering aroma of spicy food filled the air. She clung to Chad's arm, the anticipation making her giddy with laughter. He positioned her to face a certain direction, then removed the mask.

An enthusiastic, smiling crowd and shouts of "happy birthday" filled the room. Her hands flew to her face. Megan and Tasha were the first to rush over and envelop her in a hug.

"I thought you two had plans this evening," CiCi said.

"We *did*—plans to decorate for your party," Megan answered, gesturing to the hundreds of tiny blue lights that twinkled overhead. Colorful balloons were wrapped around support pillars, and banners decorated the walls. Two servers attended the food stations near the kitchen. The bar had a line of customers, and guests milled about or sat at tables around the room.

She threw her arms around Chad's neck. "Thank you so much!"

"Happy birthday, sugar." He kissed her with passion, then realized others were clamoring for her attention. "We'd better mingle with your guests."

They circled the room, chatting with everyone who came to celebrate her special day. Mark and Pete were there, and several of Chad's co-workers she'd gotten to know over the last year. She greeted neighbors and the complex manager, Brian. Her boss and mentor, Floyd, and several co-workers sat together at one table. Art from the hardware store kissed her on each cheek and wished her a happy decade. Pastor Young, his wife, and three couples from church congregated together along one wall.

CiCi enjoyed the compliments on her glamorous watch and praised Chad for having chosen the perfect gift. When music drifted from the overhead speakers, Megan pulled her boyfriend, Dennis Browning, to the dance floor, and Mark asked Tasha for a dance. Several couples joined them, and CiCi was happy to see everyone having a good time.

"Happy thirtieth birthday," Chad whispered as he and CiCi blended into the crowd, their bodies swaying in sync to the music. She smiled and nestled her head against his shoulder.

"You're certainly good at keeping secrets."

He chuckled softly. "As a detective, I've been trained to keep sensitive information on a strictly need-to-know basis."

"Do you realize this is my very first surprise party?"

"I wanted you to feel special and know how much I love you."

"Mission accomplished. Now I feel bad for not celebrating *your* birthday earlier this year."

He shook his head. "Don't feel guilty. It was just another day to me. Besides, you had just gotten out of the hospital and were in no condition to party."

When the music stopped, they drifted over to the bar, where Chad and Mark ordered a drink. CiCi declined and turned when the door to the clubhouse opened. A late arrival stood at the entrance clutching a package adorned with a large ribbon.

CiCi's eyes widened. "You invited Katherine?"

Chad grinned, putting his dimples on display. "What's a party without family?"

By the time CiCi made her way across the room, Katherine had deposited her package on the gift table. CiCi gave her aunt a hug and kissed her cheek. "What a surprise! I'm so glad you came. Let me introduce you to a few of my favorite people."

CiCi took Katherine's hand and introduced her to Megan,

Tasha, and a few other guests. CiCi then excused herself to visit the ladies' room. When she returned, she found Katherine talking with Chad, Mark and Pete.

"Oh, here's the birthday girl," Katherine said. "Chad introduced me to Mark. Of course, I know Detective Mason."

"Now, Katherine, Pete will do," chided the former detective. "I'm retired, remember?"

"Old habits are hard to break. Anyway, we've been chatting, and I was about to tell them how much I appreciate you talking to Jenna's friends."

"She's good at asking questions, as long as that's *all* she's doing," Chad said, directing his attention to CiCi. A hint of warning colored his remark.

Suddenly, CiCi's stomach growled loud enough for all to hear. She smiled at her good fortune. "Katherine, I'm starving. Why don't we get something to eat?"

CiCi turned and led Katherine away from the group.

EIGHTEEN

On Sunday morning, Chad and CiCi attended worship service at the First Baptist Church. After the last hymn and benediction, they exchanged pleasantries with other members of the congregation as the crowd shuffled toward the exit. At the door, they shook hands with the pastor and his wife.

"I'm surprised to see you both this morning," Pastor Young said. "I take it your party ended quite late." He grinned at CiCi and gave her a mischievous wink.

"Sorry, Pastor," she said, her face flushing with heat. "I couldn't seem to stay awake during the sermon."

He chuckled. "That's all right. I have the same problem when we have visiting speakers, but I have an advantage over you." He leaned in and whispered, "When my eyes are closed for too long, people assume I'm deep in prayer. Bessie knows better. She sends me a text, and the vibration from my phone brings me back to the here and now."

CiCi chuckled. "I wish Chad's elbow nudges were as subtle as Bessie's texts."

Chad grinned and lifted his shoulders. "Didn't want you snoring during the message."

"See you tomorrow evening?" Pastor asked.

"Yes. We're looking forward to it."

After lunch, CiCi reread the birthday cards she'd received while Chad removed the crossword puzzle from the Sunday paper. She tucked the gift cards into her purse and ran her fingers over Katherine's present. The rich brown suede and leather eyeglass holder had twelve slots, an adequate number if CiCi kept her purchases under control. "This is exactly like Jenna's, except hers is red. I fell in love with it the moment I saw it. I can't believe Katherine had one made for me."

"When did you see Jenna's?" Chad asked, glancing up from the clues.

"Oh, Katherine showed me Jenna's room when I went back with the photo album." She held the organizer up against the wall. "It's perfect here, don't you think? I've been wanting to make a few changes. I think I'll move the flash drive collection upstairs next to the computer."

"Any particular reason she showed you Jenna's room? That seems a bit odd."

CiCi tensed, and the framed flash drive collection slipped from her grasp as she removed it from the hook on the wall. She quickly recovered and caught it before it crashed to the floor. Keeping her back to Chad, she shrugged. "Jenna's my cousin. I think she wanted me to get a feel for who she is as a person."

"Maybe." He frowned and went back to the puzzle.

Before he had a chance to ask any more questions, she made a show of glancing at her watch. "It's getting late. I'll bet Mark is expecting you at the gym."

He chuckled. "Trying to get rid of me?"

"Certainly not. Besides, I'm going to catch a movie this afternoon with Tasha and Megan."

"I can stay a bit longer and we can finish the puzzle together… or maybe talk about what you found interesting in Jenna's room."

"There wasn't anything in her room you'd find of interest."

He leaned over and gave her a lingering kiss. "If you say so. I'll call you later."

"Have fun. I love you."

"Love you, too," he replied, walking out the door.

As she changed out of her church clothes, the phone rang. "Hello?"

"CiCi? This is Heather, Jenna's friend."

"Hey, Heather. What's up?"

"My boyfriend and I are moving today, and I found some of Jenna's things in the basement. I called her mom, but she didn't answer. I'd wait, but the movers will be emptying the storage unit in the next hour. Think you can swing by and grab her stuff?"

"Um, sure. I can be there in fifteen minutes."

"Great. See you then."

CiCi had only driven two blocks when she noticed a black sedan several car lengths behind her vehicle. With each turn she made, the car followed. She sped up and pulled into a gas station. The mystery car drove on past. She couldn't identify the driver because of the tinted windows. She waited to see if the sedan circled back. When it didn't, she continued on her way.

She turned onto Polk Avenue and scanned the street for a place to park. On her second lap around the block, a car pulled away from the curb three houses down from Heather's apartment. CiCi parked and walked back toward Heather's building. A black sedan parked on the opposite side of the street, blocking a private driveway.

This is ridiculous. I'm going to find out why this guy is following me. The moment she headed for the sedan, the driver revved the engine, put the car in reverse, and backed down the street. At the intersection, it made a U-turn and sped off.

CiCi paused and let out a breath she hadn't realized she'd been holding. She turned, skirted around the large moving truck in Heather's driveway and went inside. In the hallway, a mover strapped a stack of boxes to a dolly. CiCi sidled by him and rapped on the open door. Heather appeared a few seconds later, looking hot and frazzled.

"Wow. That was quick," she said, flashing a weary smile. "Follow me."

She hustled down the common hallway to a door that lacked an apartment number. She flipped a wall switch and bounded down the stairs. The basement was divided into four equal spaces, one for each tenant. The walls separating each storage area were made from slatted wood pallets. Heather removed the padlock from her unit and swung the door open. She reached up and yanked on a chain, bringing two four-foot LED shop lights to life.

"This is the rest of the stuff I couldn't fit into the apartment after my boyfriend moved in. I seldom come down here. Maybe that's why I forgot Jenna used this area as a make-shift office to work on her newspaper assignments. It was impossible for her to concentrate with three of us crammed into the small space upstairs." She pointed to an old roll-top desk. "That belonged to my grandmother."

CiCi eyes widened in admiration at the decades old piece. She ran a reverent hand over the dark walnut finish, her fingers worshiping the excellent craftsmanship. The finish had faded in places and the piece needed a good cleaning. Scratches and gouges marred the work surface. *If this desk could only talk.*

"I started boxing up a few of her things but kept getting interrupted." Heather waved her hand to a cardboard box, and then pointed to a small stack of albums and magazines sitting on the corner of the desk. "I found those just after I called. You might want to take a second look through the drawers to make sure I didn't miss anything. I'd say take your time, but the movers will be emptying this room next."

"Did she use her laptop down here?"

"Yeah, but I haven't seen it. Must've taken it with her. Well, I need to get back."

"Thanks." She glanced over her shoulder, but Heather had already left.

CiCi quickly fingered through the stack on the desktop, but nothing stood out as being out of the ordinary. One by one, she checked each drawer and cubby. She shoved her arm inside every open drawer and felt around to make sure a wayward paper hadn't gotten stuck in a crack. Every pencil, flier, notepad, and sticky note went into the box, even the blurry photos. After a thorough search of the desk itself, she dropped to her hands and knees. Using her phone as a flashlight, she found another pencil, empty gum wrappers, and lots of mouse poop. *Ew!* Satisfied she had covered every inch, she added the albums and magazines to the carton before closing the lid, brushed off her hands and knees, and carried the container upstairs. Two movers paused at the top to let her pass. *Not a moment too soon.*

She thanked Heather for the call, wished her happiness in her new home, and asked her to stay in touch. With the cardboard box tucked under her arm, she exited the building and scanned the street for the mystery vehicle. Relieved to see it hadn't returned, she climbed into her Jeep and headed home. She tried to think of anyone she knew who drove a dark sedan *and* who wanted to keep tabs on where she went. Serena came to mind. *Maybe.*

CiCi found Megan and Tasha waiting on the porch. She stashed the box on the floor next to the buffet, grabbed a light jacket, and locked up, leaving behind any worries about the mystery vehicle.

NINETEEN

Late Sunday afternoon, after Tasha and Megan had dropped her off at home, CiCi swept her porch and checked the bird feeder. Empty again. A quick glance at her watch told her she had an hour before the hardware store closed, plenty of time to pick up a fresh bag of seed. She grabbed a pair of sunglasses from the new wall display and set out on foot.

Walking to and from the square had become a part of her recovery program after the attack four months ago. At first, she could barely walk a block with Chad's help. As her stamina increased, so did her distance. Eventually, she was able to complete an entire lap and then some.

One of her frequent stops on the square, other than the bakery, library or bookstore, was Art's Hardware. She and Art Bahtzman, the elderly proprietor, had developed a relationship one might expect between a grandfather and granddaughter. She looked forward to their visits, and he was always ready to share a corny joke or a little neighborhood gossip. He kept a stash of her favorite truffles behind the counter, though he would only hand out one at a time to keep her coming back. He often patted a big hand across his heart and joked that if he were only forty years younger …

The wooden floorboards creaked beneath her feet as she entered the store, and the distinctive odor of the aged building made her smile. Art stood in his usual spot behind the cash register, a denim apron tied around his ample waist. White hair ringed his head like a halo. Bushy eyebrows overshadowed his bespectacled brown eyes and plump, ruddy cheeks.

Her presence brought a look of panic to his face. He pulled her behind the counter and past the curtain that separated the front register from his office. He took a truffle from his apron pocket, shoved it into her hand and put a thick finger to his lips.

"Not a word," he whispered.

He quickly disappeared, leaving her alone and bewildered. She took a seat at his desk as heavy footsteps approached the front counter.

"Damn shame I have to pay these prices. Highway robbery is what it is," the customer groused.

Her father's voice sent chills up her spine, and her heart rate spiked. The cash register dinged, change counted back, and a "Thank you for shopping at Art's Hardware" offered. Her dad grunted. An awkward silence filled the air, then the floorboards creaked under his weight as he left the building.

She hadn't seen Jack in months. Despite their estranged relationship, deep down she still loved him. After all, he was the only father she'd ever known. As a child, she'd been a daddy's girl. By the time she entered high school, booze had become the gleam in his eye. His drinking and physical abuse during her junior and senior year severely damaged their relationship. That he chose liquor over her hurt almost more than the abuse itself. After she graduated and married, she limited her contact with him out of simple self-preservation.

Art poked his head through the curtain. "Come, he's gone." He shook his head. "That man's nothing but trouble. He gave me the oddest look before he left, but I can't imagine he knows you're here."

"Thanks, Art. He's the last person on earth I want to talk to."

Art fetched a three-pound bag of birdseed and rang up the

purchase. They chatted until another customer approached with a question. CiCi scooped up her sack and Art slipped a second truffle into her hand with a wink. Stepping outside, she waved goodbye through the store's large front window. Art waved back.

At the corner of the building, two hands yanked her into the alleyway. It happened so fast, she didn't have time to think, let alone yell for help. The bag of birdseed flew from her grasp as someone slammed her against the brick exterior of the store. Her gaze traveled up the denim-clad arms that restrained her, and her eyes widened.

"Well, well, look who we have here," her dad snarled. "I knew you was close by. I could smell that gawdawful perfume you and your granny always wore. Did you think I'd forget?"

"What do you want, Dad?"

"My rightful share of the inheritance! Helen was my wife, and it belongs to me."

It had been a shock to them both to learn Helen had a hidden estate worth several million dollars. Overnight, CiCi became owner of the family farmhouse, ninety acres of rich Kansas farmland, rental properties, investments, and several bank accounts. Her dad, on the other hand, received a monthly allowance of a thousand dollars and the option to live rent free in the farmhouse. To say he was angry was an understatement.

"The lawyer explained this to you before. According to the terms of Mom's estate, I'm forbidden to give you any of the inheritance. It's not my choice."

"Check again," he snarled. "There's always a loophole. Until you make things right, there'll always be unfinished business between us. And now I hear you been talking to Katherine." He spat on the ground. "I should've known that would happen eventually."

"Who I talk to is none of your business. Now, let go!" When her efforts to free herself failed, she opened her mouth to scream. His calloused hand clamped over her mouth and his grip on her arm tightened.

"I'd let her go, if I were you."

Although startled by the forceful voice, she felt relief to know someone was gutsy enough to intervene. From the corner of her eye, she saw Art standing at the head of the alley. Though impressed by Art's boldness and confidence, she worried for his safety. He stood a good eight inches shy of her dad's towering six-foot-four frame and was older by at least twenty years. The odds weren't in his favor.

"Mind your own business, old man."

"My name's Bahtzman. Some call me Bat Man...should I show you why?" Art pulled a wooden baseball bat from behind his back and smacked it across the palm of his free hand. The old bat looked worn and well used.

"This is none of your concern, Art. You're too old to fight other people's battles."

"*I'm* not too old," said a newcomer. Pete Mason rounded the corner and stood next to Art, his stance wide and ready for a fight. His steely blue eyes were hard and never wavered from Jack's face. The look Pete gave could've seared paint off a car.

Jack chuckled. "You ain't got what it takes either, so get lost."

"Oh, I got what it takes," Pete said, his voice low and threatening. He moved his right hand behind his back, as though reaching for something in the waistband of his jeans. The gesture spoke volumes.

"We'll finish this conversation later, *in private*," Jack whispered in her ear. He released his grip and gave her a shove. She fell and cried out in pain as bits of broken pavement and sharp pieces of gravel dug into her hands and knee. When he chuckled, she tossed an angry glare over her shoulder.

Art rushed to her side. Pete took a menacing step forward. Jack raised his hands in surrender and retreated down the alleyway. "And don't come back," Art shouted.

CiCi's body trembled as Art and Pete helped her to a bench in front of the store. A small tear escaped from the corner of her eye, which she quickly brushed away. Art rushed inside and returned with a bottle of water, an alcohol wipe, and a hand towel. Pete looked on as Art inspected her scrapes. "I'm fine. Really. Thanks for your help."

She grimaced as Art used the dampened towel to work bits of grit from her palm. He pulled a clean, white handkerchief from his pocket and wrapped it around her hand. She stopped him when he reached to inspect her throbbing knee through the hole in her jeans. "I'll take care of it at home, Art. You've done enough."

"If you're sure." He sighed. "Let me get you a new bag of bird seed before I close up for the day."

She gently touched his arm. "It can wait. I'll come back for it later." He nodded and went inside.

Pete, his face hardened with anger, pulled his cell phone from his pocket and snapped photos of her injured hand and knee.

"What are you doing?"

"Taking pictures. I'm going to send these to Chad," he said, squinting at the screen.

Her eyes widened. "Don't do that!" She stood and snatched the phone from his hand.

"After what he did? Chad deserves to know. Now, give me the phone." His mouth pinched into a firm line.

She swallowed hard, realizing Pete had taught Chad much of what he knew before Pete retired from the police force. "You're right. He does deserve to know, but not right this minute. You and I both know how he'll react."

"As he should. Now, gimme the damn phone."

"On one condition—that you don't tell Chad today." She held up a hand to stop his protests. "I know this sounds crazy, but tomorrow is a big day at Five Star. If Chad finds out about this before then, he'll have me knee deep in a police report."

"You need to get your priorities straight, missy."

"All I'm asking is for one day. I promise to file for a restraining order tomorrow afternoon, and I'll tell Chad everything after he gets off work." *By then, I'll have a lot to say that won't make him happy—like how I discovered Jenna had a second job, and that she had a fight with a guitar player named Derek shortly before she disappeared. And he'll go ballistic when he hears someone in a black car has been following me.*

He stared at her for several seconds, then looked away and shook his head. When he turned back, she knew he'd relented.

"You've talked me into crazy stuff before, but this beats all. I'll give you until tomorrow night. If you haven't told Chad by then, *I* will."

She nodded and handed Pete his phone. "How did you know I needed help?"

"I'd just finished replacing a broken security camera at the deli when I saw you walk out of Art's. When I turned back, you'd disappeared. Then Art went tearing around the corner of the building with a baseball bat. I knew right then something wasn't right." He glanced up and down the street. "Where's your Jeep?"

"I walked. In hindsight, it doesn't seem to have been a good idea."

"I can take you home. Besides, I want to make sure Jack isn't lingering around waiting for you."

"Can I talk you into staying for a cup of coffee and a slice of banana bread?"

"I wouldn't think of turning down anything you baked." He smiled, took her elbow, and helped her to his work truck.

She climbed inside, thinking it wouldn't hurt to have Pete's security and surveillance truck parked in front of her place for a while. As they drove, she thought about asking him what prompted the police to close Jenna's case and whether he thought they had just cause to do so. But, being a former detective, he was bound to ask questions and discover she'd been doing more than just talking to Jenna's friends. She was fortunate he agreed not to tell Chad about her father's attack for now. To ask him to keep quiet about her trip to The Tap & Keg would be like asking him to give up coffee.

"Well, looks like there'll be no banana bread for me today," Pete said as he pulled in front of her townhome. Chad sat on the porch scrolling through his phone. Pete turned to CiCi. "I'm not staying. Chad will know something's up the minute I set foot outside of this truck. I'll be checking in on Tuesday to make sure you kept your end of the bargain."

"I understand." She laid an aching hand on his arm. "Thanks, Pete, for everything."

As soon as CiCi slid from the vehicle, Pete gave a small wave to Chad and pulled from the lot. CiCi walked to the door, trying her best to conceal the slight pain in her knee. Her torn, bloody jeans didn't escape Chad's keen eye.

"Are you all right? What happened?"

"I'm fine." She waved him off, forgetting the handkerchief tied around her hand. Chad took her elbow and helped her inside. "Can you get the first aid kit from the bathroom upstairs?" By the time he returned, she was sitting at the dining room table trying to enlarge the hole in her jeans to get a look at her knee.

"It'd be better if you take off your jeans."

She cocked an eyebrow and gave him a crooked smile. "Really? Better for *who*?"

He grinned and knelt in front of her. "Just trying to take your mind off the pain."

"I know where your mind is, and it isn't on my knee."

He winked and brushed a soft kiss across her lips. "Can't blame a guy for trying. Here, let me help. I'm guessing these jeans are going in the trash." At her nod, he ripped the hole large enough to clean, disinfect, and bandage her knee. As she reluctantly showed him her scraped and swollen palm, he asked, "What happened?"

"I went to Art's for birdseed and fell after I left the store. Pete saw what happened and gave me a lift home." She pushed back a twinge of guilt for not telling him the whole truth.

"You must've taken quite a spill to rip your jeans." Chad kissed her hand. "I'll thank Pete the next time I see him."

Without a moment's pause, she said, "Don't bother. I think he'll appreciate a loaf of my banana bread more than your thanks." She let out a sigh of relief when he hesitantly agreed.

Chad snapped the lid shut on the first aid kit. "I was going to ask if you wanted to go bowling tonight, but I think we'd better skip that idea."

"Yeah. Plus, I've got a big day tomorrow and want to turn in early tonight."

He pulled her close and pressed his lips against hers. "I'd wish you luck, but you don't need it. You'll do great."

"Thanks," she said, her body eagerly responding to his touch.

TWENTY

A low buzz filled the breakroom as eight Five Star real estate agents, appraisers, and office personnel chattered nervously. Off to one side, the caterer checked her list and added final touches to the buffet table. The aroma of hazelnut-flavored coffee scented the room. Party plates, napkins, and a decorated sheet cake sat on a separate table.

CiCi looked at her co-workers as they anxiously waited to learn the fate of the company and their jobs. The shredded tissue in her hand suggested the waiting had gotten the best of her, too. She brushed a piece of lint from her slacks and then fingered her necklace, making sure it was centered. Tasha, who stayed behind to lock the front door and transfer incoming calls to the answering service, slid into the empty seat beside CiCi.

As if on cue, Floyd Masters stepped into the room. The dark blue suit, starched white shirt, and patriotic tie was a departure from his usual khakis and polo shirt. Five Star's lawyer entered next, followed by a man and two women. The foursome sat at the nearest empty table.

After a short speech, Floyd introduced three new employees:

real estate agent Troy Miller, researcher Linda Pearson, and part-time accountant Ginger Otey. After sharing a brief recap of their work history and background, Floyd welcomed them to Five Star. His announcement that Tasha would be promoted to office manager elicited a round of congratulations from her co-workers.

Floyd cleared his throat and waited for the chatter to die down. "As you know, the last few months have been difficult for Five Star. There were days when I didn't know if the company would stay afloat. But then, like an answer to prayer, someone stepped forward and made me an offer I couldn't refuse." Floyd chuckled as the small crowd groaned at the use of a line from his favorite movie.

"My new partner loves this company almost as much as I do. She holds a bachelor's degree, with a major in accounting and a minor in business. She is very familiar with the research aspect of the business and received her certified general appraiser license this past July. Under our combined leadership, we believe Five Star has a bright future ahead, which means job stability for all of us." Several people let out a sigh of relief. "It's my privilege to introduce my new partner—" Floyd paused, and the room fell silent. "—Miss Cecilia Winslow."

After the initial shock faded, the room erupted in applause. With a broad smile on her face, she walked to the front of the room and let her gaze sweep over the people she'd become so fond of over the years. Everyone smiled in return, except for Ashley, who appeared as sullen as ever. Chad stood at the back of the room, his face beaming with pride. Over his shoulder, she noticed Serena and Jimmy from *The Ripley Review*. CiCi paused. *What are they doing here?*

Floyd leaned over and whispered, "Did I mention I invited the press? With the unfortunate publicity we had earlier this year, I thought this would give us an opportunity to show the community and our clients we've turned a corner."

"Oh, um, that's a great idea, Floyd. Good publicity is like money in the bank."

Serena pulled out a notepad while Jimmy snapped photos of the new partners shaking hands. CiCi smiled and launched into a small speech, hinting of positive changes that would be forthcoming in the new year, and stressing that she would always be available for comments, concerns, or questions.

She stepped aside and let Floyd take control. He reminded them the office would be closed for the rest of the day, which garnered another enthusiastic response. He then ushered Troy, Linda and Ginger to the buffet table and invited others to follow. As CiCi's co-workers filed past, they offered heartfelt congratulations.

Tasha pulled CiCi into a hug. "You should be ashamed for keeping secrets from me."

Glancing over Tasha's shoulder, CiCi's happiness dimmed when she caught Ashley's cold, hard stare. She mumbled something under her breath before fleeing the room. *She's not taking the news well. Did she really expect to inherit her uncle's share of the business after what he did?* CiCi disengaged from Tasha and started to follow, but a firm hand caught her upper arm.

"Let her go," Chad said. He smiled and pulled her into a hug like no other could give. He planted a kiss on her cheek and said, "Congratulations. I'm so proud you."

"Thanks, hon. I didn't know you were coming."

"Wouldn't miss it for the world." He cocked his head towards Tasha. "Your new office manager let me in."

Tasha chuckled. "Well, what should I call you now? Boss, or your highness?"

"If you call me either," CiCi smirked, "I'll be looking for your replacement."

"Guess your grandma's inheritance came in handy, huh?"

"I suppose it did," CiCi said. She refrained from saying more. Very few people were aware of the windfall from her mother's estate, and she intended to keep it that way. She'd seen first-hand how money could destroy relationships.

"Want something to eat?" Chad asked.

"Yes, I'm starving. I was too nervous to eat this morning." She stopped when she heard her name called.

"CiCi, what a surprise." Serena smiled as she approached the group. "When Mr. Masters asked if the paper would cover Five Star's new partnership, he never mentioned *you* were the new partner."

"Hello, Serena. Have you met my fiancé, Chad Cooper?"

Serena offered her hand. "Nice to meet you, Chad. Do you also work at Five Star?" she cooed, fluttering her eyelashes at Chad. "If so, I might have something that needs, um, *appraising*."

"No, ma'am. I'm a detective with the Ripley Grove Police Department."

"Oh." Serena disengaged her hand from his and glanced about the room. "Um, if you'll excuse me, I need to speak with Floyd."

As she walked off, Chad frowned. "I'd say she has an aversion to law enforcement, since hearing we were engaged didn't stop her from flirting."

"So I noticed." *Now I know how Jenna felt.*

They watched as Serena stood talking to Floyd about Five Star's humble beginnings. When the interview concluded, Jimmy readied his camera and Floyd waved CiCi over.

Chad leaned over and kissed her temple. "I'll fix us both a plate while he takes photos."

"Thanks."

CiCi's co-workers snuck away the moment it seemed appropriate, leaving her the afternoon to get settled in her new office. As she boxed up the items in her cubicle, she realized those co-workers were now her employees. Becoming a co-owner of a business might take a little getting used to. She hoped it wouldn't affect the friendships she had cultivated.

"Don't worry about getting everything done in one day, CiCi. You've plenty of time."

She whirled around and slapped a hand over her heart. "Floyd! I thought you'd left."

"Sorry. Didn't mean to startle you. I needed a refill," he said, lifting his coffee cup. "Troy and I are going over his benefits package in my office." He paused. "I'm sorry to drag you in so early tomorrow. With any luck, the meeting with the new client will be short. I would have scheduled it later in the day, but he flies to France in the afternoon and will be gone for a month."

"Not a problem." She stopped packing and glanced down the hall toward the empty office that once belonged to Bruce Owens, one of Floyd's former partners. "I, uh, have an office desk and chair being delivered this afternoon. I hope you understand it's not my intention to erase Bruce's memory. I just need to …" *Replace the desk where the cleaning lady found his body.*

Floyd's expression softened as he placed a gentle hand on her shoulder. "I think it's wise to start fresh. Well, I need to see if Troy has any more questions. See you in the morning?"

"Bright and early."

She watched him leave her office, then returned to her packing. She brushed off her hands after stacking the last box in the corner of her new office. The size of the room was more than adequate, with large windows that looked out onto the parking lot. To fill time until the furniture arrived, she transferred folders to the file cabinet.

By three-thirty, the desk and leather executive chair had been delivered. She'd found the two pieces at a local second-hand store and fell in love with the rich dark wood on the desk. She paid the asking price, pleased she hadn't let her inheritance go to her head and splurged on new furniture. After arranging two pictures on the desk, she plugged in the lamp and glanced at her watch. *Whoa. It's late. I need to file for that order of protection before the courthouse closes. It might keep Chad from blowing a gasket when I tell him about Dad's attack and what I've learned about Derek.*

As if on cue, Chad called. "Hey, sugar, just wanted to let you know something's come up and I'll be working tonight. I rescheduled our counseling session for tomorrow night. Will that work for you?"

She sighed. "Sure, but there's something important I wanted to talk to you about."

He paused. "Go ahead."

"No, not on the phone; in person."

In the background, someone shouted Chad's name. He angrily muttered under his breath. "Look, can it wait until tomorrow?"

"I suppose one more day won't hurt."

"Good. We'll talk then. I promise."

As she disconnected, she looked up, surprised to see someone other than Floyd or Troy in the room. "Ashley, what are you doing here? Is there something I can help you with?"

"I know what you did," Ashley said, her voice seething with anger.

"What are you talking about?" The hairs on CiCi's arms stood on end.

"You planned it all along, didn't you? He promised to leave me his share of the company and you stole it out from under me." A tear trickled down Ashley's face.

"I know you're upset, Ashley, but it wasn't like that." *Has she gone crazy?*

"You're a liar and a thief!" Ashley took a step forward, her hands fisted. Her eyes were filled with hatred as she closed the distance between them.

CiCi glanced around. There wasn't anything nearby she could use to defend herself if things got out of hand. She stepped to the side, putting the desk between them. "Ashley, listen to me," she said in a soothing tone. "I didn't—"

Ashley screamed and lunged across the desk, knocking the lamp over. CiCi blocked as many blows as she could before they both tumbled to the floor in a tangled heap. Seconds later, Floyd and Troy rushed in and pulled them apart. Ashley continued to kick and fight as they dragged her from the room. CiCi got to her feet and sank into a chair.

Moments later, Floyd returned. "Dear God, CiCi," he said, "are you okay? No, you're not. Your nose is bleeding." He pulled a handkerchief from his pocket. "Here, use this."

"You want me to call the police?" Troy asked, tucking in his shirt that had come undone in the scuffle.

"Please," Floyd said.

"No!" CiCi shouted as she stared at the ceiling, the hanky pressed to her nose. "I'm fine. If word of this gets out, it'll just give Five Star another black eye."

"Speaking of black eyes, let me get some ice. Looks like you have a bit of swelling under your eye," Troy said.

"I don't know, CiCi." Floyd shook his head and rubbed the back of his neck.

"Trust me, Floyd. I'm fine."

"If you're sure. At least she won't be harassing you at work anymore. I just fired her."

"Thanks. If you didn't, I would have."

When the ice pack had melted and her nerves had calmed, she gathered her things, said goodbye to Troy, and let Floyd walk her to her vehicle. According to the clock on the dashboard, the courthouse closed ten minutes ago. She'd have to file for that restraining order in the morning, right after meeting with the new client. With nothing else on her agenda, she decided to stop at Penny's Deli on the square. After the day she'd had, she needed a pick-me-up.

The slight swelling under her eye received a second look from the young girl who took her order. CiCi smiled, paid for her food, then looked for a table. Near the back, Abigail waved and motioned for CiCi to join her and her young daughter. CiCi smiled as she took a seat. "Thanks. Chad's working late and I didn't feel like going home just yet."

"Wow. What happened to you?"

"I ran into something at work." The half-lie flowed from CiCi's lips with ease. *I feel like I'm back in high school, making excuses for the bruises Dad gave me after one of his drunken fits.* She smiled at the red-headed little girl to avoid Abigail's reaction. "You must be Ava."

The little angel gave an endearing smile. "I'm five and I just got my hair cut."

"You did? It looks very pretty."

Abigail laughed and shook her head. "Tell CiCi *why* you got your hair cut." The child lowered her eyes, stuck out her lower lip and refused to say another word. "Seems little Ava took a nap with her daddy who stayed home sick today. When he woke up and got out of bed, he had terrible pain on the left side of his chest—thought he was having a heart attack."

Abigail chuckled, and CiCi wondered if she'd misunderstood. "Is he all right?"

"Oh, he's fine. You know how men blow things out of proportion. Anyway, he felt fine except for when he moved his left arm. After a lot of whining and cussing, he discovered a big wad of bubble gum stuck in his armpit. Every little movement pulled the hairs out by the root."

Abigail and CiCi doubled over in laughter and tears sprang from their eyes. Abigail tilted her head to Ava. "I found more gum in her hair, hence the haircut."

CiCi used her napkin to wipe her eyes. "I've never heard anything so funny."

"Believe me, Dan wasn't laughing. So, how are things going? Have you turned up any leads on your cousin?"

"No, nothing definitive."

"You talk with Serena?"

"Yes, on Saturday." CiCi thanked the young girl who delivered her order—a turkey, bacon, and avocado sandwich on wheat, a side of chips, and a drink. "She was helpful to a point. The point being is she wants first chance at writing the story if I discover a dark side to Jenna's dream of becoming a famous journalist."

"That sounds like Serena—always looking out for number one." Abigail took a sip of her drink. "I overheard her talking with Tyler today about Jenna. I planned on calling you."

"What did she say?"

"It's what *he* said that caught my attention. Mind you, I didn't catch the whole conversation, but he said 'I'll never sell the cabin or the property and leave Jenna behind. I'm closer to her there than anywhere else.'" Abigail's eyes widened as she took a large bite of her sandwich.

CiCi stopped mid-chew. "What did he mean by that?"

"I don't know," Abigail said after she swallowed, "but it sounded odd to me. I hadn't heard him mention Jenna in a long time. For a brief second, I wondered if Tyler could have—"

"What? Hurt Jenna?"

Abigail waved the notion away. "Forget I said that. I feel guilty for even thinking it."

Why? It's the first thing that popped into my head.

TWENTY-ONE

CiCi glanced at the wall clock. If she didn't leave soon, she'd be late to the meeting with Floyd and the new client. After grabbing a bottle of juice from the fridge, she dashed out to her Jeep. She stopped in her tracks. Her jawed dropped, as did her bottle of juice, which splattered across the asphalt when the lid popped off. Her heart sank as she circled the vehicle. Vile four-letter words and slanderous accusations, "thief" being the most frequent, had been spray-painted in neon yellow on the black exterior. Even the windows took a hit.

Blinking to keep the tears at bay, she pulled a rag from her emergency bin in the cargo area. A few swipes in different locations proved to be a waste of time. Tears turned to anger as she snatched up the empty bottle of juice, jumped into the driver's seat, and started the engine.

"Darn you, Ashley! What were you thinking?" she mumbled as she drove through morning rush hour traffic. Horns honked and people pointed, making her angrier by the minute. She backed into her usual parking spot, got out, and slammed the door. One last look at her vehicle made her wish she had a tarp to throw over it. After taking everything into consideration, there was only one thing to do. She pulled out her cell, scrolled through the contact list, and called her insurance agent as she made her way inside.

Tasha, the only person in sight, stood at the copy machine replenishing the paper supply. "Morning. Where is everyone?" CiCi asked.

"Out doing inspection. Floyd is in his office. Mr. Perniciaro is running late." A worried look washed over Tasha's face when she caught sight of CiCi's bruised cheek. "What happened?"

She sighed. "Yesterday, after everyone left …"

Tasha shook her head as she listened to a quick recap of the attack. Her eyes widened when she glanced out the window. "Lord Almighty. Who did that to your Jeep?"

"Take a wild guess. We'll talk later," CiCi said as she walked towards Floyd's office.

After the meeting concluded, her insurance agent arrived. He was a gem and went above and beyond her expectations. He arranged for a local body shop to pick up her Jeep and give it a new paint job. Her policy would pay for a rental vehicle to use in the meantime. After he left, Tasha poked her head into CiCi's office.

"You got company and he doesn't look happy." Tasha tipped her head toward the parking lot, then disappeared to answer the phone.

CiCi stepped over to the window and watched with dismay as Chad circled her Jeep. He was on duty and it showed. As he snapped pictures of the damage, Mark pulled up. He, too, inspected the Jeep as he talked with Chad. The two men frowned and looked toward her office window. Though certain they couldn't see her, she took a step back just in case.

Two minutes later, Chad and Mark strode into her office and closed the door. Chad stared at her for a moment, then walked over, hooked a finger under her chin, and tilted her face upward to get a better look. "What happened?"

She touched the swollen spot under her eye. With all that had happened since yesterday, she'd nearly forgotten about it. "Ashley came back yesterday afternoon and let me know what she thought about my purchasing her uncle's share of the company."

"You okay?" He gently stroked her cheek with his thumb.

"I'm fine, although we're now short one employee."

He went to the window and peered through the blinds. "Why didn't you tell me?"

"About Ashley's attack? I decided it could wait until we had a chance to talk face-to-face, remember?" She pursed her lips and looked away. "How'd you find out about the car?"

"Guzman was on patrol this morning."

"You think Ashley tagged your Jeep?" Mark asked.

"That'd be my guess."

"Put her name in the police report."

"I'm not filing a police report," she said.

Chad crossed his arms over his chest and frowned. "Why not?"

"Someone in your office will talk." She planted her hands on her hips and returned the frown. "I've already explained this to Floyd. It wasn't long ago someone murdered two employees here. Five Star doesn't need any more negative publicity. I'm fine, and my insurance will cover the paint job."

A soft rap drew her attention from Chad's stare. Pete stood in the doorway with a scowl on his face. "That man is the devil incarnate. First, the assault, then Art's windows, and now your Jeep. You filed for that protective order, didn't you?"

She tried to wave Pete off, but he paid no mind.

"Man? What man?" Chad stiffened. "What assault?"

"She didn't tell you?" Pete pinned CiCi with an icy glare. "Your time's up, missy. Hey, what happened to your eye?"

CiCi ignored the hardened look on Chad's face. "Pete, what happened to Art's windows? Was he hurt?"

"Forget Art's windows. What's Pete talking about?" Chad demanded.

"Art's fine," Pete said. "We had a deal, missy. Are you gonna tell Chad, or should I?"

"Tell me *what?*" Chad's voice grew louder and angrier.

CiCi pressed her fingertips to her temples. "Stop! Please, stop. I told you last week and again last night we needed to talk, but now is not the time or place."

Chad glared; his jaw muscles tensed. "I promise; we'll be having a long talk tonight."

She stared into his stormy eyes before looking away. She walked to the window and expelled an irritated sigh. Through the blinds, she saw Serena talking to the driver from the body shop. "What is *she* doing here?"

Chad stepped up behind her. "Isn't that the reporter from the newspaper?"

CiCi nodded and reached for the cord to raise the slats. Her vision blurred and she missed on the first try. And the second. She blinked several times, but her vision only worsened.

"CiCi, are you okay?" Chad asked.

"Does it matter?" She turned away, upset at being pushed into a corner and angry at having a problem she refused to acknowledge still existed. Three steps later, the floor shifted, and the room spun out of control, just like her life had been doing the last couple of days. Panic set in, and she couldn't breathe. She leaned against the desk and closed her eyes.

Chad rushed over and wrapped his arms around her. "I've got you. Relax and take slow, deep breaths, hon."

"Chad?" she whispered.

"Pete, grab a chair," he commanded. Her knees buckled, and he tightened his grip. "Too late. Mark, help me ease her to the floor."

Her head wobbled, then fell against his chest as her world went black.

Faraway voices filtered through the outer edges of the fog. "...call 9-1-1?...not yet...get me a bottle of water...use my hanky...is she okay?" A damp cloth traced a line across her forehead. A soft moan escaped from her throat. The moist cloth caressed her face again and trailed down the side of her neck. Someone patted her hand.

"Can you hear me, CiCi? Open your eyes, hon."

Chad's voice pulled her from the depths of darkness. The fog in her head slowly dissipated, and she forced her eyelids open. Three blurry faces loomed overhead. Startled, she tried to get up, but a firm hand on her shoulder held her down.

"What happened?" she whispered.

"You passed out," Chad said, his face etched with worry as he checked her pulse. She closed her eyes and shook her head in response. "You did, whether you want to admit it or not. You were out cold for several minutes."

A flash of light from the doorway drew their attention. Serena had her phone's camera aimed at CiCi and Chad. Mark jumped to his feet and chased her from the room.

"Squeeze my hand, CiCi. Again." He glanced over at Pete, who nodded and came to kneel at her left. "Watch her while I go make a call. Don't let her get up."

CiCi closed her eyes and counted to forty. She opened her eyes and took a deep breath. "Help me up, will you, Pete? I feel ridiculous lying on the floor."

"Not until Chad says so. I have a hunch he won't be happy with me as it is."

When Chad returned, he and Pete helped her into a chair. Floyd came in with a bottle of water for her and informed them Mark was keeping the press away.

CiCi took a few sips. "Thanks. I'm feeling much better now."

Chad sat on the edge of her desk, his eyes clouded with worry. "Dizzy spells and double vision are not something to be taken lightly. This is the second time in a week you've had an episode, and they seem to be getting worse."

The phone on her desk rang. She reached for the handset, but Floyd grabbed it first.

"Five Star, Floyd Masters speaking…I'm sorry, she's unavailable and won't be back in the office until next week…that's right…Yes. Yes, I'll make sure we adjust the square footage. Thanks for calling. Goodbye."

CiCi frowned. "Who were you talking about? Certainly not me."

"Yes, you. You're taking the rest of the week off."

"But—"

"I don't want to hear it. I own fifty-five percent of this company and have final say. And I say go home. You've been working more hours than your doctor prescribed. As your former boss, I should have put a stop to it earlier. As your friend and business partner, I aim to rectify that right now. Go home, CiCi."

"Well-played, Floyd," said Chad, which earned him a scathing glare from CiCi.

A young man appeared in the doorway. "Um, excuse me? I'm from Midwest Body and Paint. I need the keys to the Jeep."

She signed the authorization slip and handed over her car keys. A few minutes later, he returned to give her the camo jacket he'd found in the back seat of her Jeep. After Floyd refused to budge about her work schedule, CiCi grabbed her purse and jacket before letting Tasha know she'd be taking a few days off. Chad scanned the parking lot to make sure the reporter and photographer had left.

She slid into Chad's truck and buckled up. "Would you drop me off at that car rental place over on Ash?"

"Not gonna happen," Chad said with a firm set to his mouth.

"Why not? I'm going to need a car."

"Not today, you don't. You want to tell me what Pete was talking about earlier?"

"Not today, I don't," she parroted. She cringed the moment the words left her lips, but she wasn't in the mood to talk about what happened outside the hardware store.

After that, there was little discussion. She closed her eyes and leaned back against the headrest and took advantage of the quiet to mull over the last twenty-four hours. When the vehicle came to a stop, she opened her eyes and frowned. Chad hadn't taken her home; he'd brought her to the hospital.

"What are we doing here?"

"I called Doc earlier. He wants to check you out, maybe run tests."

Her pulse spiked and her breathing hitched. Panic tightened like a vise around her chest. "No, I…I can't. Take me home."

"Not gonna happen. There are things I'll compromise on, but this isn't one of them. You need to get checked out."

Chad walked around and opened her door. Fear of the unknown kept her frozen in place. She stared straight ahead. A lone tear trickled down her cheek. He leaned in and brushed it away.

"There's nothing to be scared of," he whispered. "It's just a few tests. It's clear you're not fully recovered, and you can't fix this if you don't know what the problem is."

Her eyes lowered to the diamond and sapphire ring on her finger she'd been twisting in circles. *Maybe I don't want to know. If it's bad news, it could mean the beginning of the end—the end of our engagement, the end of our future together, the end of us.*

"Come on. Doc is waiting." After planting a kiss on her forehead, he stepped back and held out his hand.

She hesitantly took it and slid from the cab. "What if the tests show …" She tightened her grip and choked back a sob. "What if you decide not to …"

He pulled her into his arms and tilted her face upward. "Look at me, CiCi. No matter what happens, I'm not going anywhere. Haven't I proven that to you by now?"

Tears stung her eyes as she leaned upward and wrapped her arms around his neck. There were no words to describe her love for him. He tightened his embrace and brushed a kiss across her forehead. He slipped his arm around her, and together they walked into the hospital.

TWENTY-TWO

Chad paced the waiting room, eager for news. He'd sent numerous texts to friends wanting an update and drank enough coffee to make a camel cross its legs. He flipped through an outdated magazine, then tossed it back on the end table. A mind-numbing soap opera played on the wall-mounted TV. Finally, a middle-aged hospital volunteer approached with a smile.

"Miss Winslow is asking for you," she said.

He checked his watch. *Five hours. It's about time.* After arriving at the room number given to him, he rapped on the door and hesitantly poked his head inside. CiCi sat on the edge of the bed, buttoning her blouse. Her slight smile was encouraging. He walked over and tenderly kissed her forehead. "How's my girl? Since you're getting dressed, I take it they aren't keeping you overnight for observation."

"No, thank goodness. Besides, they'd have to tie me to the bed first."

"Sounds interesting." Chad winked and gave her a dimpled smile.

"Stop that!" she teased. "Doc should be here any minute."

Doctor Cunningham entered the room, nodded, and pulled up

a chair. He patted several pockets before finding his glasses atop his graying head. He put them on, opened the folder in his hand, and began to review her chart.

"Cecilia, Chad," he said. "We ran several tests and compared them with those done a few months ago. I detect very little change. I'll go over the results again after the various departments report their official findings."

CiCi sighed with relief. "I told you it was nothing."

"I disagree. You say these episodes started again after you returned to work?" Doc rubbed a hand across his chin and frowned. "Are you working over twenty hours a week? Resting at regular intervals?"

"Not exactly. I've had a lot on my plate and work is stressful right now."

He grunted when she avoided his steadfast gaze. "I should've known. Let's take a step back. No work for the next two weeks. Get plenty of rest. Cut back on the computer, TV and electronics to give your brain a rest. If you have any more episodes, I want you back in my office pronto. Understand?"

"Two weeks?"

"Yes. I'll see you in two weeks, and hopefully not before."

"But—"

"No buts." Doc remained firm as she argued for a more lenient list of restrictions. Finally, he stood, patted her shoulder, and shook Chad's hand before he left the room.

Chad turned and tucked a strand of hair behind her ear. *She looks stunned, like someone told her she's allergic to sweets.* "You ready to go home, sugar?"

Chad held her hand as he drove and refrained from idle chitchat, allowing her time to process the delay in her recovery. He parked and followed her inside. After she tossed her purse on a chair in the living room, she headed to the kitchen to make a fresh pot of coffee. His phone buzzed as he took a seat at the breakfast bar. He checked the message and texted one back.

"That was Pete. He wanted to know how you're doing."

Her shoulders tensed at the mention of Pete's name. "Is that all he said?"

"Yes."

She set two mugs on the counter and let out a deep breath.

"Worried he told me your secret? He didn't, but you and I need to have a talk about what's been going on. After the day you've had, it can wait until after you get some rest. You look exhausted."

"I am. You might as well head back to work. I'm not going anywhere but to bed."

"I know, because I'll be here to make sure you do."

She started to protest until she saw the determined look in his eyes.

A soft tapping on her bedroom door startled her awake. CiCi checked the time. She'd been asleep for nearly three hours. As she sat up and swung her legs over the side of the bed, Chad poked his head in the room.

"Dinner's about ready. You hungry?"

"Starving. They didn't give me anything to eat at the hospital. I'll be down after I freshen up." He gave her a nod and lumbered down the stairs. She followed five minutes later.

Chad placed their drinks on the table as the oven timer dinged. He waved her away, so she took a seat in her usual spot next to the bay window. She enjoyed watching the bunnies play tag and the squirrels gather nuts in the wooded area just beyond the complex's property line. It was now October. By the end of the month, the trees would be ablaze in rich shades of red, orange, gold and magenta. Chad interrupted her visions of fall splendor when he set two steaming plates of baked pasta on the table along with crusty garlic bread.

"I used your last can of cream of mushroom soup and the leftover rotisserie chicken."

"It looks wonderful," she said. "I didn't expect you to cook dinner, but thank you."

He handed her a napkin. "Taste it before you thank me."

"It's delicious," she said after taking a bite. "Maybe I'll try a few new recipes while I'm off."

"You need time off, considering *everything* you've been doing these last few weeks."

Her fork slipped and clattered against the plate. "Chad, I need to—"

"Let's eat before it gets cold. We'll talk later."

The look in his eyes and the firm set of his jaw told her she'd be talking with Detective Chad Cooper. She picked up her fork and ate without tasting, drank without being refreshed, all while strategizing how to explain the events that had her on edge.

They cleared dishes and put away the leftovers before moving to the living room. She settled on the sofa while Chad took the upholstered chair to her right. He crossed his legs and sipped his coffee, his silence lending a heaviness to the air. She tapped her foot against the hardwood floor, drawing attention to the stillness in the room. "Want to watch a movie?"

"Not tonight," he said. "Are you trying to delay the inevitable? Where would you like to start? With Ashley's attack—or your dad's?"

She gasped. "How did you find out?"

He set his cup on the coffee table. "I'm a detective, CiCi. This is what I do. I take a clue, or in this case a slip of the tongue, and follow the trail. When Pete mentioned trouble at Art's, all I had to do was make a call. Art filed a police report after the windows of the hardware store were smashed during the night. His statement mentioned an altercation on Saturday. Your name, Pete's, Jack's—it's all there in black and white."

"Oh. So, okay, I understand why you're mad, but—"

He leaned forward and braced his forearms on his knees. "Damn right I'm mad! You know what Jack's capable of. I should've been the first person you called."

"In my defense, I told you I needed to talk to you about something." His eyes bore into her and she glared back. "I'm sorry I didn't tell you earlier. I just couldn't deal with him, and you, and the restraining order stuff the day before the big announcement at work."

"Priorities, CiCi. Your safety is a priority. So, tell me what happened." His hardened face showed his irritation.

He had every right to feel that way. She would if she were in his shoes. She stood and paced the floor while recounting each event. "Before Ashley went crazy in my office yesterday afternoon, I had every intention of going to the courthouse to file for a protective order, but I didn't leave work in time. Then, when I went outside this morning and found my car vandalized, everything snowballed, and I couldn't stop it."

Frustrated, she paused and took a deep breath. Crossing to the window, she stared out into the darkness beyond her reach and rubbed her forehead to ward off the start of a headache. Chad left the chair and closed the distance between them. His reflection in the window towered over hers. His expression softened as he placed his hands on her trembling shoulders, as though worried the continued stress might bring on another attack.

"All the more reason you should have told me. I worry now that your dad's back in the picture. I'm glad Art and Pete were there. Pete should have called me, even if you didn't."

"Don't blame him. I begged him not to."

A low chuckle rumbled from his chest. "That man has a soft spot for you—you and your banana bread."

She turned and gazed into his eyes. "And you don't?"

"Not when it interferes with keeping you safe." He pulled her into his arms, and she surrendered to his warmth. "You know how I feel about your dad, so I'm not going to waste my breath." He kissed the top of her head. "I think you know what you need to do next."

She frowned. "No, what?"

"File for a protective order. Get your laptop and we'll fill out the application together. Do you still have copies of the evidence you submitted a few months back?"

"I do." She retrieved the envelope with the Protection from Abuse order she had filed against her dad months earlier. When she missed the court date because of her hospitalization, the case was dropped. She'd saved the packet, thinking the evidence might be needed one day. *I guess deep down, I knew it would never be over.* An hour later, she pulled the updated paperwork from her printer and reviewed the form for mistakes. She printed the photos Pete sent from his phone and added them to the stack. "Done. I'll take everything to the courthouse tomorrow."

"I know, because I'm going with you. I'll pick you up on my way to work."

"That's not necessary. I can go by myself."

"Oh? How do you plan to get there?"

She wrinkled her nose. "I forgot I don't have a car." Glancing about the room, she asked, "How about that movie now?"

He shook his head. "Doc said to cut back on the electronics, and you just spent an hour on the computer. How about we take a walk instead?"

She grabbed the first available coat on her way outside. Chad followed, helping guide her arms into the sleeves of the fitted, hip-length jacket.

"I've never seen you wear camouflage, but it's cute on you. Is it new?"

"No, it belonged to Jenna. She left it in Edna's closet at the nursing home."

"Remind me who Edna is."

"Katherine's mother-in-law and Jenna's grandmother. She's so sweet, but a bit confused. She thinks I'm Jenna and I don't have the heart to correct her. On my last visit, she insisted I take the jacket home. I did to make her happy, and Katherine didn't seem to mind."

She zipped the jacket and pulled the collar up when a slight breeze kicked up. The cool, crisp air tugged at her hair as they walked around the block, stopping at times to chat with neighbors out walking their dogs. It was well after dark by the time they arrived back home.

He seems to have calmed down. Maybe now's the time to tell him about my visit to The Tap & Keg and the car that's been following me. As she started to speak, his phone pinged. She glanced at the screen as he pulled it from his pocket. Evan. Chad read the text and cursed under his breath. "Your undercover agent having problems again?" she asked.

"Yeah. I need to go," he said, tucking the phone away. "Are you sure you're okay staying alone tonight? I'm sure Megan wouldn't mind staying over."

"I told you I'm fine. Once my head clears and the weakness fades, I can't tell anything happened."

Chad stopped next to his truck and pulled her in for a quick goodnight kiss, generating a welcome heat that did more than warm her lips.

She stood on the porch, waving as he drove from the lot. Sticking her hands in one of the jacket's many pockets, her fingers brushed against a piece of paper. She withdrew the paper and unfolded it. There was no name, only an address that was located just outside of town.

TWENTY-THREE

CiCi strummed her fingers on the arm of the wood chair as she waited for the court clerk to call her number. The courthouse teemed with activity, and the air was thick with impatience. Chad took her hand in his and smiled, easing the jitters that knotted her stomach.

"You're doing the right thing," he said.

"I know. It's just that …" She sighed. "I know."

Twenty minutes later, she tucked her copy of the restraining order into her purse and followed Chad into the lobby. "I'm glad that's over. Now I can move on with my life without worrying what Dad will do next." She glanced at her watch. "We're done earlier than I expected. Can you drop me off at Smitty's before you head back to work? I need a rental car."

"Is driving a good idea? Maybe you should wait until your test results come back."

"Doc never said I couldn't drive."

"That's because he was too busy arguing with you about your workload. Maybe we should call—"

Chad's suggestion was cut short when her phone rang. She held up a finger and answered, grateful for the interruption. "Hi,

Katherine. How are you? What? No, no, I'm fine. A little dizziness brought on by stress." She turned away from Chad's raised eyebrows and shook her head. "Yes, I'd love to get together. I just finished some business at the courthouse…don't worry, I have an errand or two to run. Would you mind picking me up at Sadie's Bakery? My car's, um, in the shop…perfect. I'll see you then."

"I take it you don't need a ride home?"

"No, but thanks. Katherine wants to discuss ideas for my wedding dress. Then we'll have lunch and visit Edna afterward."

"Sounds like fun. I'll see you tonight." He leaned in and brushed a kiss across her cheek.

As he strode away with a slight swagger in his step, she couldn't help but notice the heads that turned to watch. *Yes, ladies, and he's all mine.* Glancing around, her eye caught the sign for the county appraiser's office. A thought popped into her head that she couldn't ignore.

She pushed through the door and reached in her purse for the slip of paper she'd found in Jenna's jacket. The information she wanted would've been easy to access if she were at work, but since she wasn't, she might as well do it now. Ten minutes later, she had the name of the business that occupied the fifty-acre parcel of land in her hand: *Greenleaf Growers.* The owner of the business was a corporation she'd never heard of.

She walked down the steps of the courthouse and strolled along the streets of the town square. At the stationery shop, she bookmarked her favorite wedding invitations, preferring to pick one after getting Chad's input. Next, she paid a visit to Sadie's bakery and arranged for a cake tasting after lunch on Saturday. With any luck, they could also narrow down the venue for the reception.

She left the shop in time to see Katherine pull up in a white CRV. After CiCi hopped into the passenger seat, she was pulled into an awkward hug across the console.

"I hope you're feeling better," Katherine said. "If you start feeling under the weather, just let me know and I'll take you home."

"I'm fine. Honest. Nice car, by the way. So, what's first on the agenda?"

"I need to drop off a replacement veil at Sybil Taylor's home. Her wedding is Saturday, and a candle used during a photo shoot caught her veil on fire. She's not the first bride that's happened to. After that, I thought we'd go to the shop. I sketched a few ideas that were tumbling about in my brain, but I need to get a feel for what you like and what you don't."

"I can't tell you how thrilled I am that you're designing my gown."

At a stop light, Katherine reached into the back seat, grabbed a newspaper, and handed it to CiCi. "I picked up an extra copy for you to keep as a souvenir. Congratulations on your new business venture. I had no idea."

"Thank you. I'm so excited. Believe me, it was a win-win situation. I helped the company avoid financial ruin *and* saved myself from looking for a job."

On the front page of *The Ripley Review*, under a bold "New Partnership" headline, was a picture of CiCi and Floyd shaking hands. The crisp photo caught CiCi's winning smile. Surprisingly, Serena's write-up cast Five Star in a favorable light, with no mention of the murders earlier in the year. CiCi flipped through the pages to find the Scene About Town column. She sighed with relief when she saw there weren't any photos of her vandalized Jeep.

After stopping at the Taylor's, they drove to Blissful Creations, where she studied Katherine's drawings. The formal ball gown was the first to be eliminated. Each of the other drawings had elements she found appealing, prompting her to ask if they could be incorporated into a dress similar in shape to Jenna's. Katherine promised to do her best when she drew a second round of sketches.

Over a lunch of soup and salad, Katherine peppered her ham and potato soup and spoke of the upcoming wedding plans of a councilman's daughter. Afterward, she paused and then asked if CiCi had learned anything from Jenna's friends that might be helpful.

CiCi speared a cucumber slice and took a bite. "I did. Among other things, I learned Jenna had a second job."

Katherine paused and set her fork down. "A second job? Are you sure?"

CiCi nodded. "She was a waitress at The Tap & Keg in the evenings."

Katherine frowned. "Jenna's had a lot of jobs over the years, but never at a bar. I mean, she doesn't even drink."

That you know of. "Maybe she wanted the extra income to help pay for the wedding."

"Could be, although Tyler was paying for most of it."

"I've spoken with him and a few people at the newspaper. Like any workplace, there was friction between some of the employees."

Katherine shrugged. "That's not uncommon. Tyler wasn't happy about the crush some photographer had on Jenna, but she laughed it off. Jenna complained about a girl at work getting too friendly with Tyler, but he insisted they were just old friends. Jealousy is never good for a relationship."

"One of the co-workers mentioned Tyler has a cabin."

"Yes. He owns several acres outside of town on Hunters Point Road. Although the cabin needed a lot of work, they planned to move in after the wedding. Jenna loved the rural setting."

"Did she have plans to put in a garden or flower beds at the cabin?"

"I don't know. You'd have to ask Tyler. Why?" Katherine dabbed her mouth before placing the napkin to the left of her empty plate.

"There was an address for Greenleaf Growers in the pocket of her camo jacket."

"Hmm. That name sounds familiar, but I can't recall why."

CiCi smiled. "I have the next two weeks off work. Maybe I'll check it out."

"I can't tell you how grateful I am you're looking for her."

"Why wouldn't I? We're family." She patted Katherine's hand. "Now, what kind of pie should we take Edna? I say strawberry-rhubarb or coconut cream."

"Those are her favorites. How did you know?"

"They were my grandmother's favorites."

CiCi and Katherine found Edna in fine form when they arrived, sitting in her wheelchair on the patio, bundled up against the slight chill in the air and telling tales to whoever would listen. Katherine pushed her mother-in-law back to her room, where they unboxed the slice of strawberry-rhubarb pie. Edna's eyes lit up as if she'd been given a puppy for Christmas. She settled into her favorite chair and polished off every last crumb. Katherine and CiCi entertained her with funny stories they'd read in the newspaper and caught her up on recent happenings around town. Tired of sitting, Katherine stood and fussed about, straightening up the room. On Edna's windowsill sat two ripe peaches.

"Where'd you get the peaches, Mom?"

"Mabel's daughter. She's trying to get on my good side because her mother keeps eating my pudding. Got them at the farmers' market a few days ago, or so she says."

"I'm sure she did. The market stays open until the end of September, which was this past Saturday." Katherine snapped her fingers. "That's it, CiCi! Last summer, Jenna mentioned someone at Greenleaf Growers wasn't happy about the newspaper's photographer taking their picture to go with an article she was writing about the farmers' market."

CiCi exchanged looks with Katherine. "Wonder why? Seems a business would jump at the chance for free publicity."

Katherine shrugged. "Who knows? People can be so fickle."

Edna stared off into space, her eyelids drooping with each second that passed. Katherine smiled at CiCi and whispered, "I think we should go."

CiCi nodded and lowered the shades while Katherine helped Edna into bed. On the way to Katherine's SUV, CiCi said, "I need to rent a car for a few days while mine is in the shop. Mind dropping me off?"

A short time later, CiCi slid behind the wheel of the rental. The sedan sat much lower to the ground than her beloved Jeep and made her feel as if she were driving a toy car. All things aside, at least she had her own transportation. While stopped at a red light, a van sporting the Greenleaf Growers name and logo passed by. Any thoughts of going straight home evaporated. She pulled the slip of paper from her purse and typed the address into the GPS app on her phone.

The directions led her to the outer city limits of Ripley Grove. A large sign at the juncture of Hunter's Point Road and Hickory Lane pointed the way. *Hmm, Tyler's cabin must be nearby.* She passed acres of farmland before driving through the wide gated entrance to Greenleaf Growers. She eased to a stop in front of a building that housed a produce stand that was open to the public. A sign by the door read *Shop Local, Buy Organic.*

CiCi stepped inside. An older woman stood with her back facing the door. By the slight tilt of her graying head, she'd heard someone enter. When she turned, her face blanched.

"What are *you* doing here?" she said. "The manager's still angry about those photos you took last year, and I understand his boss wasn't too happy, either."

"Is the owner here?"

"No. Never met the man. Leaves everything up to the manager." Her eyes darted past CiCi and scanned the parking lot, as if looking for someone. "If you're smart, you best be gone before he gets back." The woman turned and stalked off into a back office and shut the door.

CiCi left the building, sat in her car, and pulled up the story on her phone. An old saying said there's no such thing as bad publicity, but CiCi knew firsthand that wasn't true. She read the article promoting the open-air venue and fresh produce, but there weren't any pictures attached. *So, what photos made the owner and manager so angry?*

TWENTY-FOUR

The question puzzled her as she drove through the square toward home. Perhaps Katherine had been right; people are fickle. She put aside any further thoughts on the matter when she noticed the small crowd gathered on either side of Art's Hardware. She parked and walked across the street to see what had attracted everyone's attention. Working her way through the gathering, she found Art, front and center, watching two men replace the store's broken windows. After getting a nod of approval, the workmen collected their gear and the crowd dispersed.

She shook her head and began to pull out her checkbook. "Art, I'm so sorry about your windows, and I feel somewhat responsible. Let me write you a check for the damage."

"You'll do no such thing, unless you were the one who threw the bricks."

"Art! I would never——" She stopped short, seeing the twinkle in his eyes.

"I know you wouldn't. But you listen to this old man." He shook a finger at her. "Never take the blame for something you didn't do. Now, come inside. I have a bag of birdseed set aside for you."

They talked as though nothing had happened. He gave her a

new bag of seed to replace the one that spilled in the alley days before. When she turned to leave, he took her hand, turned it over, and inspected the scrapes.

"It's healing. I'm glad you weren't hurt." He patted her hand, placed a wrapped chocolate in her palm, and folded her fingers over it. "Take care of yourself."

She smiled, happy to have such a kindhearted friend. As she deposited the seed in the sedan's trunk, Mr. Rivera drove by in a red BMW and waved. Before she could get behind the wheel of her rental, someone called her name. Tyler waved and darted between vehicles as he crossed the street. Over his shoulder, she spotted Jimmy taking photos of the man painting the hardware's name on the new windows. Some would have opted for vinyl lettering, but not Art. He was old-school and determined to keep a dying art alive.

"Have a minute to talk?" Tyler asked as he pulled a pen and paper from his pocket.

"About Jenna?"

"No, about Art's windows. I heard rumors it stemmed from something to do with an altercation between you and your dad a few days ago. Any comment?"

"Did you ask Art?"

"I did. Said it was a simple case of vandalism."

"Who am I to call Art a liar?" She flashed him a smile and leaned against the door.

"I also hear you've been talking to some of Jenna's friends. Learn anything new?"

"Yeah, I did. Why didn't you tell me Jenna had a part-time job at The Tap & Keg?"

Tyler's face darkened. "I didn't think it was important. Jenna assured me the job was temporary. 'A means to an end', she said."

"What did she mean by that?"

He shrugged. "I don't know, and at the time, I really didn't care. All I wanted to do was smooth things over, get married, and move to the cabin."

"Katherine told me about the cabin. I heard a rumor you might be selling it."

"Where'd you hear that?"

"Oh, here and there. You know how people talk."

"I'll never sell. It's where Jenna…where Jenna …" The muscle in his jaw ticked, and he looked away.

She waited for him to continue, perhaps to say it was where Jenna liked to write, or cook, or ride horses. When he didn't, she asked, "What were you going to say?"

"It's where Jenna is."

"What? She's…she's at your cabin?" she stammered. *Is he admitting he had something to do with Jenna's disappearance?*

"Yes, but only in spirit. It's where she and I spent a lot of time together." He took in the shocked look on her face and gave her a sly grin. "If you want to know more about your cousin, come with me. I'll show you where we were going to live after the wedding."

Her pulse quickened as she slid into the passenger seat of Tyler's car. *Is this a good idea?* Just then, her phone rang. *Perfect timing.* "Hey, Chad."

"I have a few minutes to spare," he said, "so I thought I'd call. How was your meeting with Katherine?"

"Great. After going over the sketches, I was able to give her a better idea of what I'm looking for in a dress."

"Where are you now?"

"On the square. After visiting Edna, I dropped by the hardware and talked with Art. The workers just finished replacing the broken windows."

"Stay put. I'll come by and give you a lift home."

"Thanks, but don't bother. I picked up a rental car this afternoon." A dead silence filled the air. "Are you still there?"

An exasperated sigh filtered through the phone. "Yes, I'm here."

"I ran into Tyler Quinn, Jenna's fiancé. He's going to show me the cabin where he and Jenna were going to live. It's a beautiful day for a drive in the country. I'll call when I get home. Love you." She disconnected and slid the phone into her purse. *At least Tyler knows that Chad is aware of who I'm with and where we're going.*

They were about five miles outside of town when CiCi noticed a dark sedan in the side mirror. The vehicle held back far enough that she couldn't identify the make or model. At the Hickory Lane turnoff to Greenleaf Growers, the car disappeared. They continued on, leaving the smooth pavement behind and traveling along a winding gravel road. At a fork in the road, they took the dirt path on the right that headed east.

Tyler never slowed as his tires thumped over the rickety bridge that spanned a small creek. A mile further, he turned down an unmarked road. It wasn't long before he came to a stop in front of a log cabin nestled in a woodland paradise. The picturesque setting nearly took her breath away.

"It's absolutely beautiful," she whispered.

Tyler nodded and exited the vehicle. "I own twenty acres and the cabin. It belonged to my grandparents once upon a time. I've renovated most of the inside and added a sunroom on the back. There's still plenty of work to do."

CiCi followed. With an appraiser's eye, she surveyed the surroundings. About fifty feet beyond the twelve hundred square foot house, two sturdy trees acted as bookends to a row of stacked firewood. A large outbuilding served as a garage and storage shed. The well-built cabin had a covered porch, new windows, a tin roof, and a rainwater catchment system. She stepped onto the porch as Tyler unlocked the door and led the way inside. CiCi's gaze traveled from the beamed ceilings and reclaimed hardwood floors to the outdated country-style kitchen. A floor-to-ceiling stone fireplace added rustic charm to the living room.

"Do you live here?" she asked, noting that several pieces of furniture were covered with sheets to protect them from dust and sun damage.

"No, I don't. It wasn't until recently that I started working on the place again. I hope to move in by Thanksgiving."

He walked through the main living area and out to the new addition at the back of the cabin. She followed. The three hundred square feet space had oversized windows that allowed an unobstructed view of the landscape. There was a cozy seating area on the left side of the sunroom. The other half served as an office. A stuffed KU mascot sat atop the cluttered, dusty desk. Jenna's desk.

Taking in the entire structure, she said, "This isn't what I expected. Katherine's description didn't do it justice."

His chest puffed with pride. "Thank you. I've made quite a few improvements since Katherine last saw it, but there's plenty more to do."

"Did you do the work yourself?"

"Most of it. Jenna helped. I built the addition for Jenna as a wedding gift, a place where she could write no matter who she worked for. She loved this place. We spent a lot of time here before she decided she needed some space."

"Is that her desk? It's beautiful."

"It is, and it weighs a ton. Jenna bought it on the final day of an estate sale for fifty percent of the asking price. She was over the moon." He stopped as something drew his attention to a small hill west of the cabin. "Come with me. I'll show you Jenna's favorite spot."

CiCi followed him to the back deck and across the spacious yard until they came to an opening nearly hidden among the pine trees. The unmarked trail led up a small hill and through a wooded area. Birds squawked, squirrels jumped from tree to tree, and chipmunks darted in and out of the dying undergrowth. Scraggly bushes scraped against her pant legs, and Tyler held the occasional wayward branch that would've required dodging to avoid getting whacked.

She stopped once to catch her breath and almost lost sight of her guide. Pressing on, she found Tyler at the crest of the hill, hands in his pockets, gazing into the distance. Her jaw dropped at the view. Marsh grass lined a large pond that reflected the late afternoon sun. Ducks lazily swam in circles, while a gaggle of geese sunned themselves on the opposite bank. Park benches, each painted a different color, sat at intervals along a path that circled the shoreline. In the far distance to the east, pumpkins dotted a neighboring field like orange confetti. A tractor chugged along as a small band of workers cut and loaded the last of the crop into a trailer. Bordering the opposite side of Tyler's property, beyond the small creek in the ravine and a grove of trees, lay acres of land in various stages of harvest. Several large structures with semi-transparent walls lined the back of the property.

"What are those buildings?" She pointed to the western border.

"Hothouses and greenhouses. Greenleaf Growers owns that land. They've been trying to get me to sell the back half of my property to them, but I promised Jenna we'd never sell. I aim to keep my promise. Serena thinks their offer is good, above what the land is worth, but I just can't do it."

Across the pond, a squirrel rooted for nuts in a six-foot rectangular patch of dirt. "What's that?" she asked, pointing to the bare plot.

"Oh. That?" he said, tipping his head. "I, uh, had plans to pour a concrete pad and add another bench for Jenna, but I never got around to finishing it. No matter what time of day, I wanted her to have a place to sit in the shade."

"That was thoughtful of you."

Tyler remained silent, lost in thought, staring at the squirrel digging in the earth.

CiCi strolled down the path and sat on the nearest bench, one painted a bright, cheery red. Closing her eyes, she breathed in the cool, crisp air and listened to sounds city girls like herself seldom heard. A rustle of leaves to her right startled her. She turned. Tyler stood a mere two feet away, staring as though in a trance, his hand outstretched as if to touch her hair. She drew back and called out his name to break the spell.

He shook his head and blinked several times. "I'm sorry. That's Jenna's favorite bench. She'd sit there for hours—reflecting, writing, taking photos of the ducks and geese. With the sun setting behind you, you remind me so much of her." He pulled a hand down his face as if he could erase the traces of pain and sadness. He started to speak again, but instead turned and walked away.

It suddenly struck her that, unlike Katherine, Tyler always spoke of Jenna in the past tense. One seemed hopeful, the other hopeless.

Left alone, she wandered to the other side of the pond, scoping out the land while sidestepping the bird poop. Most of the ducks ignored her, but one goose resented her presence. He became aggressive, hissing and flapping his wings until she was forced back to the other side of the pond. She sat a few moments longer on Jenna's bench, taking in the surroundings before heading down the trail to the cabin.

Tyler sat on the back deck, awaiting her return. They walked through the cabin and left by the front entrance. He locked up, then placed the key on the frame over the door. When he noticed the puzzled look on her face, he said, "I have contractors coming over the next few weeks to install a new heating system and update the electrical. They're trustworthy, and I can't leave work and drive out here every time a worker needs to get inside."

On the drive to town, Tyler seemed unusually quiet, but his words replayed in her mind. There's no doubt he loved Jenna, but something seemed amiss. It wasn't until later CiCi realized she'd forgotten to ask him about the story Jenna had written about the farmers' market.

CiCi chattered away during dinner that evening, telling Chad about her trip to the country to see Tyler's property. "It was beyond beautiful," she sighed. "The cabin, the woods, a pond with ducks and geese, and a view to die for. It looks like a picture straight out of a travel brochure. I don't see how Jenna could up and leave the man she loved and the cabin they were renovating together."

"Stranger things have happened," he said, reaching for another helping of spaghetti.

"As peaceful as the setting was, something seemed off. I can't put my finger on it. Do you think Tyler was involved with her disappearance?"

"I can't say. I understand you wanting to get acquainted with Jenna's fiancé, but I don't like you spending time alone with him."

She sat back and grinned at the hardened look on his face. "Chad Cooper! Are you jealous? You, sir, have nothing to worry about. My heart belongs to you, and only you."

He leaned over and pecked her cheek. "I know. But think about it. We don't know what part he played in her disappearance. According to you, he still loves her, and you're almost a dead ringer for his missing fiancé. Sorry, that was a bad choice of words, but you get my drift."

"I'll keep that in mind."

"You do that," he said.

"So, have you read Jenna's missing person report?"

"Yes, but keep in mind I do have two other cases on my desk that need my immediate attention. From what I've looked at so far, I keep running into roadblocks. Detective Logan isn't the most thorough person. His interviews and follow-up calls are sloppy, and his organizational skills are terrible. Several forms are missing, so I have Stacy combing through backlogs trying to find them."

She gathered their empty plates and loaded them in the dishwasher. "If there's something off, I'm sure you'll spot it. Want to watch a movie?"

"Is that a good idea?"

"Don't worry. I've followed Doc's orders and haven't touched my computer or watched TV all day. One movie won't make my head explode."

He picked up the remote and winked. "Okay, but it's my turn to pick."

TWENTY-FIVE

After tossing and turning most of the night, CiCi finally managed to drift off to sleep. The alarm clock went off the moment she closed her eyes, or so it seemed. She stifled a yawn as she ate breakfast, checked her email, and read through the daily posts on Facebook. Spider Solitaire kept her occupied until she tired of winning. She glanced at her watch. *Where has the time gone?* She slipped on a jacket and a pair of green plaid sunglasses on the way out the door to meet Katherine at the bridal shop.

"I love them both," CiCi said as she sat beside Katherine in a consultation room, going over the recent sketches. "I wish Mom were here to help me choose." CiCi's voice caught and her eyes glistened with tears.

"I know you do, honey, but imagine your mother looking over your shoulder and smiling at what a beautiful bride you are. To honor her, we could attach one of her favorite pieces of jewelry somewhere on the dress, or maybe put her photo in a heart-shaped locket and clip it to the bridal bouquet. There are lots of ways to keep her memory alive on your special day."

"Those are wonderful ideas!"

"Give it some thought. Now, about the dress. Do you need more time to decide? Keep in mind I can always shorten your second choice and reduce the embellishments if you want a different look to wear at the reception."

"No, but thank you." CiCi studied the designs again. "In my heart, the first dress speaks to me the most. It's simple, but elegant. I can imagine walking down the aisle and Chad's face lighting up when he sees me in it."

"All right then, dress number one it is. Now, let me show you the fabrics that would best suit the style you've chosen. There are several options."

After picking a fabric and taking measurements, CiCi hugged Katherine. "I'm so glad to have you in my life."

"I feel the same." Katherine's shoulders sagged, and her joy was short-lived. "I wish Jenna were here to meet you."

CiCi clasped her hand. "I do too, and I'm sorry I haven't been able to turn up something that would tell us where she is."

"It's not your fault, dear. I know you're trying."

"Well, I'd better let you make another bride as happy as I am." CiCi's phone pinged as she placed a kiss on her aunt's cheek. "I'll see you later."

Outside the shop, she pulled up the text message. A Jeanne Glidewell book she'd placed on hold at the library was ready for pickup. CiCi drove across town and found a parking spot not too far from the entrance. Off to one side, she noticed Serena interviewing a city councilman. Their exchange looked tense. The newspaper's photographer stood a few feet away, taking pictures of a newly installed sculpture. Three large stainless-steel orbs, each with a single stem reaching skyward, dotted the library's limited green space.

CiCi approached the photographer. When she came within touching distance, he turned and took a quick step back. His mouth moved, but no words came out. She stifled a laugh and extended her hand. "Sorry, I didn't mean to scare you. My name's CiCi. I'm Jenna's cousin."

"I...I know. Abigail told me your name after you came to see

Tyler. You're just as pretty as Jenna." He winced and his face flushed. "Did I say that out loud? Sorry."

CiCi chuckled, hoping to ease his embarrassment. "You did, but I won't hold it against you. So, what's with the big silver balls? I hope they aren't decorating for Christmas already. It's only October."

He wrinkled his nose. "Nope, nothing to do with Christmas. According to the city's illustrious art committee, these are a modern representation of 'planting seeds for future growth,' or something like that."

"In whose world? They look ridiculous."

"I agree, but you didn't hear it from me." He placed a cap over the camera lens and scrolled through the shots he had taken.

"That's a pretty fancy camera. You must know a lot about photography."

"Enough to keep my job."

Before she could ask another question, Serena appeared. "CiCi, what do you think of city's new artwork?"

CiCi wrinkled her nose. "It's a bit too modern for my taste." She nodded to the departing councilman. "He doesn't look happy."

"I suppose not. He cast the deciding vote to award the contract to Miller's Metal Sculptures. I did a little digging and found out Miller is his wife's maiden name, and she owns the company."

"That's not good."

"How's the investigation going? Did you turn up any leads yet on your cousin?"

"No, and I'm not investigating. I'm simply talking to a few of Jenna's friends."

"But you'll call if you uncover any new information, right?"

"Yes, I'll call." *Right after I call the police.*

Jimmy stepped over and spoke to Serena. "I'm finished. I'll see you back at the office—or not." He slung the camera bag over his shoulder, smiled at CiCi, and left.

Serena shot him a dismissive look, then turned back to CiCi. "I've called your office several times, but you're never in. I need some info."

"Oh? About what?"

"The catfight you had with someone at work Monday afternoon. Floyd wouldn't talk, and that gal named Tasha hung up on me."

CiCi tensed. "That's because it's none of your business."

"I'm a reporter. Everything's my business." Serena said. "Did it have any connection to *this*?" She pulled up several photos on her phone, each showing a different angle of CiCi's vandalized Jeep in all its glory. "These photos could create quite a backlash, especially after the story about your new partnership. People might wonder where you came up with the money to buy into an established business like Five Star when they see the word thief painted on your vehicle. Your integrity, and the company's, might come under attack, warranted or not. By the way, where *did* you get the money? You might as well tell me. I'll find out eventually."

"Like I said, it's none of your business."

Serena cocked her head and smiled ever so sweetly. "Ah, but it is. I get paid to dig up things that are none of my business."

"True, but it'd be a real shame for you to miss out on the story of a lifetime."

"What are you talking about?"

"Well, if you make trouble for me, or Five Star for that matter, I doubt I'll feel like sharing any information I come across that pertains to Jenna." CiCi waited while Serena processed the information. "Okay, let me put it this way. Which will earn you the most recognition? A story about a twelve-year-old Jeep that's been vandalized, or the story about a young Ripley Grove woman who's been missing for over a year?"

"Okay, okay, I get your point." The phone with the photos disappeared into Serena's purse. "I won't print the pictures—for now—but I expect to be the first reporter you call."

"Thank you." CiCi let out a sigh of relief. "Since you're so good at digging up information, maybe you know why Greenleaf Growers wants to buy Tyler's property. They're not even using all the land they own now."

Serena folded her arms across her chest. "Who knows? Big

farms buy up smaller pieces of property all the time." She cocked her head. "How'd you hear about it?"

"Tyler. He took me out to see the cabin yesterday and gave me a tour of the property. It's a beautiful place."

"It is," Serena said, lost in thought. "We spent a lot of time there together as teens when his grandparents owned the place."

"Really? Tyler never mentioned that."

"I'm not surprised. When Jenna came along, he forgot all about the great times we had together." She turned suddenly and checked the time. "Look, I need to go. We'll talk later."

Before CiCi could pursue the subject further, Serena walked away. *Is she still interested in Tyler? Is that why she urged him to sell the property—because it's a constant reminder of Jenna? It seems Jenna not only stood between Serena and a promotion, but she also stood between Serena and Tyler. Hmm.*

At home, lunch consisted of a peanut butter and banana sandwich and a cold glass of milk. As she ate, CiCi thought about her visit to Tyler's cabin. Serena's talk of digging up information moved CiCi's mind in a different direction. *Should I?* She thrummed her fingers on the countertop. *I have to. I'll never rest until I know for sure.* After changing into jeans, a flannel shirt, and duck boots, she grabbed the camouflage jacket off the hook by the front door and headed to the car.

When the turnoff to Tyler's cabin appeared, her nerves forced her to drive right on past. A half-mile down the road, she took a deep breath, made a U-turn, and tried again. As she pulled in front of the cabin, the scenery bathed in the soft afternoon light set her at ease. After surveying the surroundings, she sighed with relief that neither of Tyler's contractors were on the premises. She walked around to the back of the house, wondering if she could see the opening to the trail she and Tyler had taken the day before. *There it is.* She noted the spot, then made her way across the expansive yard to the outbuilding.

With a gentle—okay, maybe not so gentle—nudge of her shoulder, the side door flew open. She batted the cobwebs away from her face as she entered. Dirt-smudged windows let in just enough light to see. It was a typical garage with an attached workshop. Mice scurried to find a hiding place as she walked across the dirty floor to the workbench. Tyler had all the tools necessary to build whatever he desired, and there wasn't a doubt in her mind she would find what she needed. She lifted one of several shovels from a peg on the wall and grabbed a nearby pair of work gloves. They were a tad too big, but trespassers can't be choosy. On a whim, she snagged the binoculars on the workbench before heading up the path through the trees.

The view from the pond was more beautiful than the day before. She zipped up her jacket to ward off the chilly breeze. Sitting on Jenna's favorite red bench, she turned her focus to the buildings at the far edge of the Greenleaf Grower's property, just beyond the fence line. There were several translucent commercial greenhouses and hothouses, and two structures possibly used for supplies and machinery. She sat in silence, reflecting, perhaps the same as her cousin might have done. A hawk flew overhead. Two ducks waddled down the path, but the geese were gone. A strong gust of wind blew across the pond and the shovel she had leaned against the bench toppled to the ground, reminding her she had a suspicion to put to rest. She dared not say it out loud, lest she sound crazy as a loon.

A quarter way around the pond, she stopped. Her breathing had quickened, and it wasn't from the walk. *What am I doing? Tyler admitted to digging up a small plot of ground to pour a concrete base for another bench. He wouldn't lie about that, would he? Maybe not, but why fill it back in?* She couldn't rest until she knew for certain if Tyler had buried Jenna there.

With a firm grip on the handle and one foot on the top of the blade, she forced the shovel into the ground. She found the digging easy the first several inches, though the gloves—too large for her hands—chafed her skin. The deeper she dug, the more effort it took. Six inches down, the metal tip struck a large flat rock. After filling the hole, she moved to another section, only to have the same results. She took off the jacket and wiped the perspiration from her forehead. The third spot yielded a hard layer of Kansas clay, as did the fourth. She tossed the shovel aside in defeat. Not accustomed to the physical labor, her hands ached and felt swollen. She looked at the patch of dirt. True to his word, Tyler had only dug deep enough so that the concrete pad he had planned to pour would be thick enough to withstand a hard winter freeze without cracking.

After filling in the remaining holes and tamping down the mounds, she scuffed her shoe over the area and scattered a few fallen leaves to cover any trace of her presence. Slipping on her jacket, she grabbed the shovel and binoculars. She turned to leave, but movement drew her gaze to a nearby bush. A small piece of string tied to a branch fluttered in the breeze. It appeared to mark the location of an overgrown path. *Wonder where it leads?* Curious, she laid the shovel aside and slipped the strap to the binoculars around her neck and stumbled as far as she could down the hillside. When it became too rocky and dangerous, she gave up and hiked back to the path. She returned the tools to the outbuilding, pulled the stubborn door closed, and headed to her car. She'd satisfied her curiosity. At least, for now.

Walking by the newer addition to the back of the house, her gaze landed on Jenna's desk next to the oversized window. She stopped. Her reflection made it appear as if she were sitting at the desk looking out. It was an eerie feeling, one that sent chills down her spine. *Is this how Tyler felt when he saw me sitting on Jenna's bench? If Tyler were here now, would he see my reflection in the window, or Jenna's?*

The thought brought an overwhelming sadness to CiCi's heart. Jenna's absence affected so many people, left so much pain, broke so many dreams. *If only I could find her and bring their nightmare to an end. A happy end, if possible.*

She felt exhausted by the time she arrived home. Maybe the fresh country air made her tired, but more likely, it was the physical exertion from using a shovel. She couldn't imagine people having to dig graves for a living in times gone by. After a shower to wash away the dried perspiration and dirt, she ate dinner. She perked up at the sound of Chad's ringtone, but her elation quickly faded when she learned he had plans to go to the shooting range with Mark after work. She disconnected the call and glanced around the room before picking up the remote.

"Tonight, I think a romantic comedy will do just fine."

TWENTY-SIX

CiCi took a bite of a toasted bagel and hugged a cup of coffee the next morning as though it held magical powers. She wished it were true, because the first thing she would do is banish the haunting scenes of freshly dug graves that kept her tossing and turning all night. After she finished eating, she called Megan and Tasha, hoping they were free for lunch. Both agreed to meet; however, Megan's schedule had her booked until one o'clock.

The doorbell rang as CiCi poured herself a second cup. When she approached the door, she glimpsed the tan uniform of a sheriff's deputy through the foyer window.

"Deputy Arnold. How are you?" She and the deputy had met for the first time about five months earlier when he delivered a copy of a restraining order she had taken out on her dad.

He tipped his hat. "Fine, just fine, Miss Winslow. I suspect you know why I'm here. I came to give you notice that I served Jack Parker with a restraining order late yesterday afternoon. Like last time, I'll need your signature showing I've delivered your copy."

"I remember," she said, stepping over to the patio table with the papers. She took his proffered pen, signed her name on the bottom, and then handed everything back. "Did he give you any trouble?"

Officer Arnold smiled. "He wasn't happy to see me, but he kept himself under control. Folks seldom like to make a scene at their place of business." He separated the copies and handed her one. "Your court date is in bold type on the bottom of the page. Keep the original with you at all times and call if you need any help. Good day, ma'am." He tipped his hat again, turned and left.

CiCi marked the date on every calendar at her disposal. Her attitude had come a long way regarding her relationship with her dad. Filing for a restraining order no longer felt like a betrayal, but more like setting boundaries and standing up for herself. As she rinsed her cup, she pondered what to do with her morning. Pulling out a bottle of furniture polish and a soft cloth, she set about giving the living room a good dusting. She moved on to the dining room, wiping down the table and each chair. When she came to the buffet, the box of stuff taken from Heather's basement caught her eye. She set it on the table and removed the lid.

Given the number of bridal magazines, Jenna had been gathering ideas for her wedding. CiCi browsed through the notes in Jenna's three-ring binder, thinking how similar they were when it came to making plans for a wedding. CiCi wondered if Katherine had seen the binder. If not, she'd probably love to see it.

CiCi moved on. The first few photos she glanced at were out of focus. She set them aside, assuming there must be a reason Jenna saved them. As she flipped through the pages of a spiral notebook, several receipts fluttered to the floor. She gathered them up. Each receipt showed Jenna had paid cash for 'services rendered' at Captured Moments. Putting the blurry photos and the receipts together made her wonder if Jenna had taken one of Flash's photography classes. *Maybe, but why didn't Flash mention he'd had business dealings with Jenna?*

She glanced at her watch and realized time had slipped away. She'd looked at more than half of the contents, and nothing seemed to be of any value. She repacked everything, grabbed another cup of coffee, and headed upstairs to take a shower. Ten minutes under the pulsing spray brought clarity to her thoughts. She shut off the water and dressed. It was fast approaching one o'clock, and she didn't want to be the last to arrive for lunch.

"You look tired," Tasha said a short time later between bites of her BLT. "Time off is exactly what you need."

"Maybe, but I miss being at work. Anything going on I need to know about?" CiCi reached for a napkin after swirling her French dip in au jus and taking a bite.

Tasha chuckled. "Floyd said you wouldn't make it through lunch without asking about work. Everything is fine. Say, I thought you were taking it easy. What kind of relaxing gives you blisters like that?"

CiCi looked at her hands. Sure enough, small blisters had formed on the fleshy part between her thumbs and forefingers. "Um, I was helping Katherine yesterday." *By trying to dig up her daughter.*

Megan ate the last of her fries and licked the salt off her fingers. "Speaking of Katherine, have you chosen the design for your wedding dress yet?"

"Yes, but it's going to be a surprise."

"What are you giving Chad for a wedding gift?" Tasha asked.

"I've been trying to think of something other than the usual watch or engraved pocketknife. I saw a video the other day advertising concealment furniture—you know, furniture with hidden compartments." She pulled up the video on her phone. "Watch. This one looks like an ordinary floating shelf, but when you swipe an RFID card across a specific spot, the underside of the shelf slides forward and tilts down to reveal a hidden storage compartment for valuables, documents, or firearms."

"That's so cool," said Megan.

Tasha frowned. "What's an RFID card?"

"Radio-frequency ID card. It's like a smart card that emits a signal to the receiver in the drawer that controls the locking mechanism. The shelf would be a perfect place for Chad to store his weapons." CiCi closed the video and resumed eating her sandwich.

"I think that's a great idea," Tasha said.

"I'm working on ideas for your bachelorette party," Megan said. "I'm taking care of the food and games. Tasha's handling the entertainment."

CiCi swallowed. "Entertainment? Don't get too crazy. I like simple."

"Where's the fun in that?" Tasha said. "I plan to meet up with Juan tomorrow night at The Tap & Keg. If he's as good a dancer as he claims to be, maybe I can hire him to entertain us at the bridal shower. I'm sure I could scrounge up a 'naughty cop' costume."

CiCi choked and sputtered on her tea and shook her head. Megan clapped CiCi on the back and Tasha chuckled.

"Hey, I was just kidding." Tasha said. "Besides, you'll have your own 'naughty cop' as soon as you say 'I do.'"

Thinking of Chad stripping off his uniform and dancing brought heat to CiCi's cheeks.

"Let me know if you change your mind," Tasha said with a wink.

"Why let the guys have all the fun?" Megan asked.

Tasha nodded. "Mark said he and Pete will be throwing Chad a bachelor party."

CiCi turned, surprised. "When did you talk to Mark?"

Tasha paused to take a long drink. "Oh, the other day. After all, he's the best man and I'm the maid of honor. It's only natural we would compare notes, right?"

"Hmm, I guess."

"So, what's on your agenda this afternoon?"

"I thought I might sign up for a photography class."

Tasha lifted one eyebrow. "You've taken appraisal photos for years and no one has ever complained. Why now?"

CiCi pulled her wallet from her purse, avoiding Tasha's questioning glare. "There's always room for improvement."

"Where do you plan to take classes?"

"Captured Moments." A smile played at the corners of CiCi's mouth.

"I'm not sure what you're up to, but sign me up, too."

"Count me in," Megan added. "Sounds like fun."

After saying goodbye to her friends, CiCi slipped on her sunglasses and drove across town to the Captured Moments Photography Studio. The sound of a hammer assaulted her eardrums the moment she walked into the foyer of the building. *Flash must have a crew working on the third-floor renovation.* She entered the studio, and a soft buzzer announced her presence. From the number of cars in the parking lot, she was surprised to find it empty. She stepped forward to admire the photo of the young girl on the park bench, but a man's voice from the back room of the studio drew her attention away.

"I'll be with you in a moment," he called.

CiCi walked over to the wall of shelving that showcased a variety of cameras. Flash had organized the collection according to age, with the antiques that used film and flashbulbs at the top and the newer digital versions on the bottom shelf. Everything was coated in a thin layer of dust. *Hard to keep everything clean with construction going on.*

"How can I help you?" Flash's eyes widened when she turned to face him. "You again? If you're here to get more information on the guitar player, I can't help you."

"No, my two friends and I would like to sign up for a photography class."

He rubbed a hand across his narrow jaw and looked back at his desk. "Good. That's good. Have a seat and I'll see if I can fit you in." CiCi took a seat while he tapped away at the keyboard. "You're in luck. The next session starts Sunday afternoon and I have three spots left. Let me get you information packets that will tell you what to expect."

He stood and left the room. She thrummed her fingers on her thigh, then stood to admire a photo hanging behind the desk. As she returned to her seat, she gave a quick glance at the computer screen. The calendar for the current month had very few entries. There were only three photography classes, one wedding, and a birthday party on the schedule. She looked over her shoulder before clicking the back button. The schedules for the months of August and September were nearly the same. At the sound of footsteps nearing, she returned the current month to the screen and scurried to her seat, and just in time.

"Here you go. I only had two packets, so I made another copy."

"Business must be brisk."

"It is, it is. You can return the applications with the fee at the first class. It's a three-week course. We meet two hours every Sunday afternoon at one o'clock. Any questions?"

"No, no questions. See you then." She exited the building, feeling his eyes upon her back. Once in her car, she inhaled a deep breath and took in the structure. New windows were being installed on the third floor. *I wonder where he gets the money to renovate. Not from his photography studio. Rich parents, maybe?*

When she arrived at The Alley that Friday night, the parking lot was teeming with cars and trucks. Inside, eighteen lanes of four bowlers each vied for a win over the opposing team. Chad's Strike Hard, Spare None team held the lead over The Bowling Stones by seventy-five pins in the seventh frame. She waved to Mark, Pete, and Frank, and then slipped into a seat beside Chad and gave him a kiss on the cheek.

He wrapped an arm around her shoulder and slid a paper boat of jalapeño cheese poppers and ranch dressing within her reach. "Glad you could make it."

"Wouldn't miss it," she shouted over the noise. Pointing to the scoreboard, she said, "You keep this up and you'll end up around two-forty."

"I hope so. Frank is off his game tonight, so the rest of us need to pick up the slack until he figures out what he's doing wrong."

"Chad! You're up," Mark shouted.

Pete filled Chad's empty seat and shot her a wide grin. "How you doing, missy?"

"Fine, Pete. Looks like you're rolling hot tonight," she said, nodding to his score. "One-fifty so far. I'm impressed."

"Not bad for an old man." He chuckled and took a sip of his beer. After smoothing his graying mustache, he leaned in close. "You feeling better since your episode?"

"Yes," she sighed, "although the doctor ordered me to take some time off work."

"Won't hurt you none. I'm sure you'll find something to fill your time."

If you only knew. "Katherine tells me that when her daughter Jenna went missing last year, you worked on the case before you retired."

He pinned her with a suspicious glare. "I did. Why're you asking?"

"Um…just curious. Do you recall if there was anything unusual about the case?"

Pete leaned back and crossed his arms over his chest. "Chad's been combing through her file and he asked me to go through the notes I kept to see if something stands out. There's no need to worry yourself over it if Chad and I are looking into it."

Looks like he's not willing to share information. She dipped a fried cheese ball into the creamy sauce and popped it into her mouth to avoid his gaze.

"Pete! Eighth frame and you're on a spare. Make it count," Frank shouted.

Chad took Pete's seat and finished off the rest of the poppers.

The next two hours went by in a flash, with CiCi cheering on her favorite team every step of the way. Strike Hard, Spare None lost the last game of the night, but won total pins, giving them a three-to-one victory. The losing team congratulated the winners and promised to get even. After securing his bowling ball and shoes in a locker, Chad walked her out to her rental.

"I can't get used to seeing you drive something so…so small."

She leaned against the door and tucked her hand in his. "It's okay, but I'll be glad to have my Jeep back. Maybe I'll check on it in the morning. Don't forget we're looking at invitations and have a tasting at the bakery tomorrow afternoon."

"Um, yeah, sounds fun."

"Jeez, don't sound so excited. Remember, the wedding isn't just about *me*. It's about *both* of us."

"We could get married right here at The Alley for all I care. The sooner, the better." He pulled her close and brushed his lips across hers.

"That's not exactly what I had in mind. I want a simple wedding, but one we'll both remember for a long, long time." She tilted her head and groaned as his kisses trailed along her jawline. "By the way, do you still have your old patrol uniform?"

He stopped and frowned. "I suppose. Why?"

She smiled and slowly ran her fingers down his chest. "I thought it might come in handy on our wedding night. I love a man in *or out* of uniform."

He planted a solid kiss on her mouth, then turned and headed to his truck.

"What's the hurry?"

"I need to make sure I still have that uniform."

TWENTY-SEVEN

Early Saturday morning, CiCi pulled several dozen cookies from the freezer, placed them in a tote bag, then grabbed a pair of red sunglasses and headed to the car. The air was crisp and the sun was glaring as she drove across town to a small, century-old church that tried hard not to show its age. A line flowed from the side door that led to a small dining hall. Inside, she emptied her stash of goodies on the counter as Maxine and her volunteers passed out sacks of food and non-perishable grocery items to those struggling to make ends meet. Instead of donating her accounting service to the non-profit organization as she had in the past, CiCi brought homemade treats to bolster A Hand Up's generic offerings. Once the doc lifted her work restrictions, she hoped to be back crunching numbers. Until then, the least she could do was help the volunteers hand out food and words of encouragement.

She smiled at familiar faces and greeted children who clung to their mothers' legs. First-timers were easy to spot because they were often too embarrassed to make eye contact for more than a few seconds. Pride was a double-edged sword, and it took a strong person to admit they needed help. Many of these folks who had fallen on hard times had to lay that pride aside to help their families.

Her heart ached when she looked into the eyes of the innocent children caught up in life's injustices.

I'll contact my lawyer and see what type of funding A Hand Up receives. As the city's "anonymous" donor, I'd be more than happy to step up and provide financial help. After all, this is my community...no, it's our community.

During lunch, she and Chad discussed plans and ideas for the wedding. Afterward, they looked at invitations and chose a simple design that reflected both of their personalities. Next, they headed to Sadie's Bakery.

Sweets were CiCi's weakness, and the prospect of tasting a variety of cake flavors made her glad she hadn't finished all of her lunch. They sampled slices of lemon cake with raspberry filling, strawberry cake layered with a berry puree, and white chocolate cake with a decadent dark chocolate filling. The confetti cake added a surprise pop of color, but it seemed more appropriate for a child's birthday party.

"My favorite is the lemon with raspberry filling and Italian buttercream icing. The flavors would be lovely for a spring wedding. What do you think, Chad?"

"I like the chocolate cake with the gooey salted caramel filling."

CiCi wrinkled her nose. "Well, it *was* delicious, but—"

Sadie splayed her hands open and offered a suggestion. "Why not have both? The lemon with raspberry filling as the main attraction, and the chocolate for the groom's cake. You'll each have something you both like and it'll give your guests options."

"That's a great idea," CiCi said.

After CiCi finished her slice of lemon cake, they walked hand in hand across the square to the florist to discuss what flowers would be available in the spring. The wedding plans were taking shape, and she was happy Chad provided input and seemed to enjoy the process.

As they drove from the last of three possible sites for the

reception, she asked, "Would you mind stopping at the store on the way home? I'm out of milk and bread."

"No problem. I need to pick up stuff for the game tomorrow anyway," he said, making a quick turn at the next corner.

Chad, Mark, Pete, and Frank had tickets to a Kansas City Chiefs football game the next day. Though the game didn't start until one o'clock, the tailgating ritual would begin the moment the parking lot gates opened five hours prior to kick-off. The four guys took turns supplying the meat, and tomorrow that task fell to Chad.

At the store, they each grabbed a shopping cart and went their separate ways. She selected a few bananas and apples as she passed through the produce aisle, then added milk, bread and a few baking basics to replenish her supply. Twenty minutes later, she met Chad at the check-out counter, where he stood chatting with the young clerk as she sacked his purchases.

CiCi grinned sheepishly at Chad as she transferred the goods from her basket to the conveyor belt. "Sorry to keep you waiting. I decided to stock up on a few things instead of making another trip tomorrow."

"I expected as much."

He grinned, loaded her bags into his cart, and headed to the truck. At her townhouse, they carried her sacks to the kitchen, and he lingered while she packed a variety of treats from her freezer into a small crush-proof container.

"My little contribution to your party."

"Thanks." Chad gave her a tender kiss and waved goodbye.

Around nine o'clock that evening, CiCi parked her car at The Tap & Keg and checked in the rearview mirror one last time to make sure the black wig sat straight on her head. She hadn't attached it as well as Tasha had, but it would do in a pinch. She smoothed her blouse and checked her watch. *Tasha said she'd be here, but I don't see her car. Maybe she rode with Juan.*

Once inside, she edged her way to the bar and ordered a virgin pina colada from the bartender. The crowd made it difficult to spot Tasha, but her dad's familiar green ball cap at a far back booth caught her attention. Her heart raced. *Talk about bad timing, but I doubt he'll recognize me in this wig. At least, I hope not.* As she turned and scanned the crowd again, someone poked her in the ribs.

"What's up, Foxy?"

She turned and smiled. "Hey, Juan. I'm looking for Tasha. Have you seen her?"

He shook his head. "I called. She said some guy came by the house as she was leaving and asked her out to a movie."

The cat lover? I hope not. So, now what do I do? "Is your mortician friend here tonight? What was his name? Eddie? I need to talk to him."

"Should be here soon. Why don't you join me at my table until he shows?"

CiCi paid for her drink and followed Juan. While she listened to the music, she studied Derek as he sang. His charismatic stage presence had women of all ages under his spell. Between performances, several ladies sidled up to him and tucked slips of paper into his shirt pocket. CiCi wondered if he drew a name from a hat whenever he got lonely. She finished a second drink and then stood to leave. Eddie was a no-show and spending any more time waiting seemed pointless. Suddenly, a strong pair of hands pulled her to the dance floor.

"You came back. Miss me?" Mace asked, his eyes twinkling with amusement.

"No. I was about to leave."

"But you haven't danced yet." Mace led her across the floor.

"You been watching me?"

"I can't help myself." He smiled and cocked his head. "I still think I know you from somewhere."

"I doubt it." She glanced up and caught Derek looking straight at her. *Is it my imagination, or did he miss a few chords and stumble over the lyrics?* She turned her head and leaned into Mace, hoping to avoid Derek's gaze. *Relax,* she told herself, *there's no way he'll recognize me in this wig. No way.*

"Now that's much better." Mace pulled her close and swayed in sync with the music.

He was a good dancer for a man of his size. After the song ended, he escorted her back to Juan's table. She felt Derek's eyes follow her every step. It took every ounce of willpower she had not to run for the exit, but that would only confirm his suspicions. *Maybe I should just get it over with—tell him who I am and ask if he knows what happened to Jenna. And to satisfy my curiosity, find out what she'd taken that caused the big argument.*

"Wait here; I'll get you another drink," Mace said, breaking into her thoughts.

Juan, now sitting at the table with a redhead, introduced his lady friend to CiCi. They chatted until a tipsy gentleman at the next table said something to a dark-haired beauty passing by. She laughed, and he tugged her onto his lap. He whispered into her ear, and she laughed again. The man's date, who had just returned from the restroom, did not. Angry words were exchanged, and pushes escalated to shoves. The table was overturned, and a hair-pulling catfight erupted. Friends of the two women joined the fray, scratching and clawing at each other. The inebriated crowd cheered them on until Mace and another man stepped in to break up the fight.

Unfazed, the women continued to lunge at each other. Somehow in the frenzy, someone mistook CiCi's black wig for her rival's hair and knocked her to the floor. During the scuffle, a hand latched onto the wig and pulled it off CiCi's head. Her eyes widened as her dark blonde curls fell to her shoulders. She pried the wig from the woman's grip, scrambled to her feet, and made a dash down the hall toward the restroom.

Footsteps pounded behind her. Seconds later, an arm snaked around her waist and a hand clamped over her mouth to muffle her screams. She fought as he dragged her outside to the dimly lit alley and pushed her up against the building.

"I thought that was you," Derek hissed as he held her firmly against her will.

"Let go of me! I'm not who you think I am," she said, squirming as the rough texture of the brickwork dug into her back.

"You can say that again."

"I'm not Jenna, you idiot; I'm her cousin."

He studied her face under the dim light. Doubt flickered in his eyes. "Prove it."

"Prove it? How?"

"Show me your tat."

"My what?"

His eyes narrowed and his mouth twisted into a sly grin. He wrapped one of his big hands around both of her wrists. With his other hand, he tugged down the elastic waistband of her pants far enough to reveal the smooth, tender skin over her hipbone. She fought back, but he pressed her against the wall until she had no room to move. When he didn't see the tattoo he'd been looking for, he released her hands.

"Satisfied?" she asked, rubbing her wrists.

He slammed both hands against the wall on either side of her shoulders, pinning her in place. "I don't care *who* you are, but if you're related to Jenna, it's all the same to me. You tell her my boss is out for blood. She'd better cough up the rest of those photos, because he's not paying another dime until he has them all." He jerked her chin up, forcing her to look at him. "You tell her that, you hear?"

Her heart pounded against her chest, and her brain whirled with confusion. *Photos? What photos?* Suddenly it made sense. Jenna and Derek hadn't argued over some *thing* she'd taken; they'd argued over *photos* she'd taken.

Over Derek's shoulder, a beefy hand appeared and gripped the top of his shoulder until he winced and released his grip. CiCi tried to peer over his shoulder, but all she saw was a familiar green ball cap. Her fear jumped into the double digits.

"Let her go."

"Back off, Jack. This gal and her cousin are robbing my boss blind and he aims to put a stop to it."

Jack glared at her, then spat a loogie on the ground. "Yep, she's good at stealing from folks, but you best let her go. Now."

CiCi froze in place. She couldn't believe what she'd heard. *Dad's coming to my rescue? Does he think he's the only person allowed to abuse me, or is this a ploy to use when he contests the restraining order?*

The exit door flew open, slamming against the back wall. Mace stepped into view. His eyes darted from one person to the next as he assessed the situation. His gaze fixed on CiCi. "There you are, babe. I've been looking for you." The muscles in his jaw twitched and his hands fisted at his sides as if to challenge the two men to argue.

"She's with you?" Derek asked.

Without batting an eye, Mace replied, "She is. You got a problem with that?"

Derek held his hands up in surrender. He retreated and went back inside. Jack turned to follow but stopped before crossing the threshold. "I was here first. You know what that means."

"Don't worry," she said. "I'm leaving."

The door swung shut behind him, and her legs turned to rubber. As she leaned against the building for support, Mace asked, "You all right?"

"I'm fine. Just fine." She turned and went inside, walking ahead of Mace to avoid answering questions. She scooped up the wig from where she'd dropped it earlier, then headed to her car. Mace kept pace and, once they were outside, grabbed her arm to slow her down.

"I remember you now. You and your friend were at the trailer park. Juan said you were looking for Derek. Look, I don't know what your game is, lady, but you're in way over your head," he growled. "Those two belong in a dark alley. You don't."

"It's not like I had a choice." She stopped beside her car. "Thanks for your help. You'd better get back to your friends. They're waiting."

Mace glanced over his shoulder at the small crowd watching, then turned to face her. "Derek's trying to decide if we're a couple or not. Don't give him a reason not to trust me. You owe me."

He wrapped his arms around her, pressed her against the

vehicle, and kissed her long and hard. Shocked by his sudden overture, it took her a moment to resist. She pushed him away amid the hoots and hollers from onlookers. Mace muttered something about 'take a hit,' and she was more than willing to oblige. She pulled her arm back and slugged him in the eye. She felt the impact as much as he did, and immediately regretted her decision. *Ow! That hurt!*

Mace fell to the ground, stunned. Two of his friends staggered over and helped him up. With a couple of good-natured slaps on the back, they offered to buy him a beer. CiCi turned, jumped in the driver's seat, and started the engine. As the small crowd dispersed, she sped from the lot, wondering how the night had gone so wrong.

Her hands were still shaking as she unlocked the door to her townhouse. She kicked her shoes off and made herself a strong cup of coffee. Leaning back against the sofa, she closed her eyes and went over the events of the evening. An hour later, the noise from the icemaker startled her awake. She grabbed her shoes on the way to the bedroom.

After taking two aspirin, she slipped out of her clothes and into something comfortable. Her hand moved to her wrist, and her heart stopped. *My watch—it's gone!* Frantic, she went through her clothing and emptied her purse. She grabbed a flashlight and searched the car. Her efforts netted her thirty cents and an expired gift card. The watch was nowhere in sight. *It must've come off during the scuffle, or in the alley, or maybe when I fought off Mace's kiss. OMG, did that really happen?* She called the bar, but no one answered. The phone call was pointless anyway, she reasoned. Anyone who found the watch would most likely keep it.

She returned to the bedroom and flopped on the bed. Tears stained her pillow. *How am I going to explain this to Chad?*

TWENTY-EIGHT

CiCi woke up Sunday morning in a dark mood. Considering her current state of mind, skipping church seemed the most logical thing to do. It'd be impossible to concentrate on the sermon or fake a smile and shake hands with other members as though nothing had happened the night before.

The plan she'd thought was foolproof had snowballed into a messy situation. Somehow, she'd gotten mixed up in a catfight and been dragged into a dark alley by a person she suspected had something to do with Jenna's disappearance. On top of that, Foxy was "dead" and no longer viable as a cover to get information. She sighed. Her trip to The Tap & Keg had been in vain—or had it? Derek's remarks were thought-provoking.

Who was Derek's boss, and why was he out for blood? What pictures did Jenna take that he wanted so bad? Had she been hired for a photoshoot and refused to turn over all the photos he'd paid for? The thing that bothered her the most was that Derek expected her to relay his threatening message to Jenna. *Derek's warning would indicate he doesn't know where she is. But, had his boss caught up with Jenna and settled the score without Derek knowing?*

And then there was her dad. Considering his past actions, his interference on her behalf had been a total shock. He could've easily taken advantage of the situation. Instead, he warned Derek off. That took her by surprise, as did Mace's arrival on the scene. His timing couldn't have been more perfect, but what did he mean when he said she was 'in over her head'?'

Her gaze fell on her naked wrist. How would she ever face Chad and tell him she'd lost the watch less than a week after he'd given it to her? He's been so proud at having chosen the perfect gift. He'd be hurt, not to mention angry when he learned where she'd lost it.

Maybe he didn't have to know. She grabbed her keys and threw on a jacket. She wouldn't rest until she found that watch. In case the errand took longer than expected, she grabbed the camera she'd need for the afternoon photography class.

It was nine o'clock when she arrived at The Tap & Keg. As she pulled into the parking lot, a car whizzed by, causing her to slam on the brakes. She craned her neck to get a better look at the driver. *Was that Serena? What would she be—oh!* CiCi's eyes widened at the scene before her. She parked and walked toward a familiar face in the small crowd gathered at the edge of the lot. A few yards away, the burned-out shell of a compact car sat amid a black ring. The liquefied residue of the foam firefighters used to extinguish the blaze covered the ground around the charred remains. *I guess I'm lucky my Jeep only needed a paint job.*

"Hey, Jimmy, what happened?"

"Oh, hey, CiCi. Suspicious car fire early this morning."

"Anyone hurt?"

"No," he said. He snapped a final shot as a tow truck operator used a hydraulic winch to load the charred hunk of metal onto the bed of the trailer.

"Who's the unfortunate owner?"

"Didn't catch her name, but Serena did. I guess several women got into a brawl last night. After the bar closed, one of the women involved couldn't get her car started. She left it parked here, hoping to have her brother look at it today. Fire department got the call about five o'clock, but it was too far gone to be saved."

"Sounds like someone carried the argument a little too far."

"I'd say so."

Fascinated by the process underway, CiCi's attention stayed fixed on the transfer. When Jimmy stood after packing up his gear, she asked, "Was that Serena that drove off in a red BMW a few minutes ago?"

"Yeah, why?"

"I thought I saw her driving a black sedan the other day."

He chuckled. "You probably did. She and Rivera swap cars whenever she feels like it."

"Hmm. Hey, I have a photography question for you. I found a few of Jenna's photos in a box of her stuff. Is there any way to make them less blurry?"

"Maybe. I'd have to see them again."

"Again?"

"If they're the ones I'm thinking of, I saw them once on Jenna's desk. They were awful. I asked where she'd taken them, but she wouldn't say. I offered to see if I could salvage them, but she said she had it covered." He shook his head. "She could paint a picture with words but couldn't take a decent picture to save her life. I told her the next time she needed photos for a story to call me."

"Do you know what story she was working on?"

"No, I don't."

"Do you remember the article Jenna wrote about the farmers' market last year?"

"Sure. I went along and took photos. She took a few with her cell phone."

"I read it, but I don't recall seeing any photos."

He shrugged. "For whatever reason, Rivera chose not to print them."

"Do you still have them? I'd like to have a look if you do."

He cocked his head in thought. "I think I do. Rivera told me to delete them, but I don't think I did. Looking for something specific?"

"I don't know. I'm hoping I'll know it when I see it."

He glanced at his watch. "I can meet you at the newspaper, say around noon? That'll give me time to download these pics for Serena."

"Great. I'll see you then."

CiCi walked over to where she'd parked the night before. She scanned the ground for her watch before retracing her steps to the bar's entrance—nothing. Though they wouldn't be open for business until eleven, she tried the door anyway. It was locked. She rapped on the window. No answer. Not one to give up, she walked around the building to the employee entrance where Derek had pinned her against the wall. She searched every inch of the barren landscape. Using the toe of her shoe, she pushed aside the debris that littered the ground, but the watch was nowhere to be seen. Behind her, the door banged open.

"What're you doing back here?" a voice growled. "Oh, it's you."

Startled, she turned. Steve, the bartender, stood in the doorway with a full trash bag in his hand. "I'm looking for something," she said. "Has anyone turned in a watch? I lost mine when I was here last night."

"You've got to be kidding! Hon, if you lost it here, you might as well kiss it goodbye." When her shoulders sagged, he rushed on to say, "But who knows? It could turn up. I'll keep an eye out for it."

"Mind if I come inside and look?"

"Suit yourself. I was just getting ready to sweep the floor."

After a disappointing search, she gave Steve her contact information before returning to her vehicle. Chad called twice, but the noise at the stadium made it impossible to hear a word he said. Finally, he texted to say he loved her and was having a great time. She smiled, knowing she was lucky to have such a good man in her life. After a quick glance at the clock on her dashboard, she pulled from the parking lot.

She stepped from her car and lightly rapped on the door to *The Ripley Review*. Jimmy unlocked it and waved her inside. Their footsteps seemed to resound in the empty office, or so she thought until she heard muffled voices coming from Mr. Rivera's office. Jimmy led her to his desk and pulled up an extra chair. His fingers spun the wheel on the mouse with precision as his eyes stayed glued to the screen. The deep voice down the hall grew stern and sharp.

"Is Rivera always so gruff?" CiCi asked as she took a seat.

"Why do you think Serena calls him Grumpa? Not to his face, of course." Jimmy cast a nervous glance over his shoulder. "I didn't expect him to show up today, so let's see if I can find those photos before he and Serena finish their argument."

CiCi cleared her throat. "Jimmy, have you spoken to Jenna since she left?"

He stopped scrolling, but his eyes remained on the monitor. "Me? No, I haven't. We weren't that close, not that I didn't want to be. She was so beautiful and talented. There's not many women like her in Ripley Grove."

He resumed his search, but she grew impatient. "Any luck yet?" she asked.

"Yeah. They should be right after these shots I took during one of the summer school sessions. Jenna wrote a fantastic article on the high school students' science and biology projects. Did you read it?"

"Sorry, I didn't."

"You should. Here we go. This is the section we're looking for."

"Can you make the pictures bigger?"

The voices from Rivera's office grew louder and angrier. The conversation between Rivera and Serena sounded anything but amicable.

Jimmy tensed. "There's no time. Rivera will have my head if he comes out and sees these still on my computer."

She leaned in as he hastily scrolled through the photos, hoping that something would catch her eye. The candid shots showcased the farmers' market, its vendors, and the general public who frequented the outdoor venue. Sellers hawked a variety of products. Some sold fresh produce, honey, meats, and cheeses. Others opted to sell homemade crafts, baked goods, jewelry, and bath products. The photos seemed to confirm that Jenna had spoken to every vendor who rented space under the pavilion's green metal roof. Jimmy narrowed the search to the six photos specifically of Greenleaf Growers. A door opened and Rivera's voice floated down the hall.

"Jimmy, can you copy them and send them to my email?" CiCi whispered. "I'll look at them later."

"Sure." Jimmy typed in her email, attached the photos, and hit send.

Her phone pinged, alerting her to an incoming message. "Thanks."

Jimmy deleted the original photos and then glanced at his watch. "Sorry, I need to get going. I promised to take my grandma grocery shopping."

"Thanks, Jimmy," she replied. She stood to leave when she heard raised voices and footsteps behind her. She turned in time to see Serena storm out of the building.

"CiCi, what brings you by on a Sunday?" Mr. Rivera asked as he strode across the room like a man on a mission. Jimmy whispered, "Not a word," as he slipped by her and headed for the door.

She smiled. "Just talking to Jimmy about a photography class I'm taking this afternoon."

"Oh? And how's your search for Jenna coming? Making any headway?"

"Some. From what I've learned so far, I'm beginning to wonder if her disappearance is somehow connected to the story she wrote about the farmers' market. Jenna told her mother that one of the vendors complained about Jimmy taking photos."

He scoffed at the idea. "Which is why I had him delete them. No need to ruffle the feathers of a company that runs an ad in every paper we print, am I right?"

"That makes sense." *Maybe.*

"Well, if you find Jenna, let me know. I'd like to talk to her."

"Really? About what?"

"Why, uh, to convince her to come back and work for the paper. She has too much talent to let go to waste."

"I'll keep that in mind," CiCi said. "Oh, look at the time. I need to get going. I don't want to be late to class."

"Trying to follow in your cousin's footsteps?"

"Maybe."

He nodded. "Don't follow too close, CiCi. After all, she left and never came back."

She arrived at Captured Moments with a few minutes to spare. She sat in the car, opened her email, and browsed through Jimmy's photos. At first glance, nothing stood out. Upon a second glance, she stopped. One of the workers at the Greenleaf Growers stall seemed vaguely familiar, though she only had a profile to rely on. And if she didn't know better, a few of the scruffy customers seemed unusually camera shy. *But why?*

Five minutes later, two cars pulled into the lot and parked on either side of her Jeep. Tasha and Megan waited at the back of her vehicle and the three of them walked inside together. Flash greeted them and ushered them to the classroom area at one end of the room. Four other students at the two tables nearest the front chattered excitedly about the class. Flash checked his watch and then clapped his hands together to get everyone's attention.

"Let's get started. I see you each brought a camera and the cords needed to download the photos to my computer. Kudos for remembering the basics. You'd be surprised at the number of people who show up empty-handed."

Flash explained how a camera works and how to use the shutter functions. Next, he went over the various modes programmed into most cameras and encouraged them to get comfortable using something other than Auto mode. Although informative, CiCi thought the Auto mode was most suitable for taking pictures required for her appraisal reports. During the last half of the class, he demonstrated simple methods to improve any photo by cropping, adjusting the saturation and color balance, and eliminating shadows and dark spots. He answered questions with the patience of an elementary school teacher before assigning homework.

"Next week," he said, "we'll see how well you've mastered the basic editing skills before moving on to the more advanced techniques. We'll also discuss the photo-editing programs on the market today."

Thinking of the poorly taken photos she'd found in Jenna's box, CiCi raised her hand.

"Yes, CiCi?" he asked.

"I recently found a small stack of photos that are blurry and out of focus. Can the editing programs sharpen the images?"

He paused before answering. "It's possible, depending on the program you use. I'd have to see them before giving a definitive answer." He glanced at the time. "Well, our time is up for today. I hope to see each of you next Sunday. The sheets at the end of the table have the homework assignment for next week."

After disconnecting his laptop, Flash disappeared through an open door at the back of the studio. CiCi picked up her camera and lingered, waiting for him to return, but he never did. As she turned to leave, her attention was again drawn to the striking photo of the blonde on the park bench. *That's one photo I may have to buy.*

"Want to grab a bite to eat and catch a movie?" Megan asked as they walked to the parking lot.

"Might as well," CiCi replied. "I don't expect Chad back until seven or eight. Are you coming, Tasha, or do you have another last-minute date?"

Tasha grinned sheepishly. "Sorry about last night. I should've called."

"Yes, you should've. So, who's the guy? Is it the cat lover?"

"No, it's not the cat lover. What movie do we want to see?"

"Hey, you didn't answer my question," she chided. "Who's the mystery man?"

"Just some guy my mom sent over." Tasha shook her head.

"What's wrong?" Megan asked. "Didn't you have a good time?"

"I did. He's nice looking and has a great sense of humor, but …"

"But what?"

"He's forty-two, unemployed, and perfectly content to live in his mother's basement." Tasha sighed. "I need to have a serious talk with my mom about boundaries."

Megan and CiCi urged Tasha to do just that. When CiCi reached her vehicle, she glanced back at the photography studio and momentarily froze in place.

Flash stared at her from the window.

It was just after eight when CiCi said goodbye to her friends and headed home. A group of three teenagers blocked the entrance to her complex, talking, laughing, and performing tricks on their skateboards. When they refused to move and let her pass, she honked her horn. They stepped aside, glaring as she drove by. She'd never seen them before and wondered if they belonged to the family that recently moved into the rental property around the corner.

She had just poured a cup of hot tea when Chad called. She sat at the dining room table, sorting through yesterday's mail and listening as he shared highlights of the game.

"Chad, I think—" The window beside her exploded, sending shards of glass across the room. She screamed and dove for cover.

"CiCi! What's wrong?" Chad asked. His excitement over the game vanished in the blink of an eye and his voice took on the serious tone of a cop. "CiCi, answer me! What's happening?"

She took deep breaths as she assessed the situation. All was quiet except for the rapid beating of her heart. The curtains fluttered as a cool breeze drifted through the hole in the window. "I don't know, Chad. I think someone threw something through my window."

"Are you hurt?"

"I…I don't think so," she said, her voice faltering.

"Stay away from the window and call 9-1-1. I'll be right there."

With sirens blaring and lights flashing, two cruisers screeched to a halt in front of her townhouse. An ambulance arrived next, along with a small crowd of onlookers. Chad barreled through the door and found her sitting at the breakfast bar. One EMT monitored her vitals, while another tended to a small cut on her arm.

"Are you okay?" Chad asked, checking her over and then pulling her into a quick hug.

"I'm fine."

Chad turned to the officer taking notes. "Well?"

"Someone threw a brick through the window. Could be the kids she saw loitering out front when she came home. It's next to impossible to get fingerprints off a brick. We'll canvass the neighbors to see if they saw anything."

Chad stepped outside to speak with Brian, the complex manager. The paramedics were packing up, ready to leave, by the time Chad returned. "Thanks, guys." They nodded and gave a friendly wave as they left.

Chad shook his head and stood with his hands on his hips. "I spoke with Brian. He can't board up the window tonight, so he offered to camp out on your recliner. He'll call in the morning and see how soon he can get it fixed."

"I suppose that's all we can do at this point."

"It'll get chilly in here tonight. I think you'd better stay at my place."

"Thanks. Let me bring down some blankets for Brian and sweep up the bulk of this glass. I'll get the rest tomorrow when it's easier to see."

Chad stared at the jagged hole in the window. "It's odd. Art had a brick thrown through his window a few days ago, and now you. It doesn't sit well with me."

Was it my dad? I doubt it, not after he came to my rescue last night. But that's a discussion for later, after Chad's had a good night's rest. "It's called a coincidence. My bet is on those new kids from around the corner."

He frowned. "Maybe."

TWENTY-NINE

CiCi yawned and rolled out of the familiar bed in Chad's spare bedroom. She'd stayed in his guest room several months back while recovering from her head injury. He had gone to great lengths to make that stay comfortable. He'd painted the walls a pale lemon color and furnished the room with items dear to her heart. The iron bed once belonged to her grandmother, as did the blue and yellow quilt covering the mattress. Once she'd been able to manage stairs, she moved back into her townhome. Home, sweet home. Well, it was until the brick-throwing incident last night. Despite feeling safe under Chad's roof, it had taken a while to fall asleep.

After dressing and pulling up her hair into a loose ponytail, she headed to the kitchen. Chad stood at the counter, wearing a crisp white shirt, a blue tie, black dress slacks, and a pair of alligator boots. His shiny police badge was clipped to his belt. He impatiently drummed his fingers as he waited for the coffee to finish brewing.

"Morning," he said. He gave her a hurried kiss before turning to slip on his suit jacket. "I forgot to tell you I have to be in court this morning, like in fifteen minutes from now. Can I swing by later to take you home?"

"Don't worry about it. I'm sure Brian won't mind picking me

up," she said as she straightened his collar. "Hey, I still need to talk to you about something. It's kind of important."

"Can it wait? I really need to get going." When the coffee maker beeped, he turned and filled an insulated to-go cup with his morning dose of caffeine.

"I suppose." Her smile was half-hearted as he gave her another kiss, grabbed a folder from the counter, and headed out the door. She was trying to do the right thing, and putting off *the talk* only made it more difficult.

An hour later, she stood in the dining room of her townhouse and inspected the damage. Brian had nailed a large sheet of plywood over the gaping hole in the bay window, which gave her a less than desirable view from inside. According to the note he'd left, workers would install new glass later that afternoon.

She opened the blinds in the living room and on the two smaller windows that flanked the boarded-up window in the dining room. In the light of day, minuscule pieces of glass shone like glitter on the wood floor and tabletop. She grabbed her cleaning supplies and set about sweeping and damp-mopping the room. As she moved the furniture back in place, the doorbell rang. She half-expected to see Brian when she opened the door. Instead, she found Pete holding a copy of *The Ripley Review*.

"I dug this out of your bushes. Heard you had some excitement last night."

"Let me guess. Chad asked you to check up on me."

"Maybe," he said with a twinkle in his eye. "I would've come regardless after I heard."

"Excitement, yes, but not the kind I want. Stupid neighborhood kids." She ignored the lift of his eyebrows. "Well, come on in. I just finished cleaning up the glass."

While she made a fresh pot of coffee, he tossed the newspaper on the counter and slipped outside, she assumed, to inspect the crime scene and the temporary fix to the window. By the time he returned, she had poured them both a cup of coffee and thawed two slices of banana bread, Pete's favorite. She took a seat beside him at the breakfast bar and filled him in on the evening's events pertaining to the window. When she glanced at the copy of *The Ripley Review* that lay between them on the counter, it came as no surprise to see a short story underneath a photo of a vehicle ravished by fire. *Serena didn't waste any time.*

"I'm glad that wasn't my car," she said.

"I'm surprised something like that doesn't happen there more often," Pete said, tapping his finger on the picture. "Not a week goes by without the police being called. Assault, theft, drugs, vandalism, you name it."

"What do you know about Derek, the guitar player? I'm sure his name must've come up when the police were looking into Jenna's disappearance."

Pete sobered and narrowed his eyes as he sipped his coffee and ate a slice of banana bread. "Don't recall that it did. How do you know about *him?*"

She stared straight ahead. "Oh, um, well, I...I heard from Jenna's friends she worked at The Tap & Keg and the two of them became quite friendly."

"He's no good and has a wicked temper. Same for that singer in his band. Heard she got out of prison recently."

Her eyes widened. "*Red's* been in prison?"

"So, you know her name, do you? What are you up to, missy?" The disapproval in Pete's tone was unmistakable.

"I...I've been talking to Jenna's friends." *And a bit more.*

"Does Chad know you've been to The Tap & Keg?"

She winced. "Not yet. I plan on telling him tonight." *After all, he'll find out when I tell him where I lost my new watch.*

"I'd like to be a fly on the wall when that happens," he muttered as he stood. "Well, I'd better be going. Thanks for the snack. Try to stay out of trouble."

She sat in the living room after he left, nursing another cup of coffee, when her attention fell on Jenna's box. *Might as well sort through the rest of her stuff. I haven't found anything of value so far, but maybe today I'll get lucky.*

She slid the box over to the end of the coffee table. Sitting on the sofa, she opened the flaps. She set aside all the paraphernalia she'd hastily shoved in the container the day before in order to sort through the section that Heather had packed. She stacked papers with any reference to Tyler on her left. Those that mentioned Derek, or The Tap & Keg, went in a pile to her right, and the blurry photos went into a third pile in the center.

Tyler's pile contained a diary of sorts that detailed Jenna's heartfelt thoughts about their upcoming marriage, her hurt at finding out he had spent time with Serena, and her hopes of putting all that behind them and spending the rest of their life together. There were numerous poems and drawings. Jenna was quite the artist, adding a touch of flair to each poem. One poignant poem detailed her struggle with her sense of self-worth, of her need to prove herself to her fiancé. From what CiCi had heard, everyone thought Jenna was very talented—everyone but Jenna herself.

Derek's pile contained scrawled notes, doodles, and a list of dates and times. Several flyers promoted his band and the occasional dueling guitar gigs. A random smattering of references to Crystal caught CiCi's attention. It seemed odd Jenna would mention Crystal.

Next, she sorted through the small stash of photos. Those of deer, geese, and squirrels had obviously been taken at Tyler's pond. Three or four showed a table lined with glass jars, tubing, and gallon jugs. She assumed Jenna had taken those with her camera phone at the science fair Jimmy had talked about. From the quality of the pics, the lighting must've been poor or her lens dirty. Two pictures appeared to capture rows of potted plants and a greenhouse behind a chain-link fence with a warning sign attached. The rest seemed to be of a group of buildings, each taken from different angles. *They're not good photos. They're blurry, off-center, poorly lit. So why did Jenna keep them?*

She thought the question over as she finished her coffee. After setting the cup in the sink, she returned to the box. Partially hidden under a flap in the bottom of the container lay a KU key chain. The attached key had no engraved markings and looked far too small to be a house key. It didn't have the same shape as the keys to her mailbox or safe deposit box. She set the key chain aside, wondering if it would be the lucky charm needed to find Jenna. Using pages from the newspaper to separate each layer, she repacked the box and placed it on the floor next to the buffet. The key and a few of the blurry photos went in her purse until she could figure out their significance.

Restless, she grabbed her sunglasses, purse, and a jacket and drove toward the area of town known as Commerce Park. The businesses that lined the streets weren't your typical retail shops. There were several automotive shops, a store that sold cement statuary, an HVAC business, a construction company, a fence contractor, and a business that offered paving stones and decorative rocks in a variety of sizes and colors. She double-checked the address on the receipt she'd been given when her Jeep was towed from Five Star's parking lot. She stopped in front of a building missing a digit in its address. When she emerged from her vehicle, the faint aroma of paint told her she was in the right place.

As she entered the small, cluttered lobby, a bell chimed somewhere beyond the front desk. To her right, a young man rocked a vending machine back and forth, trying to dislodge a bag of chips. His black, shaggy hair curled along the collar of his work uniform. Tattoos covered the back of both hands, but dirt, grease, or paint made the designs unidentifiable. When the chips fell to the tray below, he retrieved his prize and turned.

"What can I do for you, lad—" He froze upon meeting her gaze, the word lady sticking in his throat. His eyes narrowed to menacing slits as he looked her up and down. "Come for your Jeep, did ya?"

CiCi took a step back and tried to place where she'd seen him before. He certainly wasn't among her circle of acquaintants, yet he seemed to know her. "How did you—"

"Zach!" barked the older man who emerged from the office. "Leave the customer alone. And how many times have I told you to quit shaking the vending machine?"

"But my chips got stuck," he argued.

The older gentleman stuck his hand out. "My name's Jeb. What can I do for you, miss?"

"I came to see if my Jeep's ready. My name is Winslow, Cecilia Winslow."

Jeb's eyes widened. "That was *your* vehicle? Sorry, but considering what was spray painted on your car, you're not the type of person I expected to see." He glanced at Zach and sighed. "Somehow your vehicle was taken out of the queue before I discovered the error. I pushed it to the front of the line, so it will take a little longer than I expected."

"What goes around comes around," Zach muttered, earning him a heated glare from his boss.

"You waiting for an invitation to go back to work? How about I write one on the bottom of my boot? Now, git!" Zach turned and scrambled for the door. Jeb shook his head. "If I wasn't friends with his dad, I'd fire that kid in a heartbeat. I don't know if he smokes too many joints or sniffs the paint, but he needs to get his act together. Lucky for me, he only works three days a week. Enough about my problems." He turned and ran a finger down a ledger behind the counter. "Looks like your Jeep will be ready tomorrow. If the delay causes you to pay anything out of pocket for the rental, I'll take care of it."

"That's kind of you, but not necessary. Hey, Jeb, has Zach worked here long? He looks familiar, but I can't place where I know him from."

Jeb removed his cap and scratched his head. "I doubt you and him travel in the same circles." Responding to her frown, he continued, "You're an appraiser, right? I saw the newspaper article about your new partnership with Floyd Masters over at Five Star. Maybe you saw Zach on a building site. He sometimes picks up odd jobs wherever he can find one."

"Yeah, maybe that's it. Well, I'd better be going."

"I have your number. I'll call when your car's ready."

CiCi slipped her sunglasses on and left, not wanting to linger anywhere in the vicinity of Zach. *Where have I seen him before? He seems to know me, but why the hostility? And why the remark about getting what's coming to me?*

She shook her head, realizing how paranoid she sounded. Chad would say she needed a nap, and she might agree if she didn't have another issue to tackle. Out of all of Jenna's pictures, the only ones she came close to recognizing were those showing rows of potted plants in a greenhouse setting. And she knew exactly which greenhouse to visit.

THIRTY

CiCi pulled into the drive-thru lane at a fast-food joint and ordered a cheeseburger and a large drink. She thrummed her fingers on the steering wheel while she waited for her order to be filled. *If I want to know why Greenleaf Growers keeps popping up in my search for Jenna, I'll have to pay them another visit. Will the older lady who manned the counter let me wander around the property to satisfy my curiosity about the photos? Probably not. She wasn't too friendly the last time.*

Fifteen minutes later, she pulled into Greenleaf's lot and parked at the far end of the rustic produce building. Bales of hay flanked by cornstalks and pumpkins lined each side of the entrance, a sure sign of fall. Nearby, a mother snapped pictures of her toddler sitting on a porch swing next to a life-sized scarecrow. Like the child, it wore a plaid shirt, overalls, and a straw hat.

As CiCi stepped inside, a bell tinkled above the door to announce her arrival. The same older woman from before stood behind the counter helping a customer. Her smile pinched into a tight line the moment she spotted CiCi. CiCi nodded and meandered about the store, biding her time and wondering how she could search the areas off-limits to the public without being discovered and thrown off the property. When the last customer left, she picked up an apple and approached the register.

"I don't know why you insist—," she said.

CiCi raised her hand. "Please," she said, glancing at the woman's nametag, "Bernice. I owe you an apology. The last time I was here, you thought you were talking to Jenna, but you weren't. I'm her cousin. I should've corrected you—I didn't, and I'm sorry."

"Okay," Bernice said skeptically.

"My name is CiCi and I'd like to talk to you—or your boss—about the possibility of Greenleaf Growers donating produce to a charity organization that provides food to the needy in our community."

Bernice appeared unmoved by the request. "Leave your contact information and I'll pass it on to the manager. I can't promise he'll get back with you."

"What about the owner, Mr. Greenleaf? Is he around?"

"Mr. Greenleaf died four years ago. His son sold the business two years ago and moved out of state."

CiCi pulled a pen and paper from her purse and wrote a name and phone number. "Maxine is the woman in charge. I'll let her know to expect a call."

"Like I said, I can't make any promises." Bernice glanced at the information and recognition flickered across her face. "A Hand Up?"

CiCi smiled. "Yes. Have you heard of it?"

"I have," she said, her voice softening. "They've been a godsend to my daughter and her family ever since her husband lost his job."

"I'm glad they've been able to help. Is he still looking for work?"

"He is," she said hesitantly.

"I have a friend who owns a security and surveillance company. He recently had an employee quit. I don't know the specifics of the job, but if your son-in-law is interested, have him give Pete a call." CiCi scribbled Pete's number on another slip of paper and handed it to Bernice.

A small smile appeared. The wall Bernice had erected seemed to have developed a crack. "That's mighty kind of you. I'll pass the information along."

"Thanks. By the way, who's the new owner? I'm surprised they didn't change the name of the business."

"Don't know his name and never met him," Bernice said. She leaned forward and whispered, "I don't know that anyone has except the manager, and he's not too forthcoming with information, if you know what I mean. If I ask too many questions, I might be the one looking for another job."

After paying for the apple, CiCi tucked her wallet and the fruit into her purse. "Mind if I take a walk around the property?"

Bernice hesitated. "Well, they frown on people wandering off on their own. There's a tour that starts in fifteen minutes, if you want to wait."

"Thanks, I think I will."

This might be easier than I thought. CiCi sat in her car and finished her drink, waiting for the tour to begin. A text from Chad arrived, telling her he would be in court most of the day. She glanced around the parking lot, wondering where everyone was. Suddenly, a bright orange-yellow color filled her rearview mirror and both side mirrors. A school bus pulled up behind her and coughed up about a thousand energetic grade school kids.

A frazzled teacher blew a shrill whistle and the frenzied mass calmed to a dull roar. Three young women, who were most likely parents, helped corral the group into two lines, with each child holding the hand of a classmate. When the tour guide started his spiel, CiCi got out of the car, threw her empty cup away, and went to the back of the line. She rummaged in her purse for an elastic band and pulled her hair up into a loose ponytail. A little girl about six, with pigtails and freckles, took CiCi's hand and gave her a big grin.

"Look, I lost a tooth!" she said, proudly showing off the gaping hole in a row of tiny white teeth.

CiCi bent to the child's level. "How exciting! Did you leave the tooth under your pillow for the Tooth Fairy?"

Freckles' eyes shone with excitement as she bounced from foot to foot. "I did, and I got a dollar and a princess toothbrush."

"Wow, you did good."

"I did, 'cause my mommy said I'm precious."

CiCi smiled. *Yep, I want a child like this someday—with Chad.* The line moved forward, and Freckles tugged at CiCi's hand.

Partway through the tour of a hothouse full of plants, CiCi gave Freckles a weak excuse for leaving and paired her with the two classmates in line ahead of them. CiCi slipped off by herself, watching for employees who might steer her back to the guided tour. After peering inside greenhouse after greenhouse, she found none of the structures' contents resembled the photos she had in her purse. She eventually found herself in a secluded area at the far back portion of the property. It was there she detected the faint aroma of chemicals. *I thought Greenleaf boasted of growing only 100% organic produce.*

She froze in place as angry voices cut through the air. One man swore and ordered another man away from an area that was off-limits to those without authorization. Footsteps neared. She scurried to the nearest building and knelt behind a stack of fifty-pound bags of fertilizer. When the men moved on, she peeked around the corner. They had to have come from the restricted area where a large outbuilding sat inside a chain-link fence with a locked gate. *Ah, the building in Jenna's photo. Maybe that's where Greenleaf develops their famous hybrid plants. Could they be using chemicals to enhance the results?*

Movement to her right caught her attention. Three Greenleaf employees were huddled together, talking. One pointed in her direction. *I need to hide, and quick.* Before she could make a move, a hand clamped around her waist and dragged her out of sight and around the corner of the building. Warm breath tickled her ear as a male voice shushed her. Her heart thumped against her chest as she wondered what his intentions were. She didn't know whether to be relieved or afraid when he loosened his grip. She turned to face her abductor. *Mace!*

"What are you doing here!" she whispered.

"Unlike you, I work here."

"How did you find me?"

"I've never seen a bag of fertilizer sprout a ponytail before." He peeked around the corner. "It's clear. This area is off limits. You need to leave before Derek catches you. I don't know what you're up to, but you're not safe here, even if he does think you're my girlfriend." He grabbed her hand and pulled her alongside him as they headed toward the public parking lot.

"Wait! What's Derek doing here?"

"He's the manager, and the one who got me this job."

CiCi jumped into her car, shocked to discover both Derek and Mace worked at Greenleaf. She fished in her purse for her car keys. When she pulled them out, the key fob she'd found at the bottom of Jenna's box fell in her lap. She tossed it back into her purse and drove from the lot, never once looking back. She wondered if Jenna had uncovered information about Greenleaf's newest hybrid and taken pictures to prove they indeed used chemicals. *Is that why Derek's boss had been so furious with her—because her photos could ruin their reputation and cause them to lose their USDA organic certification? Maybe. It would be a huge hit to their reputation, not to mention the financial repercussions.*

At the end of the lane, she came to a stop. She could turn left or right. Both would lead back to town but turning left would take her past Tyler's cabin. *I still have a set of pictures to identify, and I'm certain I know where to go.* Taking out her cell, she called the newspaper.

"Hey, Tyler. It's CiCi." She paused. "Um, would you mind if I visit the cabin and sit for a spell at the pond? I need someplace quiet to think."

Tyler hesitated, as though considering her request. "Sure, go ahead. It was always Jenna's favorite spot to gather her thoughts." A commotion erupted in the background and Mr. Rivera's booming voice reverberated through the phone. "Yes, sir. Be right there," Tyler shouted before the line went dead.

It had taken less than five minutes to drive to Tyler's cabin. As she stepped from the car, she realized she should have made a pit stop before leaving Greenleaf Growers. Ordering a large drink had been a bad idea and her bladder felt ready to burst. She glanced around. The clearing surrounding the house offered no privacy, and who knew what lurked in the overgrown brush? *Tyler won't mind if I use his facilities, right?* Standing on her tiptoes, her fingers fumbled along the top of the window frame until she found the key to the cabin. Once inside, she raced to the bathroom, hoping the rustic cabin had running water. She was in luck—and in time.

When she returned to the living room, her gaze swept across the interior and settled on the addition at the back. Seconds later, she stood in front of Jenna's desk. *Should I see if Jenna's key fits one of the drawers? No, I shouldn't—but I'll never rest until I know. If it doesn't, Tyler will never have to know. If it does, I'll have to explain and beg his forgiveness later.* She brushed the dust from the chair's worn seat and sat down. The desk was high quality, made of walnut with a leather inlaid writing surface, a far cry from the desk in Heather's basement storage unit.

After removing the key from her purse, she determined it was too small to fit the large lock on the center drawer, which slid open with little effort. Other than a few pencils, paper clips, rubber bands and a roll of tape, there appeared to be nothing that raised any suspicions. The top drawer to her right turned up two blank writing tablets, and the one below held empty file folders. To her left, between the first drawer and the desktop, she found a narrow indentation. She pulled and found a writing shelf with a sheet of paper taped to the surface.

As her finger traced down the list of names and phone numbers, she felt something beneath the paper. Peeling back the tape, she found a plastic card. It had no identifying logo, barcode, or magnetic strip. *What is it?* Then she remembered the video she'd watched for the concealment furniture she considered buying for Chad as a wedding gift. Each handcrafted piece came with an RFID card to access the hidden compartments. Those RFID cards looked identical to the one taped under the phone list. *Could it be?*

She slid the card along the spots as shown in the video, hoping that the batteries in the receivers weren't dead. At the bottom of the desk, she heard a muffled snick. With a slight tug, a panel below the bottom drawer gave way. Inside the hidden compartment lay a flat, red metal lockbox. She placed it on the desktop and almost broke a nail trying to open the lid. Crossing her fingers, she inserted the key. It fit but wouldn't turn. When she tried to remove the key, it wouldn't budge. *Dang it! Now what?*

She stood—or sat—at a crossroads. *What should I do? Give the box to Tyler? I should, but I'd have to admit I snooped in the desk without his permission. Using the restroom seemed innocent enough, but now I've crossed the line.*

She stared at the box. *Jenna kept the box hidden and locked for a reason. I should put it back, but I can't. I need to find out what's inside.*

After finding two other secret compartments empty, she replaced the RFID card and re-taped the edges of the phone list. She carried the metal box to her rental car and locked it in the trunk for safekeeping. With thoughts of Greenleaf Growers still on her mind, she rounded the cabin and walked another thirty feet to the outbuilding. After grabbing the binoculars from the workbench, she headed to the pond. The surroundings were familiar to her now and the setting so tranquil, she almost wished she could stay for a spell.

At the top of the rise, she walked around the pond until she came to Jenna's red bench. After removing the binoculars from their case, she scanned the area surrounding the pond and spotted a small doe eating berries from a bush. *So beautiful.* Within minutes, it disappeared down an overgrown path. She turned her sights on the outbuildings at the back of the Greenleaf property. She pulled Jenna's photos from her purse, holding each one aloft. From the elevated position of Tyler's property, those buildings behind the security fence in the distance looked like a match.

She looked through the binoculars again. There seemed to be quite a bit of activity down below. Workers loaded trucks with merchandise from one of the greenhouses. At one of the smaller buildings, a man smoking a cigarette leaned against the building. He straightened and threw down his cigarette as Mace approached. They argued, and the first man pushed Mace and a brief scuffle ensued. After another worker escorted Mace out of her line of sight, a dark sedan pulled up. The smoker leaned against the vehicle, nodding his head as he spoke to the driver.

Her phone rang, making her almost drop the binoculars. "Hey, Chad, what's up?"

"Now that you're supposed to be resting, you're harder to pin down than when you were working. Where are you?"

"Um, well, I'm looking into something for Katherine."

"That didn't answer my question."

"If you must know, I'm at Tyler's cabin." The silence that followed worried her. "Chad, are you there?"

"Is he there? I told you I don't want you meeting him alone."

She winced at his harsh tone. "He's not, and I thought that was a suggestion."

"Don't play word games with me. Did you know that after Jenna disappeared the police dragged his pond looking for her body? I don't want you alone with him. Get in your car, CiCi, and leave. Now."

She looked over her shoulder at the pond. Knowing it could've been Jenna's final resting place sent chills down her spine. *Perhaps I should be glad Chad is overly protective.* "Okay, okay, I'm leaving."

"I'll pick you up at six-thirty. We have a counseling session tonight. Afterward, we need to talk."

"That sounds serious."

"It is. I'll see you later."

The line went dead, leaving her to wonder what he wanted to talk about. Whatever it was, he didn't sound pleased. She sighed. *Maybe I'd better postpone telling him about my watch, or what I've been doing to find Jenna. And he certainly won't like hearing that Derek jerked me into the alley and threatened me.*

She took one last look through the binoculars and sucked in a breath. The smoker was also looking through a pair of binoculars, and they were pointed in her direction!

THIRTY-ONE

CiCi slid into the passenger seat of Chad's truck. On the drive to the counseling session, he remained unusually quiet. "Are you okay?" she asked as they neared the church.

"I'm fine."

"Is something bothering you?"

"There is, but we'll get to that later," he said, pulling into the parking lot. "We're here."

They followed the brick pathway to the church. Not one to let his emotions override his manners, he held the door open, letting her enter first. Pastor Young greeted them with a friendly smile and robust handshake before leading them to his study. Though she took a seat next to Chad, she sensed a distance between them. Chad looked straight ahead, and it tore at her heart.

"Having missed our last session, it's good to see both of you again. I'd like to revisit the topic from a few weeks ago concerning money. It's a difficult subject, and often the downfall of many marriages. It's not so important how much you have, but how you agree to manage it. Let's get started."

Over the next hour, Chad and CiCi discussed their views on paying off debts, making investments, managing household expenses, and handling financial emergencies. Their only point of contention revolved around the prospect of combining their assets.

Pastor Young looked at Chad. "Are you worried you're not entering the marriage as equal partners, per se?"

"Somewhat. I do okay on a detective's salary, but my net worth is nothing compared to hers."

"It's a fact that almost thirty percent of today's women make more than their husbands," Young said. "Your situation, however, is more extreme than most, and it's something you should commit to resolve now rather than after you're married."

"I agree," CiCi said. "But the Bible says when a man and a woman marry, they are joined together as one flesh. That 'joining together' includes their goals, their dreams, their hurts, their possessions. They're to share everything, leaving nothing hidden. It's symbolic of having total trust in one another."

Chad stared at her and gave a tight smile.

"Marriage is about compromise," she said, addressing Chad. "What if your salary and my salary from Five Star were put into a joint account for everyday living expenses, and the money from the inheritance placed in a separate account? I was hoping in the future we could use a portion of that money for emergencies or special projects that benefit people in Ripley Grove."

Pastor Young smiled. "I often counseled your mother and grandmother when they sought advice and prayer for humanitarian projects. Their anonymous philanthropic efforts were a blessing to this community. I'd be thrilled if the two of you continue in their footsteps, but that is something you both need to agree on."

Chad turned to her with a curt nod. "That sounds like a possibility, but we'll need to talk about that later. I think our time is up."

Pastor Young looked at his watch. "Oh my, you're right. Well, Lord willing, I'll see you in two weeks. Our next topic of discussion is communication." He glanced at Chad and smiled. "That should be interesting, and the timing couldn't be more perfect, wouldn't you say?"

CiCi unlocked the door to her townhome and Chad followed her down the wide hallway and into the living room. She hung her purse over the back of a dining room chair and took a seat on the couch, leaving Chad's usual seat beside her empty. He hesitated, then sat in the upholstered chair at the end of the sofa.

She frowned. "What's wrong with you tonight? Are you still upset over the inheritance? What does it matter? What's mine will be yours once we're married. In fact, I see no reason to wait until then to add your name to the accounts and properties. I'll call the lawyer this week. I'll feel better knowing everything is in good hands if something happens to me."

"Why would something happen to you?"

"I'm not invincible, you know. I could die in a car wreck, get hit by a bus, have a heart attack, or—"

"—or have your dad throw a brick through your window?"

His steady gaze made her heart race. She sank back into the cozy chenille cushions, hoping to look more comfortable than she felt. "Those neighborhood kids—"

"You don't believe the neighborhood kids did that any more than I do."

"They might have," she said, refusing to concede the point. "It's not worth arguing about, so let's change the subject. How was your day? From the mood you're in, I'd say not so good."

"I'm glad you asked." He leaned forward, laced his fingers together, and braced his forearms on the top of his thighs.

A tingling sensation crept up her spine. She knew him well enough to know he had shifted into cop mode.

"Thinking there might've been a connection between your busted window and the one at the hardware, Mark and I went to talk to your dad this afternoon. Imagine my surprise when he said he saw you the other night at The Tap & Keg."

Words stuck in her throat. *How much did Dad tell him?*

"I didn't want to believe him," Chad continued, his expression steely, "so I drove to The Tap & Keg and spoke with Steve. He and I are old friends. I showed him your picture, and he said you'd been in—not once, but several times. Don't recall hearing a word of this from you."

She took a deep breath. "That's what I wanted to talk about this morning. You were in a hurry, remember?"

"Three visits, that I know of, CiCi. You had plenty of opportunity."

"I know, and I'm sorry I didn't say something earlier. When I found out Jenna worked there part-time, I went to ask a few questions."

"But it went beyond that," he said. "Way beyond."

Her heart began to race. "I suppose it did. Steve and two old guys at the bar told Tasha and I that Jenna had a huge fight with a guitar player named Derek, so we went back one evening to check him out. I wore a wig and glasses so he wouldn't think Jenna had returned to pick up where they'd left off." A hint of surprise flashed in his eyes but vanished before she could determine what it meant.

He stood and placed his hands on his hips. "And you thought that was a good idea?"

"Yes, I did, although I never expected to see my dad there."

"And even though you have a restraining order against him, you stayed. You stayed, had a drink or two, and danced with other men."

"I was waiting for someone who might have information about Jenna, but he never showed. I got pulled to the dance floor on my way out. It was never my intention to dance with anyone."

The muscles in his jaw tightened and his eyes hardened. "You told Pastor Young tonight you believe couples should share everything, but your actions say otherwise. You shared none of this with me—why you went to The Tap & Keg, what you found out, or who you kissed in the parking lot."

She sucked in a breath, then stood to set the record straight. "I didn't kiss anyone! That guy forced himself on me." She paused, then fisted her hands at her sides. "Wait, are you accusing me of—"

"*No*, I'm not *accusing* you of anything," he growled.

"Is that what this is about? You're jealous?"

"No! Yes! *Of course*, I'm jealous, but that's not the point."

"Then what is the point?" she said, planting her hands on her hips.

"The point is you put yourself in danger. I know the kind of people who frequent that place, and that guy could've done a lot more than kiss you. It's no place for you to be."

"That's for me to decide. You can't protect me from everything, Chad."

"But I can try." He raked a hand through his hair. "What's done is done, but you should've told me before I had to hear it from someone else."

"I tried tell you several times," she snapped, "but you were always busy."

"I'm not busy now." His icy stare pinned her in place.

She threw up a hand to ward off any further conversation. "No. You're angry, I'm angry. The timing's not right for everything I have to say."

He narrowed his eyes. "There's more? What else haven't you told me?"

She opened her mouth, then closed it before she made matters worse. When he reached for her hand, her shoulders sagged with relief. *He's going to apologize for over-reacting.* Her hopes vanished when he held up her wrist and stared into her eyes.

"Where's your watch?"

Her heart stopped, and the seconds ticked by. "I…I lost it."

"Where? The Tap & Keg?" His mouth twisted into a tight line when she nodded and looked away. He released her hand, turned, and stalked toward the front door.

"Chad, wait!"

The door slammed shut, leaving her alone with her thoughts. *He has every right to be mad. This wouldn't have happened if I'd confided in him from the very start.*

Later that evening, she reached out to him by text several times.

I'm sorry.

Can we talk?

Every text went unanswered. She climbed into bed but couldn't sleep. She tossed and turned enough to burn five hundred calories. Throwing back the covers, she slipped on her robe and went to the kitchen. Holding a pint of pralines and cream ice cream in one hand and a spoon in the other, she dug into the frozen treat as though the answer to her problems could be found at the bottom of the carton.

As she paced the floor, she glanced out of the window overlooking the parking lot. Startled, she stepped back out of view before taking another peek. In the far corner of the parking lot, a dark sedan faced her townhome. A shadowy figure sat in the driver's seat, the lit end of a cigarette punctuating the dark interior. She flipped on the porch light. The car started its engine and sped from the lot.

She thought of calling Chad but, considering his refusal to respond to her texts, decided against it. She double-checked every lock and turned on every light before heading upstairs to her bedroom and repeating the process. She climbed into bed, removed the gun from her bedside caddy, and settled in for a long, sleepless night.

THIRTY-TWO

CiCi reluctantly cracked an eye open. Sunlight poured through the French doors of her bedroom, bathing the room in light. She dressed and took extra time with her make-up to conceal the dark circles under her eyes. She frowned after checking her phone for the umpteenth time. By nine o'clock, Chad still hadn't responded to her texts. Her shoulders sagged with disappointment. A text from the auto body shop said her Jeep was ready to be picked up. *Well, at least one thing in my life will return to normal.*

She grabbed a pair of sunglasses and headed out to take care of business. First, she needed to return the rental car. The older gentleman behind the counter stepped outside to inspect the vehicle for damage. When he returned, he had a red metal box in his hand.

"I think you left something in the trunk," he said with a smile.

"I guess I did. Thanks."

"I don't see anyone with you. Do you need a ride somewhere?"

"I do." She accepted his offer and voiced her appreciation, bringing a blush to his weathered cheeks.

Though a bell announced her arrival as she entered the lobby of the auto body shop, no one came to greet her. "Hello? Is anyone here?" A muffled sound followed by a giggle came from the room just beyond the front counter. A few seconds later, a young woman appeared, with Zach close behind. Without looking up, she hastily fastened the top two buttons on her blouse and said, "Can I help you?"

Zach sneered and slid his arms around her waist. "If I were you, babe, she's the last person I'd be offering to help."

CiCi took a step back. *Wow. Zach's as friendly today as he was yesterday.* When his love interest looked up, CiCi's eyes widened. "Ashley? What are you doing here?"

"I work here."

CiCi turned her gaze from Ashley to Zach. *That's why he looked familiar. Zach is her boyfriend, the guy who flipped me off when he picked up her from Five Star. I'll bet one or both of them vandalized my Jeep after she lost the court battle for her uncle's share of the company.*

"I'm sure I'll find a better job soon," Ashley said, "one that treats me with more respect than you and Five Star did."

"You're lucky I didn't press charges against you for assault. And to set the record straight, the outcome of the court proceedings had nothing to do with me, and everything to do with your uncle's poor decisions."

"You might believe that, but I don't."

A door down the hall opened and closed, and footsteps could be heard approaching from the back end of the building.

"Everything all right in here?" Jeb appeared in the doorway. "Zach, what did I tell you about hanging out in the office? Ashley has work to do, now git."

Zach winked at Ashley and sidled by Jeb.

"Now, Miss Winslow, how about I find the keys to your Jeep? I imagine you'll want to inspect the work we've done. I hope it meets your expectations."

CiCi smiled at Jeb and followed him from the room. After signing off on the paperwork, she put the red box on the floor behind the driver's seat and drove from the lot, happy to have her own vehicle back. A quick glance at her phone revealed no new texts or missed calls. *Chad must still be angry.* Her heart skipped a beat when the phone rang, but the caller wasn't who she'd hoped to hear from. "Hi, Katherine. How are you today?"

"Fine, just fine. I wanted to remind you that today the staff at Sunflower Village is preparing a special lunch celebration to honor those who have a birthday in October. Edna is really looking forward to it. She'll be eighty this month. I should have called you yesterday, but it slipped my mind. If you can't make it, don't worry about it."

"I wouldn't miss it. I'll see you there."

CiCi turned at the next light and drove toward the square. *What type of present do you get someone who lives in a nursing home? Edna can't see well enough for books, puzzles, or crafts. No doubt she has a dozen fleece blankets and fuzzy socks.* CiCi browsed the aisles of her favorite gift shop and settled on something that reminded her of her grandmother. After picking out a gift bag and tissue paper, the salesclerk rang up her purchase and wished her a wonderful day.

She arrived at Sunflower Village earlier than she expected but doubted it would pose a problem. She found Katherine in Edna's room, helping her to get "dolled up" as Edna called it. Katherine guided Edna's arms into a soft cable-knit sweater that had a large novelty "Happy Birthday" pin attached to the collar. She greeted CiCi with an infectious smile and asked her to get a necklace from the dresser.

"I like your necklace. It's very pretty," CiCi remarked, as she slipped the gold chain around Edna's neck and fastened the clasp.

"You should, dearie. You have one almost like it."

"I do? I must have forgotten." CiCi cast a quick glance at Katherine.

"Don't you remember? We bought the necklaces on vacation one year. Mine says 'Gram-cracker' and yours says 'Firecracker.' You haven't lost it, have you?"

"Um, no, I haven't." *Can't lose something I never had.* To change the subject, CiCi presented Edna with the gift bag. "I got you a little something for your birthday. I hope you like it."

Edna smiled and her eyes lit up. "You didn't have to do that." She wasted no time in pulling the tissue paper from the bag and unwrapping the small bottle of cologne. She unscrewed the lid and swooned with delight. "Oh, my favorite. I haven't worn *White Shoulders* in years. Thank you, sweetheart."

"I'm glad you like it."

Edna dabbed a bit under each ear, then carefully smoothed and folded each sheet of tissue and had Katherine put them in a drawer for later use. "They should start serving lunch in twenty minutes." Edna patted her hair. "Do I look all right?"

"You look beautiful. Shall we go?"

Katherine pushed Edna in her wheelchair and CiCi followed along as they headed to the dining hall. CiCi's phone rang. She glanced at the screen and saw the name of a salesman who'd been trying to convince her to buy a new car. She let it go to voicemail. It rang again during lunch. Noticing it came from the same number as before, she ignored the call. At the end of the meal, her phone pinged, and she pulled up the text.

Where are you? We need to talk.

Chad! Her heart filled with hope. *But why didn't he just call? Must be someplace he can't talk.* Not wanting to be rude, she excused herself from the table and slipped into the hall where she could respond to his text: **At Edna's birthday lunch.** She waited for his response, her thumbs hovering over the screen.

We're looking over Jenna's case and have questions. My office. 3PM?

His words were brusque. Her heart sank with disappointment that he'd chosen to ignore her earlier apology or pleas to talk things out. She typed **I'll be there** and hit send.

She rejoined Katherine and Edna as the Activities Director led the room in a chorus of "Happy Birthday." Edna blew out the candle on her lemon cupcake with one huff and grinned with delight. By the time the festivities had concluded, Edna's energy had faded. After settling her in for an afternoon nap, CiCi and Katherine left the building together.

"Is everything alright? You seem distracted," Katherine asked.

"I'm fine. Well, maybe. Chad and I had an argument last night and a lot of it hinges on the fact that I haven't been honest with him about what I've been doing to find Jenna."

"I'm sorry. I shouldn't have gotten you involved. Maybe if I talk with—"

"Thanks, but no. We need to work this out on our own. It's not the first time our personalities have clashed. Sometimes my independent tendencies clash with his over-protective nature."

THIRTY-THREE

CiCi arrived at the Ripley Grove police station at two o'clock instead of three, hoping to have time to clear up things with Chad before they talked about Jenna's case. After checking in, the officer escorted her down the hall to a conference room. She stepped inside. Mark stood beside a long table covered with loose papers and stacks of documents. He rifled through a pile, pulled out a sheet, and ran his finger down the page.

She cleared her throat to get his attention. His eyes met hers and he greeted her with a curt nod. "Come in," he said. "Chad will be back shortly."

"What's all this?" she asked.

"We've been comparing the official file to some of the private notes Pete took after he was assigned to help with Jenna's case."

She glanced around the room. "Where's Detective Logan? Isn't it his case?"

"He's, uh, been reassigned," Mark said, his tone crisp and professional. He nodded to a chair. "Have a seat. I have a few questions for you."

Sensing tension in the air, she chose to stand. "That's what Chad said in his text. I was hoping to talk to him before we get started."

"That'll have to wait." Mark propped his hands on his hips. "Last night you told Chad that Jenna and a guitar player at The Tap & Keg had a huge fight before she disappeared," he said. "The bartender never mentioned it when we went to follow up on your dad's claim that he'd seen you at the bar."

"Well, the bartender knows more than he's telling. That's part of what I wanted to tell Chad last night, but things didn't exactly go as I planned."

"From the mood Chad's in, I figured as much. When he told me that Jenna had a fight with Derek, I started wondering if there was a connection to ..."

"A connection to what?" she asked. A familiar voice drew her attention to the hallway. Her heart fluttered the moment she saw Chad walk past with a prisoner in tow. "Chad!" she called, resisting the urge to run to him, throw her arms around him, and apologize.

Chad turned. He glanced at his watch. "You're early."

"I know. I thought we might have time to talk."

"If it's about Jenna's case, then yes," he said, his face revealing little emotion.

So, I guess he's still mad.

Chad's prisoner angled himself around Chad. When the man caught sight of CiCi, his face broke into a wide grin. "Hey, Foxy. Didn't expect to see you here. Miss me, darling?"

CiCi gasped. Mace sported a fresh bruise on one cheek underneath what appeared to be a days-old black eye. His knuckles were scraped, and the shirt he wore that barely contained his muscles had tears in several places.

Chad stiffened. "Hold on. You two know each other?"

Mace nodded. "She's the gal I told you about who's been snooping around The Tap & Keg and Greenleaf Growers. She's also the one who gave me this black eye."

CiCi smirked. "You told me to take a hit, so I did."

"I said to *fake* a hit."

"You deserved it for forcing yourself on me."

"Wait. *He's* the one who kissed you?" Chad turned and shot daggers at Mace.

Mace grinned. Behind her, Mark sucked in a deep breath.

"Yes, he is." Heat flamed across CiCi's cheeks. "The jerk deserves to be locked up."

"Might as well have him join us," Mark said to Chad.

Chad pushed the man into the conference room, shut the door, and removed the handcuffs. Mace rubbed his wrists and grumbled, "Next time don't make them so tight."

CiCi frowned and took a step back. "Why is *he* here?"

Chad huffed an exasperated sigh and then introduced the two people who *thought* they knew each other. "CiCi, meet Evan McIntosh," he said, before turning a heated gaze to Evan. "Evan, this is Cecilia Winslow, my fiancée."

Evan cocked an eyebrow as he looked her over. "I had a feeling your name wasn't Foxy." He sank into a chair, laced his hands behind his head, and chuckled as he glanced up at Chad. "Hey, man, that kiss? Purely in the line of duty. You'll be proud to know her punch knocked me on my ass afterward." Evan grinned. "I must say, you are one lucky bas—"

Chad held up a hand. "Stop!"

CiCi frowned at Chad. "He told me his name was Mace. What's going on? Is this some kind of joke?"

Chad sighed. "It's no joke. Evan and I went through the police academy together. He's an undercover officer on loan from another jurisdiction."

Evan snapped his fingers and straightened as though he'd just thought of something. "Mark, can I get my personal effects back?" A few minutes later, Evan opened the sealed pouch, removed an object, and dangled it from his fingertips. "This yours?"

CiCi's hands flew to her mouth. She took the watch from his hand and clutched it to her chest. "Thank you," she whispered. "Where'd you find it?"

"Out back when Derek and I left for the night. The clasp must've broken when he jerked you into the alley."

Chad stood. "That was *you*? Why didn't you tell me?"

She lifted her chin in defiance. "I would've, but you stormed out last night and never returned my calls." She stared. His mouth opened, then closed. *Was that regret that flickered in his eyes, and an apology that died on his lips?*

"Okay, that's enough," Mark said, the tone in his voice commanding their attention. "You two can work things out later. Let's get back to the topic at hand. CiCi, have a seat." After she and Chad sat, Mark took a seat, pulled out a pen and small spiral notebook from his shirt pocket, and turned his attention to her. "As I said earlier, when Chad told me that Jenna had a fight with Derek before she went missing, I started wondering if there was a connection to a case we've been working on. But we need to know more about what you've uncovered about Jenna."

"So, you think there's a connection between her disappearance and your case? What case?" She folded her arms across her chest.

Mark tightened the grip on his pen, glanced at Chad and Evan, and then leaned forward and pinned her with a stare that made her want to run from the room. "CiCi, this information goes no further than this room. Understood?"

His deep voice chilled her to the bone. She nodded and released a breath she hadn't realized she'd been holding.

"Okay, then. We suspect someone at Greenleaf Growers is using The Tap & Keg and the farmers' market to distribute drugs. We're trying to find out who runs the operation. Greenleaf is owned by a shell corporation, but our guess is there's a local connection."

She frowned and reeled back in her seat. "Are you saying Jenna got mixed up with drugs?"

"No, I didn't say that," he said. "But she may have discovered something that put her life in danger."

She stared at the table, digesting his words. "And I suppose Mace, er, Evan is the undercover agent working the case."

"That's right," Chad said. "He's developed a friendship of sorts with Derek, who got him the job at Greenleaf. We faked his arrest this morning for a traffic violation in order to pass along some information, so he might as well stay and hear what you have to say."

Mark opened the notebook and turned to a clean page. "All

right, CiCi. Tell us what you've discovered from talking to Jenna's friends."

She cleared her throat. "I don't know who knows what, so I'll give a condensed version from the beginning. I've spoken with Jenna's fiancé, her employer, and numerous friends. She worked at *The Ripley Review* and, from what her fiancé told me, she was working on a story that would guarantee her a promotion. After looking into it, I suspected Jenna's big story somehow involved Greenleaf Growers."

"And you thought she took a job at The Tap & Keg to get close to Derek." Mark said.

"Exactly," CiCi said. "Tyler became jealous and it caused problems between them." She shot a pointed look at Chad. He opened his mouth to speak, but she continued. "Jenna moved out of his apartment and in with a friend named Heather, but never called off the wedding. That's another reason I believe she was simply using Derek to get her story."

"And that's why you went to The Tap & Keg? To check out Derek?" Chad asked.

CiCi nodded. "After the bartender told me Derek and Jenna had a fight over something she'd taken, I thought it would be smart to first get a sense of who he was. That's why I borrowed a wig and fake glasses from Tasha."

Mark's head jerked up. "Tasha went with you?"

"Of course she did. We're best friends."

As Mark mulled over the information, his mouth pinched into a tight line.

"Logan's report mentions Jenna's second job," Chad said, flipping back through Pete's notes, "but there's no indication he ever followed up."

"Have you talked to the owner of the bar?' she asked.

"No," Mark said firmly. "Rivera owns The Tap & Keg, and we don't want him to *accidentally* print something in the paper that would jeopardize the investigation."

"Continue with your story, CiCi," Chad said.

"Well, while I was there, I met a guy who remembered Jenna

and said he would ask around. That's why I went back the next week, to see if he'd found out anything."

"And did he?"

"He never showed, so I thought I'd hit a dead end. Then about a week ago, Heather called. She'd found some of Jenna's stuff in the basement while she was packing to move."

"Wait. This friend found some of Jenna's belongings from the time of her disappearance and never thought to call the police?"

"I guess not. She called me only because she couldn't get ahold of Katherine. Otherwise, I would've never known about it." CiCi shrugged. "Among other things in the box, there were quite a few pictures, most of them blurry. After thinking about what Derek said when he yanked me into the alley, I thought Jenna might've been exhorting money from Greenleaf's owner. Then I realized Jenna hadn't taken *something*, she'd taken pictures. The pictures are what led me to believe they were Jenna's proof that Greenleaf was using chemicals on their produce. I mean, we all know their reputation rides on their promise to provide 100% organic produce and plants. That alone would make headlines around here."

"So," Mark said, "you thought Jenna planned to write a story that would expose Greenleaf for misrepresenting their product?"

"Well, yeah. I thought so at the time. It would be a huge deal to lose their USDA organic certification, not to mention expensive. I've read the government can fine an offender as much as fifteen hundred dollars each time a product is falsely sold or labeled as organic. In fact, the Kansas City Star ran an article not long ago about a Missouri man who was sentenced to more than ten years in prison for fraud. He made millions of dollars marketing and selling non-organic grain as though it was organic."

Chad shook his head. "If that was the case, I'd think Serena would've jumped on the story after Jenna left."

"No one knew what Jenna had been working on, not even Tyler or Mr. Rivera. And Jenna and Serena didn't get along. Serena has been doing all she can to find out what dirt I dig up about Jenna's disappearance. I wouldn't be surprised if she's the one who's been

SHIRLEY WORLEY

following me around town. Of course, it could be Ashley. She hates me with a vengeance."

Chad looked up from his notes. "Wait. Someone's been following you?"

"Well, yeah, but I haven't actually seen who's been behind the wheel."

"When's the last time you saw the car?"

"Early this morning, outside my house. When I turned on the porch light, it took off."

Chad leaned forward. "Why didn't you call me?"

She pursed her lips. "Seriously? You really want to go there?"

Their exchange was clipped and tense. Mark stopped taking notes and glanced from Chad to CiCi, and back again. Evan shot Chad a questioning look. Chad ignored them both.

"Anything unusual you noticed about this car?" Mark asked.

"Not really."

Mark shot a serious gaze to Chad and Evan. Evan shook his head, and Chad gave Mark a barely perceptible nod. She remained quiet so as not to interrupt their silent conversation. Mark tossed his pencil on the table, stood, and walked over to the window. Chad and Evan joined him. They huddled together, discussing the situation in whispered tones. Chad tapped something into his phone. A few seconds later, the group disbanded and reclaimed their seats.

Evan cleared his throat. "You say there are photos?"

"Yes. They're a bit blurry, but a couple of them show tables loaded with chemicals and toxic liquids."

"Where are they?" Mark asked sternly.

"A couple are in my purse. The rest are at home in the box of stuff I got from Heather."

Mark glowered at her. "Looks as if you've poked your nose right in the middle of our investigation—again."

"That wasn't my intention."

Chad shook his head. "I knew you were talking to Jenna's friends. But when I heard you'd been to The Tap & Keg several times, I realized you were doing more than just talking." When she opened her mouth, Chad pinned her with a glare and held up a hand to stop her protests. "You were supposed to tell me the moment you found anything pertaining to her disappearance. Investigating is *my* job, not yours. Do you realize how many times you've put yourself in danger?"

"I never thought about it being dangerous until recently."

"Was it when Derek assaulted you in the alley," he said, his eyes turning dark and stormy, "or when the brick crashed through your window, or when you picked up a stalker?"

"Okay, you're right. I should've been more careful, and yes, more forthcoming. But since I haven't been able to go to work, I've had time—"

"To *rest*. That's what you're supposed to be doing, remember?"

"Easier said than done. Anyway, I've had time to ask questions and piece together the information I've gathered. The trips to Tyler's cabin were a big part of that, because you can see Greenleaf Growers from his pond. I think that's where Jenna may have taken some of the pictures. There's an overgrown path on the other side of the pond that leads down the hillside. I suspect it ends behind the outbuildings in the photos."

"Did Tyler show you the path when he took you to the cabin?"

"Um, not exactly." She searched through her purse for a mint, or gum, or anything that would keep her from looking into Chad's penetrating eyes.

"CiCi."

His tone said it all. She glanced up and took a deep breath. "Okay. I saw it the time I went to the pond to dig up what I thought might've been Jenna's grave. But it wasn't."

Chad dropped his head into his hands. "Dear Lord, help me."

"Nope." Mark threw his notebook on the table. "Not touching that. No way I'm writing that down."

Evan shook his head. "Lady, you've got guts, but what were you thinking?"

"I had to know!"

"Tell me about the trips to Tyler's property," Mark growled.

"I went with Tyler the first time and he gave me a tour of the cabin. Afterward, we hiked up a hill to the pond. He said it was

Jenna's favorite place to think. That's when I noticed the six-foot patch of earth across the way. Later, the image kept popping into my head because it reminded me of a grave. So, I went back."

"To dig up Jenna's body?"

She nodded. "I couldn't dig very deep because of the rocks."

"Did you notice anything else unusual during your visits to the cabin?"

She stopped and her breathing hitched. She gnawed on her lower lip to keep the words from gushing forth before she had a chance to gather her thoughts.

"CiCi, answer the question," Chad said.

She sighed. "Yes."

"What did you see?" Chad leaned forward, as did Mark and Evan.

She swallowed hard and took a deep breath before continuing. "Evan arguing with some guy, and the guy made him leave the area. Then, a car that looked exactly like one that's been following me pulled into the restricted area at the back of Greenleaf Growers. Even with binoculars, I couldn't see the driver. After the car left, I noticed the guy Evan argued with watching *me* through a pair of binoculars."

The room fell silent. Chad raked a hand through his hair while Mark rubbed the back of his thick neck.

Evan pulled his phone from his pocket and flipped his fingers across the screen. "Tell me if any of these guys look familiar."

CiCi took the phone and scrolled through the pictures. "This one."

Evan took the phone back, glanced at the photo, and shook his head. "That's not good."

Chad exhaled. "What else did you find, CiCi?"

She pursed her lips and glanced away. After a few seconds had passed, she looked Chad square in the eyes. "You're not going to like this, but it's one of the reasons I needed to talk to you. I found a key in the bottom of Jenna's box."

"And?"

"I kept it in my purse, hoping to ask Katherine or Tyler if they knew what it went to."

"And? What does it have to do with Tyler's cabin?"

"That's where I found another box." She explained her urgent need to use the bathroom, entering Tyler's cabin using a key he'd hidden over a window frame, and later letting curiosity get the best of her when she tried the key in Jenna's desk. "The metal box had been tucked away in a secret compartment. I don't know what's inside. The key is stuck in the lock and I can't get it open."

"Holy crap, CiCi! You entered Tyler's cabin without his permission and took his property? What the hell were you thinking?" The alarm in Chad's voice echoed in the room.

"I'd been so focused on finding Jenna, I guess I wasn't. I figured the contents were important. After all, she'd gone to the trouble of hiding that box where even Tyler couldn't find it. I had to know what was inside."

"Where's the box now?" Mark asked.

"On the floor of my Jeep behind the driver's seat."

He took her by the elbow and tilted his head toward the door. "Let's grab that box from the back of your car and give Chad time to breathe."

THIRTY-FOUR

CiCi followed Mark back to the conference room. He closed the door behind them and took a seat next to Chad. Evan stood off to one side, drinking a cup of coffee. Her eyes moved from face to face, but their attention remained riveted on the red metal box in her hands. They seemed to be mesmerized by the key that dangled from the lock. She placed the box in the middle of the table.

No one moved. No one said a word. No one touched the box.

Chad's eyes narrowed and his mouth twisted into a tight line. He leaned over and, in whispered tones, conferred with Mark. Mark checked his watch, shook his head, and whispered back. They bantered back and forth before coming to an agreement.

Mark nodded to her and leaned back in his chair. "We're going to have Tyler come to the station so we can straighten this out. For now, the box will remain in our custody. Can you be here at ten tomorrow morning?"

"How about eleven? Chad and I have a meeting with the lawyer at eight-thirty. Chad should be finished by nine, but I'll need to stay a bit longer to take care of other business."

Chad's phone rang. He answered, and within seconds his eyes

darted in her direction. He stood and paced the room as he listened. He nodded to Mark, who gathered his notes as though he'd been privy to the conversation.

What's going on? Whatever it is, I think it involves me.

Mark stuck his head out of the room and called for an officer. "Take this man back to his cell." Evan was cuffed and led from the room.

Chad hung up, came around the table, and stopped in front of her, a mixture of anger and concern written on his face. "That was your complex manager. He's been trying to reach you."

She quickly pulled out her cell phone and sighed. "It's dead. I guess I forgot to charge it last night. I'll bet he's looking for his measuring tape. He left it on my counter the other day. But why call? He has a key."

Chad paused before delivering the news. "Someone broke into your house."

It took a few seconds for the news to register. She turned and ran from the room. Chad reached out for her, but she evaded his grasp.

"Wait! I'll drive, just give me a minute," he called.

"No. I'll meet you there." She dashed out of the building and didn't stop until her butt was firmly planted in the driver's seat of her Jeep. She gunned the engine and peeled from the lot, her mind reliving the damage done to her home when it was vandalized five months earlier.

Her lead foot proved to be of little help, as the lights at every intersection turned red the moment she approached. On the final stretch, wailing sirens and flashing lights forced her to momentarily pull to the side of the road. She fumed when Chad's and Mark's vehicles whizzed past. *Cheaters!*

When she arrived, they stood at her front door talking with Brian and Officer Guzman.

"It looks like he climbed up the trellis to the balcony," Guzman said, "broke out a pane of glass, and entered through the bedroom."

Mark scanned the area as he spoke to Guzman. "Talk to the

neighbors. She lives in the end unit next to a wooded area, so I doubt anyone saw anything."

When she'd calmed down enough to understand the damage inside was minimal, Chad handed her a pair of gloves and gave instructions to touch as little as possible until the place could be dusted for fingerprints.

She entered, expecting to see a disaster, and sighed with relief when she didn't. Mark pulled out his phone and snapped pictures as they walked through the area. The hall closet door hadn't been closed all the way and storage boxes had been pulled from the top shelf. The dining room chairs sat askew from the table. The sliding glass door stood open. She pointed to the empty spot beside the buffet. "Jenna's box is gone."

While Mark showed the crime scene tech where to start dusting for prints, CiCi turned and went upstairs. Chad followed. Her heart raced, and her breathing quickened. She glanced around the room, taking it all in. The closet doors were open, as was the drawer to her nightstand. She checked her jewelry box, but nothing had been taken. Her laptop sat on the desk next to the printer. She stepped over, slid her hand into the bedside caddy that hung from the side of her mattress, and checked for the gun she kept hidden behind a book in one of the pockets. "Well, my gun, laptop, and jewelry are still here. At first glance, I'd say Jenna's box was the only thing taken."

Chad gently placed a hand on her shoulder. "You okay?"

She lifted her chin. "I will be. It just reminds me of ..."

Chad nodded. "I know. The damage is minor, but the danger's the same. Pack a bag. I want you back at my place."

"Thanks, but I'll be fine. There's plenty of daylight left and I'm sure Brian will have the windowpane fixed in no time."

"That's not the point, CiCi, and you know it. Your home has been vandalized twice now. I've told you this before. I protect those I love—no apologies, no regrets. Nothing has changed."

She shook her head, turned away, and rubbed her temples. "I just don't know if that's a good idea. I'm so confused right now.

What with the two cases overlapping, the break-in, and the tension between *us*, I don't know if I can handle any more."

"These are rough characters we're dealing with, CiCi." He placed a gentle hand on her shoulder and softened his tone. "Stay with me so that I know that you're safe. Besides, aren't we long overdue for a talk?"

"We are," she whispered.

CiCi grabbed her phone charger and packed a small overnight bag. After Chad conferred with Mark and Guzman, he escorted her to his truck. She slipped on her sunglasses and leaned her head back against the seat, listening to their favorite country music station. He remained silent, she assumed mulling over the events of the day. Were it not for the break-in, she had no doubt he would've stayed to help Mark or gone back to the office to review the notes they'd taken earlier. She thought of the break-in as he drove through town. Her mind barely registered when the truck pulled to a stop at a scenic spot in Meadowlark Park. The area was deserted except for the ducks and geese that pecked at the ground beneath the picnic tables hoping to find errant crumbs to eat.

Chad shut off the engine. "I thought some fresh air would be helpful."

They got out and walked across the grass and down the beaten path to the south side of the large pond. At the end of a short pier, they leaned against the wood railing and listened to the water lapping against the shoreline. The sun sat low in the sky and cast a shimmery orange streak across the surface of the water. The crisp October breeze felt chillier than it had in town. Chad removed his jacket, wrapped it around her shoulders, and turned her to face him. His kind gesture was that of a fiancé, but his demeanor was all detective.

"Why didn't you tell me what you've been up to?" he asked.

"I should have, and that's on me. I never really thought my asking questions would lead anywhere."

"But it did. It landed you in the middle of a police investigation, *again*."

"It wasn't intentional, and I didn't want to worry you for nothing. Unlike your Detective Logan, I'm perfectly capable of asking questions, getting people to talk, and gathering information."

"That might be true, but talking to people you view as suspects in your cousin's disappearance is dangerous business. I don't want to see you get hurt."

"I know you don't. When things got out of hand at The Tap & Keg, I knew I had to tell you. And I tried—several times, but you were busy and, well, truthfully, I didn't push the matter because I was scared to bring it up."

"You should never be afraid to talk to me about anything. Don't you get it? I want to be the first person you turn to, in good times and in bad."

"I wanted to explain last night, but—"

He looked out over the water and shook his head with regret. "I know. When I heard you'd been kissing someone else, I was shocked. Angry. Jealous."

"For the record, *he* kissed me." She placed her hand on his forearm and leaned her head against his shoulder. "You should know by now you're the only man I'll ever love. We are meant to be together."

The corners of his mouth lifted. "I know. I should've listened to Mark. He told me there had to be more to the story, and he was right. If I'd known it was Evan that kissed you, I wouldn't have gone crazy."

CiCi frowned. "I'm confused. So, now you don't mind that Evan kissed me?"

Chad chuckled. "Sugar, you're not his type."

"Oh? And what type would that be?"

"It's complicated."

"Complicated, my foot. This caused a rift in our relationship. I deserve to know what you're talking about." She waited while he debated whether he should or shouldn't give her an explanation.

"Okay, and I'm only telling you this because Evan gave me

permission to if I needed a 'get out of jail' card. It's not something anyone else needs to know. Understand?"

"Um, okay?" she said hesitantly.

"CiCi, everyone can see you're a beautiful, desirable woman, but Evan's flirting and kissing—it's all just an act. Acting is a big part of being an undercover officer."

"Well, he's certainly good at his job."

"And that's all it is to him—a job. Outside of work, he prefers someone with a higher level of testosterone than you'll ever have."

She let the words sink in, and the light of understanding dawned. "Oh!"

"No one on the force here knows but me, and I aim to keep it that way. It's his story to tell, if and when he wants to."

The puttering sound of a motor neared, and they turned to watch a small boat cruising toward the marina.

"Forget Evan. Let's get back to us." Chad sighed and took her hand in his. "I owe you an apology. I'm sorry I doubted you, sorry I left the way I did, sorry I didn't return your calls. Will you forgive me?"

"Yes. I didn't react much better than you, and it was my lapse in judgment that got us into this mess. Forgive me?"

"Yes." He cupped her face and gave her a gentle kiss.

"So, what's next?"

"For us? After last night, I'd say we need to work on our communication skills before our next meeting with Pastor Young."

He pulled her into a hug and brushed a kiss across her forehead. She held on tight, refusing to let go. When his stomach growled, he rolled his eyes. "I'm hungry. How about you?"

She nodded. "I didn't eat much for lunch other than birthday cake. The food at Sunflower Village is rather bland."

"I know just the thing," he said.

Holding hands, they walked back to the truck and drove to the Speckled Pig. Chad placed their order while CiCi grabbed two drinks and picked out a booth. A minute later, he slid into the seat across from her. When the server called their ticket number, Chad retrieved their food: a slab of ribs with extra sauce, a large barbeque beef sandwich, seasoned fries, coleslaw, baked beans, Texas toast, and a cookie.

Chad laughed at the startled look on her face. "The cookie's yours, but I thought we'd share the rest. I grabbed a takeout box for whatever we don't eat."

As they ate, she answered his questions in detail about her conversations with Tyler, Mr. Rivera, Serena, and Heather.

"Who's Flash again?"

"The photographer. He and Derek lived in the same apartment building at one time, and Jenna took photography classes from him. He's the one who told me where Derek played and gave me his current address."

Chad sat back and stopped eating. "You went to his house?"

She nodded and dragged several fries through a mound of ketchup. "Trailer. He wasn't home. That's why I decided to look him up at The Tap & Keg."

"You said you wore a disguise. How did he recognize you?" he said, tossing a rib bone on a spare plate and then sucking the barbeque sauce off his fingers.

"There was a catfight, and someone yanked my wig off. I realized I was in trouble the moment he dragged me into the alley. Did I tell you my dad came to my rescue before Evan showed up? I couldn't believe it."

"Don't trust him, CiCi. He's fully aware your court date is coming up."

She sighed and then took a drink. "I know."

"And who knows what either of them might've done if Evan hadn't come along."

"Yeah, he got me out of one mess and kissed me into another."

He grinned. "Should I be worried he's a better kisser?"

"No comparison." She put a rib on her plate and stared at the woman at the counter. "There's Serena."

As Serena stepped aside to wait for her order, she noticed CiCi sitting nearby. She glanced around as if to hide, but realized she'd been seen. She held her head up and approached with an air of confidence. "Hey. I guess we're both craving barbeque."

"Yeah, what a coincidence. At first, I wondered if you were following me."

"Why would I do that?"

Chad stood. "Someone's been checking up on her comings and goings. Know anything about that?"

Serena looked puzzled. "No, why would I?"

CiCi shrugged. "The first time I noticed the car following me was after I asked you about Jenna. I thought maybe you were trying to see if I dug up any leads for your story."

"Sorry, not me. They're calling my number. Gotta go," She scurried to the counter, grabbed a take-out bag of food, and made a dash for the door.

"I'll be back," Chad said. He caught up with her just as she slid behind the driver's seat of her vehicle. He leaned a forearm against the roof of her car, his height making him more intimidating than usual.

CiCi watched with interest and answered her ringing phone without hesitation. The gravely, muffled voice on the phone sent a chill down her spine. Moments later, Chad returned. Stunned, she still held the phone in her shaking hand when he slid into the seat across from her.

"Sugar, what's wrong?" He took the phone from her hand, but the screen had gone blank.

"He...he said he wants the other pictures—the *good* ones—*or else.*"

"Who was it? Did you recognize the voice?"

"No, but how did he get my number?"

He stood. "Let's go. Now."

"But we haven't finished—"

"Leave it. We'll grab something later."

She hastily folded the foil wrapping over the slab of ribs and stuffed it into a take-out box. He took her by the elbow and whisked her out to the truck. He made a couple of quick phone calls and drove straight to the police station. Once there, she gave a statement. Mark took her phone, copied down the last incoming number, and began the process to obtain a trace on the call. When there was nothing more to be done, CiCi and Chad left for the night.

The cab of his truck was heavily scented with the aroma of barbeque as they drove in silence. Chad gently held her hand as he continually checked his rearview mirror. The planes of his face were hard, and his jaw was tight with tension. He took a couple of U-turns and backtracked twice before turning down his street. He carried her bag inside while she brought in the leftover food. He double-checked all the locks and pulled the blinds.

"Looks like I made the right decision to stay here for a few nights."

He snorted a laugh. "If that's how you want to remember it, fine. Now, let's finish off those ribs."

THIRTY-FIVE

Early the next morning, CiCi scampered down the hall, hoping to beat Chad to the shower. His bedroom door stood slightly open and the room was dark. The aroma of coffee scented the air. From the hallway, she peeked into the kitchen. The coffee pot was filled with a dark brew, but the room was otherwise empty. Living room, also empty. She turned and bumped into him as he exited the bathroom. He reached out and kept her from falling.

"You okay?" he asked.

Words failed to form as her eyes skimmed over his chiseled, half-naked body. A few strands of damp hair fell across his forehead. Beads of water dotted the fierce tattoos on his broad shoulders and biceps, and his woodsy aftershave lingered in the air. Her eyes followed the tufts of curly dark hair that spanned his chest, tapered at his waist, and disappeared into a pair of low-slung sleep pants.

Oh, my. A flood of desire washed over her. She swallowed hard and looked up to find him taking inventory as well. His eyes had a hungry gleam, and it was evident he wasn't thinking about breakfast. To his amusement, she crossed her arms over her chest, certain he could see the rapid beating of her heart—and more—

through the thin material. She stepped aside to let him by. He leaned in for a kiss, but she turned and offered her cheek. "Haven't brushed yet."

He chuckled, then nibbled on her ear before pressing light kisses down her neck. His hand slipped under her top and caressed the sensitive skin along the side of her ribcage. "Sure you don't want to move up the wedding date?"

A small moan escaped her lips. "Believe me, it's tempting, but we both agreed on a spring wedding. Remember?" She stepped back and playfully shoved him in the direction of his bedroom before heading to the kitchen for a cup of caffeine.

"I know. I want you to have the wedding you've always dreamed of, but March seems so far away," he called from the bedroom.

"March will be here before we know it," she said. She savored her first sip and then pushed away from the counter. "It won't take me long to get ready, and then you can drop me off at my place so I can check on things. If we both drive to the lawyer's office, you won't have to come back to get me when I'm finished."

"Not gonna happen. I'll drive us this morning, and Pete will pick you up when you're finished and bring you to the station."

"Oh." Hearing his western boots thump against the hardwood floor, she turned and saw him walking down the hallway fully dressed, except for his shoulder holster. *How does he do that? I suppose wearing the official black or tan pants and a RGPD polo takes the guesswork out of getting dressed in the morning.* "Wow. That was fast."

"I know when to pace myself," he said, giving her a wink.

"Good to know." She looked away to hide her smile. "So, Mark never told me why he wants to see me at eleven."

"You're going to tell Tyler you stole his property."

CiCi and Chad followed Saundra down the hall and stopped in front of the door that had "Dennis Browning, Attorney-At-Law" printed in bold letters across the frosted glass in the upper half of the door. She rapped twice and then opened the door. Dennis stood the moment they entered and came around the large mahogany desk to greet them. Saundra softly closed the door on her way out.

His warmth and friendliness eased CiCi's mild case of jitters, though she had no reason to be nervous around Dennis. They first met while settling her mother's estate and remained in contact to deal with the business end of the inheritance. Since Dennis and Megan, Chad's sister, were dating, CiCi and Chad also occasionally saw him on a personal level.

Everyone took a seat. Dennis shuffled through papers on his desk as they made small talk. When he'd found what he'd been looking for, he turned his attention to the task at hand.

"I've drawn up the paperwork that will ensure the entirety of your inheritance will transfer to Chad should something happen to you. Let's go over each document before I answer any questions you have."

They spent the next forty-five minutes studying the documents, asking questions, and listening to Dennis' explanations. At the conclusion, Dennis called in Saundra to witness the signatures. CiCi signed, then handed the pen to Chad.

He paused. "Are you sure this is what you want?"

"Positive. We've talked about this. We'll be married soon, and what's mine is yours. I'll feel much better knowing everything will be left in good hands should something happen, not that it will."

He squeezed her hand and then scribbled his name on a half a dozen signature lines. When he finished, his phone buzzed. He glanced at the screen and sent a quick text. "Sorry about that," he offered. Dennis waved off his apology.

Saundra signed her name and gave a notary stamp of approval where required by law before leaving the office. Dennis double-checked the documents, then gathered the papers and placed them in a folder. "Now," he said, "let's move on to the next item on the agenda."

Chad stood. "If you don't need me any longer, I need to get to work." He shook hands with Dennis and brushed a kiss across

CiCi's cheek. "Pete will be waiting in the lobby whenever you're done here. No hurry."

She nodded and watched him leave.

"Having car trouble? I could've given you a ride if you'd asked."

"No, no car trouble." In response to Dennis' questioning look, she added, "While searching for my cousin who disappeared last year, I seem to have crossed paths with a police investigation. Someone broke into my house last night, so Chad is taking extra precautions. You know how he is."

"I do, and I'm sure he has reason for concern. We've only known each other for six months, but I have the utmost respect for his professional judgment." Dennis picked up the phone and instructed Saundra to keep Pete supplied with coffee whenever he arrived.

"Now," he said, "let's proceed with your request to bolster the ongoing needs of A Hand Up. It's an excellent organization, but it struggles to stay afloat as much as the families they try to help. Your mother and grandmother would be pleased with your choice."

"I'd like to think so."

"I assume you'll want to do as they did and keep your identity concealed. That allows you the freedom to enjoy life without being pestered to support every cause that comes along."

"I do. Thank you." Once she reviewed the paperwork and approved the clause concerning how the money could be spent, she signed her name.

CiCi slipped on her sunglasses and slid into the passenger seat of Pete's truck. She zipped up her coat against the chill and glanced at the clock on the dash. "Can we swing by the jewelry store on Maple? I need to get the clasp fixed on my watch."

"Sure, we have plenty of time." He cast a sideways glance at her. "I hear you got yourself mixed up in a police investigation again."

"Let me guess. You've been talking with Chad."

"I have. Wasn't especially smart on your part, missy, breaking into Tyler's cabin."

Pete must've taught Chad everything he knew about giving a frosty glare. "I know. I'm guessing Mark expects me to smooth things over with Tyler today."

After leaving her watch at the jeweler's, they headed toward the police station. As Pete pulled to a stop and shut off the engine, CiCi asked, "Where are we?"

"This is a side entrance for employees only. We thought it best to be discreet in case someone is watching you. Since I've been consulting on the case and sharing my private notes, Chief Dougan gave me the entry code. We should be good to go."

CiCi led the way up the stairs and Pete followed. She had taken a couple of steps when the ground shifted beneath her feet. *No, please, not now.* She swayed, then stumbled. Pete, or his double, caught her and eased her onto a step. As he mumbled something into his phone, she closed her eyes, hoping to lessen the dizziness.

"Just relax, missy," Pete said in a soothing tone.

She nodded without opening her eyes. "I'm fine, Pete, really," she whispered.

A few moments later, the door behind her whooshed open and footsteps rushed down the stairs. A hand gently brushed back a strand of windblown hair from her face, and then cupped her cheek. She leaned into the familiar touch and sighed. "I'm fine, Chad. Just a little dizzy. It wasn't near as bad as last time."

"That's not saying much. If you rested more instead of chasing leads and trying to dig up bodies, you might not have *any* dizzy spells."

"She *what?*" Pete sputtered.

"Oh, I didn't tell you about that, did I?"

Pete shook his head in disbelief. "I'm not sure I want to know."

CiCi stood and brushed off her backside. Chad led her inside to Mark's empty office, while Pete headed to the conference room. She removed her jacket, draped it over a chair, and took a seat. Chad sat in the chair beside her. Seconds later, Mark entered the room. He nodded to Chad, then walked around his desk and took a seat. She squirmed under his intense gaze.

"Pete said you had another episode. You okay? If not, we can do this another time."

"I'm fine. Let's get this over with."

"We have only a few minutes before Tyler gets here. We've dusted the box for prints. Has anyone other than you touched it?"

She frowned. "No, no one. Wait. Yes, when I returned the rental car. I'd left the box in the trunk and the attendant found it when he inspected the car."

"Okay, that'll probably match the third set of prints we found, but we'll check to make sure. I assume the other two belong to you and Jenna. I haven't told Tyler why—"

A rap at the door cut him off, and Stacy leaned in. "Mr. Quinn is here."

Chad stood as Tyler stepped into the room and shook hands with the two detectives.

"Please, call me Tyler." His friendly smile faded when he caught sight of CiCi. "I didn't expect to see you here."

She swallowed hard and looked away.

Chad gestured to the empty chair. Tyler nodded and took a seat.

"CiCi has something to confess," Mark said.

"Like what? That she went inside my cabin without my permission?"

CiCi eyes widened. "How did you know?"

"The bathroom towels were hung up nice and neat, and the dust on Jenna's desk and chair had been disturbed. It's called the process of elimination. Both of my contractors pushed back their work for one reason or another. You're the only one who's been to my cabin recently and knew where I'd hidden the key."

CiCi opened her mouth but closed it without uttering a word.

"If it had been anyone else, I'd file charges," Tyler said, giving her a pointed look.

"Let's take a breath, everyone," Mark said. "CiCi, I think Tyler deserves to hear why you were in his cabin, and what you found there."

CiCi swallowed and started from the moment she drove onto his property. In her mind, her actions sounded reasonable for someone willing to do whatever it took to find a loved one—Tyler's loved one. "I'm sorry, Tyler. I had this key of Jenna's and my curiosity got the best of me. When I found the box, I became convinced it held a clue to her disappearance. Otherwise, why would she hide it so well?"

His eyes fell on the red metal box and the key fob dangling from the lock. "Is that it?"

She nodded. "The key fits, but it's stuck and won't open."

"I went through that desk more than once. That box wasn't there."

"I'm sure you did. But what you didn't know is that the desk is custom-made and has hidden compartments," she said.

After digesting the information, Tyler turned to Mark. "Well, now what, Detective?"

"I think it's best if the box is returned to you."

CiCi frowned and started to protest. "But, Mark—"

Mark held up a hand to CiCi. "I can't have you turn in stolen merchandise, especially if it contains anything that relates to Jenna's disappearance. That would make the evidence inadmissible in a court of law." He then turned to address Tyler. "However, as the rightful owner of the box, *you* can turn it in. Once we get it open, we'll examine the contents and compare it to our notes. The box and any items that don't relate directly to Jenna's disappearance will be returned to you."

Tyler sighed, then looked at CiCi. "I'm not happy that you entered my home uninvited, but I admire your heart and tenacity. I remember doing a few foolish things myself when I first searched for Jenna." With a curious look, he lifted the box from the desk and shook it. He ran his fingers over the key fob, then nodded to the detective. "Do whatever you need to do if it'll help find out what happened to her."

Mark pulled a form from his desk drawer, filled it out, signed the bottom, and handed the receipt for the box to Tyler. After reading the form, he folded it and tucked it into his shirt pocket. Mark picked up the box and shook Tyler's hand. "Tyler, if you don't have any other questions for me, I'll get started."

"Fine. Just keep me posted on what you find."

Mark nodded and left with the box.

Chad looked at CiCi, then turned his focus to Tyler. "I have a question for you. Did Jenna ever mention anything about Greenleaf Growers?"

Tyler frowned. "Not that I recall. Why?"

Chad shook his head. "Just wondering."

"I think Greenleaf plans to expand their operation. After Jenna disappeared, they made me an offer to buy the acreage that backs up to their land. I refused. Then a few months ago, I caught a couple of guys lurking around the pond. Said they thought the property was for rent," Tyler said, making air quotes with his fingers. "I figured they were from Greenleaf, so I sent them packing."

"Interesting," Chad said, rubbing a hand across his chin.

"Tyler, I have a few pictures that Jenna took," CiCi said. "Most are blurry. Why is that? Was she a nervous sort of person? Taking medication?"

Tyler stood, put his hands into his pants pockets, and walked over to the window. He stared outside for several moments, his shoulders seeming to sag with an unknown weight. When he turned, his eyes glistened with moisture. "Can this stay just between us?"

CiCi and Chad nodded and waited for him to continue.

"Jenna suspected she had early-onset Parkinson's." Tyler paused to compose himself before continuing. "She was terrified of how her life would change. I told her I loved her, that I would be by her side no matter what. She resisted, wanted to be as independent as she possibly could for as long as she could. Said she didn't want to hold me back, didn't want to be a burden. But I loved her far too much to ever think of her as a burden."

CiCi's breathing hitched as if a knife had pierced her heart. *Jenna's fears were identical to my own, right down to how my episodes might affect my relationship with Chad.* She cleared her throat to ward off the emotions that threatened to surface. "Did she ever confirm she had Parkinson's?"

"No, she never did. That's another thing we fought over. I wanted to know *exactly* what we were dealing with instead of living under a cloud of uncertainty. The slight shaking could've been caused by any number of things. I thought it was most likely a side effect of her new asthma medication, but she assumed the worst. That's partly why she moved out, to have some space and decide what she wanted to do. She never gave the engagement ring back or called off the wedding, so I thought we'd work through it together. She was intent, though, on snagging that one big story before …"

CiCi glanced at Chad. Though his expression remained professional, his eyes said otherwise. He, too, had made the connection. CiCi looked away. "Did Katherine know?"

Tyler sighed. "No, and I promised Jenna I wouldn't tell her."

"She must've had a good reason."

"What reason could ever be good enough to keep something like that from the people who love you, from people who would rather take your place than see you suffer?"

CiCi glanced over and saw Tyler's pain mirrored in Chad's eyes. She swiped away the tear that trickled down her cheek. *I've been so selfish. I haven't given much thought about how my refusal to address my health issues might affect Chad.*

Tyler cleared his throat and addressed CiCi. "I know it must've been a shock to suddenly find out you have a cousin who's missing, and I appreciate you wanting to find her. It's just that…after all this time, it's reopened old wounds and brought the heartache back to the surface. It's difficult, because I still love her."

She lowered her head. "I'm sorry, Tyler. I was only trying to help."

"I know." He laid a gentle hand on her shoulder as he passed. He reached out and shook hands with Chad, who thanked Tyler for his cooperation and promised to keep him apprised of any new developments.

CiCi stared at the floor, her mind reeling with guilt, sorrow, and questions. When she looked up, Chad stepped forward. She stood and wrapped her arms around him and held tight until the ache in her heart subsided.

"I know you probably feel like talking," Chad whispered as he stroked her back, "but I don't think now is the time or the place."

"You're right. It can wait."

"Did you have pictures to show me?"

THIRTY-SIX

CiCi turned her focus to the task at hand. "Can I use your computer? The pictures Jenna took at the farmers' market last year were sent to my email. I glanced at them on my phone, but not on a bigger screen. Maybe we can spot something that caused Greenleaf to throw a fit about the publicity. From what I've pieced together, that's about the time Jenna became chummy with Derek."

"Sure," Chad said. They walked down the hall to Chad's office, where he rounded the desk and nudged his computer awake.

She slipped into his office chair, logged into her email account, and found the photos she'd gotten from Jimmy. They scrolled through the pics, one by one, the larger screen making the details more visible. "There!" she exclaimed, pointing at the screen. "I knew that guy looked familiar. That's Zach, Ashley's boyfriend. He works part-time at Midwest Body. I think he's the one who spray-painted my Jeep." She squinted and leaned closer to the screen. "There's Bernice. That's Derek, selling herbs to Zach."

Chad knelt beside her and tapped a few keys, fast forwarding through the next few shots, and back again. "Looks like he took something from his apron and slipped it in the bag with the herbs. Money is exchanged in this next shot, and then the cash goes into his apron, not the money box Bernice uses." Chad scrolled through a couple of more pictures. "These guys," he said, pointing to another picture, "Neither of these guys strike me as someone who knows their way around a kitchen, let alone knows how to use herbs."

A rap sounded at Chad's door. Mark stepped inside. "We got a video from the neighbor's doorbell camera. She lives across the street from CiCi, so it might be too far away to make a positive identification."

Chad straightened. "Let's take a look."

"It's in the conference room, along with the box. One of the guys got the key out and the box unlocked, but we haven't opened it yet. Thought you'd want to do the honors. Oh, and Pete left, but said he'd be back soon."

Chad nodded and motioned for her to follow them to the conference room, where they sat and pulled up the neighbor's video. In it, a man, presumably the neighbor's husband, pulled into their driveway at the same time a rusty green pickup pulled up across the street. The driver of the pickup got out, rang CiCi's doorbell, then peered in the windows when he didn't get a response. After glancing around, he walked down the side of the building and disappeared around back.

"Chad, that looks like Zach, Ashley's boyfriend," she said.

"I'll have an officer bring him in." He turned his attention to the box on the table. "Well, let's hope this little box is worth all the trouble it's caused."

He opened the lid and removed a small stack of photos. Determined to see it through, he spread them across the table. Mark, Chad, and CiCi studied each one.

"Chad," CiCi said, "I think some of these are edited versions of the originals I found in Heather's desk. These must be the ones Derek's boss wants. Jenna must've taken a lot of photography classes in order to be able to sharpen the images this good. Here's some of Derek and Crystal and several of their amps. That's odd."

"Do you recognize these, CiCi?" Mark asked, holding a few pics aloft.

She looked at each and nodded. "I think that's the inside of the building that's off-limits at the back of Greenleaf Growers. From the angle, I'd say they were taken from the ravine just beyond Tyler's pond."

She frowned and looked at the images spread across the table. "In this picture, the wall behind the chemicals on the table looks like the inside wall of that building. I don't know much about this stuff, but these pics make me think of what a meth lab might look like."

She glanced at the hardened faces of Chad and Mark as they poured over the pictures yet again. Chad and Mark exchanged a cryptic look.

Her eyes widened. "Is that what Jenna discovered—a meth lab?" Stunned that her guess was right, she slumped back in her seat, her mind whirling with questions.

Mark turned and sent a text. A few minutes later, he read the reply and nodded to Chad when he'd finished. "Evan will be here soon. Nothing we can do now but wait. How about I order pizza?"

"Good idea," Chad said, sitting back and raking a hand through his hair.

Evan and Pete showed up shortly after the delivery guy left. Between the five of them, the pizzas disappeared in no time. After the boxes were disposed of, Pete and Evan were filled in on the latest developments. While they rehashed the old information and the new, CiCi excused herself to freshen up. She applied a fresh coat of lip gloss and swept her hair up into a loose ponytail. As she came back down the hall, she heard raised voices. She paused outside the room and listened to Evan vent his frustrations.

"I'm telling you, man, I don't know who's in charge! I've talked to him once on the phone, but that's it."

"Try harder," Mark shot back. "We don't have any more time to waste."

CiCi slipped into the room and took a seat.

Evan snatched up a couple of photos and waved them in the air.

"I haven't even been able to get a look inside the outbuilding. These pictures are as close as I've come."

Mark nodded. "I think we have cause to go in and shut down the operation, but we need to nab the head guy to make it a clean sweep. Otherwise, he's just going to open up shop in a different location."

Evan glanced over at CiCi and held up a picture. "Tell me why you think this was taken from Tyler's property."

She walked over and took a closer look. She briefly glanced at the four men in the room, then looked away. "Well, um, after I dug what turned out not to be Jenna's grave, I hiked down a trail until it became too steep to continue. From where I stopped, I could see the back and side of the building. One of the windowpanes had been broken out, same as in this picture. It's a high window, though. Jenna would've had to stand on one of the metal barrels to see inside."

"That area is surrounded by fencing."

"Where there's a will, there's a way. And Jenna must have found a way. I'll bet she wore her camo jacket to blend in on the trail."

The men mulled over the possibilities and looked over the aerial map of the adjoining properties. CiCi's phone rang and she stepped aside to answer the call. Her heart nearly stopped the moment she heard the menacing digitized voice.

"Got the pictures?"

"Who is this?" she asked. A pause ensued. "A name, or I'll hang up," she commanded. The sharpness in her voice caused the men to stop and give her their undivided attention.

"Just call me Chief."

"What kind of name is *that*?"

"I'm not in the mood to play games with you," he snapped.

"I'm not playing games." She tilted the phone away from her ear as the men gathered around to listen.

"Good. Then let's meet. I want those pictures."

She took in the serious expressions on the faces around her. Her grip tightened on the phone and she struggled to keep the panic from her voice. "What makes you think I have them?"

"You're nosy, just like your cousin, always meddling in other people's business."

"Like your *side business* at Greenleaf?" she taunted.

"I see you've figured it out, which you couldn't have done if you didn't have those photos. Have you told that cop boyfriend of yours?"

The moment she caught a glimpse of Evan, an idea formed—one sure to get her out of meeting the meth king. "That controlling jerk? No way I'd tell him. Besides, we broke up after I started seeing Mace." She locked eyes with Chad, who gave a slight nod to her plan to put Evan in contact with the head of the drug operation.

"I don't believe you."

"No? Why don't you ask Mace yourself? He's right here."

Chief paused. "Put him on."

CiCi handed the phone to Evan, who conjured up his alter ego in a matter of seconds and stepped away from the crowd. "Yeah, boss?" He scowled at CiCi as he listened. "Yeah, she can be a handful. I guess that cop wasn't man enough to keep her in line, but I know how to handle women like her." He paused, and his mouth pinched into a tight line. "Sure, you can count on me...okay, here she is." He handed the phone back to CiCi.

"Chief? I'll hand the pictures over to Mace and you can get them from him."

"Not good enough. I want *you* to deliver them."

She swallowed the huge lump in her throat. Her plan had taken a sudden detour. "Why me? I didn't have anything to do with the arrangement you had with Jenna."

"So you say, yet you suddenly had enough money to buy Five Star. I can only assume Jenna funded your new business venture with some of *my* money."

"That's crazy!"

"Perhaps. We'll talk about it when we meet."

"What if I refuse or disappear like Jenna did—and take the pictures with me?"

Chief swore under his breath. "Then you'll force me to have a private talk with Katherine. Is that what you want?"

CiCi's heart skipped a beat. "You stay away from her! She knows nothing about this."

Mark, Chad, and Pete exchanged glances. Mark nodded, and Pete hurried from the room.

"Tomorrow evening, seven o'clock, at Greenleaf. You and Mace come alone and bring the pictures." Without waiting for an answer, he ended the call.

CiCi stared at the phone in disbelief. Chad, Mark and Evan started talking at the same time, each trying to be heard.

"What did he say, Evan?" Mark asked.

"He'll make it worth my while if I make sure she comes alone and brings the pics."

Mark copied down the number on her phone. "He probably called from another burner phone, same as before."

Evan walked to the table and studied the aerial map of the area. Chad pinned her with a steely glare. She turned to face him, her stance as determined as her voice. "Don't look at me like that. I never intended to get this involved, but I am. *He* called *me*, remember?" She crossed her arms over her chest.

"These are dangerous people, CiCi. You're not going to Greenleaf tomorrow, with or without the pictures. Not. Gonna. Happen."

"Mark," she said, as he walked over to diffuse the situation, "Evan admitted he hasn't been able to flush this guy out. Well, now's your chance. Besides, I'm not going to give him a reason to hurt Katherine." Her eyes widened. "Katherine!" She pushed past the two men and snagged her purse as she bolted for the door.

Chad grabbed her arm. "Where are you going?"

"Katherine's," she said, trying to pry herself from his grip. "I need to warn her."

"Pete's already on his way. He'll put Katherine somewhere safe until this is over."

"Chad," Mark said, "this is what we've been waiting for. We don't have much time to pull together a plan."

He let go of her arm, shook his head, and raked a hand through his hair. "Maybe we can put one of our female officers in disguise and let her take CiCi's place."

"Oh, that's a *great* idea," she scoffed. "Let's see," she said, glancing out onto the work floor as a couple of officers walked past. "She might work if she were five-six instead of five-eleven. Or maybe her, the Korean with the black hair." She turned to face the two men. "Chief has my cell phone number. He knows my name and where I live, so I assume he knows what I look like. Don't you think he'll spot an imposter the moment he gets close?"

"I don't like this either, Chad, but she's got a point," Mark said.

"I'm the only logical choice you have. I can do this, Chad. I'll give him the photos and then get out. After he's arrested, you can find out about the money he's been paying to Jenna, which might lead us right to her. Besides, my new *boyfriend* will be there to protect me."

He cocked an eyebrow. "Is that supposed to make me feel better?"

"I thought it would be reassuring."

"It's not," he sighed. "We'll talk it over, and by *we*, I mean me and Mark." He pulled out his phone and sent a quick text. "Since it looks like I'll be busy here most of the night, I'll have Pete swing by and pick you up after he takes care of Katherine."

Chad, Mark, and Evan studied the map of the area—pointing here, drawing a circle there. Chad dialed a number. "Tyler, I need your help." He moved out of hearing distance and spoke rapid-fire. Mark made several calls, asking for back-up. Evan left to continue his undercover work. The wheels were being set in motion. A short time later, Chad escorted her to the side door, gave her a fierce kiss, and walked her out to Pete's truck.

CiCi buckled up as Pete drove from the lot, his grip firm on the wheel. "You okay, Pete?"

"I'm okay. Are you? I heard what's going down. I don't like it, but it's not my show."

"I'm as surprised as you, but I have no choice. What did you tell Katherine?"

"Very little. You can decide how much to tell her when you see her."

CiCi frowned. "Is she staying at Chad's?"

He shook his head. "No. We're stopping off at Chad's to get your clothes. With him working late, it'd be best to have you and Katherine under the same roof where I can keep an eye on both of you."

After CiCi packed a change of clothes, Pete drove her to a two-story building not far from where she worked. Lacking signage, the nondescript brick exterior gave no clue as to its occupant. He drove around back and keyed in a code to open the wrought iron gate, which closed automatically after they entered. The underground garage surprised her. It was well-lit and ran the entire length of the building. He passed several cars and parked in a space marked "Reserved." He grabbed her bag, took her elbow, and walked a short distance to a nearby elevator. After they stepped inside, he typed in a sequence of numbers and the doors shut.

As they rode to the second floor, she asked, "What is this place? A safe house?"

He gave a half-smile. "In a manner of speaking. PM Security and Surveillance occupies the first floor. The second floor is where I live."

Before she could respond, the elevator doors opened to reveal a large living space decorated in masculine shades of blues and browns. Katherine popped up from the leather sofa and closed the distance in seconds, wrapping CiCi in a crushing hug. She returned the hug while Pete carried her bag down a hallway. When he came back, they gathered around the kitchen table. Katherine fidgeted, eager to hear why Pete had whisked her away from her shop before closing time.

"Let me make a pot of coffee; then you can tell me what all this is about." Katherine stood and filled the reservoir with water, then poured coffee into the filter. A bundle of nervous energy, she wiped down the already clean counter and placed a couple of plates in the dishwasher. Once the coffee pot gurgled to a stop, she took three cups from a cabinet and filled them. CiCi raised an eyebrow at Katherine's familiarity with Pete's kitchen.

Pete grabbed the cream and sugar as Katherine set the cups on the table. She took a seat next to Pete and remained silent as CiCi summarized the day's events without going into too much detail. *No need for her to worry about something she can't control.*

Regardless, Katherine fretted over CiCi being dragged into a dangerous situation. CiCi answered questions as best she could, which did little to reduce Katherine's anxiety. Pete gently placed his hand on hers and gave a slight squeeze. He draped an arm over the back of her chair and said, "Kat, CiCi is tougher than you think, and you can be sure Chad and Mark won't let anything happen to her."

"You're right," Katherine replied, her eyes misting, "but the thought of something—"

"Shake those thoughts out of your head. What do you say? Should we watch a movie after dinner or play a game of Scrabble?"

The corners of Katherine's mouth lifted slightly, and she bumped her shoulder against his. "I'll leave that up to you. But if we play Scrabble, there'll be no swapping out tiles when my back is turned. CiCi will make sure of that."

Pete grinned at CiCi. "She's just sore she lost. Twice."

Katherine stood. "I'm going to freshen up, and then I'll fix us something to eat."

CiCi watched her aunt walk down the hall. Once she was out of earshot, CiCi turned to Pete and smiled. "Should I ask?"

Pete's eyes twinkled as he peered over the rim of his coffee cup. "You can. Doesn't mean you'll get an answer."

THIRTY-SEVEN

Mid-afternoon the next day, CiCi gave Katherine a quick hug before leaving Pete's living quarters, hoping she wouldn't notice the trembling. Despite faking a brave smile, CiCi's nerves were on edge over what the day would bring. She grabbed a jacket, followed Pete to his vehicle, and climbed in. They passed through the iron gate and headed to the edge of town. He navigated a narrow, winding road for about five miles, then veered down a seldom traveled route through the countryside. Once Pete spotted a wayward strip of black cloth tied to a roadside bush, he drove about a quarter-mile farther before taking a dirt path to the east. He slowed to avoid kicking up a dust cloud behind the vehicle. Two miles later, the backside of a rustic shed appeared. He pulled close to the building and parked next to Chad's and Mark's vehicles.

She looked around. "Where are we?"

"Tyler's cabin. Mark and Chad are using it as a base camp of sorts. We came in on a trail Tyler's grandparents used years ago."

"No wonder I didn't recognize it. Who do those vehicles belong to?" Two black vans were parked in the deep shadows of a nearby tree line.

"Reinforcements. Since the main road in passes the turnoff to

Greenleaf, they came in the same way we did so as not to attract attention." He glanced at her. "You ready?"

Conversation stopped and heads turned as they entered the cabin through the back door. The interior seemed crowded. A dozen or more officers were on hand. All were dressed in either black or camouflage, from their long-sleeved shirts to their combat-style boots. Some sat in the living room, bulging duffle bags at their feet. Others drank coffee at the kitchen table. In the addition at the back of the house, two women and two men stood alongside Chad and Mark, studying a map taped to the window. She and Pete walked over, and Mark introduced them to the team he'd assembled from nearby law enforcement communities. Chad glanced at his watch and nodded to Mark.

"It's time," Mark said, clapping his hands and spurring the group into action.

Chad led CiCi by the elbow outside to the front porch. Her brows knitted in puzzlement. "What's happening?"

"They're suiting up and checking their weapons. Mark wants them in place a couple of hours early." He sighed. "You sure you want to do this?"

She nodded. He wrapped his arms around her, and she melted into his embrace, savoring the moment.

"You know I don't like this," he said, "but I need you to know how proud I am of you."

She looked up at him and smiled. "You are? That means a lot to me."

They broke apart at the sound of Mark giving last-minute instructions. They went inside and followed the team into the back yard.

Several men, heavily armed and wearing bullet-proof vests and helmets, formed a circle, each with a hand on a comrade's shoulder. They bowed their heads and prayed for a successful and safe mission. After an "Amen," they dispersed to their assignment. Three men trekked up the trail toward the pond; she assumed, to follow the long path down the steep incline to the rear of the Greenleaf property. The others piled into the back of one of the vans and drove away.

Back inside, Mark gave her an overview of how the operation would go down and went over her part in the general plan. They had talked earlier of having her wired for sound, but vetoed the idea, thinking it too risky if she were searched. Same for wearing a Kevlar vest. At Mark's prompt, Pete dashed out to his truck and returned with a small bag that read PM Security and Surveillance on the side.

"I mentioned this earlier to Mark and Chad. This will take the place of wearing a wire," he said, fishing out a small box. Inside, a two-inch lapel pin was nestled safely in foam. A cute dog and the words "Adopt, Don't Shop" were printed on the face of the button. "Just push the dog's nose to turn on the device. I can monitor and record everything that's said from this end." He pinned it to the shoulder strap of her crossbody purse and made sure the latch was secure.

"Your only job," Mark said, "is to draw this guy onto the property and give him the set of duplicate pictures. That's it. Nothing more. You go in with Evan, you leave with Evan. We'll execute the warrants once you're safely out of the way."

She studied the map and locations of the borrowed officers, asking questions to distract herself from the knots in her stomach. Heads turned at the low rumble of a motorcycle cruising to a stop out front. Chad, hand on his weapon, peered through the opening in the curtain, then gave an "all's-well" sign.

Evan knocked twice and strode through the door. He nodded to Chad and Mark before winking at CiCi. "Hey, Foxy. Ready for our date?"

Before she could answer, Chad growled, "Knock it off, Evan. This isn't a game."

Evan sauntered to the living room, shucked his leather jacket, and plopped on the sofa to watch TV. Mark shook his head and muttered, "That guy acts like he's God's gift to women."

CiCi smiled, his comment easing her tension.

Chad moved to block Evan's view. "Well?"

"Well, what?" Evan countered. "We can't leave now. They're expecting me to go into town to pick her up, and that takes time. Now move so I can see."

Chad took a step forward. "You'd better not let anything happen to her, or—"

"Relax, man. I know how to do my job. Have I ever let you down before?"

"No, you haven't, so don't start now."

The two stared at each other before Chad walked away to put on his gear and check his weapons. Mark followed suit. At the appointed time, Evan slipped on a bulletproof vest and zipped his leather jacket over it. "You ready?"

The time had come. She nodded and put on her jacket. After stashing the envelope of pictures inside her purse and slipping the shoulder strap over her head, she kissed Chad goodbye.

"Be careful, sugar. Get in and get out. Period. We'll handle the rest."

"You be careful, too. I don't want anything to happen to you."

She donned a helmet and hopped on the back of Evan's motorcycle. Her grip tightened around his midsection as he sped down the road and headed to Greenleaf Growers. The business had closed an hour before, leaving the parking lot empty. They drove through the wide gate and to the back corner of the property, where Derek stood in front of a small building.

Evan parked, cut the engine, and lowered the kickstand. CiCi dismounted first, and Evan followed. He removed his helmet, then took hers and set them on the bike. He brushed a strand of hair from her face and whispered, "It's showtime. Remember, my name's Mace, not Evan." He kissed her, then took her hand and walked over to Derek. "Where's the boss man?"

"He'll be here," Derek shot back. He walked over to CiCi and looked her up and down. "Is she wired?"

Mace shook his head. "She's clean."

"Chief wants me to check. Hold her."

CiCi's breath caught in her throat. She turned as if to flee, but Mace stopped her. He removed her purse and jacket and handed them to Derek, who checked every pocket and seam. He tossed them on the ground when he found nothing of interest. Mace gripped her wrists and held her arms out and away from her body as Derek's hands ran over her torso, butt, and up and down both legs. Facing Mace, she stared into his cold eyes. He gave the slightest shake of his head, warning her not to fight it. He turned her around at Derek's command and held her wrists behind her back. With a smirk, Derek slowly ran his hand around the inside waistband of her pants, and back again. Next, he felt the straps of her bra, down the sides, under the band, and then followed the curves of her breasts.

Arching one eyebrow, he stopped. "Well, what do we have here?" he said, his fingertips exploring her cleavage. She struggled when he pulled her shirt up, exposing her chest, but Mace held tight. A grin crept across Derek's face as he eyed her black lace bra. "Jenna could've learned a thing or two from you." His fingers ran over the area he found suspicious.

CiCi's eyes flashed with anger and indignation. "That metal piece is the underwire in my bra, you idiot!" He smiled back in amusement as his hand poised to cup her breast.

"Don't even think about it," Mace growled from over her shoulder.

Derek stopped mid-grope, looked at Mace, then stepped away. Mace released his grip. CiCi pulled her shirt down, picked up her jacket and bag, and moved closer to her "boyfriend." *If that's the worst that can happen, I'll be okay.* Goosebumps formed on her arms. The sun had disappeared, and the air had turned chilly. She slipped on her jacket and zipped it up.

Derek whipped out his phone and placed a call. "Chief? Yeah. She's here, and she's clean." He paused. "Yeah, full crew in the lab tonight." He disconnected, then lit a cigarette.

Ten minutes later, a car rolled to a stop beside the motorcycle. *That's it—the black sedan that's been following me.* Mace slipped his arm around her shoulders and gave a reassuring hug. She barely noticed because her attention remained focused on the vehicle. When the driver emerged, her eyes widened.

"Not who you were expecting, CiCi?" the man asked.

She ran her fingers over the button attached to the shoulder strap of her bag and pressed the dog's nose, hoping the device worked as planned. "That's a clever nickname you gave yourself, Mr. Rivera. I should've made the connection, but I didn't."

With a sinister smirk on his face, the esteemed editor-in-chief of *The Ripley Review* walked over, ignoring Mace altogether. She glanced back at the vehicle.

"Are you expecting someone else? Serena, maybe?" He shook his head. "She borrowed my car tonight to go clubbing with friends in Kansas City. Besides, she doesn't know about my side venture, and I'd like to keep it that way."

"So it was *you* who's been following me?"

"Let's not worry about that. Did you bring them?" When she nodded, he took her by the elbow. "Let's go inside. It colder out than I expected."

Mace grabbed her arm. "Hey, I thought we were just dropping off photos."

Rivera pinned him with a steely gaze. "She and I need to talk—in private. If that's a problem, you can leave."

"If she stays, I stay."

Rivera nodded to Derek, who clearly relished the idea of putting Mace in his place. Derek stepped forward, and CiCi quickly intervened, placing a hand on Mace's chest. "It's okay, hon. Mr. Rivera and I won't be long."

She followed Rivera inside. The building was multi-purpose. There were tables and folding chairs where the field workers probably ate lunch, as well as a couple of cots along the back wall where they could catch a nap. In the small kitchen area, the trashcan overflowed, and the small sink held dirty dishes. Cases of bottled water were stacked six high next to an older model refrigerator.

Rivera turned, his expression cold and callous. "Let me see them."

Tightly clutching her purse, she said, "First, I want to know where Jenna is. I found the pictures, but not Jenna. Where is she?"

Rivera leaned in close, inches away from her face. His mouth twisted in disgust. "If I knew, we wouldn't be here. The way I see it, you passed along my message and Jenna sent you the pictures to avoid any problems."

"You're wrong."

In one swift motion, he clamped a hand on her shoulder and forced her onto a chair. "Sit. You're just like your cousin. Stubborn to a fault. Now give me the damn pictures." He sat across from her at the table. After she removed the envelope from her purse, he snatched it from her hands, emptied the contents on the table, and flipped through the photos.

"Is this all of them?"

"As far as I know."

"This could've been avoided if she hadn't been so greedy."

"So, what happened? Did she discover your secret and blackmail you?" she asked as he shoved the pictures back into the envelope.

"Yes. After she left, I got an email demanding money. She threatened to write an article, exposing my operation. I couldn't let that happen, so I wired money every month to her overseas account. In exchange, I received two pictures for every payment. Then you came along, like an answer to prayer, looking for her. I knew you would lead me to her—or the pictures."

"How could you poison our community? Is money the only thing you care about?"

"What? You think I make a fortune running the newspaper? My income from the bar isn't much better. No, meth is where the money is. And speaking of money, I want the money back Jenna gave you to buy Five Star."

"What? That came from my inheritance, not Jenna."

"You're lying!" He stood and paced the floor, essentially blocking her exit.

She eased from the chair. "Look, I gave you what you asked for. Since you can't tell me where Jenna is, there's no reason for me to stay."

"Did you really think I'd let you leave?"

Her heart raced. She tried to push past him, but he grabbed her arm with a vise-like grip. She winced in pain. A shot rang out. They both froze as shouting erupted outside.

Rivera grabbed the envelope and dragged her through the doorway. Derek and Evan were embroiled in a vicious struggle. In the distance, police swarmed the meth lab behind the security fence, demanding the occupants come out with their hands up. Shouts came from inside the building. A firestorm of shots pierced the night. Looking as panicked as she felt, Rivera dragged her toward the sedan. She kicked and struggled until she had yanked her arm free. Evan shouted for her to run, and run she did.

She raced around the corner and down the narrow path between two smaller buildings. She turned left. *A dead end.* She spun and retraced her steps. When she rounded the next building, she found herself staring into the barrel of Rivera's gun. She stopped. Her heart lodged in her throat. With her hands raised, she prayed he would show mercy.

Rivera growled, "You should've come alone like you promised."

Her mind barely registered the sound of boots hitting the ground when a hulking shadow lunged in front of her as Rivera fired. Mace tackled her to the ground. He grunted and his body jerked, leaving her no doubt he had taken the bullet meant for her. They landed hard, forcing the air from her lungs. He rolled to keep his body between her and the shooter, his weight pinning her to the ground. She panicked when he went limp. *Dear God, please don't let him die.*

"Drop the weapon, Rivera!" Chad shouted. "Now!"

From the corner of her eye, she saw Rivera hesitate, then spin and fire his weapon. His actions left Chad no choice. He returned fire, and Rivera fell to the ground.

THIRTY-EIGHT

As soon as the back doors of the ambulance slammed shut, the driver engaged the flashing lights and started the engine. From her seat next to the EMT, CiCi watched Chad's face disappear as the vehicle pulled away from the chaotic scene. Though shaken and bruised, she had convinced him to stay behind while she rode to the hospital with Evan. A bump in the road brought a moan from the stretcher, drawing her attention to the man who saved her life. When Evan caught her looking, he smiled through gritted teeth, as if embarrassed to have someone see him in pain. She squeezed his hand, and he squeezed back.

They were separated in the ER, where they each underwent thorough examinations. An hour later, she was released after having minor cuts and scrapes tended to. She inquired about Evan and was told he'd been taken for tests. She left her name and took a seat in the waiting room. It was then she realized she had his motorcycle jacket. The bullet-proof vest he'd worn must've been left at the crime scene. She shook out the jacket to fold it and noticed the hole in the back. Tears sprang to her eyes. *He could've died.*

A gentle hand touched her shoulder. She swiped at her eyes and glanced up to find Pete standing beside her chair. "He's going to be all right, you know. The bullet-proof vest did its job. He'll have a lot of bruising, maybe a cracked rib or two, but he'll recover. How are *you* doing?"

She nodded as he took a seat beside her. "Fine."

His eyebrow lifted. "Fine. That seems to be your go-to answer. I'm sure you'll be stiff and sore tomorrow and have a few bruises of your own."

She shrugged as she stared at the jacket in her lap. She poked a finger through the hole. "Evan doesn't strike me as the type of guy who'd be overjoyed to get flowers. Do you think he'd like a new leather jacket instead?"

"Missy, a new jacket would almost make Evan forget he'd been shot."

That night, angry shouts to surrender and images of Rivera's lifeless body robbed CiCi of much-needed sleep. As the sun rose, so did she, with the hopes of grabbing a short nap later. The thought proved to be a frivolous idea because the constant ringing of the phone made it impossible to rest. The gossip train in Ripley Grove was running at full speed, and inquiring minds wanted the details about her part in taking down a drug lord. The most important call came from Chad, telling her to come to the station that afternoon to give a statement.

After lunch, she browsed online stores for motorcycle jackets. The styles and materials available were overwhelming and abundant, but she decided to play it safe. She chose one similar to what Evan currently wore, but with upgraded features like a zip-out lining, extra ventilation and plenty of pockets. It was the least she could do for someone who put his life on the line to save hers.

Tyler called wanting an exclusive interview about her involvement in the raid, but she declined. "I promise to call the moment I get the okay from Mark or Chad. I'll ask when I go to the police station this afternoon. How is Serena handling the news? I feel bad for her."

"She's devastated, of course, and the entire office is in turmoil. It came as a shock to us all. Especially the owner of the newspaper, who lives somewhere in Arizona. I spoke to him this morning. Lucky for us, he has a soft spot for Ripley Grove and plans to fill Rivera's position as soon as possible." Tyler blew out a sigh. "Maybe you can tell me this. Did Rivera say anything about Jenna?"

"Nothing I can talk about." *He'll eventually hear about Jenna blackmailing Rivera, but not from me.*

After Tyler disconnected, she sank onto the sofa, troubled over what Rivera had said about Jenna's demands for money. *Something doesn't fit. Jenna's life never revolved around money. She drove an old, battered Jeep, and had been content to live in Tyler's dated cabin after they married. Her fiancé and her job were the focus of her life, not making a fortune or living high on the hog. So, why would she resort to blackmail?*

The situation nagged at her as she tidied up the house. After a mid-afternoon snack, she applied a touch of makeup to conceal the dark circles under her eyes, grabbed her purse and sunglasses on the way out the door, and drove to the police station.

She checked in at the front desk and was promptly directed to a room down the hall. The station's conference room was teeming with activity when she passed by. Several of the officers she'd met at the cabin were on hand, as well as a few she'd never seen before. Mark and Chad were fielding phone calls, giving orders, and making notes as various men gave reports. Chad caught her eye and waved her in. She hesitantly stepped through the doorway and stood off to one side. He approached with a determined set to his whiskered jaw and the look of a man running on empty. Behind him, Mark seemed to fare no better and looked equally haggard and weary.

Chad gently ran a finger over her cheek and his bloodshot eyes studied her face. "You doing okay? Doesn't look like you got much sleep last night."

"I could say the same about you." She tipped her head to the hubbub in the room. "What's going on? I thought everyone would've left by now, and you and Mark would be wrapping up the case."

"I wish. We just got word they've arrested Crystal near the Colorado border."

"Crystal? Arrested for what?"

"She sold drugs for Rivera at bars across Kansas. Those identical amplifiers she and Derek used were fitted with false bottoms to hide cash and drugs."

CiCi nodded. "Ahh, and they exchanged amps whenever she came to town."

"Right. She traded the cash she collected for a fresh supply of drugs." Chad glanced over his shoulder as the chatter in the conference room grew more excited. "There's one more thread to follow before we can call it quits. If we're right, it seems Jenna isn't the one who—"

"Chad! You need to see this!" Mark shouted.

Chad brushed a quick kiss across her forehead before leaving.

"Wait. You didn't finish. Jenna isn't the one who *what?*" Her question was swallowed by the excitement in the room.

A female detective CiCi had met only once before stepped forward and said, "Miss Winslow, are you ready?"

She nodded and was led to a small room down the hall, where she answered a few questions and gave her statement. Her phone rang during the process, but the look she received from the officer made her think twice about answering it. *Probably Tyler, wanting to know if I got the okay to give an interview.* She set her phone to vibrate and apologized for the interruption. By the time she had finished, the conference room had cleared. She checked, but Chad wasn't in his office either. She flipped open her phone, intending to listen to Tyler's message, but the message she heard wasn't from Tyler. Flash had left a message saying he'd found the cord to her camera. *Hmm, I never even missed it.*

She left the police station and drove directly to Five Star, where she checked in with Floyd, caught up on the latest happenings in the office, and offered suggestions on handling a dispute with the county appraiser. As five o'clock neared, Tasha talked her into having dinner at Stella's, one of their favorite haunts. Stella seated them in a booth tucked away from the crowd. They stayed far longer than they intended. At eight o'clock, they called it a night, hugged, and went their separate ways.

On the drive home, CiCi caught a red light at the corner of Beaker and Lemont. She glanced over and noticed lights ablaze in the Captured Moments Studio. *Flash must be working late. Might as well pick up the cord to my camera.* She parked out front and sat for a minute to gaze up at the night sky, wondering if she might spot the Big Dipper. She was surprised to see a sliver of light peeking through the boarded-up windows on the third floor. *Probably a contractor working late.* As she walked up the steps, the hearing-impaired couple were on their way out. They nodded and smiled as they passed.

She knocked on the door to Captured Moments. It swung open, so she hesitantly stepped inside. An uneasy feeling stuck to her like an unwelcome shadow. "Flash?" She frowned when she didn't receive an answer. She called again, louder. "Anyone here?" Still, no answer. *He must be upstairs talking with the contractor.*

The photograph of the young woman on the park bench drew her over, as if she had no say in the matter. As she studied the picture up close, the partial word "cracker" on the woman's necklace stirred a memory. *"Don't you remember?" Edna said. "We bought the necklaces on vacation one year. Mine says 'Gram-cracker' and yours says 'Firecracker.'"* CiCi's eyes widened. She'd been admiring a picture of Jenna all along, and Flash never said a word. *What else has he been hiding?*

She glanced around the room. Through the open door to the back workroom, she spied her distinctive red and white camera cord poking out of a drawer. *Should I?* She listened for footsteps. The silence made the decision easy. As she rounded his desk, curiosity pulled her eyes to the past due notices scattered across his desktop blotter. *Somehow that's not surprising.*

She scurried through the door to the workroom, slid the drawer open, and grabbed her cord. She gasped. Below a tangle of cords lay a small laptop. On its lid, the eyes of the KU Jayhawk stared back. *Jenna's laptop!* She reached for it but stopped short after recalling the uproar caused when she'd taken the red box from Tyler's cabin. Instead, she pulled out her phone and took a picture.

"What are you doing back here?" Flash demanded.

Her heart jumped into her throat. She quickly slid her phone into her purse, hoping he hadn't seen her take the picture. She turned with a smile and held up her camera cord. "You weren't here, and when I saw my cord sticking out of the drawer, I figured you wouldn't mind if I took it."

His gaze went from her to the drawer. "I'm guessing that's not all you saw."

She tried to remain calm, but her voice betrayed her. "I...I don't know what you're talking about." She tightened her grip on the purse strap looped across her body, surprised to feel Pete's recording device still attached. Her fingers found the button and gave it a push.

"How stupid do you think I am?" he asked, taking a step into the room.

"How did you get Jenna's laptop?"

"Does it matter?"

"She had pictures on the laptop, didn't she? The ones she asked you to clean up. When you figured out what they were, you stole them from her." She inched to the side, hoping he would mimic her movement. He didn't. He continued to block the exit.

"What of it? They were worth a fortune. All she cared about was writing her story, exposing corruption. I tried to convince her those pictures were worth far more than a stupid byline, but she wouldn't listen."

"If she wanted to print the story so bad, then why did she leave town?" she asked. His silence spoke volumes. "She didn't, did she? In fact, you were the *only* person who heard Jenna say she wanted to leave town. But that was a lie to throw off the police, wasn't it?"

His lips twisted into a sinister smile. CiCi's pulse quickened as he took a step forward. She kept eye contact, trying to anticipate his next move. *I need to keep him talking.* "So, let me guess. After Jenna was out of the way, you pretended to be her and blackmailed Rivera. Is that how you afford the renovations on this building?"

"It helps, or it did." His eyes flashed with anger. "But that's over now that he's dead."

"The police will find out you were involved."

"I doubt it, because you won't be around to tell them."

She bolted for the exit. He lunged at her but tripped. His outstretched hand caught her ankle as he fell, and she toppled to the floor. He straddled her body and twisted the strap of her shoulder bag tight around her neck. As she gasped for air, she dug her fingers into his cheeks and clawed her way to his eyes. He screamed in agony and released his grip. She bucked and heaved him to the side, scrambled to her feet, and fled to the safety of her car. Looking back, the light from the studio framed his silhouette as he raced down the steps. She fumbled for her keys, started the car, and peeled from the lot.

Her heart raced as she drove, not even caring which direction she headed as long as it was away from Captured Moments. At the next red light, she rummaged through her purse, pulled out her phone, and tapped in Chad's number. It rang several times. *Please answer, please answer.* It went to voicemail. "Chad, pick up if you're there. I need you! Flash has Jenna's computer. He was the one blackmailing Rivera, not Jenna. Call me back."

She intended to go straight through the intersection when the light turned green, but a battered truck cut her off and forced her to make a left turn. A horn blared when she barely missed clipping another vehicle. She drove another block, and the truck appeared again, forcing her to make another left. When she caught a glimpse of Flash in the driver's seat, she panicked and stepped on the gas.

She called 9-1-1, blurting out her situation before the operator could say a word. "Look, this guy Flash is trying to kill me. I'm headed west on Harper Road. I'll try to turn—" Her upper body snapped back against the seat. Flash had rammed his truck into the rear of her Jeep. She made a sudden sharp turn and accelerated, hoping to put distance between them. "—I'm headed north on Miller's Creek. He's still on my tail. I need help. Get ahold of Detective Cooper."

When the operator asked her name, address and location, CiCi hung up. She didn't have time for nonsense. Metal crunched against metal as another hit sent the tail end of her Jeep skidding along the shoulder of the narrow road. Gripping the wheel until her hands ached, she managed to keep her vehicle on the road. He slammed her again. She pressed the accelerator to the floor. With a bit of breathing room, she dialed Chad again.

"Chad, Flash is trying to kill me. I'm headed north on Miller's Creek, and I don't know how I'm—"

A sharp curve appeared in the road ahead. The roar of Flash's engine drew her eyes to the rearview mirror. The impact knocked the phone from her hand and sent her Jeep over the edge of the steep embankment. She instinctively threw her arms up to shield her face and screamed until she had no air left in her lungs.

She opened her eyes. Darkness surrounded her. *Where am I?* A tree branch jutted through the front windshield of the Jeep and out the passenger side window. She unbuckled her seatbelt and tried to open the caved-in door, but it wouldn't budge. She did the next best thing and climbed out the broken window. She slumped against the vehicle. Her head ached and every muscle in her body hurt.

Walk. Something compelled her to walk. Why, she didn't know. Despite the thick vegetation, the rocky terrain, and the moonless night, she placed one foot in front of the other and walked. Stumbled, mostly. She rested occasionally on a log or boulder but the burning urge to keep moving propelled her forward. Thunder clapped overhead and a light rain began to fall. Still, she kept moving. To where, she didn't know, and didn't care.

Her clothes were soaked and torn, her body ached, and her vision blurred, distorting her perception of her surroundings. Her foot slipped on a mossy rock, sending her tumbling to the bottom of a shallow ravine. Head spinning, she struggled to her feet, but was barely able to put pressure on her ankle. She took in her surroundings. *Which way was I headed?* She picked a path and trudged onward. It felt as if she'd walked ten miles. Up ahead, she spied something familiar. Under the dense canopy of trees, her black Jeep took on a bluish tint. She leaned against the bumper, trying not to cry. *I'm right back where I started.*

The rain stopped, and she began to shiver. In the far distance, a light panned across the treetops. *Am I dreaming?* She pushed away from the vehicle, the aches and pains increasing with each movement. The dense growth of trees and brush put a tremendous strain on her ankle and made it difficult to maneuver up the small hill. The slight pain in her side she'd noticed earlier was now more pronounced. Her knees buckled when she reached the shoulder of a road, and she collapsed on the pavement. She closed her eyes and surrendered to the blackness.

THIRTY-NINE

CiCi felt as though she were floating, higher and higher. Slowly, she reached the surface and opened her eyes. She looked around, puzzled by her surroundings. It didn't take a genius to figure out she was in a hospital. *But why?* The overhead lights had been dimmed and a bag of fluid hung from a pole next to her bed. Her eyes followed the tubing as it snaked through a complicated machine and ended at the IV needle stuck in her hand. Her swollen ankle was wrapped in bandages and rested on a pillow. She sighed and shook her head, sending a spasm of pain up her neck. The clock on the wall read five-fifteen, but she had no idea if it was morning or evening.

She shifted in the bed and something clattered to the floor. Chad, who slept in a chair off to one side, immediately jumped to his feet and came to her bedside. He smiled as he brought her hand to his lips. "There's my girl," he whispered. He picked up the remote from the floor and pressed a button. When the nurse answered, he said, "Would you let Doc Cunningham know Miss Winslow is awake?" She assured him the doctor would be paged. Chad squeezed CiCi's free hand. "You've had me worried sick, sugar."

"What happened?" she asked, her voice raspy and rough.

"You don't remember?" When she frowned and gave a slight shake of her head, he hesitantly continued. "You, ah, were in a car accident."

She uttered a soft groan. "How bad?"

"You had surgery to stop the internal bleeding. You have cuts and bruises and a mild concussion. Your ankle is badly sprained. Doc said it'd have been better if you'd broken it. Nothing that won't heal with time…and a good nurse." He winked and gave a dimpled grin that brought a tiny smile to her lips.

Doctor Cunningham entered the room with another doctor and two nurses. "Time will be our biggest obstacle because I happen to know Miss Winslow is an impatient patient. Chad, why don't you get something to eat while we take care of business here."

Chad nodded and gave her a kiss on his way out.

Chad stepped outside the room and scratched his head. Knowing the cafeteria was on the far side of the hospital, he headed to the waiting room down the hall instead. A couple of vending machines provided a variety of snacks to tide him over. Fifteen minutes later, Doc entered the room.

"Thought I'd find you here. She's sleeping at the moment. She'll be a bit groggy for a day or two from the pain meds. Her test results look fine, but I've asked my colleague, a specialist in head trauma, for a second opinion." He placed a firm hand on Chad's shoulder. "There's no reason to panic. I don't foresee any problems, but I prefer to err on the side of caution. If everything goes well, I'll release her on Monday."

"She didn't remember the accident," Chad said, his brows pinching with worry as he tossed his empty potato chip bag into a nearby trashcan.

"It's not surprising, considering everything she's been through. Give her time. I'm guessing her memory will come back before she goes home."

Chad let out a sigh and shook the doctor's hand. "Thanks, Doc."

Chad returned to her room and found her still sleeping. He passed the time watching television and texting updates to their friends and family. Megan showed up, carrying a small tote bag, a pillow, and a blanket as though she were going to a sleepover.

"Thought you'd need a break," she whispered. "Go home. Eat, take a shower, and get some sleep. I'll stay with her tonight and promise to call if anything changes."

The following day, several friends stopped by to visit and offer support. Tasha insisted on staying over on Saturday night, giving Chad time to ready his apartment for her "homecoming." Long hours at work meant he hadn't been concerned about keeping his place clean or the fridge stocked with food.

When he arrived Sunday morning, he found CiCi sitting by the window, her foot propped on a nearby chair. He hung the clothes he'd brought her to wear home in the closet before taking a seat next to her. After leaning over and giving her a soft kiss, he asked, "How are you feeling today?"

"Better, except for my ankle and a slight headache."

"I saw Doc Cunningham on the way in. He plans to release you in the morning with crutches and a boot to keep your ankle immobile. He and his colleague are pleased with your test results. I assume Doc has already spoken to you."

She pursed her lips. "Yes, he did."

"And?"

"And my course of treatment hasn't changed much. Rest, more rest, and limit electronic devices."

"And?" he pressed.

She huffed a sigh. "And no driving for at least six months, which I'm sure he told you."

"He did. I just wanted to hear you say it."

"And how exactly am I supposed to get around?"

"We can worry about that later. Right now, you're in no condition to be hobbling about town." He tucked a strand of hair behind her ear. "Besides, your car was totaled in the wreck." A tear slid down her cheek. "I know how much you loved that Jeep, but think of the fun you'll have picking out a new one once you're able to drive again."

She gazed off into the distance. "Flash. What happened to Flash?"

"Don't worry about him."

"Tell me."

Chad sighed. "Okay. He's been arrested and charged with attempted murder. I'm sure other charges will be filed. So far, he's denying he stole Jenna's laptop, says you planted it there. He also claims he never blackmailed Rivera."

"That's a lie." She leaned back and closed her eyes, soaking in the news. With a start, she sat forward. "My purse. Where's my purse?"

"Probably with the rest of your stuff. The ER staff put everything you came in with in a plastic bag. Why?"

"Can you get it?"

Chad stood and retrieved her purse from the bag in the closet. She smiled the moment he handed it to her. It had seen better days and would eventually be trashed, but the small recording device with the "Adopt, Don't Shop" slogan was still firmly attached to the strap. She removed the button and gently ran her finger over the dog's face before placing it in Chad's hand. "I forgot to give this back to Pete. I recorded my conversation with Flash. I hope it still works."

Chad turned it over in his hand before planting a kiss on her forehead. He immediately called Mark. "It's Chad." He paused to listen, then chuckled at something Mark said. "You are? Well, when you come, bring an evidence bag. CiCi has a present for you. Okay, see you later." He disconnected with a grin. "He planned to visit you later this afternoon. My guess is he'll be here within fifteen minutes."

"Does Flash know where Jenna is?" Her eyelids felt unusually heavy and she struggled to maintain eye contact.

"He's not saying, but I think he knows something. Sugar, let's get you into bed before you fall asleep."

"I'm just resting my eyes."

Despite her weak protests, he helped her into bed and dimmed the lights. She fell asleep within seconds. About twenty minutes later, Mark walked into the room. They talked for a bit, and Chad handed over the evidence CiCi had given him. Movement from her bed caught their attention. CiCi's breathing turned erratic and her face twisted in fear.

"CiCi! CiCi, wake up!" Chad placed a gentle hand on her shoulder. She opened her eyes in a panic and sprang upright. "Relax, hon," Chad said, easing her back onto the pillow. "You're having a bad dream."

She closed her eyes and tried to steady her breathing. "It was dark, and I was at Tyler's pond, splashing my bare feet along the water's edge. A man dressed in black started chasing me. I ran through the woods, but he followed. Branches clawed at my legs as I tried to get away. I tripped and fell against my Jeep. He caught up with me and …" She hid her face behind her hands. "I'm sorry. It seemed so real."

"No need to apologize," Chad said.

Mark stayed a bit longer, then decided he ought to go. "And thanks for this," he said to CiCi, holding up the bag containing the recording device. "That was quick thinking on your part. I'll take it back to the station. Get some rest, okay?"

Though CiCi had wanted to return to her townhome after being released from the hospital, she'd been glad Chad insisted she stay at his place. With stitches in her side, crutches, and a boot on her foot, she would've had a hard time navigating the stairs to her master bedroom several times a day.

Chad had proven yet again to be an attentive caretaker, though his mind wandered at times. He had been placed on administrative leave for the week, giving the review board time to investigate the fatal shooting of the town's newspaper editor-in-chief. He also had to meet with his union rep and a mental health counselor. Killing a man took an emotional toll on a person, no matter how justified the act.

Whenever he had an appointment or errand, Katherine, Megan or Tasha would "happen" to be in the neighborhood. And they seldom came empty-handed. Megan brought cozy socks and a relaxation tape she often used for her physical therapy patients. Tasha, knowing CiCi's weakness for sweets, showed up with chocolates, scones, or an occasional Frappuccino. Practical Katherine stocked Chad's freezer with several easy-to-heat meals. They were determined to help her recover.

Remembering every detail about the accident seemed to be the one thing they couldn't help her with. Over time, the pieces began to fall into place, yet she sometimes had trouble differentiating between reality and the flashbacks that appeared out of the blue.

Limited by the amount of time she could use a laptop, phone and other devices, she quickly became bored. Late one afternoon, as Chad read the newspaper, she tossed her earbuds aside, threw her head back against the sofa, and sighed. "I don't know how much longer I can do this. I'm going stir-crazy."

Chad stared at her thoughtfully, then stood and left the room. He returned, wearing a sweatshirt and carrying her jacket and crutches. "Put this on. I think what you need is some fresh air." He helped her into her jacket and out to his truck.

He slowly drove through the town square to let her drink in the sights and sounds she'd been missing. He idled in front of Sadie's Bakery and Art's Hardware so she could chat with the owners, who were happy to see her out and about.

As they continued down Ash and past *The Ripley Review*, Chad's grip tightened on the steering wheel, his knuckles turning white. Few cars were parked in front of the building. A sympathy wreath hung in the window, and a wide black band of ribbon had been taped across the door. Rivera's funeral had been held several days ago. Though she and Chad never discussed it, neither felt comfortable attending.

At Meadowlark Park, a handful of people jogged along the walking trail, and a group of high school teens practiced cheers in the grass. Chad left by an alternate exit, only to find the road ahead closed. He followed the detour and cursed under his breath.

She glanced up ahead to see what made him swear. Darkness filled the building that housed Captured Moments, and remnants of crime scene tape fluttered in the breeze around the entrance. "Chad, what did the police find when they searched Flash's business?"

"Jenna's phone, laptop, and her wallet." Chad hesitated. "I have to say you did good, CiCi. Finding that laptop helped tremendously."

"Maybe I should think about joining the police force." She winked.

Chad shook his head and chuckled. "Not gonna happen—ever. Anyway, after talking with Rivera, we concluded Jenna wasn't the blackmailer. Rivera never received a demand for money until *after* she disappeared. Since Jenna's original photos were blurry and required an expert's touch to clean them up, we knew someone else had to have been involved."

"I want to see where Flash forced me off the road."

"Is that a good idea?"

"I need to see it. There are things I still don't remember. Maybe it will help."

He made a turn at the next corner and drove until he came to the spot where her Jeep crashed through the trees and ended up in the ravine below. He pulled to the shoulder and they sat in silence while she took it all in. His hand tightened around hers and his eyes misted. "We noticed two sets of skid marks. The second set, the ones from Flash's truck, stopped just short of the edge. The broken tree limbs told the rest of the story. Mark and I grabbed our flashlights and scrambled down the embankment as fast as we could." His voice broke. "My heart stopped when I saw your Jeep. You weren't inside. Mark and I searched the hillside, screaming your name over and over. I was frantic, about to lose my mind."

"And then you found me."

He turned, shaking his head. "No. I got a call from the hospital. A guy driving home from an AA meeting found you in the road a couple of miles from here and drove you to the ER. By the time I got there, you were already in surgery."

"A good Samaritan. I'll have to find out his name and thank him."

Chad pursed his lips and looked away. "Are you ready to go home, or would you like to stop for a hot chocolate?"

"Let's end the evening on a sweet note, shall we?"

FORTY

Though CiCi still had to contend with the clunky orthopedic boot, she moved back home two weeks later after convincing Chad she was capable of being on her own. When the doorbell rang just before noon, she hobbled to the entrance and peered through the peephole. Pete and Katherine stood on the porch. After giving them each a hug, she led them to the living room. "It's so good to see you."

"Are we interrupting anything?" Katherine asked, setting aside the small tote dangling from her arm.

"Not at all. I just finished putting a chicken in the crockpot for dinner tonight. Have a seat and I'll fix a pot of coffee, unless you'd rather have tea."

"Coffee will be fine," said Pete as he settled on the sofa next to Katherine.

CiCi watched the two from the kitchen as she filled the coffee pot with water. Pete leaned back against the cushions, rested one ankle atop the opposite knee, and draped his arm around Katherine's shoulders. They looked quite cozy nestled together on the sofa. "Would either of you care for a slice of banana bread? Pete, I know it's your favorite."

Though Katherine declined, the glimmer in Pete's eyes conveyed his answer. CiCi used the microwave to thaw a couple of slices from the freezer, then poured the coffee into mugs and took everything to the living room. They asked how she'd been feeling, then chatted amiably about the weather and work—everything except Rivera, Flash, and the wreck. She knew they did so to spare her, but CiCi couldn't deny the hint of sadness in Katherine's eyes.

"Katherine, I'm sorry I couldn't find Jenna. I thought I'd come so close—"

"Don't be sorry. You were brave to try, though it almost got you killed. Had I known how dangerous it would be, I would've never asked. At least you uncovered evidence Detective Logan overlooked and helped rid our town of a meth lab. In a way, you finished what Jenna set out to do."

"Hmm. I never thought of it like that."

"In fact, I brought you something." She pulled out a small book and handed it to CiCi. "I took some of my favorite photos of Jenna and you and had a custom book made. I thought you might enjoy seeing how many things you had in common."

"Thank you."

Katherine patted the empty seat beside her. "Come. Let's look at them together."

CiCi moved closer and slowly flipped through the pages while Katherine told the story behind each picture. The contents brought laughter and tears to the surface. When she came to the last page, she stopped. In the top photo, Jenna sat on the back bumper of her older model Jeep, its exterior dull and rusted in places. The lower photo showed CiCi and Megan standing next to CiCi's graduation gift from her mother—a brand new, shiny black Jeep. CiCi remembered the day the photo had been taken and the excitement she felt.

But her gaze was drawn back to the photo of Jenna and her midnight blue Jeep. Her heart raced and her mind whirled with a mishmash of images. None of them were clear or made any sense as they flashed across her mind's eye. She felt as if she were being sucked into a fathomless void.

"Missy? CiCi! Are you okay?"

Pete's sharp tone brought her back to the present. She blinked several times before noticing he knelt in front of her, his brow creased with worry. Katherine, her eyes wide, had a firm grip on CiCi's hand.

"What? I'm...I'm sorry, did you say something?"

"You were out of it for a minute there. I was scared you were having one of your episodes."

"No, no, I'm fine. Just a bit of a headache, I suppose." She glanced away, wondering what had just happened. *Am I losing my mind?* She thanked Katherine again for the thoughtful gift and asked if they'd like more coffee.

Katherine hesitated, then glanced at Pete before giving an answer. "Maybe we should be going. You look a bit tired."

"No, please stay," CiCi insisted. "I enjoy the company." She moved to the recliner to prop her foot up and listened while Katherine gave a recap of bridal bloopers she'd encountered over the years.

CiCi awoke with a start and glanced around the living room, wondering if she'd dreamed the afternoon visit. She tossed aside the soft blanket that covered her body and headed to the kitchen. As she walked past the dining room table, she noticed the photo book and a note scribbled on the back of an envelope. It read: *You drifted off to sleep and we couldn't bear to wake you. Talk to you later. Love, Katherine.* Underneath her signature was a message from Pete. *Confession is good for the soul. I took your last piece of banana bread.*

CiCi laughed and decided she may have to share the recipe with Katherine. She placed the envelope on the table next to the book, then hesitantly traced a finger over the cover, unsure if she wanted to open the cover after what had happened earlier.

She checked the clock on the wall. In another hour, the chicken would be done, and Chad would be walking through the door. She chopped and tossed the ingredients for a salad and stored it in the fridge to keep it crisp. After preheating the oven, she placed a refrigerated roll of French bread on a baking sheet, scored it, and slid the tray onto the middle rack. Another quick look at the clock told her she had just enough time to freshen up.

She held tight to the banister as she came down the stairs from the second floor, the cumbersome boot proving to be more of a challenge coming down than it did going up. Back in the kitchen, the aroma of warm yeasty bread filled the air and made her mouth water. The timer on the oven buzzed as she set the table. She pulled the bread from the oven and slid it onto a cutting board to cool. Chad walked into the kitchen and brushed a kiss across her cheek as she sliced the loaf into thick slices.

"Can you get drinks on the table while I fill our plates?" she asked.

They talked about the day's events over dinner, Chad expressing his determination to plow through the backlog of paperwork on his desk. He nodded to the note and book on the table. "I see Katherine stopped by."

"Yes, she and Pete came by around noon. Katherine had a book made with pictures of me and Jenna at various stages in our lives."

"She called a week or so ago wanting certain pictures of you. I told her Megan would have the ones she wanted. I'll look at it after we eat. Don't want to get it messy."

After putting the dishes in the dishwasher and the leftover food in the fridge, they settled on the sofa with the book. Chad slowly thumbed through each page while CiCi gave a running commentary on each photo. Chad concocted his own silly version about the history behind a few of the pictures, causing her to erupt with laughter. The laughter died in her throat when he lingered over pictures of the two cousins and their Jeeps. She stiffened as new images flashed through her mind. She sprang from the couch. "Chad, we have to go. Now!"

He stood, frowning. "Why? What's wrong?"

"I...I think I know where Jenna's Jeep is."

Chad patiently listened to her theory, and then shook his head.

"Hon, you were in bad shape that night and in shock. You told me yourself you circled back to your vehicle."

"That's what I thought at the time. But after looking through that book, I had a vision of me leaning against the Jeep to rest," she said as she slipped on a jacket. "I have to know if it was *my* car or hers."

"Okay, okay. Calm down. We'll go look."

Twenty minutes later, they slowed at the curve where CiCi's Jeep had been forced from the road. "Someone found me about two miles from here, right? So, let's find a stopping point about midway between," she said, her nails digging into her palms.

Around the next bend, they pulled to the far side of the road where a wide shoulder gave them a safe spot to park. She shot out of the truck and gimped her way along the edge of the road. Chad retrieved a flashlight from his glove box and followed.

She stopped, transfixed by the tall trees and heavy brush. Her heart thumped against her chest as she surveyed the landscape that had permeated every flashback. She swallowed back her fear and took a couple of steps forward, intent on forging down the steep embankment. A hand clamped around her waist and jerked her back.

"What do you think you're doing?" Chad asked, panning his flashlight beam across the thick growth below.

"I'm going down there. I need to see that Jeep for myself."

"Not gonna happen." He huffed out a deep breath. "You're sure about this?" When she nodded, he didn't hesitate to pull out his phone and place a couple of calls. Within minutes, a fire and rescue truck, Mark, and several other officers were on the scene. CiCi stepped aside while Chad explained her suspicions. A flurry of activity commenced. One fireman donned heavy gloves, a helmet with a flashlight attached, and a harness, while another man hooked a cable to the harness. The first fireman grabbed a small chainsaw and then disappeared over the edge. His partner waited a few minutes before trekking down the newly cleared path. Their voices could barely be heard over the roar of the saw. Eventually, the chainsaw went silent.

Darkness had fallen and the wind picked up, causing CiCi to shiver. Chad steered her back to his truck. "Get inside, out of this wind. I'll let you know if they find anything."

She chewed the nail on her pinky nearly to the quick. Tears pricked her eyes as her mind ticked off the possible outcomes. *Please, let me be wrong. Please, let me be wrong.* Chad and Mark paced along the edge of the road, straining to hear the men below. Minutes stretched into what seemed to be hours.

Thirty minutes later, the first firefighter appeared and planted his feet on level ground. He was soon followed by his partner. The two men conferred with Chad and Mark before handing Chad a small, clear bag. Chad studied the contents and heaved a heavy sigh, his broad shoulders sagging under the weight of the discovery. He slowly turned and walked over to the truck, his eyes filled with sadness and compassion.

She jumped from the cab. "Did they find Jenna's Jeep?"

He hesitated, then held up the bag containing an engagement ring and a necklace with the words "Firecracker" engraved on the charm.

CiCi fell into his arms, the tears flowing down her cheeks.

The search was over.

FORTY-ONE

CiCi held tight to Chad's hand as they entered the sanctuary for Jenna's memorial service. Katherine and Tyler stood near the front of the church, accepting condolences from those who had come to pay their respects. It looked as though half of Ripley Grove had turned out to express their sympathy and offer support. Despite the forced smile, Katherine seemed to have aged ten years. Tyler wore a pained look of heartbreak and resignation as he shook hands.

After speaking with Katherine and Tyler, CiCi and Chad took a seat in the second row of pews. Her gaze was immediately drawn to the walnut pedestal at the front of the church, where a sleek blue urn was surrounded by a ring of white flowers. She sighed and brushed away the tear that threatened to run down her cheek. Chad draped his arm around her shoulders and gave a reassuring hug. Pete and Tyler escorted Katherine to the first pew and took a seat on either side of her. Pastor Young glanced at his watch and then stepped to the podium. Katherine dabbed at her eyes with a lace-trimmed hanky as she listened to the eulogy. After the final amen, soft music began to play in the background and the mourners began to go their separate ways.

Across the room, Jimmy stood off to one side. CiCi couldn't recall ever seeing him without a camera, either in his hand or hanging around his neck. Seconds later, Serena appeared at his side with a pen and notepad. Without making a scene, he shook his head, took them from her hand, and tucked them into his shirt pocket. *Way to go, Jimmy.*

CiCi and Chad mingled with friends and read the cards attached to each flower arrangement. As the crowd thinned, CiCi touched Chad's arm to get his attention. "I'm going to tell Katherine goodbye. I'll be right back."

Chad looked in Katherine's direction, then frowned and mumbled something under his breath. "CiCi, wait." He reached out and held her back. Glancing over her shoulder again, he shook his head. "I didn't expect to see *him* here."

She frowned. "Who?"

"Your dad."

She turned and sucked in a breath. She barely recognized the tall, well-dressed man talking to Katherine. Katherine stood as though in shock. Pete had a protective arm draped around her shoulders, his steely gaze never wavering from Jack's face. With a nod and a small smile, Katherine tentatively shook Jack's hand before walking away with Pete.

CiCi's heart thumped in her chest. "What's he doing here, Chad? He knows I have a protective order against him."

"No, hon, you don't. You had just been released from the hospital and were in no condition, physically or mentally, to appear at the court hearing. The judge had no choice but to dismiss your petition." Chad sighed. "There's something else you should know."

"What?"

"He's the man who found you in the road after the accident."

Jack walked over and stopped in front of her, careful not to invade her personal space. He looked like a refined version of his old self. His hair had been recently trimmed, his clothes, though dated, were free of wrinkles, and his eyes were clear. "CiCi." He nodded and nervously fingered the brim of his hat. "You look much better than the last time I saw you."

"I understand I have you to thank for taking me to the hospital."

He nodded, then looked away as though struggling to find the right words. "I was hoping we could meet for coffee sometime. I've been attending AA meetings, and I have a few things I need to say to you. Privately, if possible."

She paused, surprised by his request. "I'll think about it. But, *if* I decide to say yes, Chad will be coming with me."

Jack nodded and walked away.

She felt stunned yet bewildered. "He seems different. Do you think he's changed?"

Chad stared at the retreating figure. "Maybe, but——."

"But what?"

"But I wouldn't bet on it. It wasn't that long ago he assaulted you in the alley, and it'll take more than a haircut and a couple weeks of good behavior to change my mind."

She watched her father leave the church, her heart and mind at war with one another. A hand touched her shoulder, bringing her thoughts to the present.

"CiCi?" Katherine said. "Pete's going to take me home now. The service was lovely, and I appreciate the suggestions you and Tyler made."

CiCi pulled her aunt into a heartfelt hug. "You're very welcome. If there's anything else I can do, please, let me know."

Katherine hesitated before saying, "Well, there is something I'd like to take care of before I reopen for business next week. Could you come by the shop tomorrow morning, say around ten o'clock?"

"I'd be happy to."

The door to Blissful Creations was locked and a "Closed" sign hung in the window. CiCi cupped her hands around her face and peered inside. A faint glow could be seen coming from the back room where bridal gowns were magically matched with young women looking for the dress of their dreams. She rapped on the glass, hoping Katherine would hear her knock. A shadow appeared, then

Katherine. She hurried through the shop's lobby, flipped the lock, and opened the door. CiCi stepped inside and kissed her aunt's cheek.

"Come in, come in. I'm so glad you came." The smile she wore belied her red-rimmed eyes. She locked the door, and then turned and led CiCi to the back.

The bridal room was the same as CiCi remembered from her very first visit. Wedding gowns were evenly spaced in wardrobes set flush into the wall. A large changing room was positioned at the far end of the room, nearest the raised platform and large, full-length mirror. Two sofas for the bride-to-be's entourage were angled to face the platform and the small coffee table held a vase of fresh flowers.

"Would you care for a cup of hot tea?" Katherine asked.

"Yes, please," CiCi said. She removed her jacket and draped it over the back of the sofa.

Over tea and scones, they talked of Jenna's final farewell and how pleased Katherine was with the service and show of support from the community. She fell silent after a bit, then set her drink on the table.

"My goal today is two-fold. One is bittersweet; the other is not. I'd like to start with the most difficult of the two." Katherine's voice wavered.

"Okay," CiCi said hesitantly, not knowing what to expect.

Katherine took a deep breath and exhaled. "Though I've known for some time Jenna was never coming home, a mother never gives up hope. I've been giving it some serious thought, and I've come to a decision about what to do with Jenna's dress. Out of all my custom designs, I consider hers to be one of the top two creations of my career. That dress was meant to make a young woman happy on her special day, and I think that can still happen. Before I let it go, would you try it on for me? Just one more time?" Katherine's eyes glistened with tears.

CiCi's breathing hitched and her pulse kicked up a notch. *She's letting it go—to me? How can I say no without breaking her heart?* "Oh, Katherine, I...I don't know if that's a good idea," she stammered. "I couldn't—"

"I'd like to see it on you one more time before I ship it off to Chicago. Please?"

CiCi mentally shook herself and tried to keep the shock and confusion from showing on her face. "Excuse me. Did you say Chicago?"

"Yes. A very good friend of mine was in a serious car accident earlier this year. I closed the shop and left town as soon as I heard. In fact, that's why I missed your mother's funeral. I didn't hear about her passing until I returned home."

"And your friend?"

"She lingered for days, but eventually died from her injuries."

"I'm sorry for your loss."

Katherine simply nodded. "She was a single mother with a daughter who'd recently gotten engaged. She was devasted and has been struggling emotionally and financially ever since. She's the same size as Jenna, so I thought I would give her the dress as a wedding gift."

"That's so very thoughtful and generous of you. I'm sure she'll be thrilled."

"So, will you try it on so I can take a picture to have as a memento?"

"Of course. I'd be happy to."

After photos had been taken from every possible angle, the dress was laid on a large cutting table in the alterations room. Katherine carefully folded the delicate garment, tucking acid-free tissue paper between each layer of fabric. The outer covering protecting the gown was a sheet of unbleached muslin, tied with a silver ribbon. CiCi helped Katherine slip the dress and a matching veil into a waterproof bag, which was then placed in a small, sturdy box, carefully sealed, and a mailing label attached. "Fragile" and "wedding dress" stickers were placed on all six sides of the container to alert the delivery person that the contents were precious.

Katherine sighed with relief. "There. That takes care of one job. I think having you here made it a bit easier. I'll drop it by the post office on my way home."

After giving her aunt a brief hug, CiCi asked, "Now, what's next on your list?"

"As I said, there are two custom dresses I consider to be the masterpieces of my career. One is in that box, ready to be shipped."

CiCi tilted her head. "And the other?"

Katherine's eyes seemed to twinkle. "The other is *yours*. That is, if you love it."

Katherine led CiCi to the viewing room and opened the wide door to the changing room. A mannequin stood in the middle of the room wearing the most beautiful wedding gown she'd ever seen. Her mouth opened, but words failed to come. Tears sprung to her eyes as she circled the result of Katherine's genius creativity and skill. CiCi reached her hand out, but pulled back, afraid to touch it.

"Would you like to try it on?"

CiCi nodded and soon the silky folds of the gown slid over her soft curves like butter. Katherine pinned up CiCi's wavy hair and attached a veil of silk tulle that fell softly around her shoulders and ended just below her waist. After slipping on a pair of heels Katherine had on hand, she slowly made her way to the carpeted platform, careful to keep her eyes averted from the mirror. CiCi closed her eyes and concentrated on keeping the butterflies in her stomach from bursting through her chest.

"Wait! Don't open your eyes yet," Katherine exclaimed.

A few seconds later, CiCi felt a bouquet thrust into her hands.

"Perfect," Katherine said. "Now, open your eyes."

CiCi gasped at what she saw. The dress was more beautiful than she ever could have imagined. It was simple, but elegant, and captured her personality perfectly. The bodice of the simple sheath dress hugged her curves before flowing effortlessly from her hips straight to the floor. The scooped neckline and lacy off-the-shoulder cap sleeves drew the eye upward. But it was the artistic placement of the sheer lace, 3D embellishments and subtle beading that made the difference. Truly, the gown was a work of art.

Tears pricked at her eyes, and soon traced a path down her cheek. *This is it! This is the feeling I wanted to have.*

Katherine hurried to the coffee table and returned with several tissues. "I'm going to assume those are happy tears of approval. It will need a final fitting, of course, but that is best done a week or so before the wedding."

"Oh, Katherine, it's perfect. Chad is going to absolutely love it!"

"I know he will, because *you're* wearing it. Now, have you thought of a keepsake to honor your mother?" When CiCi shook her head, Katherine smiled. "Good, because I think I have just the thing." She produced a small box from behind the vase of flowers and presented it to the bride-to-be. "Cecil, your biological father, gave this pearl bracelet to your mother as a wedding gift. She later loaned it to me. I'd forgotten all about it until recently. The clasp is broken, and it needs to be restrung. I think the individual pearls and a little lace would look lovely sewn onto the comb of your veil."

"You've thought of everything. How can I ever thank you?"

"Your happiness is enough. Now let's get you out of that dress before you become so attached to it you don't want to take it off."

CiCi stared dreamily into the mirror for a final look. "It's too late for that. In fact, just looking at it makes me tempted to move up the wedding date."

FORTY-TWO

March

With nervous anticipation, CiCi sat on a tall stool in the church's nursery, running her fingertips over the sapphire and diamond engagement ring that once belonged to her grandmother. She still marveled that her mother, knowing Chad's intentions, gave him the heirloom ring just before she died. Soon, Chad would be slipping on a custom-made wedding band. Together, the two bands would symbolize the blending of her past and their future.

Megan, her bridesmaid, stepped over and applied a final touch of gloss to CiCi's lips, while Tasha, the maid of honor, took the strappy sandals from their box. Katherine unzipped a long, white garment bag, revealing the gown she'd put her heart and soul into making. Tasha and Megan, seeing the dress for the first time, fell silent, their eyes wide in awe.

Katherine glanced at her watch. "It's time."

CiCi's wavy hair was gently swept into a low, elegant chignon. Loose tendrils framed her face and a delicate pearl earring dangled from each ear. With Tasha and Megan's help, CiCi slipped into her wedding dress. Katherine attached the veil just above the chignon. The veil's comb was adorned with lace and the pearls from the bracelet that once belonged to the bride's mother. A few minutes later, CiCi stood in front of the mirror, memorizing every detail. She couldn't keep the smile from her face, and she could only imagine how Chad would react.

A short rap at the door brought silence to the room. Katherine opened the door a few inches to screen the visitor before allowing anyone to enter. Pete, dressed in a sharp black tux, stepped inside and gave Katherine a peck on the cheek.

His jaw dropped the moment he glanced over at CiCi. "Missy, you're the most beautiful bride I've ever seen. Chad's going to have a heart attack."

"Let's hope not," she said. "As a groomsman, I thought you'd be with Mark making sure Chad doesn't change his mind."

"There's no chance of that," Pete assured her. "In fact, Chad sent me to deliver this."

"A present?" She took the small velvet box from Pete's hand and opened the accompanying envelope first. "To carry on the family tradition" was written on the card above Chad's signature. Inside the box, she found a delicate pearl bracelet. "Aww, it's so beautiful. I wonder how he knew?"

Katherine smiled and busied herself straightening the room. Another knock came at the door. Pastor Young's wife poked her head inside and announced, "It's almost time. Katherine, Edna has just been seated."

Pete turned to Katherine and gave a slight bow. "May I?"

Katherine pulled CiCi into a hug and then left the room on Pete's arm. Megan and Tasha, each dressed in a knee-length blue dress of their choosing, grabbed bouquets and gave the largest arrangement to the bride.

CiCi's eyes grew misty as she looked at her two best friends. "Do you two know how much I love you? Maybe by this time next year one, or both of you, will be standing in my shoes and I'll be the bridesmaid."

"We're so happy for you," Megan whispered.

Tasha pulled out a tissue and dabbed at CiCi's eyes. "No crying, or you'll ruin your makeup. Now, let's go. There's a handsome man waiting for you at the altar."

The small group stepped into the foyer, where Abigail waited with her two children. Jimmy, the wedding photographer, snapped a candid photo as the mother leaned over the little ring bearer and flower girl and gave reminders of what they were to do and not do. When the ushers opened the doors to the sanctuary, CiCi remained off to one side and out of view. The processional music began, which was Megan's cue. She stepped forward with a smile. After waiting the appropriate amount of time, Tasha followed. The ring bearer went next, carefully balancing the satin pillow on his upturned palms. Abigail gave her daughter a gentle nudge. The little girl walked down the aisle throwing flower petals high into the air.

The music stopped, as did CiCi's heart.

"Are you ready, sweetheart?" The man who would escort her down the aisle appeared at her side and offered his arm.

She looked up into her father's clear blue eyes, smiled, and placed her hand in the crook of his elbow. Over the last few months, the two of them had been working on mending their relationship. Though Chad remained wary, she was ever hopeful and thrilled at the progress her dad had made to get his life back on track.

When the music began again, the congregation stood. The guest list had swelled to nearly a hundred, and all eyes were focused on her. She took a deep breath and smiled, intent on savoring the moment. Her father squeezed her hand, and Pastor Young beckoned them to walk forward. They slowly made their way down the center aisle and stopped at the first pew. Her father placed a gentle kiss on her cheek before taking a seat next to Katherine and Edna.

As she took the last few steps up the aisle alone, her focus remained on the only person in the world that made her heart skip a beat. After handing her bouquet to Tasha, she turned to face her soon-to-be husband. She could hardly contain her love for the handsome man who stood before her, and the look of adoration on his face was one she would remember forever. *How did I get so lucky?*

Chad's eyes glistened and his smile was one of pure happiness. "You look stunning," he whispered. Overcome with emotion, he wrapped his arm around her waist, pulled her to him, and tenderly pressed his lips to hers. She leaned into him and deepened the kiss. Soft laughter rippled across the sanctuary, and a few wedding guests clapped. CiCi blushed, and Chad stepped back with a sheepish grin on his face.

Pastor Young chuckled. "This isn't exactly how the rehearsal went last night." He cleared his throat and opened his bible. "Let's start from the beginning, shall we? Dearly beloved …"

DOUBLE TROUBLE IN RIPLEY GROVE
A RIPLEY GROVE MYSTERY, BOOK 3

After parking his truck at the curb and shutting off the engine, he slouched against the seat and took another drag on his cigarette. Outside, the neighborhood was unusually quiet for a Saturday morning; the relative silence allowed his thoughts to drift back over the last year. The more he stewed over his cruel lot in life, the darker his mood grew. From where he stood, or sat if he wanted to be literal, most of his problems could be traced back to one particular woman. The odd thing was he recently found out he wasn't the only man who felt that way about her. He took a final puff, flicked the butt out the window, and watched it smolder on the pavement. A few minutes later, a shiny 4X4 pickup drove by.

There she is. As I suspected, her husband is with her. He glanced at his watch. *Eight o'clock. They must've slept in.*

He eyed the vehicle's rugged tires, fancy bedliner, and chrome trim with envy as it passed. A low-profile, dual-lid toolbox sat under the back window and stretched across the width of the bed. Though the truck wasn't brand spanking new, it evidently had been well cared for. The new arrivals slowed and pulled into the driveway of a vacant house down the street. The couple exited the cab and took a moment to gaze at their recent purchase. Besides the satisfied smile on their faces, they each wore a tattered pair of jeans and a T-shirt—perfect attire for grunt work. She gave her husband a kiss before pulling her dark blonde hair away from her face and up into a ponytail. After grabbing a thermos from the front seat of the cab, she headed up the steps of the dilapidated house they were remodeling. Her husband followed a short distance behind after retrieving a circular saw and a few hand tools from the bed of the truck.

Even though he had parked a hundred yards away, the muffled sound of the saw could be heard from where he sat. He leaned across the passenger seat and pulled a flask from the glove compartment. After a few sips, enough to jump-start the day, he tucked it back under the truck manual and lit up another cigarette.

A screen door slammed and drew his attention back to the vacant house. The shapely blonde sprinted to the truck, grabbed a pair of work gloves and safety goggles from behind the front seat, then disappeared back inside the house. He wasn't sure if they had any experience at home remodeling, but they certainly weren't shy about rolling up their sleeves and getting their hands dirty. He'd heard rumors around town that they'd paid cash for the old house—above what it was actually worth, which meant they had more money than they had common sense. That itself was something to be envious of. From what he could tell, they were living the dream. Everything they touched seemed to flourish.

For them, yes; for me, not so much. Was it too much to ask her to bend the rules just this once, to look the other way in order to give me a leg up? Apparently, it was and that created a problem for him. The fact that they were related only made it worse.

He took another drag of nicotine. Life was a beautiful thing, until it wasn't. He knew firsthand everything could change in an instant. Maybe—just maybe—he should give them a taste of the real world, let them feel what it was like to have your dreams slip through your fingers. After all, who said life was fair?

Available in Paperback and eBook from Your Favorite Bookstore or Online Retailer

ACKNOWLEDGMENTS

Though my name is on the cover of Double Vision in Ripley Grove, there are many people behind the scenes who were vital in helping this story make it to the finish line.

I want to give a big round of applause to those friends and supporters who showered me with words of encouragement. I won't dare try to mention each individual by name for fear of leaving someone out.

There are a handful of people who most certainly deserve mention, along with my sincerest gratitude. Fellow author, Jeanne Glidewell, for her friendship, inspiration, and support. My loving husband, Bert, who is my biggest supporter and often holds more confidence in my writing abilities than I do. My daughter, Rachel, who always makes herself available to me (I should have named her Patience.) These three, along with Marla Worley, were exceptional proofreaders. Any mistakes that slipped by are entirely of my own doing.

These members of my critique group also deserve a standing ovation: Larry Hightower, Mike Flynn, and Nicole Sorrell. Their keen eye for detail and helpful suggestions allowed my story to shine to its fullest potential.

My deepest appreciation goes to Brian Paules, of ePublishing Works, and Nina Paules, of eBook Prep, for putting their faith in me. Their professionalism carries my manuscript to the next level, and Nina's cover designs are simply the icing on the cake.

Finally, I cannot forget those nearest and dearest to my heart—my family. Thank you for listening to me ramble, answering questions, coming to my aid with computer and technical help, and offering your love and support. I love you all more than you know.

ALSO BY SHIRLEY WORLEY

Double Threat in Ripley Grove
Double Vision in Ripley Grove
Double Trouble in Ripley Grove

ABOUT THE AUTHOR

Shirley Worley and her husband Bert have been married since 1969 and reside in Merriam, Kansas. They have two adult children and love spending time with them and their families. She retired from the U. S. Postal Service in 2009 with 39+ years of service. She enjoys bowling, working puzzles, playing Farkle, and having lunch with her sister every Saturday. Shirley is an avid reader, always in search of the next mystery that will keep her awake far into the night. Some days, you may find her sneaking in a nap after her husband goes to Panera for his afternoon cup of coffee.

Readers can reach Shirley through her publisher:
ShirleyWorley@epublishingworks.com

Photo by: Joseph Keehn

Manufactured by Amazon.ca
Bolton, ON